BOOK 2
CHRONICLES OF THE WATCHERS

· ⚜ ·

J. WILLIAM HAUCK

Elijah's Quest
Chronicles of the Watchers Book 2

Paperback ISBN: 978-1-7335435-4-5

White Ladder Books

Visit **jwilliamhauck.com**

Also by J. William Hauck

The Chronicles of the Watchers Series

Elijah's Awakening

Elijah's Quest

The Reckoning

The Rising

The Sojourners Series

The Sojourners

The Soul Seekers

The Searchers

The Sheep Rancher's Series

The Sheep Rancher's Daughter

The House by the River

Do not suppose anything is without purpose.
Your footsteps are being guided.
But beware, danger lurks all around you.

CHAPTER I

TEARS OF THE TASSILI

TASSILI N'AJJER
THE THIRD AGE
8,500 B.C.

Elijah's sapphire eyes gazed across the lush river valley as the gentle breeze stirred his brown, wavy hair. A formidable being, Eli stood more than a head taller than most, and his woven tunic fit tight across his broad, defined chest. Though confident in his look and manner, the smooth-faced watcher was best known for his benevolence.

As part of a collective of immortals tasked with guiding humans, Eli took his stewardship seriously. He had seen countless cultures rise and thrive in the tens of thousands of years guiding and teaching mortals. Eli and the other watchers received great satisfaction in observing the indigenous people's progress. But their work was not without disappointment. Patience and perseverance were vital traits for the watchers. Never more so than now.

Among those sworn to guide mortals was one called Lu. After violating the Grand Precept, the founding doctrine and directive the immortals had pledged to follow, Lu lured away a third of the collective. Great wars ensued, placing the survival of the mortal world in question. Then came the great cleansing. In that, the impure and fallen watchers were banished to a dark and terrible world.

The centuries after were much like starting over for Eli and the remaining true and faithful watchers. The world slowly healed.

But this world was not meant to be a utopia. A portal to the dark world was reopened, and Lu and his henchmen were secreted back. While the holy watchers believed Lu to be contained, his treachery and maliciousness spread.

Eli's pleased gaze moved across the hundreds of simple mud and bamboo huts stretching beyond the grassy plain to a smooth-flowing river. Across the river, on higher ground between broad-canopied trees, stood the temple of the plateau people, known as the Tassili. Pyramidal in shape, the Tassili's finest masons built the gleaming stone edifice using techniques shown to them by the watchers to worship the creator gods, the Holy and Great Ones. Standing the height of four giants, the temple's size was enough to set it off from the plateau people's other, more humble structures, but the Tassili distinguished the temple further by adorning it with gold and their most precious gems.

In the meadows to Eli's right grazed cattle, sheep, and goats. He saw clansmen and women armed with spears tending the herds. Beyond the grazing animals lay a vast cornfield. Eli spotted a giant cutting through and plucking ears. The six-foot cornstalks reached nearly to its chest. Beyond the cornfields, where the river diverged to form marshlands, lay rice paddies, and beyond that, misty, rolling hills. Eli was amazed the huts had spread as far away as those hills.

Eli sighed. He felt contentment with what he and the other watchers had accomplished in just a hundred years. But he also felt sadness for what the Tassili would soon endure.

Beside Eli stood a white-cloaked man with a tidy gray beard. "You've done well here, Elijah," nodded Cyrus as he scanned the sprawling valley, the mid-day sun gleaming off the golden orb atop his staff. While not as tall as Eli, the overseer had a more commanding presence and an unforgiving gaze. "They have even learned to live in harmony with giants."

"It's not always harmonious," said Eli, watching a farmer scold the corn-trampling behemoth.

"Impressive, nonetheless."

Eli watched a falcon soar above them, then turned to the overseer. "You're certain it will come."

Cyrus turned to Eli, bothered that he would question him. "Yes."

"But not for a year."

"That is right, but they will need time to relocate."

"How do you move twenty-five thousand people?" asked Eli.

"Not just them, their livestock, and everything they can carry."

Eli shook his head.

"You've done it before," frowned Cyrus.

"Not this many. What if they refuse?"

"Then they will perish."

Eli tried to ignore Cyrus's callousness. "Will they find sanctuary among the Nubians?"

"Ra will welcome them."

"What of the unrest there?" asked Eli.

"That is being handled. By the time you get the Tassili to Nubia, it should be no problem."

Eli faintly nodded, still somewhat skeptical.

"Doubt me no longer, Elijah. Your purpose is to help these people, not question me and those who send me."

Eli watched as Cyrus raised his staff, its golden orb glowing.

When an eight-foot-tall shimmering portal opened before them, Cyrus moved toward it, then paused. He turned from the glowing vortex back to Eli. "It will be some time before I come again. I can depend on you to see this through?"

"Yes, of course," replied a troubled Eli.

With a terse nod, Cyrus turned and disappeared into the swirling light.

THE TEMPLE FEAST was bustling with song, dance, and merry chatter. The mouth-watering aroma of roasting lamb spread across the meadow before the temple as families sat on skins and blankets, men plucked stringed instruments, and women sang. While most of the celebrating Tassili sat on the ground, Elijah and the clan elders sat at bamboo tables before the stone temple's entrance.

Eli smiled politely at the maiden serving him a dish of rice, snails, and lamb wrapped in leaves. Her eyes lingered on the tall, wavy-haired Eli, as did those of most young women and many of the old. The smitten maiden smiled at Eli, then giggled when shooed away by the shaman leader, Mawufe.

"Apologies, the women are always enchanted by you," grinned Mawufe.

Eli paid the compliment no mind as he turned to the bronze-skinned leader, who had dark, pulled-back hair and a long braided beard. Mawufe was not only the anointed ruler of the Tassili, but their spiritual guide as well. Endowed with the knowledge of the ancients, as his father before him, their wisdom and balance had allowed generations of Tassili to prosper.

While Eli's skin was pale compared to the Tassili's, not all the watchers were as lightly complected. They all, however, stood more than a head taller than the indigenous plateau people. And while not as large as the giants, they were easy to spot amid the celebrators. "A fine feast," Eli nodded, taking a bite from his leaf wrap.

"I'm happy you are pleased," smiled Mawufe.

Eli chewed his food as Mawufe watched him, then nodded to the towering obelisk to their right. Its elaborate engravings told the story of creation. "Your devotion and craftsmanship are very pleasing."

"If you are pleased, will the Great Ones be also pleased?"

"Yes."

Satisfied, Mawufe lifted his leaf roll and bit into it.

Eli took in the celebration. He saw people dancing, laughing, and singing. He wondered how they would respond to his message.

"It is what you have taught my father, and his father before him, that has made this land most beautiful. I hope you will teach me how to make this people even more pleasing."

Eli's face filled with concern. "Mawufe?"

The ruler looked at Eli with expectant eyes. "Yes?"

Eli sighed. *Now is not the right time,* he told himself. "Later, after the feast, we must talk."

Mawufe studied Eli, then nodded. "Yes, we will talk." While he lacked Elijah's power of insight, it was easy to recognize something weighed heavily on the guardian.

THE NIGHT SKY sparkled with countless stars as Eli walked with Mawufe atop the temple hill. In the valley below, hundreds of torches bathed the settlement in a golden hue while a pleasant breeze stirred the leaves, and crickets chirped.

"The stars are bright tonight," said Mawufe, gazing into the sky.

"Yes, they are," nodded a pensive Eli.

"It is said you come from the stars." Mawufe watched for Eli's response, wondering if he should have spoken such a thing. When he saw Eli's concern, Mawufe lowered his head and said, "I'm sorry, I-"

"Mawufe..."

The shaman leader's worried gaze raised to Eli. He knew something was wrong.

"There is something I must tell you."

"Yes?"

"Your people... Your people must leave this valley."

Mawufe looked at Eli with confusion. "Leave? I don't understand. Are we not pleasing?"

Eli shook his head. "No, you *are* pleasing."

"Then why must we leave? We have labored to make this valley beautiful. It is said the Great Ones ordained this valley for our use!"

"Yes, I know." Eli's lips faltered as he searched for the right words. "Something is coming."

"Is a storm coming? We have many storms and do not fear them. It is the dew from the heavens that blesses this land."

"No, not a storm. A star will fall from the sky. It will change this land," explained Eli.

"A star?" Mawufe asked in confusion. "Are the Great Ones sending punishment?"

"No."

Mawufe looked into the sky. "Which star will fall?"

"You can't see it yet."

"I cannot see it? But I can see many," Mawufe pointed. "When will it come down?"

"When it is time to plant the corn."

Mawufe shook his head, confused. "That is long from now. Where will it fall? Here?"

"Not here."

"If it is not falling here, why must we leave?"

"Mawufe, it will change this land."

"Change it? How?"

"The green plains and the river that brings life will dry up and turn to dust."

Mawufe stared across the glowing valley. "Why would the Great Ones do this if they are pleased?"

Eli sighed. "Do you believe my words?"

Mawufe's troubled gaze moved to Eli. "Yes, you are the guardian the Great Ones have sent us. You have made us pleasing."

"I have not made you pleasing. I have only taught you how to prosper."

"Yes, we have prospered, which gives me pain to leave this valley. It is our home."

"We will lead you to a new home."

"Will you lead us?"

"No, another will," Eli explained. "I must now help other people in another land."

"Where will we go?"

"Far away, to the north and east."

Mawufe's face filled with concern. "How many days walk?"

"Many. Nearly three moons change."

"Hmm." Mawufe's eyes flashed in thought. "That is far."

"Yes, I know."

"That is past the land of the giants to where the Nubians live."

Eli nodded.

"The Nubians," muttered Mawufe with a furrowed brow. "They are a quarrelsome and troubled people. Are the Nubians pleasing to the Great Ones?" He saw Eli's hesitation. "What if my people do not want to leave this valley?"

Eli sighed. "Then they will not prosper. They will die."

Mawufe looked up into the night sky and wondered which of the stars might fall.

NUBIA

THE BEAKED-NOSED Ra stood proudly atop the palace balcony as he gazed across the royal gardens. Ra's sunken eyes appeared even more so with his black-painted eyelids and prominent cheekbones. Below his chin hung a beard wrapped in silk. A necklace of gold and turquoise hung across his smooth, lean chest. He wore a colorful headdress and a skirt while finely crafted sandals shod his feet. Nearly rivaling the watchers in height and beauty, some mistook the Nubian king for an immortal. To that, Ra was pleased.

For three hundred years, the Nubians had prospered in the land that would one day be known as Egypt. It was Ra's father's father who was shown the ways of agriculture, order, and religion by the watchers. For hundreds of years, the rulers of Nubia worshiped the Holy and Great Ones. But Ra's fathers had gone the way of mortals, leaving him King of Nubia, and Ra chose a different path.

While some of the watchers' teachings were still practiced, many of the old ways were done away with. Nubia had changed. The dark secrets of the before times had returned, and with them, unmatched power.

Ra's gaze moved beyond the walls of his lavish retreat to the wide, flowing Nile. Beyond the river lay his city. Sandstone dwellings with brightly colored canopies shaded by towering palms stretched as far as he could see. Ra swelled his bare chest as he considered his magnificence. His gaze moved to the only manmade structure taller than his palace, a sixty-foot obelisk raised to honor the creator gods. Ra wondered how much longer he would have to look at it.

When Ra noticed a fanning palm frond in his periphery, his dark-painted eyes moved to the servant, who bowed his head in apology and lifted the cooling palm leaf farther away.

The Nubian king stood a little taller and puffed out his smooth chest when the red-bearded Lu emerged from the royal bedchamber, ducking to clear its doorway.

Like all watchers, the green-eyed Lu stood over a head taller than most Nubians and had an intimidating presence, but Lu's stern brow and stony face made him even more forbidding.

Ra tried to hide his jealousy as Lu pulled his robe closed over his broad, hairy chest. When the king gave the palm fanner an irritated glance, the servant bowed and scampered out of sight.

Ra was about to make small talk with the banished watcher when an undressed woman, glistening with sweat, passed through the same bedchamber door. Ra watched her long golden legs strut past him, the beads in her lengthy strands of braided hair lightly tapping together as she walked. When the woman brushed her breast against Lu's thick arm, Ra turned his gaze across the river. While the ruler didn't mind sharing his wife and consort with the immortal, it irked him she so much preferred Lu. Ra drew in a cleansing breath and reminded himself that the power Lu had given him should be worth any such sacrifice.

When the queen pushed her hand into Lu's robe, Ra turned to her and said, "Hathor, why don't you show Lu the exquisite gown I had made for you?"

Hathor's painted eyes shifted to her husband, pleased by his jealousy. She pushed her hand further down Lu's robe with a playful smirk. "Husband, why don't you fetch it for me?"

Ra's jaw tightened. He nodded to a servant standing against the wall behind them, and she dutifully disappeared inside the palace.

Hathor ran her hand across Lu's broad chest, looked up at him, and smiled.

Lu knew her game well but had no interest in playing. While her body pleased him, and he was more than willing to give her a child and a future king, Lu needed Hathor for other things.

An irritated Ra stared across the gardens, his hands clutching the balcony railing. Hathor pulled her hand from Lu's chest when he cleared his throat. She saw her husband's frustration and said, "You seem to have a problem with shared governance."

"Is that what you call it?" scoffed Ra, throwing a glance at Lu.

"Enough of this, children," glared Lu.

Ra shook away his frustration, squared up to Lu, and pretended to be unbothered.

When the servant returned carrying a white gown with a gold-spun collar, Hathor pulled it around her like a robe, and Ra gave a calming sigh.

"If you're finished, we have much to talk about," said Lu, glancing at Hathor.

"I'm finished for now," teased Hathor, eyeing the two-foot taller Lu, his thick vermillion hair pulled back.

"Have you quieted the dissidents?" asked Lu.

Ra nodded. "It was a small uprising. Easy for my army to manage. Hardly worth the effort."

"You will learn that a few agitators can quickly grow to many, like a rotten fruit, spoiling an entire basket," said Lu.

"The gateway is a wonderful tool. I wish I had ten of them," said Ra.

"You wish you had one of them," corrected Hathor. "You forget. I am the gatekeeper."

"Yes, of course," nodded Ra. "Shared governance."

Hathor grinned at her husband.

Lu looked past the gardens to the river and the city beyond. "More will come to your land."

"They come from far and wide now," boasted Ra.

"An entire nation will soon arrive," said Lu.

"From where will this nation come?" asked Hathor.

"From the plateau lands to the west. They are being guided here even now by others like me," explained Lu.

"My land is flowing with milk and honey; can you blame them for coming?" asked Ra.

"They will bring strange ways," warned Lu.

"Are they a peaceful people?" asked Ra.

Lu's eyes narrowed. "Yes."

"That is good," nodded Ra. "Peaceful people are like sheep. Easy to control."

"Easy to control, but fast to pollute your ways. Remember, to maintain power, you must maintain control," said Lu.

"Yes, of course." Ra's brow wrinkled in thought. "Should I not welcome those from foreign lands that bring strange ways?"

"You should welcome them. They will prove useful."

"Useful?" asked Hathor.

"They are skilled stone workers. They would make excellent laborers to build your monuments," Lu explained.

"What if they do not wish to labor?" asked Ra.

"Do not give them a voice." Lu eyed Ra. "You may quarrel with your brother, but if a lazy wanderer comes into your house to take your clothes and eat your food, are you not united with your brother against the wanderer?"

"Yes," nodded Ra, not really understanding.

Hathor's face lit up. "I see! We can use them to unify our divided people! They can become a common enemy!"

"But you said they are peaceful," said a confused Ra.

"And you believed me. What if I said they are warlike? Would you not believe that as well?" asked Lu.

Ra looked on in thought.

"The people will believe what they are told," concluded Hathor.

"But it would be a lie," frowned Ra.

"Or would it? You have much still to learn, my husband."

"That is right. Those in power write the truth. Those not in power have no choice but to believe," explained Lu.

"But what if they do not believe our lies?"

Lu turned to the alluring Hathor. "Then, as gatekeeper, you will give them a new place to live."

Ra's face tightened. "Some of my priests say I should kill those who refuse me."

Lu's cutting gaze moved to Ra. "Do you wish to bathe your hands in blood?"

Ra looked down in thought.

"There is a time for the spilling of blood, and there is a time for banishment. You would be wise to discern the two."

Eight Years Later

The Chamber of Passing was a shadowy, cavernous hall with high granite walls covered in mysterious pictographs and glyphs that even the Nubians didn't understand. Built in a forgotten age, its original purpose had been perverted. Once a doorway to other worlds, it was now a prison entrance.

In the center of the chamber, opposite two elevated thrones, was a twelve-foot-tall pewter ring. More symbols and glyphs covered the two-foot-wide sides of the dull-lustered annulus, and its base was fused into the granite floor. In the high ceiling, narrow windows let in sun rays, which cut through the murky air to the seated Ra, illuminating him like a god.

Seated on his throne of punishment, Ra looked down at the prisoner with stern, painted eyes, his cone-shaped chin beard wrapped in black silk, his broad collar necklace shimmering with gems.

Before Ra kneeled the Tassili shaman, Mawufe, his head down, his face bloodied, his tunic torn. Two Tassili elders dressed in humble gowns watched from across the court. Beside them stood four of the king's guards, wearing red skirts and boxy hats. Each held a long-tipped spear and had curved daggers at their sides. Behind the guards stood a ten-foot-tall giant. Clothed in a woven robe, the massive creature had lighter skin than the Nubians and a craggy, deformed face.

"What do you have to say for yourself?" asked a glaring Ra. "Will you command your people to return to their labors?"

Mawufe drew in a ragged breath. "Since arriving in your fair land eight years ago, my people have served you. We have only wanted peace, but you have yoked us mightily. You have forced us to build your monuments—not to the gods of our creation, but in honor of you. This we can no longer do!"

When a bruised and puffy-eyed Mawufe raised his head, a guard stepped forward and slapped his bloody face. "How dare you look upon the mighty Ra!"

Mawufe hung his head.

"Have I not treated your people fairly?" questioned Ra, glancing at Hathor seated beside him.

"You have given us a home," acknowledged Mawufe, "but the price has been dear. We are as if in bondage. My people labor for a pittance. They go hungry, and we can no longer worship as we please."

"That is because you worship false gods," snapped Hathor, her lips painted gold, a horned crown atop her head, her golden gown glistening.

"We worship the creator gods! The kings and queens that rule the heavens!" exclaimed Mawufe, "You want us to worship a man king who rules the grasshoppers!"

The guard stepped forward and clubbed Mawufe.

A fuming Hathor shook her head. "We do not need this vile man. How long will you tolerate his insolence?"

Ra leaned toward his wife and whispered, "He is the leader of twenty thousand! His people will not work without his command!"

"Is the mighty Ra afraid of stone-chipping savages? This heretic is their leader only as long as he breathes," hissed Hathor.

Ra searched his wife's cold eyes. "What should I do?"

"Cut off his head!" exclaimed the seven-year-old prince after stepping out from behind Hathor's throne, his emerald eyes wide, his vermillion hair pulled back, his skin lightly shimmering. While it was known inside the palace walls that the red-bearded watcher had sired Prince Shu, the next king of Nubia, no one spoke of it.

Ra's eyes narrowed. "I will not make a martyr; that would only give the Tassili reason to revolt and stop the work further."

"Then banish him," urged Hathor. "The gods gave me this power to clean our land of filth, just as they did in the before times. I will do this thing for my husband."

While not as cruel as his cold-blooded wife, Ra knew he must pronounce judgment or risk losing his standing. His frustrated gaze turned to the bloodied shaman, and he barked, "Take his beard!"

Hathor eyed her weak husband as guards grabbed Mawufe's arms and pulled back his head. Another guard grasped the shaman's long, braided chin beard, a symbol of his leadership, sliced it off with his dagger, and held it up for all to see.

"My beard does not make me who I am!" exclaimed a defiant Mawufe.

"Banish him!" exclaimed Hathor.

Ra's chest swelled as he glared at the kneeling Mawufe. "It has been decided. If you do not renounce your ways and command your people to return to their labors, I will banish you, and your people will have no shaman!"

Mawufe defiantly raised his head, locked eyes with Ra, and cried, "The Tassili do not need me to guide them; they are led by the Holy and Great Ones!"

"How dare you cast your eyes upon me!" bellowed Ra.

"The fool does not value his eyes! Burn them out!" shouted Hathor.

Horrified yet exhilarated by his wife's cruelty, Ra raised an arm and roared, "Burn out his eyes!"

"Do with me what you will, but you will never darken my soul!" cried Mawufe.

An eager Prince Shu watched a guard pull a glowing poker from a fired clay oven and move to the kneeling Mawufe. While two guards held the shaman's head, the other raised the glowing red poker.

Ra's nostrils flared as the guard pried open Mawufe's eyes, one by one, and pushed the hot poker into their sockets. The sound of searing flesh was lost in Mawufe's agonized cries.

After pulling the groaning, black-eyed Mawufe to his feet, his knees buckling, his searching arms extended, the guards led the blind shaman to the giant pewter ring.

Hathor breathed in her power, stepped down from her throne, and moved to the star gate. "You shall forever wander the world of darkness as a blind man!" When she touched its side, the ring hummed and vibrated until a swirling vortex formed within the annulus, casting the chamber in a churning, fiery hue.

Ra's eyes widened at the dark dreamscape beyond the rift. "Mawufe, shaman leader of the Tassili, I banish you to the world of darkness. May your soul never find the light."

With a shove from the two guards, Mawufe disappeared inside the swirling light, and the rift closed with a snap.

CHAPTER 2
THE LEADER

LANDSBERG PRISON, GERMANY
DECEMBER 1924

The black sedan's engine idled as its headlights illuminated patches of the inky night outside the three-story stone prison. Resembling a castle with its tall, round turrets and green-patinated Turkish domes, dim light glowed from the prison's barred windows. Seated in the rear of the idling sedan was a large red-bearded man wearing a suit. He paid no attention when the prison's main door opened under the keystone arch. A German policeman exited, escorting a smaller man with black, oiled hair parted high on his head and a square mustache under his nose.

The sedan's driver opened the rear door opposite the red-bearded Lu, and the released prisoner, a thirty-five-year-old beady-eyed Austrian, slid into the back seat holding a basket of his belongings.

Adolf Hitler studied the shadowed Lu seated beside him. "It was you. You had me released." Hitler had wondered how he was freed after just six months of his five-year sentence.

Lu, who had discovered the wounded Hitler in a German hospital at the end of the Great War, waited for the sedan to drive away from the prison, then turned to his sunken-eyed apprentice. "You have much to learn, young Adolf."

A slightly miffed Hitler straightened his tie. "I don't know what you mean. I've become more popular with the movement than ever."

"*The movement* will die with you behind bars. You must be free to give the party life."

Hitler shifted in his seat. "I could fill a park with those wanting to hear me tomorrow! Don't forget I spoke to 6,000 of my faithful not long ago in Munich!"

"Don't forget who got you this far," glared Lu. "Because of your Beer Hall Putsch—your failed coup d'état—you are now banned from speaking in Bavaria."

"*Pfff*, Bavarians are fools!" huffed Hitler. "I will go to Berlin. They are open-minded there. I see the Nazi Party only growing. With what those French and English fools did to our country, how could it not? How much is inflation now?"

"Sixty-million reichsmarks to one American dollar," replied Lu.

"Is that all?" laughed Hitler. "The fools, they are playing right into our hands!"

Lu eyed the would-be revolutionary like a disappointed father, but Hitler dismissed the judgment and proudly said, "I've finished it!"

"Your memoirs?"

"Yes, but I'm having trouble with the title. I'm thinking *Adolf Hitler, Leader of the Third Empire.*"

Lu sighed. "Perhaps something more subtle. You don't want to alienate everyone, not yet."

Hitler nodded in thought.

"Call it, *My Struggle.*"

Hitler's eyes narrowed as he considered the title. "*My Struggle.* I like it! It has a sense of...inevitability. I think it's inspirational!"

A humored Lu glanced at Hitler. "Yes, inspirational."

BERLIN, GERMANY
13 MARCH 1932

HEINRICH HIMMLER, a short man who wore a dark suit, spectacles, and his brown hair shaved high on the sides and back, entered the campaign office and closed the door. He mashed his cigarette into an ashtray when he saw the others were already there, then marched across the room and tossed the newspaper onto the table. All eyes moved to its bold headline: HINDENBURG DEFEATS HITLER!

The belligerent Hitler, whose brash rhetoric was as incendiary as it was captivating, had garnered a large following in depressed post-war Germany. And in a bold move, he had run for president.

Himmler turned to the beady-eyed Hitler, fuming in the corner with his suit coat off and his black tie loosened. "Now what do we do?"

"Nothing has changed," frowned Lu, sitting in the shadows at the head of the table, almost disappearing against the dark paneled wall.

"What do you mean, nothing has changed?" snapped the bony-faced Joseph Goebbels before running a hand through his black, oiled-back hair. "How can the party move forward if Adolf is not president of the realm?"

Lu sighed. The shortsightedness of mortals never ceased to astound him. "The plan will move forward."

"Chancellor Brüning has already promised he will ban the SA and the SS!" fretted Himmler.

"There are ways to leverage opposition," explained Lu.

"You tell us these things, but we have nothing to show for it!" barked Hitler, glaring at Lu with folded arms.

"You have human nature on your side," replied Lu.

Goebbels turned to Lu. Such things intrigued him.

Lu leaned forward in his chair, out of the shadows, his red beard neatly trimmed, his hair combed back, his emerald eyes piercing. "Understand, most humans are sheep. They want to be told what to do. They want to be told what to believe. If you control information, if you control the newspapers, you control the people."

"What if we don't control the papers?" asked Goebbels.

"It takes but one weevil to infest a bag of flour."

"Are you saying we are parasites?" asked Himmler.

"I'm saying you can sway the masses. Those who support Hindenburg will change their minds as Germany continues to suffer. When it takes a wagonload of reichsmarks for a man to buy a loaf of bread, that man will soon blame the government and, by extension, President Hindenburg." Lu turned to Hitler. "If you do as I say, you will be in power in a year."

Hitler sighed and unfolded his arms. "What must I do?"

BERLIN, GERMANY
10 DECEMBER 1932

BARON LUDWIG VON STROHEIM nodded politely and raised his champagne glass as a charming heiress in a stunning dress passed by. A small ensemble standing under the grand staircase played Mozart on violins as the wealthy and famous drank, laughed, and conversed. The balding von Stroheim's wealth spoke for itself, making him a must for any fashionable soirée, but it was his connections as a close friend and advisor to the German President that made his presence most desirable. Even so, the long-mustached von Stroheim thought such gatherings insufferable. His advancing age and dislike for sniveling small-talkers, as he called them, left him beyond bored. If not for his wife, he would have left the party already, but the baroness, even at seventy-five, adored the attention.

"Would you care for a chicken liver?" asked a young man in a suit with oiled-back hair carrying a silver platter.

The baron waved the boy off as he eyed a tall gentleman he didn't recognize. He thought the stranger was well-dressed with his fine dinner jacket and bowtie, and strikingly handsome with his white hair and close-cut beard. Von Stroheim stiffened when the stranger moved to him.

"Good evening, Baron von Stroheim," nodded the white-bearded man.

"Good evening, sir," nodded von Stroheim. He studied the stranger for a moment, then said, "You have me at a disadvantage, sir."

"My apologies," bowed the stranger. "My name is Cyrus."

Von Stroheim nodded, still eyeing the man. "And what is your employ?"

"Industry, like yourself," grinned Cyrus.

Von Stroheim nodded, trying to understand what he found so compelling in the man.

"And politics," added Cyrus.

Von Stroheim's thick brow furrowed, sensing the stranger's motives were to get to President Hindenburg through him.

"But I find the current state of affairs in this country abhorrent," frowned Cyrus.

"Yes, don't we all," breathed von Stroheim.

"I fear for the future of the fatherland. Especially with the communists coming to power."

Von Stroheim nearly choked on the idea. As a staunch centralist, the German communist party's rise in popularity was the worst thing imaginable, rivaling the thuggish Hitler's Nazi party. But von Stroheim's worst fears were realized nine months before when the communists gained parliament seats, leaving no clear majority to pull his country out of its dismal depression. The frustrated baron was about to turn away when Cyrus took hold of his wrist.

"Listen closely," said Cyrus, his eyes penetrating.

The baron's jowls slackened, and his face went blank as if in a trance.

"You fear the communists will take control of Germany, but there is a solution. Convince Hindenburg to appoint Adolf Hitler chancellor. His party will see that no communist ever takes power in this land."

When the steely eyed Cyrus pulled his hand away, von Stroheim stared blankly across the room. Then, stroking his mustache in thought, he muttered, "I've just had an idea."

"And what is that?" asked Cyrus, hiding a clever grin.

"If Hindenburg were to appoint Hitler chancellor, that could rally the socialists. That might be just the protection we need against the communists."

Cyrus nodded, as if intrigued by the idea. "But Hitler, he's a bit harsh, wouldn't you say? Some might call him a demagogue."

"No, he can be reeled in, just like any other politician," said von Stroheim with a dismissive wave. "They go where the money is."

"I think that is an excellent idea, but do you think you can convince Hindenburg of it?"

Von Stroheim laughed. "The poor fellow is desperate for a solution. I can convince him. We are of like minds."

Cyrus's grin was barely noticeable.

MUNICH, GERMANY
JULY 1933

CHEERS FOLLOWED the pop of a champagne cork in the wall-papered hotel room. After hastily filling the glasses, a beaming Adolf Hitler raised his and proclaimed, "We did it! The Nazi Party is destined to save the fatherland!"

"To Adolf Hitler, Chancellor and soon President of Germany!" bellowed Hermann Göring, a full-bodied man with short wavy hair and crisp blue eyes.

Cheers filled the room as Lu watched from the shadows.

Barely able to control his smile, Hitler raised his glass to Göring. "To the leader of the Gestapo, may you continue to root out our opposition!"

Göring nodded and raised his glass.

"And to my friend, Heinrich. As police president, I'm sure you will keep these damn Bavarians in place," grinned Hitler.

A beaming Himmler touched glasses with the Chancellor.

"Of course, I cannot forget Joseph, the newly appointed Reich Minister of Public Enlightenment and Propaganda! If it were not for his subtleties in controlling the sheep, I would not be here, toasting you as the leader of the Nazi Party and future president of Germany!"

Goebbels gave an accepting bow, then turned to Lu, watching with folded arms from the corner. "Don't forget Herr Stormbrewer. Without his direction, we would all be in prison right now!"

"Or dead," laughed Himmler.

"The question now, Herr Stormbrewer, is what must we do to maintain power?" asked Goebbels.

Lu's knowing gaze moved to Hitler, whose growing sense of self-importance had made it increasingly difficult to recognize the fallen watcher's role in his success. But Lu understood the neurotic Austrian's frail ego well, and said, "Perhaps you should ask The Leader?"

A thin smile formed under Hitler's square mustache as he made a fist. "We must continue to crush any opposition."

"That shouldn't be too hard with all other political parties banned," laughed Himmler.

"Long live the Nazi Party!" toasted Goebbels.

"Long live the Nazi Party," echoed the others.

"You will yet face opposition," warned Lu.

"And we will crush them!" nodded Göring. "Goebbels is doing an excellent job with the homosexuals and mentally defective."

"It helps that nobody wants them in society," laughed Himmler.

"There is no place for such filth in the pure Aryan race," glared Hitler. "And then there is the Jewish question."

All eyes were on Chancellor Hitler.

"The greatest pestilence and plague on society," frowned Göring.

"It's just a matter of time," nodded Hitler. "Joseph's plan for racial hygiene is inspired. There is no stopping the Aryan race! When it is over, the world will honor the pure race of the gods!"

"Just as it was intended from the creation," toasted Goebbels.

"From the creation," echoed the others with raised glasses.

Lu's thin smile was hardly visible under his beard. He thought it ironic that these four champions of Aryan superiority and purity looked nothing like the blonde-haired, blue-eyed stereotypes they espoused.

Himmler turned to Lu. "Thank you."

"Yes," said Goebbels, raising his glass. "You have led us from the desert to the promised land!"

A pleased Lu looked over the men. They had followed his counsel well, right down to the anti-Jewish protests and book burnings. "It is the thinkers you must now deal with. They relish upsetting the established world. They ask questions that cause others to ask."

"Yes, the intellectuals," nodded Hitler. "Our lists are growing, and we are watching them. Now, with Dachau, we have the perfect place to re-educate such troublemakers."

"Forced labor to enrich The Third Reich! A fitting place for them," nodded Göring.

"And that's if they toe the line. If they give us problems, they will face worse," glared Hitler.

"How many such camps will there be?" asked Himmler.

"As many as we need," nodded a beady-eyed Hitler.

Lu stepped forward. "While the thinkers and dreamers pose a challenge and must be watched and weeded out, even they can be of use."

All eyes were on Lu.

"If they are well-liked, if they have charm and cunning, they can be used to manipulate the masses. The four of you are perfect examples."

Hitler and the others exchanged glances, unsure if Lu's comment was complimentary or derogatory. Himmler was the first to laugh, and the others quickly followed, grinning and nodding acceptingly.

CHAPTER 3
OSTIUM MUNDOS

CHÂTEAU DE BRET
JULY 1933

Eli stared tiredly across the meadow at the grazing sheep. He surveyed their thick, wooly coats and knew it would soon be time to sheer them. Eli shook his head. He had a dozen other chores that needed his attention but had the desire to do none.

As an immortal, Eli had for millennia yearned for the simple yet fulfilling life of a man, but now that he had it, he felt its routine and mundanity numbing. With a tired sigh, Eli turned to the stable that once held Ronan's mares and wagon. It was now empty but for spiders and trampled hay.

It had been fifteen years since Eli's wife Michelle and two-year-old son Franny had disappeared into the abyss. Following that fateful night, Eli discovered most of his powers had returned. Believing he could once again make a difference to humankind, Eli had embarked on a mission of change. But his sadness over his wife and son's loss was crippling, and Eli found his powers of discernment and persuasion were limited.

After nearly a year of searching for a way to rescue Michelle, Eli came to the painful realization that, without an orb, he could not access that dark realm. Left to live out his endless existence, unbothered by angels, Lu, or even Cyrus, Eli now understood his true punishment. He was cursed to be a lonely man in a world swiftly changing beyond his recognition.

With a restless sigh, Eli turned and started back to the chateau. The sun was low in the sky, and Madame Duguay would have dinner waiting for him.

After cleaning up, Eli descended the stairs wearing the suit Ronan had purchased for him years before. He slowed when he saw a hand-rubbing Madame Duguay waiting at the foot of the stairs. Eli smiled pleasantly at the seventy-four-year-old housekeeper, her gray hair pulled back, her nose pointy but jowls droopy, a dark blue dress and white apron covering her matronly shape. With all the change happening around Eli, Madame Duguay had been a loyal and constant presence.

"Master Eli, I'm sorry, but he's here again."

Eli stopped and turned with a furrowed brow.

"I tried to tell him you wouldn't see him, but—"

"He insisted on you asking me," Eli finished, already knowing.

"Yes, sir," Madame Duguay sighed. "Should I ask him to leave?"

"He is very persistent."

"Yes, he is, sir. *Very*."

Eli gazed across the great room in thought, then said, "Invite him to dinner, if it's not too much trouble. Perhaps it's time I face this journalist once and for all."

"No trouble at all, sir," replied Madame Duguay, grateful she would not have to turn him away again.

Eli watched as she returned to the front door. He hadn't moved when the lean reporter in a double-breasted suit followed her into the great room holding his hat, his eyes wide and searching.

"Cleto Nazario, I write for the Vatican newspaper," nodded the nervous reporter, this being the closest he had come to the immortal Eli in his thirty years of trying. Nazario's olive skin was smooth for a man in his fifties. His dark, wiry hair was short, and he had a well-groomed mustache.

"Elijah Mansel, but I think you already know that," Eli said with an indifferent look and outstretched hand.

Nazario stepped closer to the foot-taller Eli and shook his large hand. "Thank you for seeing me."

Eli nodded. "Won't you join me for dinner?"

"Oh, I-I couldn't impose," stammered Nazario.

"You've been imposing for a year," mumbled Madame Duguay as she passed by them into the kitchen.

"I think you must be hungry," said Eli, turning to the dining room.

Nazario's eyes widened. "How did you know? Of course! Discernment is one of your gifts!"

Eli glanced back at the anxious reporter. "I simply surmised. It is dinner time."

"Of course."

Seated across from Eli, Nazario removed a small notepad and pen from his coat. He froze when he noticed Eli's curious gaze. "May I take notes?"

Eli breathed in and nodded. "Yes."

"Thank you." Nazario flipped open his well-used notepad. "How long have you been here?"

"Seventeen years."

Nazario blinked in confusion.

"I first came to Château de Bret seventeen years ago."

"No, I meant, how long have you been...*here?*" Nazario made a swirling motion to the surrounding space.

"The dining room?" Eli playfully asked. "Not ten minutes."

Nazario awkwardly laughed, "No, I meant...here on Earth?"

Eli's eyes narrowed. "Mister Nazario, what is it you wish to learn from me?"

Nazario gulped. "To understand you and the others like you. To learn where you came from, why you are here, and where you will next be going."

"That is a question every man, every woman asks at some point in their existence."

"Yes, of course, but you are not like any other man I know," Nazario said, his eyes wide.

Eli studied the reporter as Madame Duguay, hiding a smirk, poured wine into their glasses. "You've been following me for years. I'm curious to hear what you believe I am."

Nazario took a sip of his wine, forced down a swallow, and said, "I believe you are an immortal being spoken of in the Book of Genesis and other holy texts. A watcher, a son of God."

Eli gave a subtle nod. "Are you not also a son of God?"

Nazario's face grew more intent. "I believe God sent you and those like you here for a purpose."

"And what purpose is that?"

"To guide mankind, to prepare them."

"Prepare them for what?" asked Eli.

Nazario shook his head, "I-I don't know. Will you tell me?"

Eli eyed Nazario as Madame Duguay served plates of trout, Brussels sprouts, and boiled potatoes. "If my purpose was to guide man, wouldn't you say, looking at the world, that I've done a rather poor job?"

Nazario's eyes blinked as he considered Eli's reply.

When Nazario picked up his fork, Eli said, "If I may."

Nazario watched as Eli bowed his head and blessed the food. Then, after muttering a surprised "Amen," said, "You are religious."

"A humble man once taught me the value of being thankful."

"Of course," Nazario nodded, crossing himself.

"You are of the Catholic faith."

"Yes," Nazario nodded, tasting the fish. "As is everyone in my country. Do you follow a denomination?"

"Religion is like a puzzle. Each is a piece that holds some truth and some falsity, but they cannot be complete without the parts of the others."

Nazario cocked his head. "But what of the Eastern religions? The Buddhists? The Hindus?"

"They, too, are part of the puzzle. They teach a spiritualism lost by some."

Nazario chewed a Brussels sprout as he considered Eli's words. "If you are immortal, why do you eat?"

"Because I'm hungry."

Nazario's eyes moved to his notepad, and he asked, "How many of you are there?"

Eli cut a potato with his knife.

"Where did you come from?"

Eli's eyes were on his plate.

"What is going to happen to this world?"

Eli looked up at the reporter. "That is a question I ask as well."

Nazario sighed. "You won't answer my questions?"

Eli eyed Nazario with neither contempt nor adoration.

Nazario nodded, accepting his defeat. After a few bites, his dark eyebrows lifted, and he said, "I spoke to your wife once—after her father's funeral."

Eli stopped chewing.

"I know she disappeared. Will you tell me where she went?"

Eli gulped, his face sullen.

"There is a rumor something happened a few years before she disappeared, that she died while giving birth—that you brought her back to life. Is that true?"

Eli pushed his plate away.

"Please, won't you tell me? The world has a right to know."

"THE WORLD DOES NOT HAVE A RIGHT!" roared Eli. He pushed back his chair, stood, and stormed out of the dining room, leaving a slack-jawed Nazario watching.

When a concerned Madame Duguay entered the dining room, Nazario turned to her and closed his mouth. "I'm sorry. I must have pushed too hard."

"It might be best for you to go now," said Madame Duguay. "Master Eli misses his wife and son terribly."

"So, it is true! He has a son! Did the boy inherit his father's powers?"

With sad eyes, Madame Duguay said, "I cannot tell you."

"Did the boy disappear with his mother?"

Madame Duguay hesitated. Then, with a motioning arm, she said, "If you please."

"Did you witness it? Did you see them leave?" Nazario asked, standing and gathering his notepad and hat. "Where did they go? Was it through a heavenly gate? A doorway to another world?"

Madame Duguay's face emptied of expression.

"It was," breathed a round-eyed Nazario. He studied the speechless housekeeper. He saw her love for Eli and the missing Michelle and realized, if appropriately prodded, she could help him find his answers. "Please, I only want to help Elijah."

Madame Duguay looked toward the great room stairs. She knew Eli had retired to his chambers, where he was brooding. She turned back to the wide-eyed reporter. "How can you help him?"

"I have been pursuing and researching Eli and the other watchers all of my adult life—since my encounter with one as a young man! I have access to information that not even Eli knows about!"

"What kind of information?"

"There are other heavenly gates—some call them star gates—that lead to other worlds. I can help him find them! I can help him find his wife and son!"

Madame Duguay gulped. Her eyes shifted about the dining room as she rubbed her hands.

"Any information would be helpful," Nazario pleaded.

Madame Duguay painfully shook her head. "I'm sorry, I cannot tell you."

"But you want to! You have something to say. I can tell!" said Nazario, following her into the great room.

The fretting housekeeper stopped and turned. "I cannot betray Master Elijah." When she heard Eli's bedchamber door open, she looked up the stairs.

"Madame Duguay, see the reporter out," called down Eli.

Nazario sighed.

"I'm sorry, I want to help him too," Madame Duguay said, moving to the foyer with Nazario following.

When they reached the front door, Nazario turned and handed her his card. "Please send for me if you or Elijah have a change of heart. I will be staying in Gien. I only want to help."

After taking his card, the disappointed Madame Duguay ushered him to the front step and closed the door.

CHÂTEAU DE BRET
SEPTEMBER 1933

ELI WIPED the sweat from his brow as the afternoon sun baked down on him. He looked down the row of lush vines and hanging clusters of purple berries. He spotted a dozen other workers harvesting the grapes and wondered if it was time to hire more.

After topping a large basket with juicy berries, Eli turned his laden cart and started back to the winery. As Eli pushed the two-wheeled cart along the trodden path, he looked over the rows of grapevines stretching from one hilly horizon to the next. Eli was pleased with the year's harvest and wondered how many more years he would run the vineyard. While Ronan had handed over much of the work to others because of his advancing age,

Eli realized he would never have to stop working for that reason. Eli sighed. Fifteen years had passed since the fateful night that Lu killed Ronan, and Michelle and Franny had disappeared. Eli now understood how a single event could forever alter a mortal's life.

As Eli climbed a gentle hill and the old stone winery came into view, he noticed a man standing on the path ahead. Unlike the other workers dressed in soiled and sweat-stained shirts and trousers, this man wore a clean, cream-colored suit and matching fedora. Eli's jaw tightened as he approached the eager Cleto Nazario.

"Good afternoon," said Nazario, hoping for a reply as Eli brushed past him.

"Why am I not surprised to see you?" asked Eli, pushing his cart toward a large wooden vat.

Nazario followed Eli. "I believe it is my destiny."

Eli eyed the tenacious reporter as he hefted a basket of grapes into the knee-high vat, its wood-slat sides stained from decades of use. "Your destiny is to pester me? If I am who you claim, I have only to wait out your life."

Nazario's face filled with concern. His greatest fear was his life ending before he could unravel the mystery of the watchers. "Of that, I have no doubt. I truly wish to learn more about you. It is my life's mission—my passion. But I now believe I have an even more valuable part to play."

"And what part is that?" asked Eli, hefting another basket of grapes.

"To help you fulfill your mission."

"My mission?" Eli stopped and turned to the reporter. "If you want work, you should consider changing your clothes. Grape juice and fine linen are not agreeable companions."

Nazario's chest swelled. "I know you suffer for your lost wife and son."

Eli emptied the basket into the vat with a frustrated sigh.

"Forgive me. I don't wish to anger you. On the contrary, I wish to help you."

"Help me? How?" Eli asked, staring into the vat, his basket still resting on its edge.

"By finding your Michelle and young François!"

"You have no understanding of these things," replied Eli, stacking the empty basket and moving to the cart for another.

"I know your son is special, like you."

Eli looked down. "Every lost child is special to those left behind."

"I don't mean that. Your son has special gifts. A unique purpose. I've heard of a legend that—"

"What do you want from me?" snapped Eli.

"I told you! To help you get your Michelle back from the world of darkness!" Nazario replied with pleading eyes.

"What can you possibly know about that?" fumed Eli.

"That she disappeared into another world, and you have searched for her."

Eli turned to the chateau on the hill, its dark slate roof just visible over the trees. "Did Madame Duguay tell you these things?"

"I have many sources," gulped Nazario.

"Spoken like a true reporter," sneered Eli. "Now, if you please. I have work to do."

Nazario stepped back as Eli replaced the empty baskets on his cart and turned back to the vineyard. "I know you think you must have a golden ball to access that world, but there are other ways. There are doorways!" He helplessly watched as Eli pushed past him. Then, feeling all of his efforts were vanishing before him, Nazario blurted, "I know where one is! A natural doorway! An *Ostium Mundos!*"

Eli stopped mid-stride.

Nazario waited to see if the immortal would turn back to him.

"Where would you have learned of this?" Eli asked, his back still turned, his hands on the cart.

"You forget, I write for the Roman Observer, the *Vatican* newspaper! I have access to the Vatican Library, to its secret archives! They hold the keys to mysteries most men understand nothing of." Nazario shook his head, overwhelmed by the immensity of it all. "They hold untold treasures few are allowed to behold!"

Eli set down the cart and turned to Nazario, not in anger but in consideration. "You know where a portal is?"

Nazario gulped. "Yes. Well, mostly," he added with a faint shrug.

Eli turned back to his cart.

"No! No! I know where, but I need your help! I only understand bits and pieces, you see. You can help me put the puzzle together!"

Eli studied the reporter. "You would help me with these things?"

"Of course!" Nazario eagerly nodded.

Eli's eyes narrowed. "At what cost?"

Nazario gave a harmless shrug. "In exchange for information."

"And what information is that?"

"For you to help me understand all that God has done from the beginning to the end so that I can share it with mankind!"

Eli studied Nazario for a moment. Then, with a shake of his head, he muttered, "Mortals are incapable of such understanding."

A slack-jawed Nazario watched as Eli pushed his cart down the path. The reporter's face tightened. "You call yourself a guardian, but you're nothing of the sort! You've hidden from the world! Another war with Germany is on the horizon, and you will again do nothing! The world deserves a better protector than you!" Realizing what he had just done, Nazario clasped a hand to his mouth. He shook his head in dismay as Eli disappeared over the hill to the vineyard.

ELI STARED at the empty fireplace as the table lamp flickered beside him. The ticks of the mantle clock echoed in the stillness of the night as Jacques, a furry Berger Picard, softly snored at his feet. For hours, Eli had considered the frustrated reporter's accusations. Nazario's words were not hurtful to him; Eli had pronounced such judgment on himself years before. He recognized he was a failed watcher. Eli's futile efforts to guide humankind had left the world spiraling out of control. He doubted anything or anyone could change it.

Eli wished things were different. He wished he could be a power for good again. But more than anything, Eli wished his beloved wife and son were with him. He missed Michelle's loving touch, her soothing voice, and her warm embrace. As a watcher, Eli had gone for a hundred millennia without a woman's affection, while so many of his kind had violated their code and mated with the alluring daughters of men.

At times, Eli wondered if it was a mistake to have fallen in love with the radiant Michelle. But then he would remind himself he had lost all recollection of his divine identity and past at their meeting. Eli marveled that, even as a watcher with a celestial calling, there were so many things he didn't understand. Why the Holy and Great Ones would sanction his union with Michelle was now clear to him. The gods had anointed their marriage for a wondrous purpose and the fulfillment of prophecy, for it was only through the union of a noble watcher and a woman of the divine birthright that the

Harbinger could be born. But Eli didn't understand his son's mission. Nor did he understand why the gods would allow Michelle and Franny to be taken from him. He wondered how his son could accomplish his task from the abyss.

For fifteen years, Eli had waited for an answer, for Charmeine or another messenger to tell him what to do. But all had been silent, leaving Eli angry and frustrated. Much of his aggravation came from seeing the evil Lu's hand in world affairs. To think they were once unified in the same noble cause made Eli's heart ache. That his trusted mentor, Cyrus, had masterminded the diabolical plan was harder still and left Eli fearing all was lost.

After pulling up from his wingback chair, Eli trudged up the stairs, each step a cruel reminder of paradise lost. He topped the steps and pushed open his bedchamber door. A glowing lamp flickered off the dark paneling. Eli stood at the door, eyeing the spot on the bed where his wife had died giving birth. The pain of Michelle's passing would have been unbearable had the angels not restored her life.

Eli sighed. His heart and loins ached thinking of their too few years together. He closed his eyes and pictured their love-making. He felt her body next to his. He felt the rhythm and friction of passion, causing every part of his body to erupt in ecstasy. In Eli's eons as a watcher, he had never known such sensual gratification. He wondered if he would ever feel such rapture again.

Eli closed the door and pulled off his coat. He eyed the lonely bed like an untrustworthy friend. Tormented by dreams of what had been and what will never be, and the vivid nightmares of his wife and son alone in the darkness, Eli couldn't remember when he had last slept restfully. He told himself he didn't deserve such luxuries, not while his Michelle and Franny were lost in the abyss.

Once disrobed, Eli pulled back the covers, dimmed the oil lamp, and slid into bed. His mind went back to that terrible night, fifteen years before. Eli stared at the dark ceiling as he waited for his torment to begin.

CHAPTER 4
THE DARK REALM

The shimmering portal ruptured the blackness of the night, its swirling light illuminating the frantic Michelle standing on the edge of the chateau's back lawn in her nightgown. "Give me my son back!" she cried, charging Lu, only to be knocked back to the ground beside her dead uncle.

"Cyrus, what have you done?" gasped the battered Eli, his sweat-glistening chest heaving.

"I'm maintaining balance. I'm protecting this world from *him!*" glared Cyrus, pointing at the distraught Franny still reaching for Ronan.

"He's a little boy!" sobbed Michelle from the grass.

"HE IS THE ENDER OF WORLDS!" roared Cyrus.

With the frightened toddler clamped under his arm, Lu reached into his coat and removed the orb. It glowed at his touch, and a shimmering crimson portal opened before them.

"NO! NOT THE ABYSS!" cried Eli as Lu started toward the scintillating doorway and the dark dreamscape beyond. With the last of his strength, Eli lunged. He smashed into the back of Lu's legs and brought him down with Franny, six feet short of the shimmering red portal. While

Lu kept his hold on the child, the faintly glowing orb broke free and rolled across the grass. Eli reached for it, but his hand fell inches short.

"Don't let him get the orb!" shouted Lu as he fought for it.

Gadreel raised his sword and swung it down on Eli's outstretched arm.

"ELI!" screamed Michelle.

Eli pulled back his arm as the glistening blade chopped into the lawn, just missing his fingers.

Horrified, Michelle watched as Gadreel pulled the embedded sword from the earth and, with both arms, raised it over his head. She knew, in an instant, that her Elijah would be gone. When Michelle felt the warm pewter of the blazerod near her uncle's hand, she turned and grabbed it, raised it in her arms, and pointed it at the fierce-eyed Gadreel.

Cyrus was watching the scene unfold when a white bolt of light shot from the blazerod through Gadreel's chest. "What?" gasped Cyrus. His stunned gaze turned to Michelle, wondering how a mortal could harness the weapon's energy, but then he remembered Michelle was no ordinary mortal.

Eli lunged for the orb when Gadreel dropped the sword and collapsed on the grass. The faintly shimmering sphere came to life at his touch, and Eli felt a jolt radiate through his body.

"Get the orb!" yelled Lu, reaching for it with one hand as he held the squirming Franny against him with the other.

A teary-eyed Michelle pointed the blazerod at Lu and roared, "LET GO OF MY SON!" But Lu held the reaching Franny before him like a shield as he climbed to his feet.

Eli cried out in pain when Cyrus's boot stomped on his wrist. After prying the domain sphere from Eli's hand, the overseer stood triumphantly. When Michelle shot a bolt at him, Cyrus dodged it.

Lu took advantage of the distraction, turned to the glowing crimson portal, and hurled Franny through it.

Ten feet away, Eli reached for his son as the boy disappeared into the dark abyss. "NOOO!" bellowed Eli, clawing across the grass toward the red-shimmering doorway.

Michelle leaped to her feet and charged Cyrus with the blazerod.

Cyrus was closing the portal with the domain sphere when Michelle grabbed it from him and dashed for the shrinking doorway. She dived through it with orb and blazerod in hand.

Michelle landed hard on the other side of the portal and tumbled across the rocky ground. She turned back as the gateway shrunk and then closed, replacing the glowing lights of the château with an eerie blackness. "Franny? Franny? Where are you?" Michelle called out, adrenaline still coursing through her. She fought to see through the darkness but discerned only jagged, surreal shapes in the shadowy expanse surrounding her.

Michelle waited for her eyes to adjust to the blackness, but they didn't. The hint of light around her came from the sky, where a dark layer of clouds choked out the moonless night.

"FRANNY!" cried Michelle. She spun when she heard something stir in the shadows behind her. There was a deep, groaning sound, like an awakening bear. Michelle gulped.

Frantic to find her lost child, Michelle climbed to her bare feet, her white nightgown all but lost in the inky night. "Franny, where are you?" This time, the groaning was more of a growl. Michelle stepped back. She stopped when she felt something against her. Gasping, Michelle spun around to the prickling arm of a dead branch. "Where am I?" she muttered before calling out again, "Franny! Come to Mama! It's okay, darling!"

Michelle gasped when she noticed something move in the shadows. She frantically scanned the darkened earth for the orb and blazerod she had lost on impact as the sounds of approaching footsteps and heavy breathing drew closer. *Oh, where are they?*

Michelle made out a round shape in the darkness and reached down for it. The orb glowed at her touch, giving light to things immediately around her. When she raised back up, Michelle squealed in fright at the hulking creature in tattered robes towering above her, its craggy, long-bearded face aglow in the orb's light. The giant's reaching hand was three times hers and caused the shrieking Michelle to fall back to the stony earth, clutching the orb.

The giant looked down at her. Its droopy eyes widened at the sight of the glowing sphere, and its large hand stopped short of taking it.

Michelle scrambled backward with the shimmering orb held up between them. But its light was barely enough to illuminate the giant's wary face, his yellow teeth bent and broken.

"Who are you? What do you want?" gasped Michelle as she pushed backward on the ground.

The giant moved closer, his huge hand still inches from the glowing orb.

Michelle let out a whimper when she backed into a boulder. She was trapped. But when the boulder moved, and she fell back, the illuminating orb revealed a second giant glaring down at her. This one was bald but for wispy strands of hair, its long, knotted beard dangling toward her.

Michelle shrieked and spun on the ground. When she did, her free hand landed on the pewter blazerod. Falling on her back, Michelle pointed the ancient weapon at the leering giant and fired a bolt. The blast of light shot up, grazing the balding giant's head before disappearing into the black sky, illuminating the thick, dark clouds like a reverse lightning strike. The balding giant cried out, grabbed its head, and leaped back with the agility of a much smaller creature. The larger, tattered-robed giant pulled back its reaching hand, its drooping eyes wide with fear, and turned and charged into the blackness, its strides shaking the earth.

A trembling Michelle turned, holding up the orb to see what lurked around her, but its dim light reached barely a few feet away and made the surrounding blackness darker still. Michelle gulped as her fearful eyes scanned the suffocating night. With so little visibility, she didn't know if she was alone or if danger was lurking beyond her light. Michelle swallowed her fear and climbed to her feet with the blazerod pointed before her. "Franny!" she again called out. She gulped when the giant groaned in the blackness.

With her blazerod extended, Michelle slowly turned as she listened for the sounds of approaching danger. The groaning seemed to move farther away, but she feared the beasts were still lurking. Michelle raised the orb above her, hoping it would better illuminate her surroundings, but she saw only jagged, murky shapes beyond the orb's light.

After remembering how it had lit up the clouds, Michelle fired the blazerod. The bolt of light shot through the night, illuminating a path between the vitrified ruins as it sped along. Michelle shuddered when she spotted other shapes ducking into the shadows as the burst of glowing energy shot past them. Michelle took a few more cautious steps, her breast rising and falling, her wide eyes searching the murkiness. She fired another bolt to her right and watched the wave of light cross a hundred feet of jagged, teetering walls and piles of rubble. Sparks flew when it slammed into a strange-looking machine with bird-like wings crashed against the ruins. *What is this place?*

Michelle looked at the blazerod and wondered if its bolts were infinite and what she would do should it run out. When she heard heavy footsteps behind her, Michelle spun around. Her simply pointing the blazerod was enough to cause thunderous clomps and crashing sounds as a giant dove for cover, knocking over a wall.

"Franny, where are you?" she whispered, afraid of what any loud cries might bring. She shook off her fear and yelled, "Franny! FRANNY! IT'S MOMMY! I'M GOING TO FIND YOU!"

Her chest heaving, Michelle listened for her little boy but heard only the murmuring giants and a distant humming sound. She wondered how a two-year-old could survive in such a terrible place. Michelle looked back toward the vanished portal, hoping another doorway would open. She wondered how long she would have to wait for Elijah to rescue her. Michelle told herself it wouldn't be long, but then remembered the horrible struggle on the other side of the doorway. Michelle looked around her and wondered where she was. She looked for a moon in the dark, clouded sky and wondered how long before daylight would come.

When the orb grew heavy in her outstretched hand, Michelle lowered it to her side. She stared vigilantly into the night, looking for meaning in the strange world around her. But the murkiness revealed only indiscernible shapes and shadows. She detected movement to her left, but all was still and dark when she turned that way.

As Michelle's pounding heart calmed, she noticed a strange billowing cloud moving toward her. Approaching at eye level, it was the size of a crouching man. The cloud was black as coal at its heart, but dark shades of purple filled its roiling mass, and it made a gentle hum like a faraway swarm of bees. As it drew near Michelle, a terrible sense of dread and foreboding filled her. The closer the cloud came, the stronger the gloom. Hovering just inches before her face, Michelle closed her eyes, but the same purple mass was in her mind. She let out a whimper as memories of torn and bloodied soldiers she had cared for flooded in. She viewed her mother lying in bed, crying out in pain from her cancer, but more than that, Michelle felt her mother's agony. "Nooo," she whimpered, the pain driving her to her knees. Michelle clutched her chest when she relived her father dying in her arms. She gasped when Gadreel's sword plunged through her Uncle Ronan's chest. "Oh, nooo!" Michelle cried as the darkness swept over her like a suffocating blanket of doom.

With her chest rising and falling, Michelle opened her frightened eyes. The terrible cloud had engulfed her. Only her hand holding the orb was free. Michelle felt her grip loosening, as if the cloud were prying her fingers from the golden sphere. She breathed in determination and raised the orb into the midst of the dark cloud, parting and thinning it. Michelle dropped the blazerod, clutched the orb with both hands, and raised it above her head. "No! Go away! Leave me!" To her astonishment, the humming, roiling cloud moved away and dispersed into the inky night. Unblinking, Michelle waited for it to return, but it didn't. "What is this place?" she asked as she lowered the orb. She looked at its dimly glowing characters and wondered what they were telling her.

With her heart still pounding, Michelle retrieved the dropped blazerod. Unsure of where to go or what to do, she searched the stony ground around her with the glowing orb, then sat. Michelle tried to swallow her fear as she scanned the darkness for danger, her blazerod at the ready.

Not far away, crouching behind a crumbling wall, the tattered-robed giant eyed Michelle.

As she stared into the inky night, Michelle felt a chill through her thin, silky nightgown. She tightened into a ball and wondered when the sun would rise.

HAVING LOST all sense of time, Michelle didn't know how long she had been listening for danger and hoping for Elijah's rescue when her lonely gaze moved to the orb. She studied its strange, glowing symbols. *If I can use the blazerod, maybe I can use the orb as well.* Michelle rotated the golden sphere in her hands, touching and pressing it in different places and waiting for something to change. She looked into the hole in the orb's base and fit two fingers into it, but nothing happened.

Michelle thought back to the day Eli had returned from America. She remembered the portal to the dark abyss he opened using the orb. She remembered Eli casting the loathsome halfborn Gik into it. Michelle guessed that was where she was. She wondered how Gik had returned to her world. *There has to be a way back using the orb, but I have to find Franny first.* Then the thought struck her. *What if Franny's not here? What if he's in another world worse than this?* Michelle pushed out the thought. *No, this is where Lu cast him. It was this dark and dreadful place!*

It has to be! Michelle wiped the tears from her eyes using the side of her hand, unwilling to let go of either the orb or the rod. *Elijah's probably already found Franny. He'll come for me next. I'll stay here so he can find me.*

As time passed, Michelle frequently checked the horizons for signs of a rising sun, but all remained dark. She listened for the giants and searched for the purple cloud, but all was still. Michelle hoped she had scared them all off.

When Michelle heard a distant whimpering behind her, she spun around and called out, "Franny? FRANNY?" She held her breath and listened.

"Momma?" was the faint reply.

Without thinking, Michelle charged down the darkened path toward the sound of her son; the glowing orb held out in one hand, the blazerod clutched at the ready in her other. Moving faster than the orb's light could show her, Michelle didn't notice the jagged, teetering walls were now higher and less damaged. But when two walls formed an even darker alley and then a tunnel, Michelle's run slowed to a stop. "Franny! Where are you?"

"Mommy!" The muffled reply came from inside the tunnel and was moving away. *Someone's taking him!* Michelle charged into the tunnel, desperate to rescue her son. Her eyes widened when she spotted a light at its opening, forty steps away.

As Michelle neared the end of the tunnel, a tall, flickering torch came into view on the far side of a stone bridge. She spotted a shaggy-haired man in tattered clothes standing there. He was holding her little boy. "Franny!"

When Michelle burst from the tunnel, she glimpsed a net just before it swept her from her feet. "No! Franny!" Michelle cried as the net pulled her into the air. She pointed the blazerod at the shadowy figures scrambling around her and fired a bolt. The blast illuminated a half-dozen men and women in ragged clothing and ratty hair before knocking a dodging woman off her feet with a painful howl.

"Give me my son back!" yelled Michelle, but before she could fire the weapon again, a flat-faced man with wild, matted hair and an eye tattooed on the center of his forehead pried the blazerod from her hand. "No! My son!" Michelle sobbed, glimpsing young Franny as another pulled the orb from her. "No! You can't have those! Give them back! They're mine!" she cried, hanging sideways four feet off the ground.

The man with the tattooed eye laughed and waved the stolen orb in Michelle's panicked face.

When Franny reached for her from over the shaggy man's shoulder, Michelle pulled back her arm and punched the flat-faced thief in the nose, knocking him back on his heels. "Give me my son!"

The flat-faced man wiped the blood from his mouth and nose. Then, with an infuriated look, he raised the pewter blazerod like a club and hammered it down on Michelle's head, knocking her limp.

WHEN MICHELLE CAME TO, she was kneeling on a cracked marble floor. On either side of her, two bare-chested guards, each with a tattooed eye on their forehead, held her up by an arm. As Michelle's head rolled on her shoulders, she heard sounds around her, but all was a blur.

Squinting from the flickering torchlight and her throbbing head, Michelle looked through blurry eyes for something recognizable. The uneven light cast shifting shadows on the large chamber's high, soot-covered walls. She discerned moving shapes and muttering voices but understood none of it. *It's a dream—a terrible nightmare.*

Michelle grimaced when the putrid stench of burning flesh registered. She groaned, and her heart sank when she saw her dirty nightgown and remembered all that had happened. *It has to be a dream.* "Franny?" Michelle called out, but her voice was weak and raspy.

As Michelle's vision cleared, she noticed a black cat sitting before her, its scrutinizing eyes shimmering. Michelle gasped and pulled back when the flat-faced man moved in front of her, his cocked arm holding the blazerod like a club. Michelle braced for another blow, but he lowered the rod and backed away.

Blinking, she saw a half-dozen men and women in dingy clothes sitting in the shadows of the large, round chamber. They spoke in an unfamiliar tongue. She watched as the flat-faced man exchanged her blazerod and orb for a basket of wood scraps, then bowed and left the chamber.

"Who are you?" came a gruff woman's voice from the shadows.

Michelle lifted her aching head but could make out only faint outlines in the darkness. She turned to the source of the light, a small flame burning from an odd-shaped torch atop a knee-high platform coated with layers of dark, dried wax. Blinking to make sense of what looked like a human leg standing atop the altar, Michelle recoiled when she realized it was a leg. The flickering, putrid flame fed on the resin-coated leg's flesh and fat like candle wax, its bones a wick. Michelle groaned in disgust and looked away.

"Who are you?" repeated the stern woman's voice.

The woman's words were strange, yet familiar. Michelle strained to see into the shadows across the chamber. When a raised platform and a shadowed figure sitting in a high-backed chair flickered into view, she said, "My name is Michelle," her voice weak and cracking. "You have my son."

"*Who* are you?" the shadowed woman repeated, her tone growing impatient. "From what tribe do you come? How did you come to possess these things?"

Michelle's eyes widened at the orb and blazerod resting on a worn and stained rug before the shadowy throne.

"I command you to tell me! What tribe are you from?"

"Please, I just want my son back," groaned Michelle. Able to make out the onlookers better now, she saw their dirty faces filled with curious trepidation. Her eyes narrowed when the single, watching eye tattooed on their foreheads came into focus. Michelle gulped and looked up at the bare-chested guards clutching her arms with one hand and long, forked spears with the other. Her searching gaze moved up the high chamber walls to painted pictographs and glyphs muted by soot. On one wall stood a ragged man on a scaffold with fresh pictographs behind him. He looked down at her with a pencil brush in hand. The chamber's domed ceiling had a small opening at its top, allowing the putrid smoke to escape.

"Are you a traveler?"

Michelle turned back to the shadowed figure on the throne. "I came here through a portal, if that's what you mean." Michelle gulped as the grimy faces eagerly conversed in the shadows. "Please, will you give me back my son? I just want to take him home."

"Where is your home?" asked the shadowed woman.

"France," replied Michelle with a faltering smile. "We have a lovely château just outside of Gien. It has a vineyard and a peaceful meadow full of sheep." Michelle hoped the happy memory would snap her out of the nightmare. But her smile vanished when a fat, heavily tattooed woman's face appeared from the shadows, her head shaven, her eyes unfeeling.

"You are an otherworlder?"

Michelle gulped. "I'm not from this dreadful place, if that's what you mean." She forced another smile and asked, "Please, may I have my son back?"

"There are no children here."

"But my son is here. I saw him!" Michelle insisted.

"He is your child no longer," glared the tattooed woman.

"What do you mean?" Michelle's eyes widened when the woman, wearing a dingy red robe and a necklace of bones around her fat neck, leaned out of the shadows. Beside her stood a calm, curly-haired little boy dressed in pajamas, a thin rope tied around his neck, his small hand clenched in hers. "Franny!"

"Where did you get these?" asked the tattooed woman, pointing to the golden sphere and pewter rod.

Michelle's worried gaze lowered to the orb and blazerod.

"Why do you have them?"

"I took them from Lu when he cast my son here," Michelle replied, wondering what the evil watcher's name would mean to them.

The tattooed woman's eyes swelled. "Luqiel, the watcher, sent you here?"

Michelle gulped.

"You are no traveler but a thief!" snarled the tattooed woman.

"Please, give me my son, and I'll leave. You can have those things if you like."

"I shall have them anyway, and the boy also!"

"No! He's my son!" cried Michelle.

"Take her to the pit!"

"No! Franny! Franny! It will be okay!" sobbed Michelle as the guards dragged her from the flickering chamber.

The ordinarily calm Franny pointed at the fighting Michelle and whimpered, "Mamma."

CHAPTER 5
DEMONS

CHÂTEAU DE BRET
SEPTEMBER 1933

Eli catapulted up from his bed with a gasp. Disoriented, he looked around his bedchamber as the terrible images of his nightmare faded. He gulped and turned to the morning light spilling through the shutters and wondered what terribleness Michelle and their son faced in the abyss. With his heart still pounding, Eli rubbed his tired eyes, groaned, and plopped back on his pillow. His face distraught, he stared at the ceiling as the nightmarish images fled. Eli's eyes welled with tears, and he groaned in anguish. He turned on his side to where Michelle would have laid and sobbed.

When his chamber door opened, and Madame Duguay entered, Eli wiped away his tears and choked down his emotion. He closed his eyes when she opened the shutters, allowing in the full measure of the morning sun.

"Would Master Eli care for breakfast today?" asked Madame Duguay, trying to hide her concern.

"No, thank you," muttered Eli.

Madame Duguay gulped and stepped closer. "You must eat, sir."

"No, thank you."

With a sigh, the dutiful housekeeper turned to leave. She stopped before closing the door. "Master Eli, forgive me, but why do you torment yourself?"

"I do not torment myself. That is the universe's pursuit," muttered Eli.

Madame Duguay shook her head. "Why do you give up when there are those who wish to help?"

"Who can help me?" groaned Eli.

"The reporter, for one. He said he can help you find our Michelle and little François!"

"How can he help me?" bellowed Eli. "He doesn't understand such things!"

Madame Duguay's brow tightened. "Lady Michelle loved Aesop's fables as a child. Do you know of them?"

Eli's face dimmed. "Yes, I met Aesop once in Delphi."

Unimpressed, the housekeeper continued, "One of her favorite stories was *The Mouse and the Lion*. In it, a lion threatens to eat a mouse that wakes him from his sleep. The mouse begs forgiveness and tells the lion that such an unworthy prey would bring him no honor. The lion then agrees and sets the mouse free. Later, when hunters net the lion, the mouse hears it roars and comes to the lion's rescue. That little mouse gnaws through the ropes and sets the lion free! Do you know the moral of that story?"

Eli closed his eyes and sighed. "That mercy brings its reward? There is no reward for mercy or any other good deed! There is only punishment and misery!"

Madame Duguay's flabby jaw tightened, and her pity turned to scorn. "Its moral is that there is no being so small that it cannot help a greater! Forgive me, and you may dismiss me for saying so, but you are behaving like a spoiled little boy too used to getting his way! You must go out and fight for what you want! You must find a way to bring them home!" Bursting into tears, Madame Duguay pulled Nazario's card from her apron pocket and slapped it down on Eli's dresser. She then stormed out of the room and slammed the door closed.

Eli glared at the ceiling, then sat up and threw his pillow across the room. Tossing his legs over the side of the bed, he scowled at the rug. Eli turned to the spot where the angel Charmeine had visited him years before and wondered where the messengers were now. He wondered why all had abandoned him. Eli's chest swelled with misery. He knew Madame

Duguay's words were true but didn't want to hear them. Eli drew in a ragged breath and wiped at his tears. He thought of all the mortals he had guided in his thousands of years as a watcher. He wondered how many of his encouraging speeches were unheeded.

Eli shook his head and dropped back onto his bed. All of his existence, he had yearned to live as a man, but now, after being granted his wish, Eli had found the taste of mortality unpalatable. He thought the emotion, the mental anguish, and the suffering debilitating. Eli wondered if he was a fool for craving such things.

When Eli heard a scratching at his door, he pulled himself out of bed and shuffled across the room. He opened the chamber door to Jacques, sitting on his haunches, looking up with pointy ears and sad eyes. It was as though the dog understood his pain.

Eli kneeled, and Jacques came to him. He scratched its ears, and the dog licked his face. Eli sighed and got to his feet. Jacques watched as his master moved to the dresser where Madame Duguay had left Nazario's business card. Eli shook his head, took the card, and tore it up.

ÉLYSÉE PALACE
PARIS, FRANCE
29 SEPTEMBER 1933

SEATED on a sky-blue camelback couch with lion claw feet, Eli looked uneasily around the high-ceilinged room. He guessed an hour had passed but told himself his time would be well spent once he could speak with the French president. While Eli had not been an influence for good since before the Great War, twenty years earlier, he still had his gift of discernment and a wealth of experience and knowledge rivaled by only a few. Frustrated by the wait, Eli told himself he would have never been so inconvenienced in the old days. He was sure the new president would welcome his visit once he heard what Eli had to say.

Across the gilded room, a lovely young woman sat typing behind a white and gold desk. She wore her dark hair short and wavy and her floral dress loose. Her pouty eyes moved from her work to Eli. The watcher shifted on the couch as he felt her curious gaze. When their eyes met, Eli nodded, then looked away. Secluded at the château for years, he had forgotten the attention he often drew.

Eli's eyes drifted across the ostentatious room. His gaze climbed the gaudy wall paneling to the thick, wavy crown molding, all embellished in gold. He thought back to Louis the Sixteenth, the last king of France. It had been 140 years since that monarch had lost his head in a guillotine. Eli had tried to persuade the proud king to change his reckless and flamboyant ways and recognize his impoverished countrymen. But from the elaborate décor of the French palace, it seemed to Eli that no lesson had been learned.

When a door across the room opened, and a thick man in a suit and monocle approached, Eli took his hat and stood, expecting to be ushered in to see the president. But before the advisor said a word, Eli knew there was a problem.

"No, I must speak with him," insisted Eli.

Taken aback, the short advisor said, "Monsieur, I'm afraid that's not possible. President Lebrun is very busy."

"But I have an appointment!"

"Yes, your appointment is with me. I'm sorry for any misunderstanding, Monsieur..." the advisor glanced down at his notebook. "...Mansel."

"The misunderstanding is with you," glared Eli. When he glimpsed the president moving down the corridor through the still-open door, Eli pushed past the advisor and called out, "President Lebrun! A moment of your time!"

The lean, graying president pretended not to hear the request and started into a conference room, his advisors at his side.

"It's Elijah Mansel! You will remember me from your days as the minister of war!"

The French president stopped and turned to the approaching Eli.

"I'm sorry, sir. Should I call for the palace guard?" asked the short advisor as he waddled behind the insistent Eli.

The president raised a halting hand to his advisor and stared at Eli. "I remember you," he said, as if recalling a dream.

Eli stopped before the president and sighed. "Yes. I hoped you would."

Albert Lebrun had a round face and a long nose. His receding, combed-back hair was gray, but his smooth mustache was black. He had wide, kind eyes and looked at Eli like a fond uncle might. "There is no need to call the guards. Elijah is an old acquaintance. You others go in. I'll join you shortly."

Eli waited for the advisors to file into the conference room, then asked, "How is Marguerite?"

"My wife?" Lebrun's eyes brightened. "She is fine. She would have been delighted to see you," he smirked.

Eli paid the compliment no mind. Instead, his brow tightened, and he said, "Forgive the interruption, but there is something of utmost importance I must speak with you about."

Lebrun cocked his head. "And what is that?"

"This situation with Germany is most vexing. If steps are not taken, I fear a catastrophe."

"Oh dear. France is in no shape for another of those."

Eli locked eyes with Lebrun. "This Hitler who has risen to power—you understand he has not achieved this success on his own. Lu has groomed and guided him."

Lebrun's face went blank.

"They will not stop with Germany. They plan to rule the world. France included!"

A confused Lebrun shook his head. "My advisors tell me there is nothing to fear. Chancellor Hitler is a bit brash, but it's all patriotic rhetoric. He is simply rallying his country. Hindenburg appointed him chancellor to appease the right and counter the communists, but the Bavarians will never elect him president. He's a flash in the pan. I think you may be overreacting."

Eli shook his head. "You should know by now that Lu and his forces do not tread lightly. This is a chess game, and Lu is looking twenty moves ahead."

Lebrun sighed. "Elijah, it is good to see you again, but I believe I have the counsel I need from your friend. He has never steered me wrong before."

Eli's eyes narrowed. "My friend? Who is advising you?"

When a white-bearded Cyrus emerged from the conference room, Eli's jaw tightened.

"Hello, Elijah," said the overseer, his gray eyes penetrating.

"What are you doing here?" asked Eli, not hiding his surprise.

"I am giving support and counsel to our friend, President Lebrun. My question is, what are you doing here? Have your sheep been sheered and your vineyard harvested?" He turned to the questioning Lebrun. "Elijah has been retired and off the world stage for some time now. Fifteen years, if my memory serves me. It usually does." Cyrus's penetrating gaze returned to the stunned Eli. "Tragic what happened to your wife and son. Have you found them?"

Eli exploded in rage, grabbed Cyrus's lapels, and threw him against the wall as the French president jumped back. "This man is a traitor! You shouldn't listen to anything he says! He's behind it all!"

Unshaken by the assault, Cyrus calmly raised his arms, breaking Eli's hands loose. Then, extending his palm in a halting gesture, he hurled the larger Eli against the opposite wall without touching him. "I'm disappointed in you, Elijah. So much promise squandered. I hope you're enjoying your mortal torment."

Lebrun's eyes widened, and he backed farther away as Eli charged the overseer, only to be tossed to the carpeted floor like a child with the wave of Cyrus's hand. When the other advisors rushed to the conference room door, Cyrus pulled it closed with a gesture. "Guards!" cried Lebrun. "Call for the guards!"

The furious Eli had just jumped to his feet when Cyrus made a swirling motion with his hand. "That won't be necessary."

The French president gasped when a hole in the floor opened, and the charging Eli dropped into it. Lebrun stared at the place where the floor had swallowed Eli, but he saw only ornate carpeting. He gulped and turned to the unbothered Cyrus. "What happened?"

"Nothing for you to dwell on," grinned Cyrus. He stepped closer to the wide-eyed president and put two fingers on his forehead.

Lebrun's concern vanished. He straightened his suit coat and pushed back his hair. Then, with a smile, said, "Well, should we move on to our next meeting?"

"I think that's a fine idea," nodded Cyrus.

In a back alley outside the palace gates, Eli kicked aside a pair of trashcans and climbed to his feet. He glared at a man whose cigarette was dangling from his gaping mouth, brushed off his wrinkled suit, and stormed away.

Dachau, Germany
4 October 1933

It was a brisk fall morning in southern Germany. The Bavarian farmland and forests were quiet but for the sound of hammers echoing like gunfire. A nine-foot razor wire fence encircled the rows of newly constructed barracks, and above its main gate was a sign that read, Work Makes One Free. Not far from the barracks, beside a train track that entered the camp but did not leave, stood a large brick building with a smokestack that reached high into the crisp blue sky. Above it raised a gentle plume of smoke. Once used to manufacture munitions, the factory had been transformed for another deadly purpose.

Three men walked along the dirt road just inside the tall fence: Josef Mutzbauer, the camp's chief administrator; SS Colonel Hilmar Wäckerle, the camp's newly appointed commandant; and a much larger man wearing neither a suit nor a uniform. Dressed in a green waistcoat, tan breeches, and high brown boots, Gadreel wore his long hair pulled back and carried a sword at his side. Looking more like an eighteenth-century pirate than a twentieth-century gentleman, the banished watcher softly wheezed as he listened to Mutzbauer's dilemma. While Gadreel had survived Michelle's blazerod attack fifteen years before, the ancient weapon had left him with only one lung and scars the size of pie plates on his chest and back.

"This doctor you speak of who is prying into state business, you fear he will go to the Bavarian authorities with these claims?" wheezed Gadreel.

"Yes," nodded a worried Mutzbauer. "If news of these deaths reaches the minister of justice, that could mean all kinds of trouble for us."

"How many deaths have there been?" asked Gadreel.

"How many have there been, or how many is he reporting?" asked the fidgeting Mutzbauer.

"It doesn't matter." Gadreel turned to the stern-eyed Wäckerle. "This is your problem now. I've been told you're quite...creative."

"Why, thank you, Herr Gadreel," said the SS colonel with a sharp bow of his head. "It has been my experience that men of such noble character do better when reassigned. I'm sure the defense force is in urgent need of his medical expertise in Berlin. I'll see to it."

"Very good," wheezed Gadreel.

"I have already tried reassigning him," frowned Mutzbauer. "He declined. He is sure something nefarious is going on here and is very persistent."

Gadreel nodded. "Sadly, terrible accidents sometimes befall persistent men."

"Understood," nodded the SS colonel.

Gadreel's icy gaze moved to a group of men who had paused from building a barracks. The laborers wore matching gray and white striped pants and dingy white shirts. They had shaved heads and shared looks of fear and uncertainty.

"Back to work!" barked the colonel, his hand on his holstered pistol.

Gadreel glared at the prisoners as they moved past. "How many do you now have?"

"Just under a thousand, with two hundred more coming next week," replied Mutzbauer.

"Your camp capacity is five thousand?"

"Yes, but it will grow...and shrink," said Mutzbauer.

Gadreel and Wäckerle laughed.

"Have you gotten many Jews yet?" asked Wäckerle.

"They are beginning to come. We're still working through political dissidents and homosexuals," said Mutzbauer.

"There will be no shortage of occupants," sneered Gadreel.

When they arrived at the administration building, the three stopped and listened to an SS major addressing the new guards, his gray uniform crisp, his black collar adorned on one side with two Ss in the shape of lightning bolts, and on the other, skulls. His flat cap was peaked in the middle with another skull on its front. His leather, knee-high boots were glossy black, his arms behind his back.

"Comrades of the SS! You all know what the Führer has called us to do. We have not come here for human encounters with those pigs in there. We do not consider them human beings, as we are, but as second-class people. For years, they have been able to continue their criminal existence. But now we are in power. If those pigs had come to power, they would have cut off all our heads. Therefore, we have no room for sentimentalism. If anyone here cannot bear to see the blood of comrades, he does not belong and had better leave. The more of these pig dogs we strike down, the fewer we need to feed."

A thin smile formed on Gadreel's scarred face. All was happening as planned.

CHARTWELL HOUSE
KENT, ENGLAND
6 OCTOBER 1933

IT WAS a cozy room with hewn timbers supporting a vaulted ceiling. The British flag hung from the rafters, and below it was a prominent painting of the English countryside. Subdued sunlight washed in from the bank of windows across a desk stacked with books and paperwork. Behind a walnut coffee table, seated in a plush chair more suited for comfort than style, the round-faced Winston Churchill set his tea down. He pulled his buttoned vest down over his rotund belly and motioned to a plate of biscuits. "I must admit, I was surprised to see you again."

Eli sipped his tea, then said, "It has been a few years since Ploegsteert Wood."

"I don't say it lightly that you saved my life that day," said Churchill, staring at the table.

Eli nodded as he reflected on perhaps his last accomplishment as a watcher.

"You told me I had a great and noble purpose. And I have found it here at Chartwell with my dear Clementine and children. I've finished the first volume of my memoirs. It seems Britons have an interest in my failures," chuckled Churchill.

"And accomplishments," added Eli.

Churchill sighed. "The ghosts of Gallipoli still haunt me."

Eli's face grew serious. "Do you remember what I showed you that day?"

"Yes, of course. How could I ever forget?"

"I'm afraid your time has come."

Churchill nodded and stared across the room. "All of this trouble with Hitler. I've been following closely and not surprised in the least."

"Italy must be watched as well."

Churchill's face filled with concern. "But Mussolini is a bulwark against the communists. I don't see him as a threat."

"He will join Italy with the Germans."

"How do you know this? Oh, forgive me," said Churchill, recalling his vision in the bunker. His gaze returned to Eli. "Will you show me again with your golden ball? I'm afraid, after seventeen years, that vision seems more like a dream to me now."

Eli sat back. "I'm afraid I no longer have the sphere."

"Pity. I think that would have been very effective with Ramsay MacDonald."

"Mister Churchill, you are the only one who can do what must be done."

Churchill set down his tea. "I suppose I could raise the warning, but I'm sure the prime minister is well aware of the threat."

"That is not what is needed."

"But I am out of public light now and have no intention of returning."

"Your wandering in the wilderness will not save your country or the world," warned Eli.

Churchill gulped. "I wish I had the vision of myself that you have. Or perhaps I do not wish it. Mister Mansel, I am happy with my life here at Chartwell. I have nothing left to offer my country. I have served my time."

"Of that, you are wrong, sir," replied Eli.

Churchill drew in a beleaguered breath. "Mister Mansel, I thank you for your visit. I have much work still to do on my memoirs, but I will consider your promptings. I hope you will keep in touch."

Eli's shoulders sank. He set down his tea and sighed.

CHÂTEAU DE BRET
10 OCTOBER 1933

MADAME DUGUAY TURNED from her book when she heard the noise in the great room. With Eli gone, all had been quiet at the chateau for weeks. "Master Eli?" she called out, leaving the kitchen. She stopped when she saw a disheveled man clutching a half-empty whiskey bottle stagger through the front door.

"Master Eli?"

When Eli fell forward, knocking a vase and picture of Michelle off an end table, Madame Duguay hurried to him and gasped, "Master Eli! What has happened to you?"

Holding the picture of Michelle, a broken Eli looked up at the loyal housekeeper and rolled onto his side. "You're still here? I thought you would be gone," he stammered.

"Why would I leave, sir?" asked Madame Duguay, wringing her hands.

"Everone else hass leff mee."

When a barking Jacques charged down the stairs, Eli set down the picture and embraced the happy dog. "Jacques still luffs mee," sobbed Eli as the dog licked his face.

"I gather your trip didn't go as planned," said Madame Duguay, helping Eli to his feet.

"All is lost," muttered Eli.

"Let me help you to bed, sir."

"No, not there," sobbed Eli. "Thas where the demons come."

"You should rest, sir."

"I donn wanna res. I wanna die, but I can't."

Madame Duguay helped the leaning Eli to a great room couch. "You can rest here until you're feeling more yourself."

"I donn wanna feel myself anymore," muttered Eli, curling up on the floor before the couch. Within seconds, he was snoring.

Madame Duguay sadly watched as Jacques nestled beside the anguished watcher.

CHAPTER 6
DOORWAYS

THE ABYSS

M ichelle had lost all sense of time in her dark and damp prison cell. In perpetual night, she didn't know if a day or a month had passed. It wasn't only the absence of the day and night cycle that left her without a sense of time; other clues were also missing. While she frequently napped, Michelle had no sense of hunger or thirst. It was as though her body and its functions were in stasis; only her mind was active. But as she perpetually sat against the hard stone wall worn smooth, she sometimes wondered if she had even lost her mind.

With a bored sigh, Michelle climbed to her feet and walked the three steps along the stone wall, running her hand along the now-familiar contour until she reached its facing wall. She made a quarter turn and walked another three steps before feeling the metal bars anchored into stone. Michelle breathed in the dank air and listened for the sounds of life. She heard a muffled groan somewhere in the darkness. It seemed new to her. "Hello, is there anyone who can understand me?" Michelle called out as she had so many times before. She heard the usual grumbles and voices in languages she didn't know and sighed.

Michelle cocked her head when she thought she saw a glimmering in the blackness but concluded it was a trick of her mind, so desperately craving light.

Michelle raised her hand through the bars and thought she saw the faint luminescence of her flesh. With a sigh, she lowered her hand. Michelle studied the blackness before her, searching for any hint of light and hope. In her time in the pit, she had come to understand the different levels of darkness. There was mostly the normal murky night, smooth and uniform, endless in its bleakness. But sometimes she saw the buzzing and billowing ebony and purple clouds. With them came painful, mind-numbing anguish as she fought through her darkest thoughts of despair and self-loathing. When first engulfed by the swirling cloud, Michelle questioned everything she had ever done and wished she could simply cease to exist. That was the early time. Though the cloud still visited her, she no longer feared it.

How Michelle had learned to tame the "purple monster," as she called it, was an accident. On her twelfth encounter with the crippling entity, Michelle remembered how the orb had parted it and how she had ordered it to leave. While she no longer had the golden sphere, Michelle discovered she could still command the awful cloud by thinking of joyful things: her Franny laughing and playing, her dancing in the flowered meadow as a child, or Eli holding her in his arms. While the encounters were still terrifying, she could now shoo away the purple monster before it could fully take hold.

Michelle thought of Eli and their son as she made the short trip around her cell. She wondered if she would ever see them again. With a dejected sigh, Michelle sank to the smooth stone floor. She closed her eyes and hoped for sleep, her only respite from her bleak solitude.

When Michelle heard feet shuffling in the blackness, she sat up. Her eyes widened when the dark passageway brightened with torchlight. She raised a hand, shielding her eyes from the dazzling light as bare-chested guards led a man in navy trousers and a coat into a distant cell. She could just see the prisoner's sandy hair and beard, and her jaw fell open when she noticed his shirt's blue and white horizontal stripes.

Pressed against the bars, Michelle waited for the guards to leave and the torchlight to fade. While the jailers took a prisoner from the dungeon every few days, it felt to her like weeks since they had last brought one. Michelle guessed those taken were used to light the evil woman's council chamber and wondered with each guard visit if her turn was next. Michelle heard the man's quiet groans and called out. "Hello. Are you new?"

The groaning stopped, and the man climbed to his feet. "Yes. Where am I?"

"You speak French!" cried a jubilant Michelle. "Where are you from?"

"Montreal, and you?" asked the man, the fear lessening in his voice.

"France. Gien, actually."

"Am I dead?"

"No. I don't think so."

"If we're not dead, where are we? What is this place?"

"I wish I could tell you," groaned Michelle.

"How long have you been here?"

Michelle sighed. "Forever, it seems. Since May. How did you get here?"

"I don't know," said the man, his voice trailing off in bewilderment. "We were crossing the Lakes. There was a terrible fog. I was on lookout, and then...then I was here."

"You're a sailor."

"Yes."

"Has the war ended?"

"What war?"

"The Great War, of course," frowned Michelle.

"Do you mean the American war? That ended two years ago. The North won, but someone killed their President Lincoln," replied the sailor.

"The American Civil War?"

"Yes."

"But that...that was fifty years ago," muttered Michelle. "How long have you been here?"

"Maybe a day. Maybe a week. I've lost track."

"What year is it?" Michelle asked, her eyes searching the darkness.

"1868, of course," replied the sailor.

"What?" gasped Michelle. She sank to her cell floor. "How is that possible?" She was about to ask the sailor more questions when the passageway brightened. Michelle squinted at the torchlight as a jailer approached. When the sailor's cell door opened and two guards pulled him from within, she called out, "No! Don't take him! Take someone else!"

"Where are they taking me?" asked the sailor.

Michelle backed into her cell when the jailer glared at her, his tattooed eye shimmering in the torchlight.

"What is your name?" asked Michelle, desperate for companionship.

"Claude," called back the sailor as the guards pulled him up the passageway. "Where are they taking me? Help me!" echoed his voice as the torchlight faded.

"Goodbye, Claude," whispered Michelle as she sank to the floor of her cell and sobbed.

CHAPTER 7
THE INEVITABLE PAWN

CHÂTEAU DE BRET
11 OCTOBER 1933

When Eli's eyes opened, it took him some time to realize he was lying on the great room rug. With a tired sigh, he pulled himself up to see the pointy-eared Jacques watching him with a cocked head. Eli closed his heavy eyes and smiled when the dog licked his face. "I know I can always count on you, my friend."

"Good morning, Master Eli."

Eli grimaced as he turned to Madame Duguay, standing near the dining room. "Good morning," he muttered. He rubbed his face, then said, "I'm sorry for my condition last night. It was not acceptable."

"No, it wasn't," scolded Madame Duguay. "Not for someone of your stature."

Taken aback, Eli turned to the housekeeper, eyeing him like a disappointed mother. His gaze moved across the great room in thought, and then, with an acknowledging nod, he pulled himself to his feet.

"If you would like to clean up first, I have breakfast waiting."

Eli met his housekeeper's stern gaze, nodded, and started for the stairs. Jacques followed him.

. . .

ELI WAS quiet when he entered the dining room, his wet and wavy hair combed back, his work trousers and shirt pressed. He sat in his usual spot, where a plate of waffles, eggs, and coffee waited. "Thank you," mumbled Eli as Madame Duguay stood by with folded arms. His uncertain gaze moved to her, but he looked away when he caught her displeasure. Eli gulped, bowed his head, and muttered a blessing.

Not looking up, Eli cut into the eggs. They weren't runny, like he liked them, but he said nothing.

"I see you're wearing your field clothes," said Madame Duguay, her tone unusually brusque.

"I've been gone. There's much to do," Eli said, taking a bite of waffle.

"You're right. There is much to do, but not in your vineyard or stable or with the sheep," snapped Madame Duguay.

Eli's uncertain gaze raised to the vexed housekeeper.

"I thought I was finished raising my boys, but evidently, I'm not."

Eli set down his knife and fork and huffed, "I'm not a boy. Do you have any idea how old I am?"

"Old enough to know better!"

Eli recoiled, and his gaze returned to his plate.

"Elijah, your sulking will do nothing to bring your wife and son home!"

"I HAVE TRIED!" Eli slammed his fist on the table.

Madame Duguay's face tightened. "I had a daughter. My little girl was the sweetest and most precious thing in my life! When she became ill, I did all that I could to help her! When the doctor said there was nothing to be done, I didn't believe him. I searched everywhere. I had no money, but did all I could to help her. Some would say more than I should!" Fighting to control her emotions, she continued, "In the end, none of it was enough. The good Lord took her from me!"

"I'm sorry, but what is your point with this tragic tale?" asked Eli.

"I am just a woman—a human. You have forgotten you are more than that! But even with all that you have, you have given up! You cannot give up! You must exhaust every effort! You must look under every stone until you find a way to get them back!"

"Don't you think I've tried? Michelle and Franny are in the most terrible place you can imagine! They are trapped there! They are suffering in misery, and there is nothing I can do! She took the key with her! I cannot unlock the door and bring them back!"

Madame Duguay's expression softened. "Then find another key." She moved to the table and placed Nazario's taped-together business card beside Eli. "This man can help you."

Eli's tortured gaze moved to the card. He picked it up, studied it, and then looked up at Madame Duguay with questioning eyes.

<hr />

BERLIN, GERMANY
14 OCTOBER 1933

ADOLF HITLER STROKED his square mustache as he looked out the office window at the charred remains of the German parliament building, the Reichstag. He thought it a shame to burn such a historic building down, but just as Lu had told him, the tragedy—secretly ordered by Hitler—had galvanized the masses against common foes. Whether those foes were the Jews or the communists depended on Hitler's needs for that day.

The beady-eyed chancellor's chest swelled as he considered the plan Lu had laid out for him. One of his next steps would be restoring the burned Reichstag to its former grandeur, the first of many achievements to glorify the name of Adolf Hitler. The chancellor reveled in his growing power. Only the presidency was left, and that would come shortly. The fallen watcher had promised him.

Hitler turned to the others seated around a large walnut table. His dark gaze moved from Himmler to Goebbels and then Göring before settling on the red-bearded Lu. His brow tightened, and his square mustache twitched in annoyance. "How much longer?"

"You must be patient," replied Lu, unbothered by the narcissist's obsessions. It was dealing with such odious persons that gave the immortal his power. "Your time is not yet. If Hindenburg were to die tomorrow, I could not guarantee your ascension."

"BUT I AM THE FÜHRER! I AM INEVITABLE!" bellowed Hitler.

Lu eyed Hitler like a child in a tantrum. "Your time will come, but only if you are patient. Obtaining power is not a quick game—not if you want that power to last."

Still fuming, Hitler shook his head and turned to Himmler. "What of your research society?"

"It is coming nicely, my Führer," nodded the spectacled Himmler.

Hitler nodded. "We will prove to the world that the pure Aryan race is superior to all others by our accomplishments—our iron will!" he said, making a fist. "But we must also reveal to the world the truth of the past. That God created the Aryan race to rule the world. Once there is no doubt of our superiority, they will welcome me as the great cleanser and honor my efforts to rid the world of the filth polluting the pure bloodline!" Hitler's wild eyes turned to Lu as if for approval.

Himmler straightened up. "I am calling it The Society for the Study of the History of Primeval Ideas. It will comprise scholars and scientists of all disciplines: archeology, botany, philosophy, and even zoology. All German, of course, and all with the purpose of uncovering these mysteries lost from the world and hidden by Jews."

"I like it, but the name's too long. When will they begin?" asked Hitler.

"I have people searching the world for artifacts of proof as we speak." A proud Himmler glanced at Lu. "Our friend, Herr Stormbrewer, has provided us with unique individuals to guide the search."

Hitler rubbed his hands together and, with the eyes of a delighted schoolboy, exclaimed, "Such news thrills me! We must use everything at our disposal to accomplish our divine tasks!" But in the next breath, his face filled with grave concern, and he added, "While I do not relish in using the dark arts, they, like many things, are a means to our great and noble ends. You have my blessing to use them." Hitler glanced at Lu. "Hold nothing back. Open the doors of hell and unleash its demons if you have to!"

Himmler's face brightened with excitement. "We are working on finding that very door, my Führer!"

"Wonderful!" beamed Hitler. "It is our calling to cleanse this polluted world. Just as I am saving Germany from itself, I will bring the world peace and understanding as I build the third great empire to rule the earth!"

An amused Lu watched as the others clapped. He had seen it countless times before. Their blindness to the watcher's control over them stemmed from an insatiable appetite for power. Lu would use Hitler and his footmen as pawns as long as possible, just as they would the German people.

CHAPTER 8
THE CLOAKED ONE

THE ABYSS

Michelle was curled up on the floor of her dark and damp cell when she felt a hand over her mouth. Her eyes shot open as she fought against the unseen stranger.

"I am a friend. Do not make a sound. I will take you from here." The whispering voice was deep, warm, and calming.

Michelle noticed the faint radiance of the stranger's flesh when he removed his large hand, and she gasped at his eyes, glowing inside the hood of his cloak. Michelle gulped as she smelled the stranger's muskiness. It was strangely familiar and comforting.

"Who are you?" she breathed.

"Shh. You must be still."

"My son? Do you have him?"

"There's no time. We must hurry."

"I won't leave without him!" insisted Michelle.

"We will come back for him," whispered the cloaked stranger. "Now be silent. You must come with me. Quickly."

After taking the stranger's hand, Michelle held out her other to feel her way. Stumbling in the darkness, Michelle followed the man up the inky passageway, surprised at the speed he moved with so little light. She heard groans as they passed other cells and jumped when a hand grabbed her through the bars.

"Pay no attention," whispered the stranger, pulling her away from the reaching hands.

When Michelle tripped on an unseen step, she let out a painful gasp. "You're going too quickly! I can't see a thing!"

The cloaked stranger turned and caught the unsteady Michelle. "Close your eyes," he whispered, before reaching the first two fingers of each hand to them.

Able to see little, Michelle's heart was pounding as she closed her eyes. She at first recoiled at his touch, but when she felt the warmth of his fingers and viewed light glowing through her closed eyelids, her body relaxed with a soothed sigh. When the stranger pulled his hands away, Michelle opened her eyes and gasped as an array of colors dissolved the suffocating blackness. She saw the dungeon walls and steps outlined in a dozen orange hues. Her jaw slackened when she noticed the dazzling colors emitting from her hands and arms. "What am I seeing? It's so beautiful," she gasped, moved nearly to tears as she examined her glowing hands. She turned to the watching stranger, his gleaming features obscured by his hood.

"Shh."

"Who are you?" breathed Michelle, her eyes wide.

The stranger placed a hushing finger to her lips, removed his shimmering sword from its sheath, and led Michelle up the glowing steps.

At the top of the stairs, the narrow passage opened to a room dimly lit by an adjoining corridor. Outlined in the same strange light were three slain guards lying on the stone floor with glowing pools of blood around them. A forked spear impaled one. Another's severed head lay on its side, its tattooed eye staring at Michelle. Horrified by the gruesome, shimmering sight, Michelle's eyes moved to her rescuer. She felt both frightened and protected by his hand. She gulped and followed the stranger out of the dim and bloody chamber.

When they came to a rusted metal door, the stranger pushed it open, his sword at the ready. Michelle breathed in the fresh air and searched the eerie ruins with her new sight. She glanced back at the dungeon's entry, partially hidden by a collapsed wall. Michelle's heart was pounding as the stranger led her by the hand through the ruins. He pulled her into the shadows when a group of shabby men and women in tattered clothes shuffled past.

As they approached a long, jagged wall, the stranger motioned for Michelle to stay. She looked back and scanned the shimmering ruins behind them as the sword-wielding stranger disappeared into the shadows. Michelle's uneasiness deepened when she realized she was alone. She gasped when two bare-chested sentries rounded a corner carrying a torch. They raised their spears when they spotted Michelle in her dingy white nightgown, but before they could attack, the stranger leaped from the shadows and cut them down with a quick sword thrust and slash.

Michelle recoiled at the swiftness of the stranger's attack, but her jaw fell open when wisps of light exited the writhing sentries' sword wounds like steam from a kettle. When the leaking light faded, their bodies went limp.

The stranger turned to the breathless Michelle. "Are you unhurt?"

After an anxious nod, Michelle took the stranger's hand, and they crept along the battlement. Like the rest of the city, the defensive wall was in ruins, with some sections nearly intact while others were piled with rubble and scrap. Ahead of them, Michelle spotted a twenty-foot-tall stone watchtower, its torchlight fading. She gulped when she noticed a sentry hanging over the side of its roost.

Michelle felt more at ease when she spotted an open gate ahead, but her hand tightened around the stranger's when she noticed a dark, wiry man standing in the shadows. Michelle's eyes widened at the glowing outline of the wiry man's pasty face, his hair long, thin, and scraggly. "Gik?"

The halfborn, wearing a drab tunic and holding a short sword, turned to her with wide, sunken eyes. He bowed as they drew closer.

"You're alive!" gasped Michelle, remembering his head rolling across the château's lawn the night she entered the abyss.

"This is Gak," said the large stranger, his wary eyes just visible within his hooded cloak.

The halfborn lifted his head. "You know my brother?" he asked, his voice high and whiny like Gik's.

Michelle gave a jittery nod, still unsure what to think of the halfborn who had three times tried to kill her before swearing his loyalty and protection. "Who are you?" she asked, turning to her rescuer.

"We are yet in danger. Come with us, and your questions will be answered," nodded the cloaked stranger.

"But my son! They still have Franny! I can't leave without him!"

"Shh! You must be quiet!" urged Gak.

"If Keket's guards take us, any hope of rescuing your son will be lost," explained the stranger.

Michelle gulped. "Who's Keket?"

"The governess of Manu," replied Gak.

"That awful fat woman with the tattooed face?"

"Yes," nodded Gak.

"Is my son safe? Will she harm him?"

The stranger shook his head. "They will not."

A worried Michelle turned back the way they had come.

"You can trust me," nodded the large stranger.

Seeing no other option, Michelle followed them through the gate.

Beyond the wall, the ruined city looked much the same to Michelle as they wove their way around collapsed walls and craters, all aglow in the shimmering orange light. Crossing at an intersection where melted stone and metal flowed into the street like dried candle wax, Michelle gave the tall stranger a wary glance, then asked, "What happened to those guards by the gate?"

"I slew them," replied the stranger, with a hint of remorse.

"But what did I see coming from them as they died?"

"That was their light leaving them."

"Their light?" asked Michelle.

The stranger and halfborn looked at her strangely. "Their life force," added the stranger, sheathing his sword.

"Oh," muttered Michelle, still not understanding.

With hardly a word spoken, they continued through the dark ruins.

When Michelle heard a familiar voice, she stopped and turned. "Eli?" she gasped, her eyes wide and searching, but she saw only ruins around her.

"Did you hear something?" asked the stranger.

"I thought...I thought I heard my husband's voice," Michelle breathed. She scanned the wrecked landscape, then shook her head. "My ears must be playing tricks on me."

The stranger considered what Michelle said, then resumed walking.

"Where are we?" Michelle asked, eyeing the glistening landscape as she hurried to keep up.

"We have just left the city of Ra. We will be out of the ruins soon," explained Gak.

Michelle looked up at the low black clouds shimmering in the same orange hue. "No, what is this place?"

Gak's brows raised, uncertain why she would ask such a question. "You are in the world of the lost, the abyss."

"Am I dead?"

"No. That is another place," replied Gak.

Michelle eyed Gak, then glanced at the tall stranger. "He's a halfborn. Can he be trusted?"

"Yes," nodded the stranger.

Michelle stopped, wondering if she should trust either of them. "You still haven't told me your name."

The cloaked stranger turned and walked the few steps back to Michelle. He pulled back his hood to dark curly hair that hung in his crisp blue eyes. He had a pointy nose and wore his beard short. "My name is Remiel."

"I'm Michelle."

"Yes, we know," said Remiel with a slight bow.

"How-how do you know who I am?"

Remiel grinned, amused by Michelle's modesty.

"Who doesn't know who you are?" asked Gak.

Michelle wondered what the halfborn meant as they resumed walking. "But how did you know where I was? That those terrible people had captured me?"

"Og told us," said Remiel.

Michelle shook her head. "Who is Og?"

Gak and Remiel stopped and turned, their eyes raised over Michelle's head.

Michelle screamed when she turned to the towering giant standing behind her. The creature jumped back, just as surprised, his enormous feet making a thunderous clomp. "How long has that been there?" gasped Michelle, clutching her breast.

"Quite some time," shrugged Remiel.

"*That* is a *he*. His name is Og," said Gak.

"But I didn't hear him! I looked back, and no one was there!"

"Giants can be very sneaky when they want to be," explained Gak.

Og looked down at Michelle with large, droopy eyes and nodded.

Michelle gulped and forced a smile as she surveyed the shaggy giant. Warts dotted his deformed and craggy face, and he had a long, snarled beard that hung down the front of his tattered robe. Amazed at the enormity of the ten-foot-tall Og, Michelle's uncertain gaze lowered to the spiked club held at his side. It was the size of a small man. She gulped at the blood and hair stuck to its four-inch spikes, then turned back to Remiel and asked, "You're friends?"

"Yes," nodded Remiel. "Don't be alarmed at Og's appearance. He's as gentle as can be."

"Unless you get him riled," added Gak.

Michelle forced a smile as she looked up at the warty giant.

"We are not yet out of danger. We should quietly make haste."

Michelle gave an unsettled glance back across the ruins. "Where are we going?"

"To the land of the light," replied Remiel.

"Oh, that sounds lovely," said Michelle, still uncertain of the giant.

"Dark dweller patrols may be near. We should travel in silence," warned Gak.

Michelle gave an anxious nod and moved closer to Remiel as they continued through the ruins.

LIGHT WAS the most precious commodity in the underground city of Manu, and the increasingly rare fuel to make that light was the dark dwellers' currency. Torches made of resin and wood scavenged from the stripped remains of a once vast forest dimly lit the inner city and underground tunnels. Even the dark corridors of the keep, the governess's underground palace, were lit by flame. But it was human candles, the rarest light of all, that illuminated the governess's throne room.

Making human candles was a lengthy process that required a body. Thieves, dissidents, and those captured from other lands provided those bodies. Once selected from the pit, the candle master bound and hung the victims by their feet. After slashing their throats and draining their blood, the candle master removed their brains and organs according to the old law to process into tallow. The candle master then lowered the gutted bodies into vats of resin and mineral wax. Once saturated and cured, a human candle could burn for a week. When the candle's light faded, the minister of flame summoned the candle master, and the time-honored flame passing ceremony was performed.

A black cat meowed, and another brushed against Keket's fat leg as two candle bearers carried a marbleized body into the Hall of Flame. The governess stared with glazed eyes as the candle bearers chained the body to the iron post atop the altar. Saturated in resin and wax, she could tell it was a man by the width of his shoulders and guessed its flame would light her hall for some time.

Keket shifted on her throne in anticipation as the minister of flame poured oil atop the candle's head, raised a rod and flint above it, bowed, and struck a spark. Keket and her ministers clapped and nodded as the flame brightened the dingy chamber. But young Franny, seated beside her, sadly buried his head.

As the initial flame softened and the stench of burning flesh filled the air, the room returned to its normal flickering dimness.

On one side of the smoky thirty-foot-wide chamber was an arched entry with the tattered remains of a carpet runner leading to it. Above the entrance hung a rusty iron gate. Arched windows lined the chamber, but they were bricked closed, allowing but one entry and exit. Like an Egyptian tomb, colorful pictographs and glyphs covered the chamber's stone walls. On one side was a small scaffold on which the governess's scribe stood to make a record.

Lining the wall of the circular hall, the chamber ministers lazily sat, their faces and colored robes dingy from soot. Some of the ministers dozed while others stared at the flickering flame, seeking its hidden knowledge. A few softly chanted as they rocked back and forth.

Keket's lazy gaze moved from the torch flame to the arched entry when Sed, her lord of the chamber, rushed in. Wearing a drab, belted tunic, chin beard, and hair pulled up in a topknot, Sed's concern was plain to see in the flickering light.

While eager for a distraction from her boredom, Keket warily eyed Sed. As lord of the chamber and next in line for the governorship, she thought him ambitious—a dubious trait for a dark dweller. "What is it?"

"Governess!" Sed exclaimed with a hasty bow. "The pit has been attacked!"

Keket sat up. "Attacked? What kind of attack?"

"One of your prisoners, the female otherworlder, is gone, taken from her cell!"

"Who took her?" snapped Keket as the chamber ministers stirred and murmured.

"It's not clear, my governess. But I suspect it the work of the cloaked one. Three of your jailers were slain! Two had their heads removed!"

More whispers filled the shadows.

"Why would the watcher bother with an otherworlder?" Keket glanced at the dull orb and blazerod on the stand beside her, then turned to the curly haired Franny, his blue eyes wide and intuitive. "Find out who did this!"

"It is undoubtedly the work of the Luminaries," said Tasud, the balding and beak-nosed master of war.

"Were any others taken? Your candles are growing few, governess!" the minister of flame fretted.

"They took only the woman," reported Sed.

"Such an attack is an act of war!" cried Tasud, thumping his breastplate.

"Good! We must replenish your candles!" said the minister of flame. "Will you attack them, governess?"

Keket's dark eyes narrowed. "Send out your spies! Find out who did this! And I want to know who that otherworlder is!"

"Yes, governess," bowed Sed before leaving the smoky chamber.

Keket sat back on her throne and looked down at the watching Franny. Then, with a crooked smile, she pulled the boy onto her pudgy lap and ran her hand down his back like a lapdog.

AFTER WHAT SEEMED like hours to Michelle, the jagged landscape opened to a barren expanse. She surveyed the vast clearing, picked clean but for the thousands of tree stumps. "What is this place?" she asked, breaking the silence.

"The Lost Forest," replied Remiel.

"What happened to it?" Michelle asked, tree stumps as far as she could see.

"The dark dwellers used it to light their city," shrugged Gak.

"Oh. That's very sad," sighed Michelle. "It must have been a lovely forest once."

"Once, long ago," nodded Remiel.

Michelle guessed they had walked through miles of stumps when a line of tall, leafless trees appeared ahead, all outlined by the same gleaming light. Soon the dark, forested flat land turned to rolling hills and enormous boulders. The trees, while fewer, still had barren branches. "Does the sun never rise here?" she asked, scanning the horizons.

"No," sighed Remiel.

"But how can that be?"

Gak shrugged.

Upon realizing she would get no answer, Michelle looked up at Og, slogging beside Gak with the agility of a much smaller creature. "That was you I met when I first got here, wasn't it?"

Og nodded.

"But that was days ago...I think." Michelle turned to Remiel. "How long have I been here?"

"Well, it all depends on your reckoning," shrugged Gak.

"What does that mean?"

"We don't measure time here," said Remiel.

"How can you not measure time?" frowned Michelle.

"Because it does not pass here."

"It doesn't pass? But, of course, it does!" insisted Michelle. "Time passes everywhere!"

"Not here," sighed Gak.

"I don't understand."

"When did you last eat?" asked Remiel, his eyes scanning the way ahead.

"The night before I came here."

"And how long ago was that?"

Michelle's brow furrowed in thought. "I don't know—a few days. Come to think of it, I haven't been hungry at all. Or thirsty."

"No," said Remiel.

"I don't understand. How long have I been here?"

Remiel glanced at Gak and shrugged. "We don't know. According to the time of your world, years may have passed."

Michelle abruptly stopped, forcing Og to jump out of the way to not step on her. "What? I-I don't understand."

Remiel's expression softened. "Come with us, and your questions will be answered."

"But where are we going?" Michelle asked, eyeing the towering Og.

"You will see," said Remiel.

Michelle's face brightened. Having nearly forgotten the miracle of her strange new vision, she turned to Remiel with a gasp. "How it is that I can see? I sat in that pitch-black dungeon for...I don't know how long. But since your touch, everything around me has a wonderful glow. What did you do to me?" she asked, eyeing the glimmering outline of Remiel's handsome features.

"I simply unlocked the balance of your vision. You had learned to see only a part of the spectrum," explained Remiel.

"It is a gift," nodded Gak.

"You have it too?" Michelle asked in awe.

"We all have it," shrugged Gak.

"But the lines that I see—*the colors*—they border everything," Michelle said, looking around her. "It's as though everything is alive."

"Everything is alive," nodded Remiel. "Even here in the abyss, everything is made of elements."

"What is it I'm seeing?"

"You are seeing the molecules that give us shape, that give us animation, life," explained Remiel.

"But even the boulders," said Michelle, looking around.

"Even the rocks are made of those things. Everything in the universe is. We are all made from the same eternal ingredients."

Michelle shook her head in wonder. Her eyes widened as the glimmering patterns became richer and more detailed. She reached a hand to a leafless tree and thought she saw its trunk breathing. Even the air was alive. "It's so...*beautiful*."

Remiel looked up at Og, whose grin was lost in his shaggy beard.

"But what of the dark cloud? It visited me in the pit more times than I can remember. It was awful!" groaned Michelle.

Remiel glanced at Gak. "The dark elements. They found you?"

"Yes, they were horrible! What are they?"

"The universe must maintain a balance," explained Remiel. "Everything has an opposite. There is light, and there is dark. There is good, and there is evil. The dark elements are the countering balance to life, happiness, and peace. They fill men's souls with hate and envy. They bring about wars, sadness, and misery. Here in the abyss, the dark elements rule. They can be suffocating." Remiel's face filled with concern. "Many succumb to them after just one encounter. How did you survive them?"

Michelle shrugged. "I...I learned to command them away."

Gak and Remiel exchanged knowing glances. "We don't have much farther," smiled Remiel.

"Where is it again we're going?" Michelle asked, her curious eyes searching.

"To Luminah, the land of the light. Mawufe, the leader of the Luminaries, will be honored to meet you."

Michelle nodded and followed them through the dead yet vibrant forest.

CHAPTER 9

TEN QUESTIONS

MILAN, ITALY
17 OCTOBER 1933

The gothic cathedral, *Duomo di Milano,* stood proudly in the center of the city, its dozens of white and gray marble spires rising majestically into the sky. Eli's boots resonated off the six-hundred-year-old marble floor as he moved down the dimly lit aisle. He wore a leather coat, carried a satchel over his shoulder, and held his fedora in his hand. Before Eli, the magnificent cathedral's eighty-foot-tall columns stretched up to the vaulted ceiling like a stone forest. The watcher's steely eyes moved to the sunlight pouring through the tall stained-glass window above the altar, illuminating the shadowy expanse with a hundred hues of light. He scanned the pews that filled the 400-foot-long nave. While the cathedral could hold 40,000, Eli guessed there to be no more than a hundred sitting in thought or kneeling in prayer. He felt sadness, hope, and pain. He noticed a kneeling woman clutching her rosaries near her silently moving lips. Eli allowed himself to feel the woman's anguish for her gravely ill sister for only a moment as he passed by. He needed to focus his attention elsewhere.

Eli's gaze moved to a lean man in a blue suit with dark, wiry hair and a mustache. He was sitting alone, scribbling in a notebook. Eli walked down the pew toward him.

When the pondering Cleto Nazario noticed Eli, his eyes widened, and he gasped in Italian, "It is you!"

Eli moved beside the stunned reporter and sat. His pensive gaze turned to the altar as an organ played, and angelic voices filled the air. "I met Simone da Orsenigo once," Eli said in perfect Italian.

Nazario closed his gaping mouth, swallowed, and asked, "Who-who is that?"

"The grand architect, of course."

"The grand architect?" gasped Nazario, his mustache twitching.

"Of this cathedral. Orsenigo would be pleased to see it now."

"Yes, of course," muttered Nazario. Trying not to stare at the watcher, the reporter's stupefied gaze moved to the line of boys in white gowns and ruffs singing. "I suppose you have met many interesting people in your time."

"Many," nodded Eli. "And some not so interesting."

Nazario's gaze returned to Eli, who was taking in the light of the spectacular stained-glass window. "Forgive me, I have thought for so long of the questions I would ask you, but I can remember none of them now."

"There is no need." Eli's gaze lowered to the old pews.

"No need?"

"You will have plenty of time to think of your questions." Eli turned to the searching Nazario. "That is, if you will still help me find my wife and son."

Nazario gulped as his eyes shifted in thought. He considered proposing an offer to get the story he wanted, but the reporter was so flattered Eli had sought him out that he pushed the idea aside. "Of course! I will do all that I can to help you!"

"In exchange for a story," frowned Eli.

Nazario's eyes swelled. "If you will allow me."

Eli sighed, then nodded. "I will answer ten questions, so consider them wisely."

"Ten questions...thank you," breathed Nazario, his gaze trailing off. Then, gaining a bit of composure, he turned to Eli and asked, "How-how did you find me?"

Eli raised an eyebrow at the reporter. "Is that one of your questions?"

"No. Forgive me."

Eli turned back to the exquisite window.

"When-when I decide to ask those questions—extraordinary questions, I might add—I will notify you. That way, we can normally converse. Is that acceptable?"

"Yes," nodded Eli.

Still trying to compose himself, Nazario reached down for his notebook on the pew beside him and scribbled a note. Then, after closing the notebook, he turned to Eli and asked, "What should we do first?"

Eli locked eyes with the reporter. "At the château, you told me you knew the location of a portal."

Nazario sat up a little straighter and pulled down on his vest. "Yes, a portal. An Ostium Mundos," he anxiously nodded.

Eli stared at the reporter, waiting for more, then asked. "Where is it?"

Nazario gulped. "Well, there are many, or I should say, several possible places."

Eli's face dimmed.

"There is a place in Southern England where enormous boulders form a—"

"Stonehenge," said Eli, intrigued by the notion.

"Yes, but of course, you would know of Stonehenge."

Eli's brow furrowed in thought. "I have not been there for some time. It was once a very busy place."

"It was?" asked a wide-eyed Nazario. "But of course it was! There, you see!"

"I need to uncover every stone," muttered Eli, remembering Madame Duguay's admonishment.

"Then a place with giant stones is a good place to start," said a relieved Nazario.

Eli got to his feet. "Are you ready?"

"Right now?"

"Yes."

"I'm-I'm in the middle of a story but... of course, I will make time for you!" Nazario eagerly pushed his notebook into his leather bag, then turned to Eli with a questioning look. "Before we begin, if I may ask, who is funding our expedition?"

"I am."

Nazario's face brightened with an exuberant smile. "Then let's go to England!"

Eli followed the softly chattering reporter out of the cathedral past a pew with a family kneeling in prayer. Two rows behind them, a man in a dark suit with brown, greasy hair sat looking away at a side chapel. The man's nostrils flared when Eli and the reporter passed, as if catching a scent. His head turned, revealing gray, baggy eyes. The man in the suit gathered his hat and followed Eli and Nazario out of the cathedral.

———

BERLIN, GERMANY
19 OCTOBER 1933

"WHAT IS SO important for you to disturb me, Guerre?" glared Lu, his open robe exposing his hairy chest.

The baggy-eyed halfborn raised his head. Across the dimly lit apartment, through a partly open bedchamber door, he noticed movement in a bed. "Forgive me, master, but it is important."

"Go on." Lu moved to a credenza containing a tray of drinking glasses, various liquors, and a water decanter, then poured a drink.

Guerre gulped. "He may cause trouble for you, master."

"Who?" asked Lu, glaring over his glass at the greasy-haired halfborn.

"The watcher," breathed Guerre with anxious eyes.

"Elijah? He is powerless. Why would he meddle?" frowned Lu.

"He seeks what we seek."

"An orb?" Lu shook his head. "He can do nothing with it should he find one."

"I sensed his power in Milan."

Lu stared across the dim room in thought. He had hoped the watcher had given up on rescuing his wife and child from the abyss, and it concerned Lu Eli might still be intent on finding them. Even more concerning was the possibility some of his nemesis's gifts had returned.

"What do you wish me to do, master?" asked Guerre, his baggy eyes fixed on Lu.

"Follow him. See what he's up to." Lu opened a credenza drawer and removed a wooden box. Inside was a twelve-inch-long pewter rod flared at one end like a candleholder. A dark, onyx lens sat within the flared opening. Engraved around its opposite end were unusual characters. "I'll trust you with this. Eliminate him if you must, but find out what he's up to first. He may have learned we are also searching for a way to access the abyss. An orb would be helpful, but it is a portal that we need, and I know of only one remaining."

"You search for Hathor's Gate," said the halfborn.

"It would be truly ironic for the noble Eli to lead us to it," said Lu, his eyes shifting in thought.

"Yes, master."

"Keep me informed of his doings, and do not disappoint me," said Lu with an unforgiving look.

"I will not." With a bow, the halfborn took the ancient weapon, turned, and left the dim apartment.

Lu stood at the credenza for a time, considering what Eli's return might mean for them, then turned back to his bedchamber. When Lu pushed open its door, a young blonde woman sat up in the bed, a pulled-up sheet covering her nakedness.

"Who was that?" asked a brunette in the bed beside her, not bothering to hide herself.

"No one for you to worry about," replied Lu, slipping off his robe.

AMESBURY, ENGLAND
23 OCTOBER 1933

ELI'S EYES narrowed as he climbed out of the carriage and gazed across the lush English countryside. The grazing sheep made him miss his château, but the line of standing and leaning megaliths, just visible over the grassy hill, made him yearn for the ancient world.

"Your timing is quite good with the weather," said the coachman, who wore a coat, top hat, and bushy muttonchop sideburns. "It's been raining all day."

Nazario buttoned his coat, pulled his leather case from the carriage, and then turned to the low sun breaking through the clouds.

"Should I wait for you, sirs?" asked the coachman.

"Yes, if you would," said Eli, handing the driver a shilling.

Nazario waited until they were on the path that led to the prehistoric henge before he said in Italian, "I've never seen this place in person, just in books, but I find it magical."

"Magical is one word to describe Annwn," replied Eli, eyeing the tops of the megaliths over the rise.

"That is what this place was called?" asked a wide-eyed Nazario.

"Yes," nodded Eli.

"One shilling for entry," said an old man standing beside a gate in a raincoat and hat.

Eli handed the man coins, and they passed through the gate.

"What was it like here long ago?" asked Nazario, looking at Eli like a boy eager for his grandfather's stories.

"Much different from this," said Eli as they approached the massive leaning and toppled stones. "Time has not been kind to you, Annwn."

"Time is kind to few," said Nazario with an envious glance at the nine-inch-taller Eli.

"What remains is a small part of what once stood here. Most of it has rotted or been carried away. Only the largest pillars remain."

"English legend says it was Merlin, the magician who built this place. That he brought the stones from Ireland," laughed Nazario. When he noticed Eli in thought, he gasped. "Is the legend true?"

Eli shook his head.

"I thought not. Merlin, ha!"

"Merlin had the stones moved from here in England," said Eli.

Nazario's jaw slackened. "How-how did he move them? They're massive."

"He used giants, of course. They're quite good at such work," shrugged Eli.

Nazario's jaw hung open as Eli moved to the center of the teetering stone circle. "Giants," Nazario muttered in amazement before catching up with Eli standing in the center of the henge. He watched as Eli pushed the long grass aside with his boots. "Are you searching for something?"

"It's not here." Eli scanned the surrounding grassland. "It's been removed."

"What's been removed?"

Eli sighed and turned to the wide-eyed reporter. "There was a portal here once. A star gate."

"What-what did it look like? Maybe I can help you find it!"

"A twelve-foot round metal ring. It stood on a large platform. It was a gateway through which one could travel. It stood here before the altar stone."

Nazario gulped. "Twelve feet is quite large. I think we would see it."

Eli nodded.

"What if it rusted away? Metal does that."

"Not this metal."

"Of course."

Eli walked the grass of the ancient henge as the setting sun cast brilliant rays between the megaliths. "This was once a bustling place."

"Did people travel here to use the portal?" asked Nazario, following behind.

"Yes, but that was long ago. It was all much different then."

"I can only imagine," muttered Nazario, gazing across the henge.

Eli thought of Michelle as he viewed the setting sun. He wondered what awfulness she faced in the abyss.

When the last rays were drawn below the horizon, Eli turned to Nazario, sitting on a toppled stone, scribbling in his notebook. "There's nothing for us here. We must search elsewhere."

Nazario put away his notebook and got to his feet. "What is it we must find?"

Eli gave the leaning megaliths one last glance, then started back down the path to their waiting carriage.

"If you tell me, I can be of more help," reasoned Nazario, catching up with Eli.

"What has your research taught you about Ostium Mundos?"

"It's Latin for door of the world," Nazario eagerly replied.

"But where does this door lead?" asked Eli.

Nazario shrugged. "To other places? Other worlds?"

Eli nodded. "Are there other doorways like this?"

"It makes only sense that there would be. My research has pointed to that as well."

Eli stopped and turned. He studied his eager assistant. Eli had discerned Nazario many times before, but since finding him in the cathedral, Eli had sensed a change in the reporter's heart. Nazario's motives now seemed purer to Eli. He resumed walking. "There are two types of star gates. Those instituted for travel, such as this place, and naturally occurring doorways."

Nazario nearly walked into the wooden gate as he listened. "Naturally occurring?"

"Yes. These doorways—catches, some call them—are powered by the energy of this world. The problem is finding them."

"If you've used these natural doorways before, couldn't you simply go back to one?"

Eli nodded to the coachman as they climbed into the carriage. He said something in Italian, but the driver looked at him blankly. "Back to our hotel, please," Eli said in English. Confident they would not be understood, he continued in Italian. "The problem is, the energy of this world is ever changing. The natural doorways move. Those who accidentally find them disappear into another world, never to be seen nor heard from again. To accomplish our mission, we must find either a portal or a key."

Nazario's eyes swelled at Eli's use of *"our."* He refocused himself. "A key?"

"A domain sphere. It's a golden orb that has many purposes. It's a communication device. A director, if you will, but it can also harness this world's energy to open portals. Through those doorways, one can rapidly move about this world and beyond. I used to have one, and they're quite handy."

"Yes, I'm sure they are," said an astonished Nazario. He opened his notebook and scribbled more notes. "What happened to your orb?"

Eli's face dimmed. "Michelle took it with her into the abyss."

"Oh." Nazario thought for a moment before his dark eyebrows shot up. "If she has the orb, why can't she use it to come back?"

"She doesn't wield the power to do so on her own."

"I see." Nazario's gaze trailed off, overwhelmed by it all.

Eli looked across the darkening countryside and listened to the clomping hooves and rolling carriage wheels.

Nazario's eyes widened with a thought, and he flipped back through his notebook. Not finding what he sought, he reached into his bag for another, cursing the faltering light under his breath. After searching its pages, he turned to the watching Eli and exclaimed, "We must go to Scotland!"

CHAPTER 10

LUMINAH

THE ABYSS

To Michelle, it seemed as though they had been walking for days, but she was no more tired than had it been minutes. "What is that glow I see ahead? Is the sun rising?"

"No, that is Luminah," replied Remiel.

Michelle's eyes widened when they topped a hill, and a broad valley with a mountainous stone pyramid standing at its center came into view. She marveled at the glowing beam of light rising from the tip of the pyramid and radiating across the blanket of low, dark clouds, illuminating the grand pyramid and the city surrounding it. She shook her head in wonder. "Is this Luminah?"

"Yes," nodded Remiel, surprised by Michelle's amazement.

As they approached the lighted city, hundreds of simple stone dwellings with flat roofs came into view. "How many live here?" she asked as the path widened to a road.

"Tens of thousands," replied Remiel.

"Where does that light come from?" Michelle asked, eyeing the pyramid's beam.

"From the temple," explained Gak.

"It's beautiful," breathed Michelle. The sound of a distant bell caused her to turn to Remiel. "What's that?"

"A welcome."

"A welcome?" frowned Michelle. "For who?"

"For you," replied Gak.

Michelle's eyes swelled at the dozens of people filing out of their dwellings. As they drew closer, the shimmering crowd of eager-faced people grew, lining both sides of the road. Some waved for others to join them as if greeting an arriving monarch. Michelle noticed their looks of awe and assumed it was Og they were looking at until she spotted another giant in the crowd. When the welcoming throng chanted, "Theia, Theia," Michelle stopped and stared. When they kneeled and bowed, she turned to Remiel and asked, "What are they doing? Why are they kneeling?"

"To honor you."

"Honor me? Why?"

"Because you are the Bringer of Light, of course," explained Gak.

Michelle shook her head, not understanding. They had just started moving again when a woman hurried before them, kneeled, and then spread herself face-first on the cobbled road. Uneasily eyeing the bowing throng, Michelle turned to Remiel. "Please tell them not to do that. Tell them to stand."

"It should be you that tells them," said Gak.

A concerned Michelle turned to the gathering crowd and said in French, "Please, you don't need to kneel to me. I'm just a woman from Gien. Please stand."

The crowd didn't move.

"They don't understand your words," explained Remiel.

"French is the only language I know," shrugged Michelle.

"It is not," replied Remiel. "Find the light within you and speak your thoughts."

"What?"

"You have the power within you," urged Remiel.

Michelle scanned the growing crowd of worshipers in dismay.

"Tell them," nodded Remiel.

Michelle breathed in, then said, "You do not need to kneel to me. Please stand. I am the same as you." Her eyes widened as the words that were both foreign yet familiar caused the multitude to raise their heads and stand. An awestruck Michelle watched as the adoring crowd closed in around her, their hands reaching to touch her. "Theia, Theia," they softly chanted. Michelle felt their love. It was a sensation unlike anything she had before experienced. Her hands glowed even brighter when she lovingly reached out her arms. Michelle felt a sparkle of light leave her outstretched fingers and flow into those she touched. But it was not only her giving light; she received a portion of their luminance in return. With tears streaming down her face, Michelle glanced back at a beaming Remiel.

"They have been waiting for you," smiled Remiel. "We all have."

MICHELLE'S MOUTH opened when they entered the gleaming throne room. It was not only the elemental glow that lighted the chamber, but also the flowing river of light that moved across the ceiling from the temple. Even the chamber's high walls glistened with illuminated tapestries depicting the history of Lumina. Michelle's wonder-filled gaze followed the pictographic wall hangings up the high ceiling to the flowing stream of light. "What is this place?" she whispered.

Before Remiel could answer, a bronze-skinned man in white robes rose from the simple, gleaming throne.

"Theia!" exclaimed Mawufe, his cut beard the same length as the day Hathor cast him into the abyss, his sunken eye sockets burned closed.

Michelle was about to offer a greeting when Mawufe lowered to his knees and bowed before her. Uncertain of what to do, Michelle glanced back at Remiel before turning to the bowed leader. "Please, don't kneel for me. I don't know why everyone keeps doing that."

Mawufe lifted his head and gestured to his throne. "Please, you must take the seat of guiding light."

"No, really, I'm fine. That's your place," Michelle said, uncomfortable with all the attention.

"Welcome," nodded Mawufe as he stood. "You are among worthy company," he added, nodding to Remiel and the others.

Remiel meekly lowered his head.

Michelle couldn't hide her pity at seeing the terrible scars where Mawufe's eyes should be and wondered how his perception was so keen. "Is it you I should thank for rescuing me from that dark and terrible dungeon?"

Mawufe shook his head. "It is they alone who acted."

Michelle turned to Remiel and the others. "Thank you once again for saving me."

Mawufe cocked his head in confusion. "Forgive me, but I don't understand. Why did you let the followers of Ra take you? And how is it they still hold the prince? Is it a test?"

"I fought as best I could, but they overpowered me. They took my orb and blazerod," said Michelle.

Mawufe's lips parted, uncertain of what to say.

"Can you help me get my son back? Can you free him?"

Mawufe stood a little taller. "It *is* a test."

Michelle glanced at Remiel, not understanding.

"Do you wish us to violate our oath? Our peace and honor are most dear to us," said a concerned Mawufe. "But we will, should you command us."

Remiel moved closer to Michelle. "The Luminaries have sworn an oath of peace. They have done this to gain favor that you might persuade the Great Ones to grant them mercy."

"Mercy? I'm sure you've mistaken me for someone else!"

"There is no mistake," frowned Mawufe.

Michelle shook her head. "I just want my son back. They are a terrible, gruesome people who burn human bodies for their light! We have to get Franny away from them! I have to get him back home!"

Mawufe turned to Remiel. "Can you and your band assist Theia?"

"Why does everyone call me that?" asked Michelle.

"Because that is your name," replied Remiel. He turned back to Mawufe. "The prince is a prize Keket will not easily part with."

Michelle shook her head and muttered, "I feel like Alice in Wonderland. This is all so very confusing. Why do they want my son? He's only a little boy!"

Mawufe cocked his head, uncertain of her meaning. "As the Queen of Light, you know well the prince's bloodline—of his divine mission to usher in the Chosen One's return. You surely understand the followers of Ra and their reasons better than I."

"But...I'm *not* the Queen of Light. I'm not Theia!" insisted Michelle. She saw Mawufe's confusion and turned to the others. "Can't you all see? I'm just an ordinary French woman!" Michelle's shoulders sank at their blank looks. On the verge of panic, she said to Remiel, "We have to get my son back before they..." She couldn't bear the thought of the dark dwellers making Franny a human candle.

"They will not hurt him," replied Remiel, seeing her worry.

"But what if they learn who he is?" asked Gak.

"What does that mean?" fretted Michelle.

"They cannot see him," said Mawufe.

"He's just a little boy! I should have never left there without him!" cried Michelle, bursting into tears.

Mawufe's face saddened as he felt Michelle's anguish. "They have your domain sphere and blazerod?"

"Yes," whimpered Michelle.

"There are none among them with the power to use a blazerod," said Remiel.

"But the orb?" asked Mawufe.

Remiel shook his head.

"I don't care about those things! I just want my son back! Will you help me? If not, I'll go back myself!"

"We will do all we can to save the prince," nodded Gak.

"Thank you," muttered Michelle, wiping away her tears. "Will you then help us return to our world?"

Mawufe was taken aback by her request and turned to Remiel for clarification.

Michelle felt their eyes on her. "Well, will you?"

"But..." Remiel began, uncertain of what to say.

"That is why *you* are here," added Gak.

"I-I don't understand," said Michelle, regaining her composure.

"The prophecy," muttered Og, his voice like a bear.

Michelle turned back to the giant. "The prophecy?"

Gak studied the bewildered Michelle for a moment, then said, "It is prophesied that Theia, the Bringer of Light, will come to the world of darkness in the end times to aid in the judgment of those imprisoned. That she will open the dark gates and free the worthy before the wicked are utterly destroyed. Is that not why you and the prince are here with your domain sphere? To usher in the return of the Chosen One and to punish the wicked? To open the doors and free the innocent?"

Michelle shook her head. "You've mistaken me for another. I don't know how to use the orb!"

"You know blazerod," grunted Og.

Michelle turned to the giant. "I'm sorry if I hurt your friend. I didn't realize who you were then. I'm just a mother lost in this terrible place, trying to find her son! I'm not who you think I am!"

Gak reached a tentative hand to Michelle's arm. "Perhaps it is you who is mistaken."

Remiel nodded. "You *are* the Queen of Light. I can see it in you. All of us can."

Michelle helplessly shook her head.

Remiel's expression softened. "You will come to realize your destiny."

"But what if you're wrong? What if that's not my destiny? I only want to get my son back and go home! Will you help me?"

Remiel sighed.

"I know there's a way out!" Michelle turned to Gak. "Elijah cast your brother here, but he came back to my world! I saw it!"

"He was summoned back by Lu using the orb's power," explained Remiel.

"If we get the orb back from the people of Ra, can you use it to open a doorway?" asked Michelle.

Remiel shook his head. "While the domain sphere can open doorways to different worlds, including this dark realm, it can only do so with the proper authority."

"Theia does not need such contrivances to command the openings!" declared Mawufe. "She can do so by her word!"

Michelle sighed and asked Remiel, "Don't you have that authority?"

Remiel studied Michelle. He saw her innocence and beauty, but he also saw her divinity and power. He thought it strange she didn't recognize those elements in herself. "I no longer have the authority. I know of but one who can command an orb."

"Who?"

"The traveler," muttered Gak.

"Who is that?" asked Michelle.

"The gatekeeper of Goash," replied Remiel.

"Then we can go there after we get Franny!" said Michelle, beaming with hope. "Surely, he'd let us pass!"

"The gatekeeper is a swindler," hissed Gak. "A despicable traveler who would rob you for passage and then send you to the wrong place!"

"Gak has a history with him," said Remiel.

Og nodded.

"Surely, there must be a way back from here," groaned Michelle.

Gak's eyebrows lifted. "There is a way. Through you."

Michelle's shoulders sank. "Are there no other portals?"

"In the other world, there are such doorways. Many of my people have fallen through them and come here by mistake," said Mawufe.

"Yes, but that is in the other world. There are no natural doorways here," replied Remiel.

"Are there no other portals but this one with the gatekeeper you speak of?" asked Michelle.

"There was the Dark Gate in the depths of Manu. But it was destroyed long ago," replied Remiel.

Michelle dejectedly shook her head. "There must be another way."

"There is. By your command," insisted Mawufe.

Michelle sighed, exhausted by the exchange.

Remiel looked at his friends, then bowed to Michelle. "My queen, we swear allegiance to you. We will give our all to save the prince."

"Thank you," said Michelle, choking back her tears.

CHAPTER II
KNIGHTS' REVENGE

ROSLIN, SCOTLAND
26 OCTOBER 1933

The sky was gray, and the clouds were low when Eli and Nazario stepped off the train. Standing on the platform with steam rolling past their ankles like a low fog, the reporter eyed the dreary cobblestone station, its slate roof wet and green with moss, the tops of red and orange-leafed trees visible beyond.

"This way," nodded Eli, spotting the station's exit.

Nazario's gaze moved to the open gate as a dozen other travelers funneled to it. He opened his umbrella and held it over Eli and himself as they walked through the station gate to a line of waiting carriages. When a black automobile puttered by, he turned to Eli and asked, "How soon do you think before we see only those contraptions?"

"Not long," replied Eli, lifting their bags into the covered carriage.

Nazario joined Eli in the carriage, then turned to the waiting driver and said in English, "Rosslyn Chapel, please."

With a snap of the driver's reins, the mare snorted and clopped down the wet cobbled street.

Behind them, a baggy-eyed man in a hat with his trench coat collar pulled up, watched as their carriage rolled away. His lifeless gaze turned to the train station's telegraph office, and he went inside. Stepping in front of a waiting couple, Guerre lowered his head to the barred window and, with a thick accent, said, "I would like to send a telegram."

"Pardon me, but we were in the queue before you," huffed the irritated husband, his wife nodding. But when the ghoulish Guerre glared at them, the husband stepped back and said, "Go-go ahead. We can wait."

The telegraph operator, who had rolled-up sleeves and wore headphones around his neck, pushed a paper before the baggy-eyed halfborn and said, "Write your message down here."

Guerre's lifeless gaze raised to the operator. "Write it for me."

The operator recoiled, partly from the halfborn's command but more from his awful breath. He pulled back the paper and said, "Fine. Who is it going to?"

"Herr Lu Stormbrewer, Berlin, Germany."

The operator's eyes widened, but he didn't look up. "And what should it say?"

Guerre's nostrils flared. "A lovely day in Roslin. Going to the chapel."

The operator waited for more, then looked up with held breath and asked, "Anything else?"

"No," glared the halfborn.

A half-mile down the road, the horse and buggy moved through a misting rain.

"Tell me more of this chapel," said Eli in Italian so as not to be overheard by the driver.

A surprised Nazario turned to Eli. "Have you not been here before?"

Eli shook his head, his blue eyes surveying the wet and dreary landscape.

"How is it you have never been to Rosslyn Chapel?"

"Because I have not."

"Surely, you know of the Knights Templar?"

"Yes, I know of them," nodded Eli, somewhat troubled by their mention.

Nazario turned to the watcher. "I'm not sure what I should say. I feel like a fool trying to educate you on the past when you've lived through it and seen it firsthand."

Eli sighed. "I can only be in one place at a time. Tell me what you know of them."

"Very well. In 1119, the Roman Catholic Church founded the order of the Knights Templar. They were a unique group, exempt from all local laws and answered only to the pope. They were soldiers and bankers, among other things, and their power gave them great wealth. It is said they had a thousand castles and were always the first into battle. It's even said at the Battle of Montgisard, an army of five hundred Templars defeated an army of twenty-six thousand!" Nazario paused to see if he was irritating Eli.

"Go on."

"During the Crusades, they acquired the treasure from Solomon's Temple. Some say it was the Holy Grail or the Ark of the Covenant, or even the remains of Jesus himself! But whatever it was, it made them extraordinarily powerful.

"When they returned to Europe, the Knights Templar were a force unto themselves. This made many monarchs nervous. King Philip the Fourth of France was in debt to the Templars and hated them. He spread lies, then had them arrested and tried for worshiping false idols. Many of them were burned at the stake. But legend says some of the Templars escaped and came here with the treasure from Solomon's Temple." Nazario's eyes widened. "Your key to the doorway, a domain sphere, may be among that treasure!"

Eli gazed across the misty farmland to the forest's edge, its red and orange fall foliage half gone.

"Well?" asked a searching Nazario, "Did I get it right?"

Eli faintly nodded. "Most of it. The Order of the Knights Templar started with a noble cause, as do many, but their success and power proved their undoing, as it does with most."

"But what of Solomon?" asked an eager Nazario.

Eli sighed. "I knew Solomon as a wise and righteous king. But his standing brought him great wealth and power, and like the Templar, he became corrupt and fell. It is the sad plight of many mortals."

"But what of his temple treasure? What of the Ark of the Covenant and the Holy Grail?"

"The Jerusalem temple held the Ark at one point, along with relics from the ancient times, but whether there was an orb there, I don't know."

"Leave no stone unturned, you said."

Eli glanced at Nazario and nodded.

When their carriage stopped, Eli's gaze turned to the five-hundred-year-old brownstone church, its front buttress and arched entry damp and dripping from the cold Scottish rain. At less than eighty feet long and fifty feet tall, the Sinclair family chapel was not large, yet its arched stained-glass windows and rows of gothic pinnacles gave it a commanding presence.

With the rain now a downpour, darkening the evening to dusk, Eli and Nazario hurried to the chapel's arched entry, dodging the swelling puddles. Standing under Nazario's umbrella, Eli was about to knock when the door opened to a gray-haired woman in a scarf and coat. Once attractive, she had succumbed to the effects of time and neglect. Eli's eyes narrowed as he sensed something unusual about her.

"Oh, we're closing just now," said the woman in a thick Scottish brogue. Her eyes lingered on Eli.

"Oh, no!" gasped Nazario in English. "Please, madame, my friend and I have come far to see your chapel! We will pay for a private tour!"

She pulled her gaze from Eli and said, "I'm sorry, but I'm the only one here. You'll have to come back tomorrow."

"Please, madame."

The woman felt Eli's gaze and asked, "Do I know you, sir?"

"Perhaps," said Eli, eyeing her.

The aged woman looked out into the steady downpour. After spotting the waiting carriage, she said, "Perhaps we could strike a bargain."

"Yes, madame?" replied an eager Nazario.

"I must go down to Collegehill. If I could borrow your buggy, you can wait here until I return, as long as you promise to disturb nothing. This is a holy house, and God is watching."

"Yes, of course, madame," beamed Nazario.

"Allow me." Eli took Nazario's umbrella and led the woman through the storm to the carriage. With a gracious nod, she climbed into the buggy, and it rolled away.

"That worked out quite well," grinned Nazario as Eli pushed open the church door. After passing through the cramped baptistry, they entered the small nave. Lit by two candle chandeliers at the far end, flickering shadows embellished the stone interior's elaborate archways and carvings. The central seating area was only fifty feet long and twenty feet wide. It held eight rows of small wooden pews with a narrow path in between. Arched stone pillars lined the sides, creating a walkway between them and the outer north and south walls. Eli's gaze raised to the vaulted stone ceiling adorned with five sections of intricately carved flowers and stars.

The dim evening light muted the colorful stained-glass windows that lined the lofty walls.

"It's spectacular, isn't it?"

"Yes," nodded Eli.

"See up there," Nazario pointed to a stained-glass depiction of a knight in armor with a green dragon lying at his feet. "That's Saint George." He waited for Eli to comment, then asked. "Did you know him?"

Eli shook his head and turned to the red altar at the end of the nave. He started for it, his boots echoing on the flagstone floor.

"William Sinclair, the Earl of Caithness, had this chapel built. It is said that the Sinclair family is of the divine bloodline. That they are descendants of Jesus." Nazario noticed Eli's look of realization. "That-that is why the Templar brought their treasure here." He stepped closer to Eli. "Does that mean something to you?"

Eli turned to Nazario but only nodded.

"Here is his tomb. Come look at this!" Nazario pointed to a sandstone slab on the floor with the inscription William de St. Clair, Knight Templar. Above the name was an eight-pointed star in the handle of a key. Above that, a sword. "Some say that this star references a doorway to another realm. A star gate. Could it be telling us a key is here? That's what we're searching for, isn't it?"

Eli studied the engravings.

"It's all very curious, isn't it?" Nazario watched for Eli's reaction but, seeing none, shrugged and said, "It is for me, anyway."

They moved to the lady chapel, glowing in candlelight behind the altar. Eli surveyed the magnificent Apprentice Pillar, its intricately carved leaf motif swirling from base to cap like a candy cane.

"It took the masons forty years to build and carve all of this. To them, that was a lifetime; to you, but a minute."

Eli glanced at Nazario, then read an inscription joining two pillars. "*Forte est vinum fortior est rex fortiores sunt mulieres super omnia vincit veritas.*"

"Yes," said Nazario. "Wine is strong, a king is stronger, women are stronger still, but truth conquers all."

Eli drew in a breath and nodded. "All true." He gazed at the musical cubes carved in the archways and the green men glaring down at him, then asked, "Where is the Templar's treasure?"

Nazario gulped. "Ah, let me show you the sacristy." Turning, he ushered Eli to stairs that led down to a dimly lit crypt. Damp and cold, it too had a high arched ceiling, but its stonework was not nearly as detailed as the chapel above. Recessed vaults lined the side walls, and a lone stained-glass window let in the failing evening light. Nazario pulled out his cigarette lighter and thumbed its flint, igniting a small flame.

Eli examined a recessed door with Nazario's light and pulled on its handle. It was locked.

"Do you think it's in there?" asked Nazario.

"I don't know."

"Can you sense its presence?"

Eli's face dimmed. "My discernment doesn't work that way. It is only to sense mortal's needs and give them aid."

"Oh." Nazario stared across the crypt. "You can no doubt read me like a book, then."

Eli's gaze moved from the nervous reporter to another wooden door. He moved to it and pulled it open. It was an empty alcove. They looked around the crypt, pushing on the stone walls and searching for secret passageways, but found nothing.

Eli studied the stained-glass window that depicted the resurrected Christ standing before three kneeling saints. He searched for clues for a time, then said, "There is nothing to find here."

"The treasure could be buried underground," said Nazario as Eli turned to the stairs.

"Or not here at all."

Nazario sighed and followed Eli up the steps. He watched as Eli examined the stone carvings in the lady chapel and paused at an engraved header.

"That depicts the seven virtues," said Nazario. "And this one, the seven deadly sins."

Eli moved to a carving of a knight and another man on the same horse.

"That is a common symbol of the Knights Templar."

When Eli moved to a wall carving of an upside-down angel bound by rope, Nazario stepped beside him, gulped, and said, "That is a fallen angel. A watcher."

Eli studied the carving.

Nazario was about to comment further when a woman behind them said, "That is Semjaza. You may have heard of him."

Eli spun around to the gray-haired woman who had borrowed their carriage. Beside her stood a younger, leaner woman wearing a cape over her gown. She had thick, pulled-back hair and deep brown eyes. "Dina?"

"Hello, Elijah. It is nice to see you again," said the younger woman with a welcoming smile.

They embraced, and Eli surveyed her in astonishment. "I feared I was the last, that you and the others were all destroyed!"

"I nearly was, thanks to Lu's henchman." Her discerning gaze moved to the wide-eyed Nazario.

"Cleto Nazario," bowed the reporter.

"I've heard of you," frowned Dina. "You're the Italian journalist. Tenacious."

"Well, thank you," beamed Nazario.

"He's a friend," nodded Eli.

"Mortal friends are much needed in these troubled times," said Dina.

Eli's gaze moved to the aged woman. "I sensed something in you I didn't at first understand, but I do now. You're a halfborn."

"Yes, this is my daughter, Angela," said the forty-year-younger-looking Dina.

Nazario's jaw slackened, and his round eyes moved between the two women.

A smiling Dina turned from the stunned reporter to Eli and said, "There is much we must talk about, but not here. Come to the castle."

"The castle?" gasped Nazario.

"You are in Scotland. Everyone has a castle," grinned Dina.

AFTER A DINNER OF SMOKED HADDOCK, peas, and creamed potatoes, Eli and Nazario moved with their hosts to chairs and a couch before a large stone fireplace. Above the cozy fire hung the Sinclair family crest. Tartan tapestries and a full-size painting of William Sinclair hung on another wall beside an elk's head. A large ringed chandelier, wired for electricity, hung from the exposed beamed ceiling.

A riveted Nazario listened to Dina and Eli discuss their past as the aged daughter quietly sat. After finding a pause in the conversation, the reporter leaned forward and asked, "What was your role among the watchers, if I may ask?"

Dina's gaze moved to the open leather case near the reporter's leg. She grinned at his overpowering urge to remove his notebook and record everything being said. "My stewardship was over learning. I was a teacher. We all were, in one form or another."

Nazario's eyes narrowed. "You speak in the past tense. Is that no longer your call?"

Dina glanced at Eli. "Many things have changed."

"How many of you were there? Is it true there were two hundred?"

An amused Dina turned to Eli and asked, "Are you going to clear his mind after all this?"

Nazario's jaw slackened.

"I told him I would answer ten questions."

"Generous," grinned Dina.

"Is that how you've gone so long without being discovered? You can erase one's memory? Of course!" Nazario's gaze drifted in realization but then shot back to Eli. "But you won't do that with me. You promised me ten questions!"

"Ten questions," nodded Eli.

An engrossed Nazario sat back as Eli turned to Dina and said, "You gave birth to a mortal's baby. I thought it was only the amorous males among us who violated the precept."

Dina laughed. "I do not view it as a violation. My time as a guardian was finished, and I wished to have progeny. I fell in love with a man. We married and mated, and now we have Angela Sinclair."

"How is it being the daughter of an immortal?" asked Nazario.

An embarrassed Angela turned to Dina. "I've had a charmed life. But it is rather disturbing watching myself grow old while my mother remains youthful. It's hard on the ego at times."

Eli's face filled with compassion. He sensed the daughter's great angst regarding her mortality. "What of your father?"

"He's passed," Angela replied, sadly eyeing the tartan rug.

"Duncan died in the spring of twenty-nine," nodded Dina.

"Oh. Not long ago," replied Nazario.

"1729," added Dina.

Nazario's mustache twitched, and he turned to the downcast Angela. "If I may ask, how old are you?"

"Old enough," muttered the aged daughter.

"I'm sorry. I didn't mean to offend," said Nazario.

Angela pulled herself up from the chair and said, "If you will excuse me, it's been a long day."

"Of course," said Eli, getting to his feet.

An embarrassed Nazario joined him.

"Goodnight, my dear," said Dina, kissing the old daughter on the forehead.

Nazario watched as Angela left the light of the fireplace.

After sitting, Dina turned to Eli and asked. "What happened to you after Sarajevo?"

Eli sighed. "When the war started, I searched for a way to stop it. I was desperate, but the domain sphere was silent. Something else happened too."

"Oh?"

"I felt my body changing."

"How so?" asked Dina.

"If I pricked my flesh, I bled."

Dina's eyes widened.

"I tried to flee but couldn't. I went to France, desperate to make a difference, and joined the Army."

"You became a French soldier," laughed Dina.

"Yes, but I could not kill until..." Eli sighed. "I lived in a trench with hundreds of men who faced death daily. So many of them perished." Eli's gaze moved to the flickering flame. "It was all such a waste. I had two friends. When they died, I was devastated."

Nazario's gaze lowered, feeling Eli's pain.

"Then something extraordinary happened."

"And what was that?" asked Dina.

"A German artillery shell struck our trench. It obliterated those around me and nearly destroyed me. My body healed, but the blast left me with no memory. I didn't know who I was. It was in the hospital that I met Michelle."

Dina nodded. "So, it is true. You have a wife and a child?"

"Yes," whispered Eli.

"But no ordinary child or mother."

Eli glanced at the wide-eyed Nazario, then said, "No."

"Is it true she died in childbirth and Charmeine raised her?"

"Eli nodded."

"The Harbinger," breathed Dina.

"What-who is the Harbinger?" asked Nazario.

"The prophesied forerunner of the Chosen One," replied Dina.

"You mean, like John the Baptist?" Catching Dina's annoyed look, Nazario's curious gaze lowered to the floor, and he sank back on the couch.

"They were both taken from me. Lu cast my son into the abyss, and Michelle chased after him," muttered Eli.

"Like a true mother warrior," said a moved Dina.

"You know Cyrus is behind it all," said Eli.

Dina sadly nodded. "I'm afraid this world has little hope now. It was bad enough with only Lu and his minions, but then Gadreel and now Cyrus. In the beginning, I would have never imagined such a thing. Fortunately, Semjaza and the others are still locked away."

Nazario's eyebrows raised. "Semjaza?"

Eli shook his head, ignoring the reporter. "They've found the perfect surrogate for their evil plan. I foresee a terrible calamity with the rise of this Hitler. They will lull the German people to sleep and then wreak havoc on all the world." Eli sighed. "After all we have done... I fear humanity is lost."

Nazario's distressed gaze moved between the two disheartened watchers. "No! Humanity cannot be lost! Not when there are two such as you!"

"Tell your mortal friend he knows not what he speaks of," frowned Dina.

"I've tried," muttered Eli.

Nazario shook his head. "You cannot give up! Remember, no stone unturned! We will find a way to get your wife and child back from the abyss, and then you can sort out the rest of this mess!"

Eli's gaze moved to the fireplace. "I will get my wife and son back, but the rest... That falls upon the mortal world now."

Nazario gulped.

Eli turned to Dina. "We came here searching for a domain sphere. My friend thinks the Knights Templar may have brought one here with Solomon's treasure."

Dina nodded. "There is a treasure, but there is no orb."

Eli's disappointed gaze lowered, and he asked, "Do you know of a natural doorway? Anything that I could use to get to my family?"

"To access the abyss without an orb?" Dina shook her head. "Even if you were to find a natural gateway, there is no guarantee it would lead to the abyss. You must have access and control to do what you wish. Your only hope is finding another orb or one of the old travel portals."

"The old portals have been closed for millennia," frowned Eli.

"Just because they have been closed does not mean they no longer exist."

Eli sighed.

Dina studied the contemplative Eli, then said, "Your desire to rescue your wife and child is noble, but you must realize that their departure may be part of the grand design." She saw Eli's confusion and continued. "For millennia, we have told mortals that important things often happen for reasons unknown at the time. It is not until the fruit is ripened that it is most sweet."

Eli looked down in thought.

"It may be that the Great Ones have a work for you to do. That your quest to find your family will only be complete when you have halted the evil that Lu and Cyrus have unleashed."

"But how can I do that? I'm powerless?" said Eli.

Nazario's jaw hung as he listened.

A loving smile spanned Dina's face. "Elijah, you are not powerless. On the contrary, you, of all the watchers, are uniquely suited for this task. As an immortal guardian of humankind, the Holy and Great Ones have endowed you with power, but they have also granted you unmatched insight through your mortal awakening."

Eli sank back in his chair and stared at the fireplace.

THE RAIN HAD STOPPED, and the mantle clock struck midnight when Eli and Nazario gathered their coats and moved through the shadowy castle foyer to the tall, arched door.

"Thank you for your hospitality and advice," said Eli, pulling on his coat. "You're sure you won't join us on our quest?"

A flattered Dina shook her head and said, "My days are long spent. I must tend to my daughter's needs now."

"Wish Angela peace and well-being for us," said Eli

"I will do so."

Eli paused when he saw Dina's concern.

"A word of warning to you, brother. With the orb gone, Lu is also searching for a way to access that dark realm. Just as he has in the past, Lu will take those from the abyss that can bolster his cause. Be careful with what you find." Dina's penetrating gaze moved to Nazario. "Be wary of those around you."

"I promise you, I have only the best intentions," insisted Nazario.

"We shall see," smiled Dina.

Eli nodded. "Your advice is well received."

After giving Eli a warm embrace and shaking Nazario's hand, Dina watched them depart through the wet court to a waiting automobile. Then, with a final wave, she closed and bolted the massive door.

Dina turned and started for the grand staircase. She passed the dying fireplace and blew out a candle but paused when she felt an unusual draft. Dina saw a dim glow from within the library and moved toward it. She gathered up a still-lit candlestick and held it before her for light. Dina's steps slowed when she saw wet shoe prints on the stone floor. When the tracks crossed over a pale carpet runner, she saw it was blood.

With wide eyes, Dina looked toward the library's half-open door. She moved toward it and cocked her head to see through its opening. The draft grew colder, and her eyes swelled when she spotted an open library window through the gap in the door.

Dina placed her hand on the half-open door and gave it a push. With a creak, it opened to her aged daughter sprawled in a pool of blood. Dina gasped at Angela's severed head lying a foot away, her lifeless eyes staring at the ceiling. "No!" cried Dina, horrified by the bloody scene. She spun around when the library door closed behind her. There stood the baggy-eyed Guerre glaring at her, a bloody butcher knife in one hand and the blazerod in the other.

CHAPTER 12
THE BRINGER OF LIGHT

LUMINAH
THE ABYSS

Michelle's eyes widened as she entered the spacious room, its granite walls sparkling, its high ceiling aglow with reflected light. "This is lovely."

"It is the queen's chamber," smiled the priestess, who wore a simple ivory gown and had pulled-back hair with streaks of gray.

"But why are you showing me this place?"

"It is your dwelling," explained the woman. "Are you no longer pleased with it?"

"Oh, I'm very pleased, but...it's too nice for me."

"It is the queen's chamber, and you are the Queen of Light. Do you not remember it?"

Michelle's shoulders sank. She was about to tell the maiden she had never been there before when Remiel appeared in the entry.

"Is your habitation to your liking?"

Michelle was happy to see her tall and handsome rescuer. His cloak's hood was pulled back, revealing his dark, curly hair and neat beard. At his side, his sword's hilt gleamed, and in his arms, he held three walnut wood boxes. "Oh yes. Thank you. Everything is wonderful. And everyone is so kind here."

"These are for you," bowed Remiel.

Michelle's gaze lowered to the intricately carved boxes. The largest was flat and rectangular and reminded her of a dress box. The next was half the size but twice as thick. The third box was the thinnest of all and the size of a salad plate. "Oh, how nice. What are they for?"

"For you to wear." Remiel set the boxes on a marble table and presented her with the largest.

Michelle glanced at the watching attendant, then reached for the box's lid. Her hands stopped short as she examined the engraved image of a sun bursting with rays. "That's lovely," she breathed. Michelle removed the box's lid. Her eyes widened at the golden spun gown within. "Oh, thank you." She glanced down at her filthy nightgown. "I must look frightful!"

The priestess smiled and shook her head. "Perhaps Theia would care to be washed before she puts it on?"

"Oh, a bath sounds wonderful!" beamed Michelle.

"This is for after," said Remiel, presenting the smallest of the boxes.

"What is it?" Michelle asked, removing its lid. She gasped at the glistening crystal necklace with a starburst medallion lying atop a green velvet cushion. "Oh, it's beautiful! May I?"

"It is yours," said Remiel, puzzled by her response.

Michelle reached a tentative hand to the sparkling necklace. When she touched it, the crystals glowed. "It's exquisite," she breathed. She pulled her eyes from the necklace and said, "I would like to put it on, but I think I will accept that bath first."

"Of course."

"I will leave you," bowed Remiel as the priestess moved to an archway and parted a curtain.

Michelle's mouth opened at a marble tub filled with emerald, effervescent water. Beside the tub stood two younger women in matching ivory gowns. Michelle moved to the tub and felt the water. "It's even warm! Am I dreaming?"

"No, my queen," said the priestess.

Breathing in the sweet scent of the perfumed water, Michelle stood as the maidens pulled the tattered nightgown over her head. Upon seeing herself in the light for the first time since entering the abyss, Michelle surveyed her naked body. Aside from the glowing elements that defined her shapely figure, she thought she looked no different, having gone so long without food.

When the maidens offered their hands, Michelle took them and stepped into the bath. "Ohhh," she moaned, sinking into the sparkling water. "I've forgotten what a warm bath feels like."

Michelle looked up at the ceiling, aglow from the temple light, and thought she saw stars. She closed her eyes when the maidens poured warm water over her and bathed her. More relaxed than she ever remembered being, Michelle soaked in the soothing water.

When the water grew tepid, the serene Michelle pulled open her eyes to the attentive maidens and breathed, "Oh, that was lovely." A dripping Michelle stood from the bath, and the maidens helped her out and toweled her dry. She watched in wonder as a maiden presented a glass decanter of oil to the priestess. After anointing Michelle's head, the priestess smoothed the scented oil across her closed eyes and face. Michelle sensed the woman's energy and light. Michelle's delicate shoulders sank, and her head gently rolled as the maidens rubbed oil over her back, arms, and legs. Her skin glowed at their touch. With her body tingling and her mind floating, Michelle's eyes closed as the priestess muttered a prayer and smeared oil down her chest and abdomen. Upon opening her eyes, Michelle marveled at the growing brightness of her flesh.

With her mind ethereal, Michelle's eyes widened when the priestess placed the crystal necklace around her neck, and its starburst medallion glowed between her breasts. After combing through her hair, a maiden presented the lovely golden dress. While simple with a few pleats, its fabric was silky and shimmered like spun gold. The gown covered her ankles, but its sleeves reached just below her elbows, and the low neck slit of its loose bodice closed with a tie string. Michelle stepped into the dress, and the maidens raised it over her shoulders. Michelle felt the necklace's energy as she lifted it through the dress's neck slit, and the maiden gathered its strings. From the unopened box came handmade sandals that fit her feet perfectly.

After thanking the women, Michelle exited the washroom, hoping to see Remiel. She gave a relaxed sigh when she found him standing in the dwelling's main room beside a tall, leafless tree that reached up through the ceiling. Michelle marveled at its trunk and branches faintly pulsing with its life energy.

"You are indeed a queen," said Remiel with a bow.

"Thank you for the lovely dress, sandals, and necklace."

"They are yours. Your elegance, light, and beauty do honor to them all."

Michelle blushed. She glanced back at the bath chamber. "What happened in there? It was magical."

"They bathed and anointed you. They've done so many times before," said Remiel with a puzzled look.

Michelle sighed. "You've mistaken me for another."

"There is no mistake," said Remiel, eyeing her knowingly.

"The necklace is lovely. What does the sunburst represent?" Michelle asked, holding it out from her neck to look at.

"It represents the light and knowledge of the Great Ones," said Remiel, wondering how she could have forgotten.

"Oh." Michelle studied the glowing crystals, then said, "I don't think I should wear this."

"You're no longer pleased with it?"

"I'm very pleased with it; it's lovely. It's just…"

Remiel nodded, sensing her discomfort in her divine role. "It was made for you."

"Made for me?"

"Yes. Long ago. When you first arrived."

Michelle drew in a troubled breath. "I don't remember ever being here before. I'm not who you think."

Remiel smiled.

Michelle moved to the balcony to see the temple's luminescence. She looked in awe at the vertical stream of shimmering light rising from the pyramid and spreading across the low, dark clouds like an upside-down waterfall. "It's beautiful. How did Mawufe build all of this? How did he find so much beauty in such a dark and awful place?"

"Luminah's grandeur comes from the light of its people. Mawufe has simply taught them how to let their light shine," said Remiel.

"It is remarkable that an imprisoned people can be so inspired."

"The light is in all of us, even in the abyss. You taught us that."

Michelle sighed. She wondered how awkward it would be once they realized she was not who they supposed her to be. Michelle looked down off the balcony at the leafless trees and passing people. The vision that allowed her to view the surrounding elements was unlike anything she had experienced before, making her feel like she was living in a dream.

Michelle smiled at a woman passing on the street below, whose gown and pulled-back hair were plain and simple. The woman stopped, looked up at Michelle, and placed her raised palms together in reverence. Two men followed, carrying large hammers and chisels, their tunics covered in glowing granite dust. They set down their tools, placed their hands together, and bowed to Michelle. Unsure of what to do, she waved to them.

"Can I do anything else for you?"

Michelle turned to Remiel. Not wanting to be left alone after her time in isolation, she said, "You can keep me company. You can tell me about this place—about you."

Remiel's eyes narrowed. He wondered how Michelle had forgotten who she was. To him, her royalty was as clear as the brightness of her being. "Would you care to walk?"

"Yes. I should love to see the temple."

Remiel bowed. "Then I shall show you."

Michelle smiled.

After exiting her chambers, they started down the winding path. The grand pyramid and its rising beam of light filled the horizon before them.

How can one with such a divine mission have forgotten? wondered Remiel. *Am I to help her remember? Why would the Great Ones entrust me, a fallen watcher, to mentor the Bringer of Light? It makes no sense. Unless... Perhaps this is my redemption?*

After walking a while and taking in the flowing energy around them, Michelle looked up at Remiel. While drawn to him, much like she was to Eli upon first meeting him in the hospital, she thought it was because Remiel had rescued her. Then Michelle remembered how Elijah so frequently enchanted other women, and wondered if it was the natural draw of a watcher. Her face filled with concern as she wondered where Eli was. She wondered if Franny were safe and how she would get him back.

Sensing her worry, Remiel turned to Michelle. "You are troubled by your son."

Michelle nodded. "Yes. Who are those ghastly people who have him?"

"The followers of Ra; some call them the dark dwellers. Hathor sent them here long ago to be keepers of the Dark Gate. They are a loathsome and treacherous people led by the evil Keket."

"She's the one who took Franny and the orb?"

Remiel nodded.

"Why does she burn people for her light?"

"Because all is dark to them. They do not have the vision of life."

"Is that what you call it? Seeing the elements around us?"

"Yes."

Michelle studied the moving energy patterns on a tree trunk, then asked, "Where does this light come from?"

Remiel tried to hide his surprise. *She truly does not remember. How can this be?* "The light—our life energy—has always existed, but the creators organized it. Just as a mother and father create their child's body from the organic elements, the Holy and Great Ones formed our souls—our sacred essence—from the eternal elements. The light you see around us has always existed. You, in one form or another, have always been."

Michelle's gaze faded into the distance as she considered Remiel's words. "If time does not pass here, does that mean no one grows old and dies?"

"Mortals do not age in this world, but death is still present. They can suffer pain, and their life energy can leave them."

Michelle remembered the slain guards from her rescue. "Will the dark dwellers come looking for me?"

Remiel nodded. "They may. You will know the followers of Ra by the all-seeing-eye tattooed on their foreheads."

Michelle gulped. "Who is Hathor?"

"A dark priestess in the otherworld, the last of the noble custodians of the abyss. In Earth's ancient times, she banished many here."

"Why are you here?"

Remiel looked down in shame. "I was banished as well."

"By Hathor?"

"No."

Michelle waited for him to say more, then asked, "You're a watcher, aren't you?"

Remiel somberly nodded.

"Do you know my husband, Elijah?"

"Of course," Remiel said, not making eye contact.

Michelle studied Remiel, uncertain of his uneasiness. Her eyes moved to his sword. It had a long pewter hilt with a fleur-de-lis at its pommel end and two smaller fleurs at its guard's ends. Black leather wrapped its long sheath and grip. "You carry a sword."

"Yes." Remiel pulled the sword from its sheath. It shimmered in the light, and the engraved characters along its blade glowed. "It is called E'atura. It was forged by Michael."

"The archangel?"

Remiel nodded. "The very one."

"What does it say?" Michelle asked, pointing to the glowing script.

"May truth light the way. It is written in the ancient tongue."

Michelle watched as he sheathed the long blade. Its pewter hilt reminded her of the blazerod, a very different type of weapon. "My husband often spoke of the Grand Precept, the watcher's code."

"Yes," Remiel nodded.

"He once told me it was forbidden to save or take a mortal life."

Remiel glanced at Michelle. "You fear you are in league with a rogue?"

"No, you saved my life, and I'm truly grateful," blushed Michelle. "I was just wondering."

"You wonder why a watcher would strike so many down?"

Michelle eyed Remiel.

"My role is as a protector. At least it is now."

"Elijah spoke of his ability to discern people—almost read their minds. Can you do that? Do you know what I'm thinking or feeling?"

Remiel shook his head. "I'm afraid my senses are no longer so keen."

Michelle gulped. "Forgive me. I ask too many questions."

"You are the Queen of Light. You should be privy to all here."

Michelle sighed. "I don't know who I am."

They continued down the shimmering path, those passing bowing with hands together.

Remembering Eli had told her some watchers were punished for violating the law and taking mortal women as wives, Michelle gulped and asked, "Did...do you have a wife?"

Remiel's eyes flashed to Michelle, and he shook his head. "No, not a wife."

She saw his reluctance, but pushed further. "Do you have offspring?"

Remiel looked down and nodded.

He's fathered a halfborn. Maybe more than one. Michelle thought it strange that some watchers were punished for mating with mortals and siring the repugnant, crossbred halfborns, while her son Franny—a child of a watcher and a mortal—was revered as a prince. Michelle sighed. There were many things she didn't understand. She looked up at the dark clouds illuminated by the grand pyramid. "Why is it always so dark here? Will the sun never rise?"

"This is a fallen world. Its cycle is complete, and it is locked in time."

"That's why time doesn't pass here?"

"Yes."

They walked for a while, then Michelle asked, "What happened to Mawufe's eyes?"

"Mawufe was a holy leader in the otherworld, but Ra, the Nubian king, was jealous of him and had his eyes burned out before sending him here."

"How are there so many here in this dark place?" Michelle asked as a man and woman bowed and passed.

"The forsaken and impure have been banished here from the time of your world's creation," explained Remiel.

"But these people, the Luminaries, don't seem evil. On the contrary, they seem kind and devout," Michelle said, smiling and nodding to another passing.

"They are here for many reasons. Some were unjustly sent here by Ra and Hathor. Some stumbled here accidentally through natural doorways in the otherworld. Others were deserving of their banishment but are now penitent."

"They seem industrious and happy."

"Mawufe has taught them the skills and religion of his people. The city, the temple, all were built under his direction," explained Remiel.

"If not for the surrounding night, it seems like a lovely place to live."

"Do not forget that life in the abyss, though perpetual, is unfulfilled. Our progression is stopped, frozen in a dark world of endless stagnation. To the infinite soul, there can be no worse punishment."

Michelle's gaze drifted in thought. "Gak said the people here will one day be set free."

"Yes, that is the promise." Remiel's gaze turned to Michelle. "That is why *you* have returned."

Michelle sighed, unsettled by his words.

They continued walking, and more people passed, nodding and bowing to Michelle.

"How is it they all know me?"

"Many of them remember you, but all can see you," replied Remiel.

"See me?"

"Your light shines brighter than all. It is your divine lineage. You are the Bringer of Light."

Michelle looked down. She thought herself anything but divine or queenly. She stopped and turned when she felt the weighty footsteps of a giant approaching. The giant had patches of frizzy hair, bent and missing teeth, and a face disfigured by warts. He also placed his enormous hands together and bowed. Michelle gulped. While intimidated by the behemoth's size and grotesqueness, she sensed his adoration and smiled. She waited until the giant was a short distance away, then asked, "Are the giants also halfborns?"

"Yes, but they were bred from a different race of early humans and multiplied on their own."

"Oh," said Michelle, not understanding. "Og seems quite gentle. Are all giants so kind?"

"No. The Nephilim are a bad-tempered and vengeful lot," replied Remiel.

"Oh, I hope I never meet them."

Remiel glanced at Michelle knowingly.

Michelle's eyes widened when they entered the temple grounds. They followed a cobbled walk to the grand entrance at the center of the enormous pyramid's base. Stretching four hundred feet to either side, the smooth granite stones sloped to its glowing peak high above. The temple's immensity amazed Michelle. "It looks just like the pictures I've seen of the pyramids in Egypt—only grander!" Her jaw hung as she looked up at the glowing, rising light.

"That's because Mawufe's people built those pyramids," explained Remiel. "When they were finished, Ra sent them here. He couldn't stand the thought of them building another monument more magnificent than his."

Michelle shook her head in wonder, not noticing those around her bowing and kneeling. "The Luminaries built this?"

"Yes. They are expert artisans."

"Yes, they are," breathed Michelle. When she noticed the kneeling crowd, she gasped. "Please, stand. You don't need to kneel for me."

"They wish to venerate you," explained Remiel.

"Let them venerate the Gods of our creation, instead. I am not deserving."

As they continued into the heart of the temple, Michelle's being glowed even brighter, as if charged by the temple's upward-flowing light. A wide-eyed Remiel trailed behind her, marveling at her radiance.

As Michelle approached the temple's core, a dozen worshipers bowed and moved aside, revealing a granite altar topped by a purple mantle cloth. At its center rested a smooth, dazzling quartz stone the size of a large man's fist. Radiating from the transparent stone, the powerful white beam climbed a five-hundred-foot shaft to the pyramid's open tip, spreading its light across the low dark clouds.

"All of this light from this little stone?" asked an amazed Michelle.

"Yes," nodded Remiel. "It is the urim. The truth stone."

"How did Mawufe come upon it? I've seen no such stones anywhere else in this dark place."

Remiel's brow furrowed. "It was gifted to Mawufe to bless his efforts here."

"Gifted?" asked Michelle, her eyes gleaming in the stone's light.

"From the Holy and Great Ones. It was you who delivered it."

A stunned Michelle turned to Remiel. "I delivered it? You must be mistaken."

Remiel locked eyes with Michelle and slowly shook his head. "There is no mistake."

Michelle turned back to the brilliant stone. "I don't understand." She studied the urim for a time, then said, "If God is pleased with Mawufe and his people, why doesn't he grant them freedom? Why hold them here in this dreadful place?"

"That is why *you* are here."

Michelle gulped. She reached her hand to the brilliant stone, unable to get enough of its light. "How is it the people of Ra have not taken the stone? It must be a constant battle to keep it safe from them."

"They find no value in the stone," replied Remiel.

"But its light would brighten their dark and terrible world!"

Remiel shook his head. "It would not, for they see no light in it. To them, it would simply be another river stone to trip or stub a toe."

"How can that be?" breathed Michelle, absorbed in the flowing energy. She sensed a warming peace radiating from the light, as if standing before a fire. She reached a tentative hand to the light and felt the surging vibration of its rising particles, like a gushing fountain.

When Michelle touched the stream of light, it grew brighter still. Those watching gasped and softly chanted, "Theia, Theia..."

Michelle's eyes closed when her hand entered the stream, and her back arched as the light swallowed her.

CHAPTER 13
HIDDEN GEMS

Cleto Nazario lifted his coat collar and adjusted his scarf before hefting his bags and following Eli off the train. As they moved down the platform, low gray clouds tumbled overhead, pushed along by a biting sea breeze. Once out of the station, Nazario looked down the road. Beyond the small fishing town, he saw the white-capped blue of the English Channel. He turned to the west. Past the red-bricked building's slate roofs lay rolling hills and lush farmland. Nazario eyed the contemplative Eli and asked, "Why again are we here?"

"I have business," replied Eli, waving down a horse and buggy.

"You said that, but what kind of business?" asked Nazario, hoping for a better answer.

"Personal business."

"Oh," frowned Nazario. "Is this about the German Dina spoke of?"

Eli turned to the persistent reporter. "I want you to watch our things. I won't be long."

"I can't come with you?"

"Not for this," said Eli as he climbed into the buggy. He turned to the driver and said, "Roughton Heath, please."

With a sigh, Nazario sank onto a bench under the station awning and pulled out his notebook.

Fifty feet away, standing in the midst of passing travelers, the baggy-eyed Guerre watched.

Eli considered what Dina had told him as the buggy climbed the gentle hill out of town. The past two days had been full of such contemplation. While Eli wanted to stop Lu and the looming world calamities, his draw to his wife and son was too great. He would rescue them first and then, perhaps, return to his labors. Eli viewed this visit as a test of his abilities.

After twenty minutes on the lonely road, passing lush meadows and gray woodlands, Eli leaned toward the driver and said, "Stop here."

"But there's nothing here, sir," said the driver. "Roughton Heath is two miles over that hill."

"Stop here," repeated Eli. He stepped out of the carriage and glanced down the road before handing the driver coins. "Go on to Roughton. Stay there for one hour, then come back and find me along this road."

With a snap of the reins, the driver urged his horse on.

Eli waited for the buggy to roll over the hill, then glanced back down the empty road. Confident he was alone, the watcher started across the meadow, its long grass bent in the sea breeze. When he reached the thicket, he found a narrow trail and ducked his head to pass through.

Eli had just disappeared into the dense woodland when another cart appeared on the horizon. In it, Guerre scanned the landscape with dark, unforgiving eyes.

Eli was emerging on the other side of the thicket when he felt the cold barrel of a shotgun against his cheek.

"Stop right there! What do you want?" barked an Englishman in a rain slicker and boots.

"I'm here to see the professor." Eli's calm gaze moved across the two-acre clearing to a simple log cabin with a thatched roof. Hidden from view, the cabin's only access was a muddy road through the trees.

"He don't want no visitors."

Eli was about to reply when a small, mustached man in a sweater, coat, and rubber boots appeared near the cabin. Another man with a shotgun followed twenty feet behind. "Tell him it is Elijah," said the watcher as the small man paced, his wild gray hair lifting in the breeze, his head raising and lowering in thought.

"Elijah who?" huffed the guard.

"He will know."

"I think you best leave or lose your head," growled the beak-nosed guard as he pulled back his shotgun's hammer.

In one motion, Eli snatched the shotgun from the middle-aged guard, opened its chamber, and emptied its shells onto the grass before tossing the weapon aside.

"Blimey!" gasped the Englishman, staggering backward.

The commotion was enough to disrupt the pacing scientist's concentration, and he paused to see what was happening as the second guard moved closer. The diminutive professor studied the large Eli, then called out in German, "Elijah? Is that you?"

Eli glanced at the stunned Englishman, then answered, "Yes."

Albert Einstein waved Eli closer as he started down the road toward him, splashing in and out of puddles without a care.

Eli reached out his hand as the small scientist approached. "It is nice to see you again, professor."

"And you," nodded Einstein. "It must be fourteen years since we last spoke in Amsterdam."

"Yes," nodded Eli.

"How did you find me?"

"Dina told me."

"Of course. How is she?" asked Einstein.

"She is now somewhat reclusive."

"That is a popular thing these days," grinned Einstein. He studied the nearly two-foot-taller Eli, then said, "What you told me in Amsterdam has stayed with me. It has inspired me in more ways than one!"

Eli nodded, pleased but unsurprised by the comment.

"I have discovered many things since. Right now, I'm working on what I call the Unified Field Theory. It has been good to get away. I have no library here, of course, but I find it quite liberating to be only with my thoughts, Elsa, and my violin."

"It was good that you left Germany when you did."

"Yes, your counsel was wise. It was safe in Belgium for years, but no longer. I've been here a few months now." Einstein eyed Eli, then asked, "How did you know, so many years ago?"

Eli shrugged. "It is my work."

"It is terrifying what the Nazis are doing." Einstein gazed across the meadow. "They have killed two of my colleagues, you know."

Eli's face filled with concern. "They will kill more. Professor, you know they are looking for you. They wish to take you back to Germany or kill you. They don't want you working with the British."

Einstein sighed. "I really had no idea my head was worth all that."

"What you know—your insight and abilities—are a unique gift to humanity. But some fear what your knowledge can do."

Einstein nodded.

"You are not safe here. You must move farther away."

"To America," nodded Einstein.

"Yes."

Einstein considered Eli's words. "Do you have any more insight for me? Any more clues to the workings of this marvelous universe?"

Eli grinned.

NAZARIO SAT up when Eli stepped out of the buggy. He set his notebook aside, stood from the train station bench, and asked, "Did you accomplish what you needed?"

A gratified Eli nodded. "Yes."

"While you were gone, I think I may have discovered something," said an eager Nazario.

"And what is that?"

"Look here." Nazario opened his notebook to an elaborate drawing of a square filled with geometric patterns. There were stars within circles and circles within squares. He pointed to the central disk within it all.

"You drew this?" asked an impressed Eli.

"Yes," nodded Nazario.

"I've seen this before," frowned Eli.

"It is the Cosmati Pavement, the floor of the sanctuary before the high altar in Westminster Abbey." Nazario gulped as his finger hovered over the depiction of the earth. "I think there may be a clue here."

Eli studied the drawing, then looked up at the wide-eyed Nazario. "I must see it in person."

CHAPTER 14
THE CROSSING

LUMINAH
THE ABYSS

Michelle felt hundreds of eyes on her as she passed through the pyramid's grand entry into the gleaming temple. Her golden gown flowed as the crystal necklace across her breast beamed. With Remiel at her side, Michelle glanced back when she noticed Gak was no longer with them. She saw the wiry halfborn was still outside. "Why doesn't Gak join us?"

"He is not allowed," replied Remiel

"Because he's a halfborn?"

"Yes," said Remiel, watching for her response.

"That doesn't seem right," frowned Michelle, glancing back at Gak.

"It is their way," said Remiel as they continued into the temple.

Michelle's eyes widened when she heard angelic voices chanting a psalm. While she didn't understand their words, their song gave her goosebumps. Her gaze turned forward as she and Remiel passed rows of watching worshipers dressed in humble gowns and tunics. Ahead of them, standing in pale blue robes beside the urim altar, was the blind Mawufe. Michelle studied the dazzling white stone atop the altar, its light a brilliant pillar rising to the vaulted shaft forty feet above. She had not stopped thinking of the truth stone since first touching it and wondered what enlightenment she might receive this time.

When a welcoming Mawufe motioned to a place before the crowd, Remiel guided Michelle to it.

Michelle glanced over her shoulder and smiled at those behind her, then leaned closer to Remiel and asked, "Is this like Mass?"

Remiel's eyes narrowed. "It is the crossing ceremony."

Michelle nodded, unsure he had answered her question. She straightened when twelve white-robed women entered and stood on either side of the gleaming altar. They were of varying age and appearance but shared earnest expressions. Michelle felt their eyes on her and gulped when they bowed in unison. "I wish they would stop doing that," she whispered.

Michelle closely watched when Mawufe turned to the altar and reached for the urim. Holding the shining stone in both hands, Mawufe turned to the congregation as they kneeled. Michelle glanced back to see what was happening. When she started to lower to her knees, Remiel took her arm and whispered, "You do not kneel."

Michelle reached uneasily for Remiel when he kneeled beside her.

"Theia, you honor us with your presence," called out Mawufe, the shining stone held out before him. "Would you petition for us?"

Michelle stood breathless, uncertain of what he asked. She glanced down at Remiel, but his head was bowed. Thinking quickly, she said, "I-I would love for you to do it."

Mawufe bowed his head and raised the urim high above him. "Sovereign arbiters of light and truth, you who embrace all space and time, before whom worlds pass like the leaf wafted by the celestial winds; from the height of thy eternity, hear our vows of peace. Enlighten us with a ray of thy divine light. Warm our hearts with a spark of thy immense love. Let us be apostles of thy illumination that intelligence may cleave unto intelligence, that wisdom may receive wisdom, and that truth may embrace truth. Let thy brilliant love and light fill this dark void, that we will be found worthy at the last kneeling, that the gates will be opened, and that our light may add to thine. In the name of The Chosen One, we pray."

A wide-eyed Michelle half lowered her head as "Amen" echoed around her. When the worshipers stood, she noticed the eight-foot round opening behind the altar. It shimmered in the light of the altar stone and reminded her of the portal through which she had come.

"Theia, will you guide us through the gateway?" asked Mawufe, holding the stone before him.

Michelle's jaw hung open, uncertain of what to do or say.

"They are honored by your presence," whispered Remiel. "They normally pass through with a surrogate."

"A surrogate?" Michelle asked, her eyes meeting Remiel's.

"Yes, someone representing you."

Michelle nervously shook her head. "I don't know what to do."

"Take the stone and lead them," urged Remiel.

Michelle gulped and stepped to Mawufe. Though blind, he bowed at her nearing and presented her with the gleaming stone. Michelle drew in an unsettled breath as he lay the urim in her hands. Her eyes closed as the stone's light changed from a vertical shaft to a radiating beam that filled the temple. In a flash, Michelle viewed the immensity of space with galaxies passing by her. She experienced the boundlessness of time folding upon itself. And she felt the indescribable connection of all creation. For an instant, Michelle was with Elijah in their bedchamber, touching the orb for the first time. She felt immense joy and terrible sadness. She reached for Eli, but he disappeared.

Michelle's eyes opened when she heard the chanting choir. She gasped at the stone's brilliant light shining on the temple's round granite portal. Gulping, Michelle started for it. She passed Mawufe and the altar. She passed the twelve in robes. Michelle breathed in when she stepped through the round doorway, half expecting to be in another world on the other side.

Upon passing through the portal, Michelle found herself in another part of the temple. Instead of granite, its vaulting walls were made of dazzling white marble. She stared in awe as Mawufe, the twelve robed women, and the other worshipers followed her through the gateway, their raised palms together. Michelle's awestruck gaze returned to the brilliant stone, and her jaw slackened with what she beheld.

CHAPTER 15
COSMATI

It was well after midnight when Eli climbed over the monastery wall. He paused on the other side as a huffing Nazario pulled himself over and dropped to the ground with a thud. "Are you all right?" asked Eli, helping the reporter to his feet.

Nazario gave a painful nod as he brushed off his coat and trousers.

The half-moon was visible through the shifting clouds as Eli looked up at the nine-hundred-year-old monastery's lofty bell towers.

"What happens if they catch us? Will you use your power to make them forget?"

Eli glanced at the nervous reporter but said nothing.

Their boots crunched on the wet gravel as they crept through the seminary yard. A barking dog in the distance made Eli pause and Nazario gulp. With his blue eyes sifting through the shadows, Eli led on. Once they reached the darkened cloister, they followed the covered walkway to a door. The wide-eyed Nazario looked back to be sure they were alone as Eli checked the latch, but the door was locked. Eli moved to a window that was also secured.

"They seem not very trusting for being men of God," whispered Nazario.

When Eli found a window ajar, he pushed it up and climbed through. Inside the darkened office, Eli helped the clumsy Nazario through the window. They then moved past a cluttered desk to a door. The door creaked as it opened to a dim corridor. Nazario's eyes nervously searched the shadows as he crept behind Eli. At the end of the passageway, they descended stairs to a darkened undercroft. The reporter's eyes were round as they entered the empty crypt, where moonlight through a single window illuminated massive arches. They crept through the undercroft and climbed shadowed steps to find another door. But when Eli turned its latch, it was locked.

"We are very close," whispered Nazario. "The south transept should be just beyond this door."

Eli's face filled with determination, and his large hand tightened on the doorknob. But when he twisted the handle, it snapped off in his hand. After eyeing the broken knob in frustration, Eli put it in his coat pocket. He then pushed on the door, but it remained locked.

Nazario gulped. "Now what?" He pulled out his lighter and, with a flick, illuminated the locked wooden door with its tiny flame.

Eli was considering forcing the door further when there was a sound from within. He pulled back when the door opened to a hooded man in a robe with a rope belt around his waist. The round-eyed monk was about to cry out when Eli raised his hand to the monk's forehead and said, "Calm. You will sleep."

The man's eyes closed, and his body fell limp. Nazario stepped back as Eli caught the collapsing monk and gently laid him on the floor. "Quite handy, that is," nodded the reporter.

Eli pushed open the door and stepped into the south transept, bathed in moonlight through the arched windows high above.

Nazario let out a little gasp when he came face to face with a statue of William Shakespeare. The reporter gulped down his uneasiness and crept into the old church behind Eli, the shadows from the busts and towering pillars playing tricks on his eyes.

They quietly stepped across the stone floor to where the north and south transepts met the nave, forming a cross, the vaulted ceiling a hundred feet above them. Nazario was looking up at the enormous rose window gleaming in the moonlight when he bumped into a row of chairs. They made a barking sound as they slid across the checkerboard marble floor. "Sorry," he breathed, seeing Eli's warning glance.

When they reached the central crossing, Nazario stopped to listen for sounds of danger as Eli moved to the holiest part of the medieval abbey, the sanctuary. Not wanting to be left behind, the reporter hurried to join him, but stumbled on the steps to the raised stone floor. "Sorry," he grimaced as Eli glared down at him. Nazario's eyes widened when he realized he was lying on the edge of the twenty-five-foot square sanctuary floor. "Here it is," he breathed, his eyes wide with reverent awe, "The Cosmati Pavement!"

Eli studied the intricate mosaic of inlaid stones, faintly glistening in the moonlight.

Nazario crawled across the floor to the four-foot-wide central roundel. Eli moved closer as Nazario pulled out his lighter and flicked its flame. "Here is the inscription!" Nazario excitedly whispered.

After spotting a line of unlit candles on a side table to their left, the reporter retrieved one, lit its wick, then set it on the floor beside the worn Latin inscription. The candlelight shimmered off the gilded façade of the high altar twenty feet ahead of them. The brass chandeliers hanging above the sanctuary likewise glistened as Nazario illuminated the floor's center-piece. He ran his fingers around the red and green glass shaped like diamonds that encircled the depiction of the earth. Within the diamonds was a layer of beige marble. Within that was a ring of blue, red, and turquoise stars. A two-foot-wide colorful marble disc lay at its center. "Isn't it beautiful? It is said that these colors represent the four elements: fire, air, water, and earth."

Eli studied the ancient inlays.

"See this." Nazario's dark eyes gleamed in the candlelight as he pointed at the worn Latin inscription encircling the roundel. "It predicts the end of the world. I never tire of seeing it!" After fumbling for his glasses, he read, "*In the year of Christ one thousand two hundred and twelve plus sixty minus four, the third King Henry, the city, Odoricus, and the abbot put these porphyry stones together.*" He looked up at Eli, who was studying the inscrip-tion, and said, "That's a little tricky, but it comes out to the year 1272, the date of Henry the Third's death, and sixty minus four equals fifty-six, the length of his reign. This is the best part: *If the reader wisely considers all that is laid down,*" Nazario motioned to the floor, "*he will find here the end of the primum mobile*—the end of the world!" He glanced up at Eli and continued. "Here's the calculation. *A hedge lives for three years; add dogs and horses and men, stags and ravens, eagles, enormous whales, the world: each one following triples the years of the one before. The spherical globe here shows the archetypal macrocosm.*"

Eli's brow furrowed as he considered the riddle. "Each lifetime is compounded by three."

"That's right! The final date is calculated by a chronology based on the life spans of God's creatures and man!"

"A hedgehog lives for three years, a dog nine, a horse twenty-seven, a man eighty-one... That's nearly twenty thousand years," said Eli.

"It calculates to nineteen thousand, six hundred and eighty-three years, to be exact," said Nazario. He saw Eli's skeptical gaze and added, "The macrocosm it speaks of is the world in which we live. The microcosm is man."

Eli's eyes shifted to Nazario. "That is your interpretation."

Nazario sat back on his knees. "You have another?"

Eli kneeled and felt the cold marble earth. "In that day, many believed this world to be the center of the cosmos, that the sun and the stars rotated around it. Those who taught otherwise were burned at the stake."

Nazario's contemplative gaze returned to the inscription.

"The macrocosm is just that, the limitless cosmos, the universe. The microcosm refers to the elements from which all is made."

"Of course," breathed Nazario. His gaze moved across the shimmering mosaic. "What then of the calculations?"

Eli shook his head. "Twenty thousand years calculated from when? This world is millions of years old. I've been here for the last hundred thousand of those years."

Nazario sank to the floor and stared at the pensive Eli in dismay.

Eli's gaze returned to the inscription. "The last part is the key. *The spherical globe here shows the archetypal macrocosm.*"

"How is that the key?"

"The inscription is not referring to the marble circle it surrounds, but a spherical globe that can show the universe."

Nazario's face lit up. "A domain sphere!"

Eli nodded. He scanned the golden walls of the high altar, then looked up at the vaulted ceiling and the high gothic windows glowing in the moonlight. He was about to return to the floor inscription when candle-light flickering off the chandelier caught his eye. Eli's brow tightened, and he stood.

"What is it? Did you find something?" asked a searching Nazario.

Eli studied the golden chandelier suspended above the central roundel. His eyes widened when he noticed the gold ball hanging from its base. "There it is."

Nazario gasped upon spotting the sphere. "You did it! You found an orb!" Realizing his exuberance might get them caught, he clasped a silencing hand over his mouth.

Eli stretched his fingers to the chandelier, but the orb was four feet beyond his reach. His eyes turned to the candle table to the side of the sanc-tuary. He moved to one end and Nazario to the other. It took no effort for Eli to lift his side of the bulky table, but the reporter strained as he slid his end across the floor, toppling its unlit candles and nearly knocking over the lit candle on the floor. Once under the chandelier and orb, Eli climbed atop the table.

In the shadowed undercroft where Nazario and Eli had entered the abbey, a figure in a trench coat walked. When the baggy-eyed Guerre reached the monk Eli had put to sleep, he pulled Lu's blazerod from his coat and shot a bolt through the stirring monk's chest with a vicious snarl. The jolting blast caused the monk to go limp and left a smoldering hole in his robe. With a satisfied grin, the halfborn pushed open the door and crept into the shadowy transept.

Atop the candle table, Eli reached for the orb. Its ancient symbols glowed at his touch, but only faintly. With a twist and a pull, the orb was in his hand.

"That is incredible!" whispered Nazario, holding the candle as Eli climbed down from the table with the sphere in hand. "How long has it been there?"

"From the inscription, nearly seven hundred years," replied Eli, surveying the ball's dulled and dusty surface.

"Who put it there?" asked Nazario.

"I have my ideas."

Nazario reached a hand to the orb but dared not touch it.

"Its power runs low," said Eli, not hiding his concern.

"Will it still work?"

Eli glanced at Nazario. "Step back."

The reporter backed away.

Eli took a deep breath, held the orb before him, and closed his eyes.

Nazario gasped when a swirling orange light appeared before the high altar. "What's it doing?"

"Quiet," muttered Eli, using all of his concentration. The light of the swirling doorway turned red before revealing a dark and misty scene. Eli's eyes opened as the swirling clouds cleared to show Michelle sitting in a dark prison. "My darling!" he cried, but she couldn't hear him. When the vision faded, Eli refocused his energy. He saw Michelle walking in the darkness with two others. *Is that Gik and...Remiel?* Eli strained to view more. *What is Remiel doing with her?* "Michelle! Come to me! It's Eli!" he called out.

In the image, Michelle turned to Eli but seemed unable to see him.

Eli glared at the orb. "It's not strong enough."

Nazario's mouth opened when the scene changed to maidens bathing Michelle. He looked away when she stood from the bath.

When the watcher saw his wife gazing into Remiel's eyes, Eli's brow tightened, as did his hold on the orb. "Michelle!" She didn't hear him but smiled at Remiel instead. Eli slammed the orb onto the candle table with an angry growl, and the swirling window vanished.

Nazario gulped and eyed the distraught Eli. "What was that? What did I see?"

Eli glared at where the doorway had been, too angry to speak. Frustrated by his jealous reaction, Eli turned to the orb resting on the dented table. He knew the device had enough power for one more attempt and told himself he would have to set his human emotions aside to reach Michelle.

Having never seen the watcher upset, Nazario considered saying nothing, but that was not in his nature. "Who-who was that with your wife?"

A seething Eli turned to rebuke Nazario. But when he spotted Guerre pointing a blazerod, Eli yelled, "Get Down!" With the orb still on the table, Eli pushed Nazario aside and dove for the floor as a blast of light shot past, striking a stone pillar beside the high altar.

Guerre's baggy eyes were wide as he leaped over the candle table, his trench coat flying like a cape, and snatched the orb. "Thank you for leading me to it," hissed the halfborn.

"You can't have that," glared Eli, rising from the floor.

"Too late," snarled Guerre as he pointed the blazerod at the cowering Nazario.

Eli pulled the broken doorknob from his pocket and hurled it at the halfborn.

Guerre ducked to avoid it and had just re-aimed the blazerod at the whimpering reporter when Eli grabbed a toppled brass candleholder and flung it, striking the halfborn in the chest. The impact knocked Guerre back and diverted the blazerod's bolt through a wise man in a nativity painting.

A grimacing Guerre turned the blazerod on the scrambling Eli. The halfborn fired but missed. He was about to shoot another blast when Eli grabbed a wooden chair from along the wall and hurled it at him. The chair knocked the scrawny halfborn off his feet and sent the blazerod spinning across the floor in one direction and the orb rolling in another. Stunned, Guerre was searching for the blazerod when he spotted the orb at the edge of the sanctuary floor. He lunged for it, but a clamoring Nazario reached it first.

"I've got it!" exclaimed the reporter, jumping to his feet.

"Give it to me!" shouted Eli from across the floor. But before he could get to Nazario, the wiry halfborn pulled a dagger from under his long coat, leaped to his feet, and charged the reporter. Nazario turned to protect the orb and cried out in pain when Guerre's dagger pierced his kidney. Looking back with round eyes, Nazario's cry turned to a gurgle when the halfborn slashed his blade across the reporter's throat.

Nazario collapsed to the mosaic floor with one hand clutching his bloody throat and the other the orb. The frenzied Guerre was prying the orb from the dying reporter's hand when Eli yanked the halfborn away and flung him across the floor into the candle table. Fifteen years of frustration exploded in rage as Eli stomped across the floor and picked the clambering halfborn up by the back of his coat. Then, with the eyes of a wild man, Eli rammed Guerre's head into a stone pillar. The bone-crushing blow caused the halfborn's eyes to cross before he fell limp. Eli roared, his blue eyes pulsing, as he raised Guerre over his head and smashed him onto the steps of the high altar.

Eli's chest was still heaving when he spotted the blazerod underneath a chair. He moved to it and snatched it off the floor. Eli turned to the whimpering Nazario lying on the stonework, his legs slowly churning like a man running in slow motion, his escaped blood filling the crevices between the medieval stones.

Eli's rage faded when he saw Nazario's life leaking away. His gaze moved to the orb still clutched in the reporter's trembling hand. He knew it had enough power for one more task. Eli had hoped that task would rescue his wife, but he could not let Nazario die.

Eli lowered to his knees, took the orb in one hand, and placed his other over Nazario's sliced-open throat. The reporter's blood pulsed through Eli's fingers as the orb faintly glowed. Closing his eyes, Eli bowed his head and focused his energy on the dying Nazario. The reporter's frantic gaze turned to Eli before his body relaxed, not in lifelessness, but in a peaceful calm. Light soon radiated from Nazario's neck wound and then his eyes. But like a dying candle, the shimmering orb faded. Eli's brow tightened in concentration, willing the orb to finish its healing task, but it was not enough. When the orb's light went out, the watcher's head sank.

Eli set the dull orb on the floor with a mournful groan and turned to the lifeless Nazario. He thought of Sebastien and Jean-Pierre dying in his arms in a muddy hole in a French field. He remembered Ronan, run through with Gadreel's sword. He thought of the hundreds of thousands who had perished in the Great War—all because of his failings. Eli wondered how many more mortals would lose their lives because of him.

When Eli remembered their attacker, he drew in a ragged breath and reached for the blazerod. He thought exterminating a halfborn would be little consolation for all the pain. Eli tightened his grip on the weapon and turned, but Guerre was no longer crumpled on the sanctuary floor. He was gone.

"Where are you?" seethed Eli as he climbed to his feet. The flickering light from the single candle shimmered off the high altar's façade and cast long shadows across the north transept. Determined to find the halfborn and make him pay, Eli was about to search the shadows when he heard a cough behind him. Thinking it was the halfborn, Eli spun around with the blazerod pointed, but there was only Nazario sprawled on the decorated floor. Eli's eyebrows raised when the reporter's leg and then arm moved. He stepped closer and looked at the stone crevices that were before filled with the man's blood, but saw only seven-hundred-year-old grout lines.

Nazario's heavy eyes were slow to open. He looked up at the looming watcher and wheezed, "What did you do?"

Eli's anger softened, and he sighed.

The wide-eyed Nazario felt his neck. "He cut my throat, and you saved my life!"

Eli's tired gaze moved to the dull orb.

With an old man's groan, Nazario sat up. Blinking, he noticed the orb beside him. "You used the ball to save me?"

Eli nodded, fearful of what his compassion toward the Italian had cost him.

"Thank you," breathed Nazario. He searched the shadowed sanctuary for the attacker but saw only the side table, toppled chairs, and candlesticks. "Where did he go?"

Eli shook his head.

"Should we look for him?" wheezed Nazario, turning to the shadowed nave.

Eli said nothing.

Nazario held up the dull orb. "You used up its energy. How will you bring back your wife?"

Eli's head sank. "I don't know."

Nazario wobbled to his feet, stepped closer to the downcast Eli, and embraced him. "Thank you. Thank you for saving my life."

"You're welcome," said Eli, patting the reporter's back.

Nazario stepped back and studied the somber watcher. "This must mean we have a special bond now. That we're brothers." His eyes swelled. "Did the ball give me some of your powers? Am I now immortal? Can I read minds? What does it mean?"

Eli sighed. "It means you are alive in this world and not in the world of the dead."

Nazario's gaze drifted in thought. Then, turning back to Eli with earnest eyes, he said, "I pledge my life to you and your family for your kind deed."

Eli studied the reporter, unsure how to respond.

When a light appeared in the south transept, their heads turned.

"Is there someone here?" called out an old monk holding a lantern in his outstretched arm as he shuffled across the checkerboard floor. When he thought he heard a sound, the monk stopped and listened. He slowly turned, searching the shadows, but all was still and as it should be. When the old monk reached the sanctuary, he saw no misplaced table or toppled chairs. Even the candlesticks were in their proper place. He didn't notice the half-burned candle on the side table or the missing ball from the chandelier. Standing on the Cosmati Pavement, the old monk turned, his lantern held out before him. He paused, and his eyes narrowed when his light shined on the nativity painting. He cocked his head when he noticed a charred hole in the wise man's chest.

Outside the cloisters, Eli helped the still-wobbly Nazario over the wall, then quickly scaled it himself.

Confident they had escaped undetected, Nazario turned to Eli and asked, "Who was that man that attacked us? And why did he kill that poor monk?"

Eli scanned the moonlit alley for danger, then waved for the reporter to follow. "He was a halfborn. One of Lu's henchmen."

"A halfborn?"

"The offspring of a watcher and a mortal."

Nazario's eyes widened. "Like the aged daughter in Roslin! But he seemed quite normal. Are they all like that? I've always believed the offspring of watchers to be hideous giants. Nephilim, the bible calls them."

"Some are giants, some more like mortals. It depends on their genetic composition," said Eli, still searching the shadows as they walked.

"Their what?" asked the reporter, having never heard of such a thing.

Eli glanced at Nazario. "Never mind."

"What must we do now?" asked the reporter, hurrying to keep up.

"We must be on our guard. Lu's forces are on the hunt. He will stop at nothing if he believes us to be a threat."

Nazario raised a questioning finger. "And who exactly is Lu again? My head seems a bit foggy."

Eli gave an irritated glance. "Your head will clear."

"Of course. But what do we do now?"

"We go to a place to re-power the orb," said Eli, feeling it in one pocket and the blazerod in another.

"And where does one re-power such a thing?" asked Nazario, hoping his questions were not annoying the watcher.

Eli sighed. "France."

CHAPTER 16
PROPHECIES

Luminah
THE ABYSS

M ichelle was resting in her dwelling, considering all she had experienced, when a maiden parted the curtain and said, "The watcher, Remiel, visits you."

Michelle sat up. "Oh, please show him in." After standing, she smoothed her gown and moved to the doorway as the maiden pushed aside the curtain. Michelle smiled when she saw Remiel. She thought him handsome and kind. "Won't you come in?"

Remiel bowed to Michelle and followed her to a marble table. She motioned to a seat, but Remiel remained standing.

"As my guest, it is polite for me to offer you some refreshment, but I guess we don't do that here," Michelle awkwardly laughed.

Remiel smiled.

Michelle studied Remiel's features, trying not to get caught up in his deep blue eyes.

"Have you recovered from your crossing?"

"My crossing?" Michelle asked, coming out of her trance.

"You said leading the crossing ceremony was exhausting."

"Yes, it was," Michelle reminded herself of Elijah and turned away.

Remiel's face filled with concern. "Are you displeased with me?"

Michelle turned back to him. "No. Not in the least."

Remiel studied Michelle. "Did the stone show you something?"

Michelle gulped. "Yes, but what I saw cannot possibly be." Her eyes welled with tears.

"You should not doubt yourself."

Michelle's uncertain gaze flashed to Remiel.

"You fear for your son."

"Yes," breathed Michelle. "If what the urim tells me is true, there is much we must do. But we must first save my son."

Remiel stood a little taller and resolutely nodded.

STANDING IN MAWUFE'S COURT, Michelle listened as Remiel explained his plan to rescue young Franny. On either side of the glowing throne, two golden-robed ministers looked on as the tapestries shimmered on the walls behind them. Beside Michelle stood Gak and Og.

"If you proceed with your plan, the people of Ra will surely seek retribution," warned the stern-browed minister of peace, her gray hair bound atop her head in a golden scarf.

"Will they attack Luminah?" asked a concerned Mawufe.

"Their spies are at our borders even now," added the long-bearded minister of industry.

"If they attack us, they will break the treaty and lose their honor," frowned Mawufe.

"They must first *have* honor to lose it," replied the minister of industry. "They may not battle us, but they rob us of our people, one by one, to light their dark governess's chamber. Many of the out-dwellers live in fear they will be taken."

The minister of peace shook her head. "Remember that we, the people of light, have taken an oath of peace to prove our worthiness in the final judgment. We would sooner be the dark dwellers' torches than violate that oath!"

Mawufe thoughtfully nodded.

"You're losing sight of the point," frowned Remiel. "They have the prince, the Harbinger! He who is to usher in the return of the Chosen One! If the prince does not fulfill his calling, your salvation will be lost, and the penitent will forever be trapped with the wicked in this dark world!"

All were quiet as they considered Remiel's words.

"Perhaps the prince can usher in the return of the Chosen One now," said the long-bearded minister. "Theia could then open the dark gates and free us!"

Remiel glanced at an uneasy Michelle. "That time is not yet."

"We must yet be tested," sighed Mawufe.

"The plan will work," assured Remiel. "We are not your people and have not sworn the oath. Those who wish to fight with us may. It is the only way to save the prince. It is the only way to save us all."

"What then?" asked Mawufe. "What happens when you return with the prince? War will surely ensue. Will Theia then petition for my people, or must they suffer more?"

Remiel turned to Michelle as she stepped forward. "Keket's armies won't come here."

"Because you will not allow it?" asked a hopeful Mawufe.

"No. Because once I have my son back, we will go elsewhere."

Mawufe leaned forward. "Please forgive me! I did not mean to offend you! It would honor us to have the Bringer of Light dwell in Luminah."

Michelle glanced at Remiel. "Thank you, but I must leave this place once we rescue my son."

"You will leave us again? We have long awaited your return. Where will you go?" asked Mawufe, trying to hide his disappointment.

"To the mountain of Goash. To find the gatekeeper and return to my world," replied Michelle.

Mawufe sank back on his throne. "What of the prophecy?"

Michelle gulped. "I-I don't know how, but when I find the way back to my world, I will do all in my power to bring you with me."

"We have all trust in you," bowed Mawufe. After the four exited his court, he sighed and muttered, "But that is not the prophecy."

MANU

BUILT upon the ruins of the old world, salvaged scrap metal and reclaimed rubble littered the city of Ra, also called Manu. As such, the dark dweller's teetering and crumbling structures were in constant disrepair.

Unlike the industrious Luminaries, the people of Ra were a lazy and incurious people that existed in a state of perpetual want. Neither satisfied nor moved to improve their situation, the dark dwellers apathetically made do and often went out of their way to avoid work.

Because of their lack of know-how and ambition, the people of Ra lived primarily in the ancient's more sound underground remains. And yet, despite occupying parts of the underground city for eons, much of its below-ground labyrinth remained uninhabited and unexplored by the lazy dark dwellers. With no need to gather food stores and no value on commodities, the flame was their only treasure.

While half the population were flame-diggers and spent their time scrounging for flammables or mining wax, all were on constant watch for torch fodder. But as valuable as the flame was, once fuel was found to light their torches, the dark dwellers were content to do nothing until more was needed.

At the center of Manu stood the domed citadel. One of the few above-ground structures to survive the ancient apocalypse, it served as the seat of power for Ra's representative in the dark realm. Inside, Franny sat before the fat Keket with a leash around his neck, his one-piece pajamas shabby and soot-covered, his curious blue eyes flickering in the dim torchlight. Still not used to the stench of the human candle in the center of the chamber, Franny tried not to look at it. Instead, he watched a bony man on scaffolding attentively painting glyphs high on the chamber wall.

Shadowed figures, some dozing, others quietly conversing, sat around the large circular throne room. In its center, chained to the post atop the stone altar, was a glazed woman's body burned down to its navel. Twenty feet above was a domed, soot-covered ceiling with small chimney vents for the foul smoke to escape. Across from the arched entry, seated on her throne, the heavily tattooed Keket stared as the flickering torchlight danced across her shaved scalp. Her dingy red robe hung open to her tattooed and flabby flesh, and a bone necklace dangled below her folded chin.

"Come to Mama," commanded Keket, her plump hand patting her lap as her ebony fingernails reached for Franny's curly hair. When a black cat slinked toward her, she shooed it away with a scowl. "Not you!"

The two-year-old's wary gaze turned to the beckoning ruler, and he shook his head.

"Not this again," fumed Keket. She took hold of the frayed cord wrapped around Franny's neck and pulled him closer.

"You're not my mother," said Franny, resisting her.

"We've had this talk before," snapped Keket. "I am your mother now. The other one left you here. She didn't want you. Why would you want her?"

Franny curled up in a ball and tucked his head to his knees.

Gritting her teeth, Keket reached her clawed hand to Franny's curly blonde hair. She was about to yank him to his feet when her spymaster burst into the chamber.

"Governess!"

"Yes, what is it?" barked Keket, letting go of Franny.

The spymaster, who wore a black tunic and his hair braided to the side, blocked the flickering torchlight with his hand to see his governess. "Our spies have returned from Luminah."

"And? Are they preparing for war?" asked Keket, her eyes wide with the thought of spilling more of the self-righteous Luminaries' blood.

"No, my governess."

"Then they are preparing to defend themselves from our attack."

"No, my governess."

"Then what are they doing? They took the otherworlder from me!" Keket glanced at the watching Franny. "They violated the peace and must suffer!"

"They are doing what they always do, my governess: build and worship."

Keket shook her head, disgusted by the Luminaries' proclivity to achieve.

The spymaster gulped. "But there is more, my governess. *She* has returned."

Keket's eyes narrowed. "Who has returned?"

"Theia, the Bringer of Light! And she is coming for her son!" exclaimed the spymaster, pointing to Franny.

Those lazily lining the chamber wall sat up, and the glypher atop the scaffold stopped and looked down at the child in wonder.

"Theia?" Keket eyed the curious Franny. "That's not possible. His mother was just an otherworlder!"

"She is more than that, and she is coming to judge us!" cried the spymaster.

"Don't be a fool!" growled Keket. "She has no power over us!" Climbing awkwardly to her feet, the fat ruler turned to her master of war. "Prepare the army! Fortify our defenses! And bring me the otherworlder alive! She will be my *next* candle! I'll teach all of you who you should fear!"

CHAPTER 17
CAMELOT

Nazario's jaw slackened as he followed Eli through the mist into the long, narrow field. While he guessed the dewy meadow to be a hundred yards across, bordered by pines and orange-leafed elms to the north, he couldn't see its end to the east or the west. Fifteen yards into the field, they passed the first row of giant boulders standing on end. The gray, lichen-covered megaliths varied in shape and stood five to ten feet tall. Spaced at regular intervals, the mystical boulders formed long, straight rows that stretched far into the misty morning. Nazario counted twelve rows spaced twelve yards apart. "I've heard of this place," he said, looking up and down the rows in wonder. "Legend has it that Merlin turned a legion of Roman soldiers into stone here."

"Legend has Merlin doing many things," replied Eli. His gaze turned to sheep grazing amidst the rows of stone, and he longed for Château de Bret. He thought of his wife and son and ached to be home with them. Eli thought of how close he had come to reaching Michelle with the orb in the abbey. He wished the domain sphere would have had enough power to bring her home. Eli's face dimmed when he remembered seeing Remiel with his wife. He felt pangs of hurt and jealousy and wondered how mortals could endure such emotional turmoil.

"What is it we're looking for?" asked Nazario as he walked with Eli through the shin-high grass.

"The nodal root."

Nazario's mustache twitched, "And just what is that?"

"You will see."

The reporter sighed, frustrated by the watcher's cryptic responses. He watched as Eli stopped to pet one of the curious sheep and asked, "Who placed these stones here?"

"The ancients."

"I think I could have come up with that," muttered Nazario as they resumed their walk along the row of standing stones.

"Is this one of your questions?" asked a distracted Eli.

"No," said Nazario without hesitation.

"Very well."

Nazario studied the megaliths as they passed, hoping to see inscriptions or something recognizable on them, but he concluded they were only upright boulders. When the reporter passed a particularly tall stone, the hairs on the back of his neck stood. He stopped and eyed the towering rock. "I feel something here."

"What do you feel?" asked Eli, looking back from a few steps ahead.

"A tingling sensation on my skin. Like electricity." Nazario moved closer to the giant stone and raised a tentative hand to its rough, crusty face. The hairs on the reporter's hand stood as it hovered an inch away. Nazario held his breath as he touched the stone, and his hairs laid back down. "Ha! It's only a rock," he said with some relief.

"Were you expecting something more?"

Nazario glanced at Eli. "Well, yes. Maybe."

"Sometimes things are just as they seem. Sometimes they are not."

Nazario considered the thought as he followed Eli along the line of boulders. When Eli slowed and stopped, so did Nazario.

With the mist thinning in places, Eli turned to the dense line of trees bordering the field and started toward them. The reporter followed. After passing through a thicket, they came to a clearing with a large earthen mound at its center. The grassless earth surrounding the rise undulated with buried roots converging from all directions. At the face of the mound was a downward-sloping passageway. Filled with mist and lined by stones, the earthen ramp led down to a six-foot-tall rock slab with a massive stone header. A single monolith stood atop the mound.

"What is this place?" asked Nazario, eyeing what looked like a giant, half-buried birthday cake with a boulder as its candle. "Is it a burial chamber? A dolmen?"

Eli glanced at Nazario, then moved down the sloping passageway.

The reporter took a step, then paused, uncertain he should go any closer. He watched unblinkingly as Eli placed his hand on the massive header, and gasped when the stone slab below swung open to a black void within. Nazario took a step closer, then paused when Eli stooped and entered the dark hollow.

Nazario waited for a moment, but not knowing was unbearable to him. He crept down the dirt passageway to the mound's entry and squinted to see inside the darkened cavity.

When Nazario's eyes adjusted to the light, he saw Eli kneeling in the center of a round chamber no more than twelve feet across and seven feet high. Its floor was paved in stone, and its walls were lined by the same types of boulders he had seen in the field. Free of lichen, the hollow's walls were covered in glyphs and swirling patterns. A single, massive rock slab formed the hollow's ceiling. At its center, where Eli kneeled, stood what Nazario thought to be a three-foot-tall stone font, but when his eyes better adjusted, he noticed the pedestal was made from a dull, gray metal, similar to the blazerod. Atop the pedestal was what looked like a brass bowl.

Nazario watched with wide eyes as the kneeling Eli removed the orb from his coat and raised it to the pedestal. The golden orb fit perfectly into the bowl.

When Eli looked at him, Nazario backed away from the doorway like a child caught sneaking a look on Christmas morning.

The reporter waited halfway up the slope for Eli to emerge, his round eyes shifting in thought. After a few minutes, the curious Nazario lowered his head to look into the chamber. The kneeling Eli hadn't moved, but Nazario couldn't tell what he was doing.

When Eli finally exited the hollow, Nazario stepped back and said, "I'm sorry. Should I not have seen that?"

Eli turned from the nervous reporter and sealed the chamber by touching the stone header.

Nazario gulped. "Now what do we do?"

"We wait."

Nazario watched Eli move past him to level ground. "Did you leave the ball in there?"

"Yes." Eli restlessly scanned the field.

"What about that halfborn fellow who attacked us in the abbey?"

Eli's stern gaze returned to Nazario. "What about him?"

"Are you not worried he will come and take the orb?"

"He cannot enter there."

Nazario's curious gaze turned to the sealed stone door. "What is it we are waiting for exactly?"

"A lightning storm."

Nazario's eyebrows raised as he looked up into the misty sky.

<hr>

WEWELSBURG, GERMANY
3 NOVEMBER 1933

ON A HILL amidst a forest stood the three-hundred-year-old Wewelsburg Castle. The three-sided stronghold had sixty-foot-tall, round turrets at each corner. Baroque domes topped two of the five-story towers, while the third, ringed with battlements, stood open. A black, red, and gold striped German flag waved proudly above. While the castle was once home to prince-bishops and liege lords, and had seen splendid feasts, wars, and barbaric witch trials, it had fallen into disrepair and become the property of the Prussian state. By 1925, the once-grand Wewelsburg had been reduced to a banquet hall and youth hostel. It would soon house a new occupant.

Inside the Renaissance castle, Heinrich Himmler slapped his gloves into his palm as he walked its stone floor in thought. While intrigued by the occult, and in particular the mystifying Lu Stormbrewer, Himmler was a romantic at heart. Long obsessed with Camelot and the legend of King Arthur, Himmler thought himself the reincarnation of the first German king. Now, as the leader of the Nazi security forces, the *Schutzstaffel* or SS, he had thousands of black knights at his command. He found the castle perfect for his dark purposes.

On one side of the well-dressed Himmler walked two SS officers, their black uniforms crisp, their tall leather boots echoing with each step. On the other side walked the district's property director, Franz König, his tweed hunting coat hanging, his trousers baggy, his feathered hat in his meaty hands.

"The district of Büren is honored by Chancellor Hitler's interest in Wewelsburg," smiled the stout director, trying to hide his disdain for Hitler and the Nazis.

"The Führer is most interested and would like to purchase it."

König uneasily shrugged. "It is for lease, but I'm afraid the district has no interest in selling it."

Himmler stopped and turned. "Even to the Führer?"

König stood speechless.

Himmler frowned in disapproval. "A hundred-year lease, then."

König gulped. "May I ask, for what purpose does the chancellor desire Wewelsburg?"

"It is to be used at mine and the Führer's discretion."

König fidgeted with his hat. "Wewelsburg has a proud history."

"As a youth hostel, yes," sneered Himmler.

"Forgive me. I'm only the property director. I must report to the district officials."

"And I must report to Germany's Führer!" snapped Himmler. Then, with glaring eyes, he added, "It is to be a leadership and training school for the SS!"

König gulped. He had seen the propaganda newsreels espousing the new hereditary laws. Those deemed unfit by the Nazi party, the mentally ill or handicapped, and those with physical deformities, such as epilepsy, blindness, and deafness, would be sterilized to prevent the spread of those flawed conditions. While König didn't buy into such lies, he knew many who welcomed a purer society. Some openly spoke of the "useless eaters" and those "unworthy of life" who burdened the German state. Just the other day, he overheard a woman purporting euthanasia to rid the country of the unwanted. König feared what would come next. He knew the SS would enforce whatever "laws" the Nazis passed. König had seen enough horror with Hitler's Brownshirts and could only imagine what havoc an entire SS army could wreak at the crazed Austrian's command. He wanted no part of it.

König considered telling Himmler the district had no interest in leasing to the Nazi party and such despicable individuals, but he knew that would land him and his wife in a work camp.

"The district Büren should be honored to have such an esteemed tenant as the SS," huffed Himmler.

"Of course," nodded the increasingly nervous König. "You're-you're sure Wewelsburg is to your liking? A hundred-year lease?"

"Yes, I'm sure," said Himmler, his dark eyes glaring through his glasses.

"Very well then. I will inform the district," said König as Himmler and the two SS officers continued exploring without him.

When Himmler reached the *säulenhalle*, a large circular chamber with a ring of arched inner columns within the tower wall, he stopped in the middle of the floor and looked up at the high-ceilinged chandelier in wonder. "This is magnificent," he breathed, his wide eyes scanning the ringed colonnade. Himmler turned to the SS officers and said, "Don't you think so?"

The SS officers obligingly nodded.

"I tell you, providence has guided us here!" said Himmler, turning in a slow circle. He glanced at the property director watching from the doorway, then backed away from the chamber's center. "Look here," he said, pointing to the marble floor. "Can't you see the SS seal here?"

The SS officers nodded.

With his hands on his hips, the amazed Himmler gazed around the chamber, then said, "Here is where your men will take their oaths to the Führer! Here is where they will swear their blood and honor!"

König backed further into the shadows as the SS officers nodded.

Himmler had found his Camelot.

CHAPTER 18
THE DARK RAIDERS

MANU
THE ABYSS

A bear-chested sentinel standing atop a watchtower scanned the city of Manu. Light glowed from its depths like the embers of a dying fire. He wore a pointed metal helmet, his tattooed Eye of Ra visible below its stubby brim. The guard turned on his perch and peered into the blackness beyond the city's shabby walls and teetering watchtowers. Parts of the citadel's ten-foot-tall walls no longer stood, having been scavenged for use elsewhere in the city. Uneven piles of debris and scrap filled the gaps in the wall. With no continuous walkway atop the ramparts, guards spent much of their time inside the city walls, huddled around a torch, telling embellished stories of a forgotten world and time. The watchtowers, spaced at two-hundred-foot intervals behind the walls, were built using the ancient blocks salvaged from the rubble. Stacked twenty feet high without mortar, the towers gave an unsteady platform for sentries to stand. While each watchtower had a fire cage, they were usually dark to save the precious fuel. Now, with the fear of attack, they were all aflame, but their light was not enough and left thirty-foot black voids in the spans between the towers.

The bare-chested sentinel climbed down from his tower onto the outer wall, felt the sword on his hip, and stared into the night. His eyes narrowed as he struggled to make sense of the shifting blackness beyond the wall. The watchtower's flame gave light to the first twenty feet in front of him, but the flickering ruins and jagged landscape beyond that left much to his imagination. While he knew the Luminaries outnumbered his people, he was not concerned. The sentinel had forgotten how long it had been since their last war, and he doubted anything would happen now. To him, it was all a waste of light.

The guard was about to climb down from the rampart when he heard a crunching sound from the shadows beyond the wall. He cocked his head and listened, balancing with his spear. He spotted another sentry standing behind the wall to his left, chatting with a third. Fifty feet to the sentinel's right, a fourth guard leaned against the wall.

When the crunching sound repeated, the sentinel raised his spear. He glanced to his left, and his eyes narrowed. The two sentries standing there not five seconds before were lying motionless on the ground. When the sentinel turned forward, he gasped at the towering shape emerging from the night. But before he could let out a warning cry, Og's swinging mace struck the sentinel squarely in the chest, knocking him off the rubble wall and into the watchtower fifteen feet behind.

Og pushed a section of the wall over with a mighty shove and climbed through its opening. A forked spear thrown from his left pierced the giant's thick arm. Turning to the wide-eyed guard who threw it, Og pulled out the spear and hurled it back, pinning the fleeing sentry to the ground.

When Og turned to his right, he saw the sword-bearing Remiel emerge from the shadows beside the two slain sentries. The giant moved to the watchtower, put his massive hand on its four-foot-wide base, and pushed. The rickety tower crumbled, putting out its light and casting the opened section of wall into darkness.

Gak and then Michelle warily stepped through the fallen rubble. With her gleaming crystal necklace safely in Luminah, she wore a dark cape over her golden gown and a slim woven bag across her chest.

After climbing the wall, Remiel pushed back his hood and looked across the shadowy inner city. He saw eight other watchtowers aglow, faintly outlining the city walls, and the dim flicker of hundreds of torches leaking light from underground places. Remiel's brow tightened when he saw the domed citadel standing three stories taller than anything else in the dark city, its chimney glowing from the human torch burning within.

Remiel climbed off the wall with his sword at the ready and led the others down the darkened, rubble-lined street toward the citadel.

Michelle's wary eyes searched the darkened ruins as they walked. She remembered how frightened she was upon first arriving in the abyss and marveled at how much had changed. Michelle was no longer blind in the darkness and had friends willing to die for her. She hoped Franny was safe and that she could take him from this terrible world.

"There are eyes on us," warned Gak, creeping beside Michelle with his sword at the ready.

"Prepare to draw light," warned Remiel.

Trailing behind them, Og lifted his large spiked club.

When a forked spear flew at them from the darkness, Remiel leaped forward and struck it down with his shimmering sword.

Michelle let out a frightened cry when four bare-chested sentries charged them from the shadows. She watched wide-eyed as Og stepped forward and, with a mighty swing of his mace, knocked them off their feet and flung them across the rubble into a wall. The wall teetered and then collapsed onto the stirring, groaning sentries with a thunderous *WHOMP*.

"I think they know we're here now," said Gak.

Michelle breathlessly scanned the glimmering world around them as they continued along the cleared path. Her legs trembled with each step as heads peered from behind fallen walls and underground openings. She braced for the next attack.

"There. That's the way in," pointed Gak, his face aglow with torchlight.

Remiel eyed the arched citadel entry. He saw at least six sentries huddled in the shadows, their shimmering bodies on full display with his darksight. When they were within ten feet of the entry, four sentries charged with their forked spears thrusting. Remiel and Gak dispatched two of them after a brief metal-on-metal clash. Og's mace hammered down on the middle two, crushing one and then the other.

Horrified, Michelle backed away as the sentries' light left their mangled shells. She didn't see the dark dweller creeping behind her with a dagger, but Og did, and his swinging mace met the shabby man face-first, tumbling him backward.

"Stay near me," said Remiel.

Michelle gave a jittery nod and moved closer to the watcher.

After scanning for more danger, Remiel turned to the others. "Surprise is no longer our advantage. It will be a fight in and out. Are you with me?"

Gak and Og nodded, then crept behind Remiel with Michelle between them.

When the four reached the citadel entry, Gak turned back to Og and said, "You're too big to fit."

Og stooped to look inside the passageway, then shook his head.

Remiel turned to the sunken-eyed giant. "We'll be as fast as we can."

Og nodded as the other three charged into the dark underworld.

KEKET GULPED as the sound of fighting echoed up the dim passageway. Seated on her throne, the dark governess's fat hands clutched the curious Franny as he pointed, sensing his mother's nearness. When Tasud, the master of war, burst into the chamber, Keket cried, "How many of them are there?"

"It's unclear, my governess, but it must be an army, and they have at least one giant!" exclaimed the beak-nosed Tasud, his eyes wide.

"A giant!" gasped Keket.

"Don't worry, giants can't fit down the passageway," insisted Tasud.

When the stone walls shook, Sed, the lord of the chamber, looked up. "What was that?"

"I don't know." Tasud backed away from the chamber entrance, cringing at the fighting and dying sounds in the shadowed passageway.

Keket's dark eyes moved to Franny. "They're coming for the child."

"My governess, you must leave at once!" urged Sed as dust sifted down from the ceiling.

"Where is safety if not in my chamber?" snapped Keket.

"Governess, they are coming for you!" Sed eyed the golden sphere beside Keket's throne. "Give me the orb and blazerod. As lord of the chamber, I shall protect them!"

Keket's eyes lowered to the pewter blazerod and dull golden sphere resting beside her. She pushed Franny from her fat lap, snatched up the orb, and moved to the altar on which the human torch burned. After removing a loose stone from its base, she pushed the orb into a secret compartment and replaced the stone.

"At least give me the rod! I will protect you with it!" exclaimed Sed.

"I am the master of war! It should be me!" insisted Tasud, adjusting his pointed helmet with a trembling hand.

Keket tossed the blazerod to Tasud. "Don't let them inside the chamber!"

Frustrated, Sed pointed to the iron gate hanging above the arched entry. "We must lower the gate!"

"On my command!" barked Keket as the flickering torchlight danced across her tattooed face and shaved head. She stared unblinkingly down the dim passage as the sounds of fighting and dying grew closer. "Where is my army?"

"They are fighting, governess!" Tasud replied, fumbling with the blazerod.

"The Luminaries will pay for this!" fumed Keket, sitting defiantly on her throne.

"We don't know it is them attacking!" exclaimed Sed.

"Who else could it be?" roared Keket. "There must be hundreds of them! Where is my spymaster?"

"We don't know, governess," said Tasud, making jabbing motions with the blazerod to fire it.

The closely watching Franny got to his feet as the sounds of fighting lessened and then stopped.

Tasud, who had given up on firing the blazerod, anxiously peeked down the shadowy passageway from the chamber's arched entry. "Did we stop them? Is it over?"

All eyes were on the empty corridor, the light from another torch around a bend faintly illuminating its stone walls. When the distant torch went out, casting the passageway into darkness, Sed stepped back. He jumped, and Keket screamed when the spy master's head flew out of the shadows into the chamber and bounced across the floor, his braided hair flipping until it came to a stop near the altar.

"Close the gate!" bellowed Keket, clutching her heart.

Sed released the latch, and the heavy gate slammed to the floor, shaking the walls.

"They cannot reach us now, my governess," assured Tasud, grimacing at the spymaster's severed head.

With the chamber's torchlight extending only ten feet beyond the gate, all eyes were on the shadowed passageway.

"What do we do when our flame goes out?" asked Tasud, eyeing the burned-down corpse. "It is unlawful for the governess to be darkened."

Sed glared at the master of flame, cowering on the other side of the chamber. "There are other things to burn."

"Mommy?" Franny called out, more curious than afraid.

Keket turned to the watching boy, his little hand pointing down the passageway. "Your mommy will be our next candle," she snarled, but Franny ignored her.

Sed jumped back, and Keket gasped when the battle-worn Remiel stepped into the light on the other side of the gate, his broad chest heaving, his shimmering sword raised.

"What do you want, watcher?" hissed Keket.

"Release the child, and you will be spared!"

"Why would we do that?" asked an emboldened Keket. "What business of yours is the child? And how is it that the mighty Remiel is doing the bidding of the Luminaries? I thought you could fall no lower."

Remiel's hardened gaze moved to Tasud, still fumbling with the blaze-rod, then to the curious Franny clutched in the dark governess's lap. "I give you one more chance. Let the child go, and you will be spared."

"We are safe inside here!" exclaimed Tasud from two feet behind the gate's rusty bars. "You will never get through!"

When Remiel ran his sword across the bars, Tasud and Sed took another step back.

"Bring me this *Theia*," seethed Keket. "I want to see her."

"Will you release the child?" glared Remiel.

"Perhaps his puny corpse will fit through the bars. Or if you insist on waiting, you can watch him light my chamber," snarled Keket.

The master of flame nervously laughed while Sed and Tasud braced for Remiel's response.

"No! Don't hurt my son!" gasped Michelle, emerging from the shadows.

"Mommy!" cried Franny, fighting to escape Keket's grasp.

"It's okay, darling! Are you all right?" asked Michelle, tears spilling down her cheeks.

Franny nodded and looked up at the dark governess.

"Ha! This frail woman is nothing more than a lost otherworlder! She has no great power!" huffed Keket. "How is it you champion her?"

"Your eyes are so dim you cannot discern her true identity!" glared Remiel. "You truly are a fallen and loathsome people deserving of this black abyss!"

"And you believe she is the Bringer of Light returned to redeem you? You have listened too long to that pious lunatic, Mawufe!" sneered Keket.

"Please, I just want my son back, then we will leave you alone," pleaded Michelle.

"How would you like him?" hissed Keket, holding up a long, curved blade. "In slices or cubes? Or maybe you would care to enjoy his light? I wager only a day or two before you can have his charred bones and ashes."

"Nooo," sobbed Michelle, moving toward the gate, but Remiel held her back.

Sed and Tasud backed farther into the chamber when Gak emerged holding a forked spear.

"You have even stooped so low to keep company with a halfborn," sneered Keket. "Or is it family?"

Gak's eyes narrowed, and he raised the trident as if to throw.

Tasud gulped. "Maybe you should release the boy, governess."

"And you are my master of war," scoffed Keket, seeing his fear. "They will not enter."

"Please, my son," pleaded Michelle.

Keket raised her blade to Franny's throat. "Leave now or watch the boy bleed."

Sobbing, Michelle backed into the shadows. Remiel lowered his sword, and he and Gak withdrew.

"Mommy!" cried Franny, unsure why she would leave him.

"You see?" laughed Keket, lowering the blade from Franny's throat. "That is how you deal with such rabble." The gloating Keket was nodding to her relieved ministers when Gak's spear shot between the bars and into her shoulder, pinning her fat arm to the throne. Keket cried out in pain and reached for the impaling spear as Franny jumped from her lap and ran for the gate. But before he was halfway there, she grabbed his leash and yanked Franny back onto the floor. "You will watch him die for this!"

When the wall behind Tasud shook, he spun to see the dust settling. "What was that?"

Sed pointed at the crack in the stone wall and backed under the glypher's scaffolding.

"Help me, you fools!" wailed Keket as she pulled on the spear.

When another thunderous *thump* shook the chamber, causing more dust to sift down from the ceiling, Tasud yelled, "A giant!"

Sed gasped when a portion of the stone wall collapsed onto Tasud, crushing him and knocking the blazerod from his hands. The master of flame scrambled for cover when Og's arm reached through the gaping hole. In response, Sed pulled the spear from Keket's shoulder and charged Og, stabbing the reaching giant in the arm.

With a resonating howl, Og pulled back from the crumbled opening.

Still clutching the spear, Sed searched for the blazerod as Keket pulled Franny back to her with the leash. After spotting the pewter weapon just inside the gate, he hurried to it. But before he could reach the rod, Michelle leaped from the shadows, thrust her arm through the gate's bars, and snatched the blazerod from off the stone floor.

"LET GO OF MY SON!" bellowed Michelle as she got to her feet and pointed the weapon at Keket, who was still pulling Franny back.

Sed thrust his spear at Michelle, but the forked tip caught one of the gate's bars and bounced back at him.

The distraught Franny, fighting against Keket's leash, reached for his mother as the dark ruler picked up her blade.

"No! Franny!" cried Michelle, firing the blazerod.

The blast knocked the dark governess back against her throne, leaving a smoldering hole in her chest as her light gushed out. Sed's jaw fell open when Keket's chest ignited, and she slumped to the side, releasing her hold on Franny's leash.

"Franny!" cried Michelle as the boy scampered to the gate. He reached his arm and shoulder through, but his head and chest would not fit between the rusty iron bars. Michelle dropped the rod and reached through the gate to help him. Remiel joined her, his sword at the ready.

A furious Sed turned from his burning governess to Franny, trying to squeeze through the bars. Sed grabbed the spear and charged the little boy, but before he could impale Franny, Remiel reached through the gate with his sword, slashed the blade down across Sed's face, and knocked the spear free. The impact spun Sed off his feet and back into the altar, knocking him unconscious.

While Michelle and Remiel worked to fit Franny through the bars, Gak stared down the dark passageway they had just fought through. "More soldiers are coming! We must hurry!"

"He won't fit through. Let me try to lift it," said Remiel.

Michelle stepped back as the watcher took hold of the heavy iron gate and heaved, but it didn't move.

"Gak, help me."

The halfborn sheathed his sword and took hold of the bars. The veins in Remiel's neck bulged as they strained to raise the gate. Remiel roared as the gate lifted one finger and then two finger widths. Michelle got to her knees. She was ready to pull Franny under the heavy gate when it slammed down.

"We can't lift it," panted Remiel, his hands on his knees. His eyes widened when he remembered the hole Og had knocked in the wall. "Og! Can you reach the prince? Og!" But the giant didn't answer.

"Maybe we should come in from the outside," said Gak.

"No! I won't leave Franny here!" cried Michelle.

"We must hurry! Their armies are nearing!" warned Gak, drawing his sword and turning to the passage.

"Shoot your blazerod up there!" said Remiel, pointing to the gate's tracks overhead. "If it can cut through, the gate should fall!"

"What about Franny?" fretted Michelle.

"Move to the side, young prince," urged Remiel.

Sed was stirring to consciousness when Franny stepped over his legs and moved under the scaffolding. In the back of the chamber, beyond the smoldering Keket, crouched the trembling master of flame.

Upon seeing her son safely out of the way, Michelle fired the blazerod. After two shots and a push from Remiel, the heavy gate fell into the chamber atop Sed, smashing the altar. But the gate also brought part of the ceiling down, blocking the hole Og had made and creating a cloud of dust and soot. As the burning remains of the altar torch faded, only the growing flames of the sprawled Keket lit the chamber.

"Franny!" cried Michelle, climbing over the fallen gate to her son. "Are you okay?"

The boy wrapped his arms around his mother's neck and closed his eyes.

"We can't get out that way," said Remiel, surveying the collapsed wall. "We must leave the way we came!"

"But the orb! We must find the orb!" exclaimed Michelle, frantically scanning the destroyed chamber.

"There's no time! More soldiers are coming!" exclaimed Gak.

As Remiel led Michelle out of the rubble, neither noticed Franny's pointing arm or the golden glow coming from the smashed altar.

With Franny in one arm, Michelle grabbed the blazerod and gave the burning governess a final, horrified look, then followed Remiel.

Franny's arms were tight around Michelle's neck as they rushed down the pitch-black passageway with Gak in the lead. She gave frequent backward glances as sounds of men and clanging metal followed. With her dark-sight, Michelle viewed the shimmering light of the tunnel walls as Gak raced in front of her, his sword pointing. But as the tunnel descended, her concern grew. "Are we going the right way?" When Gak stopped and looked back the way they had come, she asked, "Are we lost?"

"We're not lost!" replied Gak, his sunken eyes searching, his sword at the ready. "I just don't know where we are."

"That means we're lost!" exclaimed Michelle in dismay.

"I think we took a wrong turn back there," said Remiel.

When Michelle heard the familiar buzzing sound, her heart sank, and she clutched Franny tighter. "Oh, no!" she cried as a dark billowing cloud passed through the stone wall and hovered before her.

"The dark elements!" gasped Gak, staggering backward. When a second cloud appeared on his side, he let out a terrified whimper.

Remiel clutched his head as the purple cloud rolled over him. He dropped his sword and turned to Michelle with frantic eyes.

"Not again. Leave us!" shouted Michelle, but the dark, swirling cloud grew closer.

"I've never felt it so strong!" groaned Remiel.

"They want the child!" warned Gak, throwing a fearful glance at the untroubled Franny.

Michelle aimed the blazerod at the larger of the two clouds and fired, but the cloud parted as the energy bolt passed through. The blast shook the tunnel walls and caused dust and rocks to fall from the arched ceiling. But Gak and Remiel were oblivious to the falling stone, engulfed by the dark element's choking gloom.

Undaunted, Michelle moved the blazerod to the hand holding Franny and raised her other toward the purple cloud. It moved closer to her as if in defiance. "Leave us!" she commanded.

The cloud didn't move. Remiel and Gak were now on their hands and knees, their useless weapons on the damp passageway floor.

Michelle stepped back as the cloud neared Franny, its core darkening even more. She thrust her fist into the cloud's heart, closed her eyes, and yelled, "Leave us!"

The purple cloud rolled back on itself and stormed in again, this time with the second cloud.

Michelle drew in a determined breath, focused her energy, and roared, "LEAVE US!" This time, light shot forth from her hand, sifting through the roiling cloud and changing it from a dark purple to a pink. To Michelle's relief, the fading cloud retreated into the tunnel wall.

As Gak's senses returned, he looked up at the breathless Michelle in wonder.

"She commands the dark elements," said an astonished Remiel.

"She is Theia, the Bringer of Light," breathed Gak, as if reminding himself.

"Are you okay, my darling?" asked a drained Michelle, kneeling to examine Franny. Her face brightened when she saw her son's inner light for the first time.

"I missed you, Mommy."

"I missed you, my love," said a tearful Michelle, squeezing her son.

"Monsieur Gik?" asked Franny, pointing to the stringy-haired halfborn.

"No, this is his brother, Gak," Michelle explained, still immersed in her son's radiance.

"Happy to meet you, young prince," smiled Gak. "You were quite a lot of trouble."

A frowning Remiel cleared his throat.

Gak half-turned to his friend, then added, "But worth all of it!"

"An honor," nodded Remiel. He shook hands with Franny before gathering up his sword.

Franny eyed the watcher knowingly.

Turning to the sounds of soldiers approaching from down the tunnel, Gak picked up his sword. "More trouble is coming."

Remiel pointed up the tunnel. "We must go back that way."

"But they're coming from that way too," fretted Michelle.

"That's the way out, and we have the advantage. They can't see us without their torches," said Remiel.

When a spear thrown from down the tunnel struck the wall beside them, Gak spun and raised his sword. But when another stabbed him in the thigh, he cried out in pain and fell back. "They're coming! Go! I will hold them here as long as I can!"

"We're not leaving you," glared Michelle. She raised the blazerod and fired a bolt. It hit the stone wall twenty feet down the tunnel and knocked large chunks from the wall as it illuminated a dozen soldiers standing three abreast. The tunnel then plunged back into inky blackness.

With her darksight, Michelle saw the apprehension in their tattooed faces as the soldiers resumed their cautious advance, their spears pointed forward. When she spotted a soldier pulling his spear back to throw, Michelle fired again, striking the ceiling a few feet before the approaching soldiers. The blast blew out more rock, including the arching stonework that supported the tunnel. Michelle groaned when stone and earth collapsed on top of the soldiers, sealing the downward passageway.

The choking dust cloud that followed, with its billions of silicone and carbon molecules, overwhelmed Michelle's darksight and left the stone passageway in a fog. "I can't see," she coughed.

"It's the dust particles. It will clear," replied Remiel.

Gak had already pulled the impaling spear from his leg when the dust cloud settled. After casting the spear aside, he climbed to his feet, hobbled up the tunnel past the others, and grunted, "This way."

With no other way to go, Michelle picked up Franny and followed Remiel.

They hadn't gone thirty feet when they came to a joining passageway. The glowing outlines of forked spears ready to plunge from around the corner were visible in the blackness.

"That's the way out," whispered the hobbling Gak, pointing to another turn beyond the junction and the hiding soldiers.

When Michelle raised her blazerod to fire, Gak looked up at the stone ceiling and nervously shook his head.

Upon realizing the intruders had detected them, the front row of soldiers moved out from the turn. Standing three abreast, the dark dwellers blocked the only way out. The soldiers shuffled forward blindly in the darkness, their spears thrusting in unison.

When the approaching dark dwellers were just twenty steps away, Remiel turned to Michelle and said, "Use your blazerod, but try not to hit the walls."

"Or the ceiling," added Gak.

With a sad sigh, Michelle raised the weapon. She counted at least four rows of soldiers before the turn. Michelle saw the worried faces of the three in front, their bare and dusty chests gleaming. She was about to fire when she had a thought. Michelle lowered the blazerod, stepped past Remiel, and called out, "I have a weapon that will surely destroy you! Your governess is dead! You have no reason to fight us! Give us passage, and you will live!"

Remiel and Gak exchanged glances, then watched with raised swords as the approaching soldiers slowed to a stop.

"Push forward! They killed our governess!" commanded a voice from the rear of the line.

The blind, rhythmic stepping and thrusting resumed.

Now just fifteen feet away, Michelle raised her weapon and, with a sad shake of her head, fired. The bolt struck the middle soldier, blowing a hole through his chest and knocking him and the next three rows back. Their emptying light briefly lit the passageway. Those still standing looked wide-eyed at the smoldering chest wounds. When the second toppled soldier lit on fire, those standing backed away in horror. His flaming chest provided enough light for them to see and did what Michelle's warning could not. The soldiers stopped and muttered their wishes not to die to each other.

"Move forward! Skewer them! They killed the governess!" came from the back of the line.

"I have no wish to take your lives! Please, move back and give us passage, and you can live!" urged Michelle.

The soldiers pushed forward.

After drawing in a ragged breath, Michelle re-aimed the blazerod.

When the leading soldiers saw her raised arm in the dim firelight, they pushed against the walls, allowing the bolt to blast through the next two rows, throwing them back onto those already down.

Michelle saw the terrified faces of those still standing in the fleeing life light. She lowered the blazerod when the soldiers dropped their spears and turned. But her heart sank when the commander skewered the retreating men and women. After a short skirmish, with puffs of escaping life lighting the dark passageway like a lightning storm, all was quiet, with only the fallen, smoldering bodies blocking the passage.

Holding Franny tight and shielding his eyes from the gore, Michelle followed Remiel and Gak as they stepped over the bodies. She tried not to look at the impaled and moaning when they reached the joining tunnel.

A hobbling Gak pointed to their missed turn and shrugged. "That's the way out."

Remiel allowed Michelle and Franny to pass, then followed, guarding their rear.

INSIDE THE COLLAPSED governess's chamber, under the fallen gate and a layer of black dust, a hand moved. With a groan, Sed raised his bloody head. Trapped under the gate resting on the crumbled altar, Sed pushed back along the littered floor until he was free. Coated in soot dust, he rolled on his side as blood dripped from his slashed face. He grimaced when he touched the sword wound that cut from his forehead, along his left eye, to his jaw. He sat up and looked around the destroyed chamber. At its head was a sprawled heap of flaming flesh. "Governess," he groaned.

Sed climbed to his feet and stumbled to the burning Keket. He dropped to his knees and gloried in her light. He wished more could behold the governess's flame.

After breathing in determination, Sed lifted her fat, fiery hand and pressed it to his slashed face. He cried out as it sizzled against his open flesh. Then, able to bear no more, Sed dropped the flaming arm.

With his wound cauterized and the left side of his face charred, Sed turned to Keket's remains, bowed, and muttered, "May you burn forever, my governess. I will avenge your death. I swear it."

Sed groaned as he pushed up to stand, but stopped when he discovered the golden orb partially hidden in the pile of altar stones. He reached for it and pulled the orb from the debris. Sed's jaw slackened when the sphere's characters glowed, but it quickly returned to its dull luster. He turned to the chamber entry when he heard voices down the shadowed passageway. "Guards! Guards!"

Three soldiers and a centurion rushed into the governess's chamber with spears in hand, but when they saw the destruction and the flaming Keket, they bowed to their knees. "Our governess burns!" exclaimed the centurion, overcome by her light.

The former lord of the chamber staggered to his feet. "I, Sed, am now Ra's chosen ruler and keeper of the Dark Gate! You will bow to me!"

The centurion's mournful gaze turned to Sed, unconvinced of his authority.

Sed raised the orb over his head and cried, "By the ancient law of succession, I claim the governorship!"

The centurion's eyes widened when he saw the golden sphere in Sed's hand.

"We will avenge the governess's death! Bring me the heads of her killers, and I will make you a general!"

The centurion's angry eyes returned to the flaming Keket. He breathed in determination. "I will do it. I will avenge Keket's murder! May Ra guide me!" he exclaimed, touching the eye tattooed on his forehead.

"Now go! Hunt them down!"

"Yes, my governor," bowed the centurion.

MICHELLE FILLED her lungs with the outside air as they rushed out of the dark passageway past slain guards. Holding Franny tight against her, she followed the hobbling Gak, his sword at the ready, while Remiel guarded their rear.

Gak limped to a stop when they came to the citadel's rotunda, light flickering through the hole hammered by the giant's mace. "Where's Og?" asked Gak, scanning the ruins for his friend.

"I don't know," replied Remiel, turning in a circle, his sword pointed. "We're being watched."

Michelle scanned the shadows and gulped at the glowing faces of hidden dark dwellers peering at them. "Will they attack?" she asked, clutching her blazerod.

"They may. Be ready," warned Remiel.

"We must find Og," insisted Gak, pushing forward.

"This feels like a trap," said Remiel as they moved along the path of cleared rubble outside the citadel.

Not taking her eyes from the hidden dark dwellers watching from the shadows, Michelle stayed close to Gak as he rubbed his stabbed leg. In her arms, Franny curiously eyed the halfborn's wound.

Remiel climbed atop a pile of rubble to get his bearings, then lowered his sword. "I found Og."

"Where?" asked Gak, hobbling toward him.

"There," sighed Remiel, pointing to the toppled giant in a courtyard beside a collapsed building.

"Oh, no," groaned Michelle, spotting the slain behemoth, his tattered robe twisted, a dozen spears piercing his torso and neck. Around him lay more than a dozen mangled soldiers.

When a bare-chested sentry emerged from the shadows and raised an ax over Og's neck, Remiel jumped off the pile and yelled, "You! Get away from him!"

Undeterred, the sentry was about to bring down the ax and claim his prize when Michelle fired a bolt into the wall behind the dark dweller. "Step away from him, you beast!"

The sentry dropped his ax and darted into the shadows.

"Og!" cried Gak, hobbling to his lifeless friend.

Remiel sheathed his sword and hung his head.

"Is he still alive?" asked Michelle, seeing wisps of light streaming from the giant's wounds.

"I think not for long," sighed Gak, feeling Og's chest.

Michelle set Franny down and reached for his hand, but instead of taking it, he moved to the dying giant. "Franny, where are you going?"

The others watched as Franny approached Og, his blue eyes fixed, his small arm extended.

"Franny?" said Michelle, her face filled with concern.

When Franny climbed onto Og's arm, Michelle moved to retrieve him, but stopped when the boy tugged on an impaled spear. Michelle's face lit up when she remembered how he had healed Gik by the pond. "Remove the spears!"

"What?" frowned Remiel.

"I think Franny can help him. Remove the spears!"

Gak and Remiel pulled out the spears and tossed them aside, then watched the little boy place his hand on one of Og's leaking wounds. Gak's eyes widened when Og's flesh glowed under the boy's hand. Remiel shook his head in wonder as the wound closed.

Gak turned to Michelle. "He can do this without the power of the orb!"

"It is the same power, only he does not need the orb to wield it!" said Remiel.

Gak stepped back when two of Og's large fingers moved.

Michelle watched with worried eyes as Franny healed one wound after another. She moved closer when Og groaned and rolled his warty head to the side. "Franny, be careful. He's waking up." But Franny was fixated on Og's gaping belly wound. It too glowed as it mended.

When Og abruptly sat up and looked about, uncertain of where he was, a worried Michelle reached for her little boy. But the giant's thrashing stopped when he noticed Franny on his chest. Og raised a gentle hand to the boy and grunted in the voice of a waking bear, "Thank you."

Franny touched the giant's finger and smiled.

"You live," beamed Gak.

Og looked from the halfborn to Remiel and nodded.

"Thank you all for rescuing my son," said the tearful Michelle, taking Franny in her arms as the giant stood.

"We're not out of danger yet," warned Remiel.

"It looks like you had your hands full," said the hobbling Gak as he viewed the carnage.

The wobbly Og surveyed the scattered bodies and nodded.

"Can you walk?" asked Remiel.

Og nodded and reached for his spiked club.

When Franny pushed for her to let him down, Michelle obliged.

They all watched as Franny moved to the wounded Gak and touched his thigh.

"It's a small wound," shrugged Gak. "It will be fine."

Franny closed his eyes and healed the spear wound.

"Thank you, young prince," bowed Gak before testing his leg.

"He healed your brother too," said Michelle, but her face saddened when she remembered Gik's terrible demise.

"We must leave. Their army is coming," warned Remiel as torchlight appeared across the ruins.

Michelle pushed the blazerod into her bag, picked up Franny, and hurried after Remiel as Gak and the teetering Og followed.

CHAPTER 19

RECLAMATION

CARNAC, FRANCE
9 NOVEMBER 1933

Nazario was scribbling in his notebook at a table near the hotel window when a restless Eli put his book down and moved to the balcony door. The watcher opened it, stepped onto the shallow ledge, and looked past the church's slate steeple to the dark and ominous clouds. The smell of pipe tobacco from the restaurant below reminded him of Ronan.

Eli sighed as he painfully considered all that had happened since that terrible night Gadreel killed Ronan, and Michelle and Franny disappeared into the abyss. Eli tried not to dwell on their plight in that dark realm, but such thoughts and worries consumed him. And now, without his labors around the château to occupy his days, Eli found himself growing increasingly irritable.

"Any sign of rain?" asked Nazario, just as eager to move on.

"Dark clouds are moving in," replied Eli, closing the door. He studied Nazario, intently writing in his notebook with three others stacked beside it. "What are you working on?"

Nazario looked up at Eli. "My notes on our adventure, of course."

"You consider this an adventure?"

"Very much so. But perhaps 'quest' is a better word for it."

"Quest." Eli stared across the room. "That's what Dina called it."

"That's what it is, a quest to bring your wife and son home from that dark and terrible place."

"Quest seems like such a...*human* word," frowned Eli.

Nazario laughed. "Well, it is that, but I think it describes your pursuit and my odyssey into the unknown."

"Unknown for you."

"Yes, of course," Nazario nodded. He eyed Eli for a moment, then asked, "But isn't some part of this unknown to you as well?"

Eli looked out the window across the square and nodded.

"Perhaps you are more human than you care to admit."

Eli's eyes shifted in thought.

"I'm also working on my questions for you."

"Still? You must think those very important questions."

"They are. Perhaps the most important mankind has ever asked."

"I doubt that," frowned Eli.

Nazario glanced down at his book. "In fact, I believe I have my first question for you."

Eli sank into an armchair beside the feather bed and studied the reporter. "Very well. Let's hear it."

Nazario scratched his head. "Okay, here it goes."

Eli waited. "Yes?"

Nazario cleared his throat. "Do you... Do you have a mother?"

Eli's face dimmed. "That is your first question for me? If I have a mother?"

Nazario sensed Eli's discomfort with the question and returned to his notebook. "I-I can ask another."

Eli's troubled gaze lowered to the floor.

Nazario flipped a few pages and opened his mouth. He raised his finger and was about to speak when a thunderclap shook the hotel.

Eli sat up and turned to the window and the gathering storm. The wind had straightened the streamers on a flagpole and chased leaves across the cobbled square. "It's starting!"

· · ·

Bundled in coats and hats, Eli and Nazario hurried down the country road as the wind bent the pine boughs and whistled through the leafless oaks and elms. The reporter wished he had brought his notebook until the rain began. A sprinkle pushed sideways by the wind soon turned to a biting downpour.

The two had just entered the stone field when a dazzling lightning bolt arced across the charcoal sky. The crash of thunder was immediate and shook the ground. "Is it safe for us to be out here?" asked a round-eyed Nazario.

"You can go back if you wish," replied Eli, his voice all but lost in the storm.

Nazario shook his head and pushed forward.

Eli was nearly across the field to the thicket when a lightning bolt struck a tall megalith with a blinding flash. The energy from the bolt blew off Nazario's hat and knocked him to the wet grass as it dissipated into smaller streams of electricity that arced from one giant rock to the next. The reporter raised a shielding hand as white streams of light crisscrossed the field. "What's happening?" cried Nazario.

With Eli's only thought on retrieving the orb and saving his family, he darted through the thicket to the chamber mound.

Still lying on the grass, Nazario frantically looked around as the shimmering megaliths absorbed the radiant energy. He gasped as a current passed under him, like an underground wave, leaving the reporter's bones and teeth tingling.

When a blinding flash erupted from the other side of the thicket, where Eli had gone, Nazario buried his head, certain he was about to die. But when he opened his eyes, there was only the steady downpour of rain.

Soaking wet, the wide-eyed reporter sat up and looked back at the giant stones. They stood motionless, gray, and dripping from the rain.

When Nazario remembered the blinding flash, he turned to the thicket. He charged toward it, tripping and falling on his face twenty yards from the field's edge. Nazario scrambled to his feet as lightning lit the dark clouds behind him. When he reached the dense underbrush, he pushed through until he reached the clearing. Once there, the huffing Nazario gasped. The chamber mound's sloping passageway was streaming with rainwater. Its rock door was blown open and tilted on its side, and the massive ceiling stone and monolith atop the mound were gone.

With rain streaming down his face, Nazario struggled to understand what he saw as he approached the smoking crater. When he was halfway down the passageway, a lightning bolt lit the clearing, revealing Eli lying in a growing pool of rainwater at the center of the hollow. "Elijah!" cried Nazario, charging into the blown-open chamber. He saw the blackened base of the pedestal, but the orb and its cradle were no more.

When Nazario reached the unconscious Eli, he shook the watcher's arm. Soot blackened Eli's face. The blast had charred and shredded Eli's coat, and his hat was gone. "Eli! Eli! Are you all right?" When Eli didn't respond, Nazario tried to pull him out of the water. But Eli outweighed the reporter by a hundred pounds and didn't move. Nazario slipped and fell into the growing pond. "Elijah! Elijah!" he shouted, tugging on his arm. Nazario shook his head in despair. He gasped when Eli's head rolled to the side, and the watcher opened his eyes. "Eli! We must get out of here. It's filling with water. Can you stand?"

Eli looked at the reporter strangely, then rolled to his knees. After looking around the exploded mound in confusion, he climbed to his feet.

Nazario moved to Eli's side but fell into the water, bringing the larger man down with him. The reporter struggled to help Eli back to his feet, and together, they slogged up the streaming passageway.

Once on level ground, the stunned Eli turned back to the smoldering crater. With rain streaming down his face, he groaned, "Michelle. Michelle."

"Let's get you back to the hotel," said Nazario, straining to stabilize the wobbly Eli as the downpour continued.

LESS THAN A DAY HAD PASSED, but the sleeping Eli's face was already less charred and bruised, and his brown, wavy hair no longer singed. Amazed at the watcher's rapid recovery, Nazario gently wiped Eli's face with a damp cloth.

Eli gasped when his puffy eyes opened to the attentive reporter sitting on the bed beside him.

"Are you okay, my friend?"

Eli grimaced as he raised his head and looked around the hotel room, the midday sun streaming through its windows. "Where am I?"

"You're in Carnac. Remember, we came here to replenish the orb."

"Carnac," groaned Eli.

"Do you remember?"

Eli painfully nodded. "How long?"

"The storm was yesterday. I would have called for a doctor, but I didn't suppose he could do much for you."

Eli tiredly rubbed his face.

"What happened?" asked Nazario, leaning closer. "What happened to the golden ball?"

Eli closed his eyes and sank back into the pillow. "It's gone."

"I'm sorry."

"They have blocked me at every turn," groaned Eli.

"Who? Who has blocked you?"

Tears streamed from the corners of Eli's eyes. "I will never get my Michelle and Franny back."

"Don't say that. There's always hope. We haven't looked under every stone yet. Remember?"

Eli turned away.

Upon seeing the immortal was in no mood to talk, Nazario sat back and set the damp cloth aside. "I will let you rest."

CHAPTER 20
THE SEA OF ARGASAY

THE ABYSS

Michelle didn't know how long they had walked when Franny wanted to be let down. With arms aching, she lowered her son and took his hand. Long out of the ruins, the vast plain on which they hiked had few stones and no trees. Not even stumps were visible, reminding Michelle of farmland back home. While the land's contour was visible with her darksight, that vision lessened after a few hundred feet, leaving Michelle wondering what lurked in the blackness beyond. "How can you tell where we're going?"

Remiel glanced back from a few steps ahead. "When you have wandered this land as long as we have, the landmarks become common."

Michelle frowned. "What landmarks? I see only a desolate plain."

"We're approaching the great scar," said Remiel.

"What's that?"

"You will see."

"It's hard to miss, my queen," shrugged Gak.

"You can stop calling me that. My name is Michelle. I'm just like you," she glanced at the immortal, the giant, and the halfborn, then added, "Well, mostly."

"As you wish," bowed Gak.

Michelle sighed.

The little band hadn't walked a hundred steps when the flatland to their left fell away. Michelle gasped when they came to the rim of an enormous crater. She could see neither the far side nor the crater's bottom, but the sloping ground within the cavity shimmered brightly. "It must be miles across! And so deep! What happened?"

"Something big," said Gak.

Og nodded.

"It happened long ago, before we arrived, when this world was yet living," explained Remiel.

"Oh. Why does the soil look different here?"

"The scar glows brightly because it is rich in elements," said Remiel.

"I see," muttered Michelle, overwhelmed by the beauty of the crater's shimmering light.

They took in the hollow's vastness for a time, then continued across the plain.

After a while, Michelle glanced up at the towering Og slogging to her left, his tattered robes dragging. "Og, I should get you a new robe the first chance we get."

Og gave Michelle a wounded look, but she didn't notice it.

"Why would you do that?" asked Gak.

"I should think he would enjoy fresh clothes," shrugged Michelle.

"A giant's robe tells a tale," explained Remiel.

"A very smelly tale," muttered Michelle.

Remiel glanced up at his offended friend, then said, "Og's robes tell his life's story. Giants take great pride in their frayed robes—the more threadbare, the better. To them, it's a badge of honor. To replace his robe would rob Og of his accomplishments."

"Well, could we at least wash them? Freshen them up a bit?"

A frowning Remiel turned back to the playful Michelle. "What you consider stench, his kind considers a proud aroma. It is Og's fragrance."

Upon realizing she had offended her friends, Michelle turned to Og and said, "I'm sorry. I didn't know."

Og nodded, accepting the apology.

Michelle sighed. Her heart ached for the lost familiarity of her own world as Franny playfully scurried ahead, his loose pajamas worn and dusty. "Is there anything here that could harm him?"

"I don't think so," replied Remiel.

Michelle was only partly comforted by his response. "Remiel, how long have you been here?" she asked, scanning the dim horizon.

"A long time," said Remiel.

"Well, when did you arrive?"

"In the middle of your earth's Second Age."

Michelle frowned. "But how long ago was that?"

"A long time ago," shrugged Remiel.

Michelle rolled her eyes. "Gak, how about you?"

"Not as long as Remiel."

"Oh." Michelle shook her head. "How about you, Og," she asked, looking up. "Can you be as precise?"

"Long time," grunted Og.

"Well, you're all very informative," sighed Michelle.

"Immortals view time differently," said Remiel.

"As a watcher, I knew you were immortal, but I didn't know Og and Gak were," said Michelle.

"All life is immortal in its own right," said Remiel.

"But most things die," said Michelle.

"Nothing truly ever dies; it simply changes form," replied Remiel.

Michelle shook her head. "I don't understand."

"That which makes up your body—the elements of life—have always existed and always will exist."

Michelle's brow furrowed in thought. "When I age and die, I will change to dust."

"That which makes up your body will return to its eternal elements, but the light of your being will live one. Just as it lived before entering your physical shell," explained Remiel.

"Does that mean that even watchers can die?"

"My kind are blessed with an exceptionally long existence, but even watchers of the divine realm can succumb—especially in this world," said Remiel.

"You say blessed, but my husband thought immortality something of a curse," frowned Michelle.

Remiel gave Michelle a sideways glance. "Eli's perspective is unique."

Michelle sighed, struggling to comprehend it all. "Well, I was going to ask, since you've all been here such a long time, what you missed most about the other world, but you probably don't even remember."

They walked in silence for a time before Gak said, "I miss food."

Michelle's face brightened as she turned to the halfborn. "So do I! Before, I sometimes thought eating was a bother, but I so miss it now! The scrumptious flavors, the delectable textures. My mouth is watering even now!"

"What food do you miss?" asked Remiel.

"Oh, where do I start? French food is the best, of course, but the Italians have a frozen cream I quite enjoy. They call it gelato. Have you ever tried it?"

The others looked at Michelle blankly.

"I suppose not. It was invented later," Michelle turned back to Gak. "What food do you miss?"

"Gumbish," Gak nodded.

"Gumbish. Oh, that sounds rather tasty. What is it?"

"Gumbish," shrugged Gak.

"But...what is it made from?"

"Wheat mash and grubs," replied Remiel.

Michelle made a sour face.

"Ale," grunted Og.

Michelle looked up at the giant and smiled. "Now that's something I could enjoy!"

A smirking Remiel glanced back at Og, whose grin was buried under his hairy face.

Caught up in the conversation, Michelle hadn't noticed the blue glow coming from ahead of them. When she spotted Franny stopped at the top of a rise, her playfulness faded, and she called out, "Franny, do you see something?"

Franny turned back and yelled, "It's pretty, Mommy!"

Michelle hurried past Remiel and climbed the gentle hill to find a sea of iridescent blue stretching as far as she could see. It took a moment for her to realize she wasn't seeing the blue expanse with her darksight but through her normal eyes as part of the visible spectrum. "It's beautiful. What is it?"

"It is the Sea of Argasay," replied Remiel, joining her and Franny atop the rise.

"A sea?" Michelle's eyes narrowed as she studied the expanse's irregular texture. It was not smooth like water, but bumpy like an endless field of stones. As they moved closer, the unusual shapes became clearer to her. "That's not water," muttered Michelle. Her eyes widened when she realized she was looking at a vast field of giant fluorescent mushrooms. "They're toadstools! Huge toadstools—millions of them! Are they poisonous?"

Remiel turned to Michelle. "No, but do not eat them."

"I wasn't planning to." When Michelle stepped closer to take Franny's hand, she saw the glowing blue toadstools were up to two feet tall and a foot wide, with no more than a half-foot length between them. Scattered throughout the sea were gangly pillars made of the same iridescent blue that stretched ten feet into the air. "I've never seen anything like it. It's lovely."

"The sea has grown," said Remiel with some concern.

"What does that mean?" asked Michelle.

Remiel turned to her. "It means this world is nearing its renewal."

Michelle shook her head. "I don't understand. The plants everywhere here are dead or dormant. Why are these alive?"

"The Sea is the beginning and the end of life. It consumes the dead and gives life to the new. As the Sea flows, it consumes and heals the land," explained Remiel.

"Watch this," smirked Gak as he stooped down beside a mushroom, grabbed it with both hands, and pulled. When the mushroom came free of the black soil, its blue light died out, and a ripple of darkness ran across the field like a wave across a sea.

"What did you do?" gasped Michelle.

"Put it back," said Remiel like a scolding father.

"It's just for fun," shrugged Gak. When he replaced the darkened toad-stool, it reconnected and glowed blue again.

"Pretty light!" laughed Franny.

"That's remarkable," breathed Michelle. "When you pulled it from the ground, it was as though all the other mushrooms sensed it? Their lights went out for an instant! How do they do that?"

Remiel turned to Michelle. "They are all connected. They each feel what one feels."

"That's incredible!" Michelle's gaze moved across the glowing blue field. "I've seen nothing like it."

"Not so incredible. Mortals are connected in the same way," said Remiel.

Michelle turned to Remiel. "How? When something happens to another, we don't feel it. Not like that."

"You *do* feel it. You have learned to ignore it, to hide away others' pain."

Michelle stared across the sea of blue in thought.

When Gak approached Remiel and whispered something into his ear, the watcher looked back the way they had come.

"Is something the matter?" asked Michelle.

"We're being followed," said Remiel.

"By who?" gasped Michelle. "The people of Ra?"

"I think so." Remiel stepped into the sea of blue and said, "Shall we cross here?"

"Wait. Are we going to walk across? Won't we hurt them?"

"Not if you're careful," replied Remiel.

Michelle turned to Og, knowing his feet could not fit between the toadstools. She stepped back when the giant pulled up his tattered robe and waded into the sea with his mace in hand. Her eyes widened when the toadstools leaned to the side, giving him a path to walk.

Franny laughed and jumped up and down. "I want to go!"

After picking Franny up, Michelle followed Remiel into the sea, but to her surprise, when she neared the first mushrooms, their blue hue turned white, and a pale wave washed across the others. Og and Remiel stopped and stared.

"I've never seen that before," said Gak.

"Did I do something wrong?" Michelle asked, holding a beaming Franny.

"No," Remiel smiled. "They recognize your light."

Michelle looked across the sea of blue with wonder-filled eyes and resumed walking, the white ripples radiating out with each step.

Not twenty feet into the sea, Franny squirmed down from his mother's arms and said, "I want to."

Seeing no harm in it, Michelle set Franny down.

Chest deep in the vibrant toadstools, their light flickered as Franny skipped around them with a joyful laugh. But unlike the mammoth Og, the mushrooms didn't part to make room for the dancing boy; instead, they leaned against him like a clowder of cats brushing against one's legs.

Michelle laughed as the pressing toadstools pushed the frolicking boy around, but Remiel watched with concern.

When Franny fell back atop a toadstool, and its collapsing cap let out a dark blue puff of spores, Remiel stepped forward and snatched the boy off the ground. Michelle was still laughing when blood-red jaws burst from the ruptured cap, snapping in the air.

"What was that!" gasped Michelle, staggering back.

"Don't agitate them," warned Remiel as the curious Franny watched the red jaws shrivel back inside the toadstool.

"My goodness. Are we safe here?" Michelle asked, looking at the mushrooms with awakened eyes.

Remiel scanned the blue sea, then set Franny down. "Yes, just don't sit on them. They don't like that."

Michelle gulped and took Franny in her arms. She glanced back to see the way clear behind them, then walked with Remiel, Gak, and Og across the blue sea, her white wave rippling before them.

CHAPTER 21
THE VANISHED SYMBOLS

Adolf Hitler couldn't hide his delight as he descended the steps of the Kroll Opera House to hundreds of his followers with outstretched arms, chanting *Sieg heil!* While the phrase came from an old German term referring to one's victory over the lower self, Hitler had given it a new meaning, "hail to victory." The day's election would mean precisely that.

With all other political parties banned in Germany, it was no surprise the Nazi parliament candidates easily defeated the communist incumbents who had, months before, made impressive gains in control of the country. But that had all changed. These former parliamentarians were now in hiding. Within weeks, they would be in internment camps or dead.

While Hitler was still only chancellor, his party now had complete control over the future of Germany. Only the presidency remained, and that grew closer to the Führer with each passing day.

Dressed in a suit, coat, and top hat, the tall, red-bearded Lu followed Hitler and his entourage down the opera house steps. Lu's green eyes narrowed when he spotted the white-bearded Cyrus standing amidst the chanting crowd. Cyrus's pleased smile and approving nod were barely noticeable.

Only a few understood the whole truth, that the fallen watcher was the chief architect of Hitler's rise. Fewer still understood the corrupted overseer's part in the deadly chess game. While the masses would never know them, the world would soon come to know and fear the name Adolf Hitler.

CARNAC, FRANCE
12 NOVEMBER 1933

NAZARIO WAS REVIEWING his diary when Eli stirred in the bed. He studied the battered and downcast watcher, then said, "Good morning."

"Good morning." Eli's voice was tired and gravelly as he pulled himself up and swung his legs over the side of the bed.

"Are you hungry? I had food brought up."

Eli pushed his hair out of his face and shook his head.

"Are you feeling all right?"

Eli didn't reply.

Nazario gulped. "What-what happened to your orb?"

Eli stared at the floor and muttered, "I don't know."

Nazario leaned closer. "There was a terrible flash and then...."

"I said, I don't know!" snapped Eli. "I don't know anything anymore, except that I'm cursed to live out my existence in misery for my mistakes!"

Nazario studied the grumpy Eli for a time, then said, "I must say, for an immortal being with eons of experience, you seem rather testy and short-sighted at times."

"What do you know? Your puny life is a spark compared to mine," grumbled Eli.

"Of that, I'm sure. But I don't plan on quitting any time soon. I plan on making the most of it to my dying day. That's why I'm sitting here babysitting you!"

"I don't need your sympathy!"

"You must have misheard me. I wasn't giving you any!"

Eli raised his head and glared at the reporter before rolling back onto the bed.

Nazario sighed. "There are still places to search!"

Eli shot back up from the bed. "Do you have any idea how many domain spheres there are in this world?"

"Until a week ago, I didn't know what a domain sphere was!"

"There were four!" fumed Eli. "My wife took one with her, and another just blew up in my face!"

Nazario shrugged. "That means there are two more to be found."

Eli angrily shook his head. "You realize we're not the only ones looking for them! Lu is on the hunt! If he finds just one, the world is lost!"

Nazario's face filled with concern. "You've given me two good reasons to keep looking. To save your wife and son and stop Lu from destroying this world! I am here to help you!"

"How can you help me?"

"If I recall, I was the one who led you to the abbey. We still have many places to look!"

Eli sighed. "Like where?"

"We haven't even started searching the Vatican archives. They may have one on a shelf there!"

Eli rolled his head toward Nazario. "Do you really think we can find another?"

"Not lying in bed."

A fuming Eli shook his head. "I am pathetic, taking encouragement from a mortal."

"I'm not only a mortal," replied Nazario. "I'm also your friend."

Eli stared at the ceiling as Nazario returned to his notebook. After a few minutes of contemplation, Eli sighed and said, "Yes, I had a mother."

Nazario turned to the watcher with wide eyes.

VATICAN CITY
14 NOVEMBER 1933

ELI REPOSITIONED his satchel and tightened his coat as the fall breeze chased a scrap of paper across the piazza. On the bench beside him sat Nazario, nervously puffing on a cigarette. Before them stretched the enormous St. Peter's Square. Tourists and religious pilgrims were scattered throughout, pointing in awe or simply enjoying the grandeur of the Catholic Church's holiest site. At the center of the cobbled ellipse stood a 120-foot-tall, four-sided Egyptian obelisk. Supported by bronze lions, the pyramid at the granite monument's top held a green-patinated cross. Beyond the obelisk loomed the towering white marble columns and giant dome of St. Peter's Basilica, its roof façade lined by statues of Christ and his apostles.

Eli's gaze moved to the Sistine Chapel's roof, just visible to the north of the basilica. He recalled the gifted and devout but uncouth Michelangelo. Eli had several encounters with the artist, once while he was painting the chapel's ceiling. It was even said Michelangelo used the watcher as inspiration for his David, but Eli didn't see the resemblance.

Eli considered Michelangelo and others like him. It still amazed Eli that some mortals were so endowed as to leave their mark throughout all human history, while most were lost in the dust without a mention. Eli knew his kind had something to do with that rare notoriety. The fingerprints of the watchers' guiding hands were evident in all civilizations across time, but many rose to acclaim on their own merits without the guiding influence of immortals. Their inspiration came from the Divine Flow, the cosmic repository of knowledge available to all humanity, and was the purest of all, Eli thought.

"He's late," said a fidgeting Nazario.

"Tell me about this man."

"Pellegrini's an assistant curator for the Vatican Museum. He used to work in the library and archives. He's a wealth of knowledge, willing to bend the rules for the right price."

Eli nodded and gazed back across the square at a huddle of pigeons bobbing and poking for food. He wondered if he and Nazario were any different from them.

"Here he comes," muttered the reporter.

Eli's gaze turned as a man in a long coat, hat, and round-rimmed glasses approached. With his power of discernment lacking, the watcher had avoided reading every passing mortal, but thought it wise to give this one a quick inspection. Eli saw an intelligent yet conflicted man who sought companionship and regretted past mistakes. He could have passed for any other mortal, Eli thought.

Nazario mashed his cigarette into the bench, then stood and reached out a hand.

"Cleto, it's been a few years," said the tall but stout Italian. His eyes shifted through his thick glasses to Eli. "And who is this?"

"My assistant, Elijah," said Nazario.

The spectacled man scrutinized the larger Eli. "He can be trusted?"

"Yes," nodded Nazario, trying not to smile.

"Where are you from?"

"France, most recently," replied Nazario for Eli.

"Pellegrini," said the spectacled man, shaking Eli's hand. He turned to Nazario and asked, "Are you still working for the *Observer?*"

Nazario shrugged. "Yes, and no. It's complicated."

"But you are a complicated man, so that doesn't surprise me. What do you want?"

"I-*we* need access to the archives," replied Nazario.

"You don't need me for that, not with your Vatican connections."

Nazario looked into Pellegrini's eyes. "The *secret* archives."

Pellegrini studied Nazario for a moment, then said, "You're still on your hunt. What will you do if you ever find one of your mythical watchers?"

Nazario choked at the question, causing Eli to look at him strangely.

"Are you all right?" asked Pellegrini.

"Yes," nodded Nazario, his eyes watering.

"It's all a waste of time, if you ask me."

"You say they are a myth, but I choose to believe differently," replied Nazario with a sideways glance at Eli.

Pellegrini shrugged. "If you want in, it will have to be at night, and it will cost you."

"It always costs me."

"More," said Pellegrini.

"How much more?"

"Three thousand lire."

"Three thousand?" gasped Nazario. "That's double!"

"There are two of you," shrugged Pellegrini. He watched Nazario turn to Eli, who gave a subtle nod. "You ask your assistant for permission?"

"He keeps the books. I just wanted to make sure we have that."

Pellegrini nodded, not convinced by the answer.

"Fine," sighed Nazario. "When can you take us in?"

"It will have to be tomorrow night."

Nazario nodded.

"How much time will you need?"

"It depends on how long it takes us to find what we're looking for," shrugged Nazario.

"More than one night?"

Nazario glanced at Eli. "Maybe. I once spent six weeks in the library, researching just one story."

Pellegrini shook his head. "That would not be possible. Not in that place. What is it you seek?"

"Information on ancient portals. Star gates or anything of the like."

Pellegrini chuckled.

"You used to be a believer," frowned Nazario.

"Believing in absurd childhood notions is no longer practical."

"It may not be practical, but it sounds like it's still profitable."

Pellegrini huffed.

"Why is it no longer practical?" asked Eli.

"Ah! The assistant speaks," quipped Pellegrini. "Why is it no longer practical?" He shrugged, then said, "The world has changed."

Eli nodded.

"There is much talk of another war, and Mussolini is leading us head-long into it. Only this time, we will likely side with the fascists."

"Such a move would lead to Italy's demise," said Eli, annoyed by the prospect.

"Perhaps," shrugged Pellegrini. "I don't get paid to make such decisions."

Nazario stroked his mustache in thought. "Do you know where we can find what we're looking for?"

"I have an idea," replied Pellegrini.

Eli's jaw tightened when he spotted a group of German soldiers approaching. "What are they doing here?"

"Forming an alliance with Mussolini, no doubt. I've seen more of them around Rome lately," said Pellegrini.

When a photographer posed the six soldiers with a red-cloaked cardinal for a picture before the basilica, Nazario waved the others to follow. They were halfway across the piazza when he turned to Pellegrini and said, "Tomorrow night then?"

"Yes, the usual place."

Eli's eyes narrowed as they approached the smooth-sided Egyptian monument at the center of the cobbled ellipse. "I don't know that I've ever seen an obelisk without hieroglyphics."

"Yes, I know, they're usually covered in them," said Nazario.

Pellegrini nodded. "It is said that it once had such markings. But when Pope Sixtus the Fifth moved it here in 1580 and placed the cross atop its pinnacle to Christianize it, the pagan symbols disappeared."

Nazario glanced at Pellegrini. "It sounds like you might still believe in such absurd notions."

"Removing engravings from red granite with a prayer? I would like to see that."

Eli eyed the obelisk as the others continued across the square.

CHAPTER 22
LAWS AND BLESSINGS

MANU
THE ABYSS

Inside the wrecked governess's chamber, Sed examined the golden orb. The left side of his face was burned and raw, and his eye was swollen shut. Beside him lay the charred remains of Keket with fine ribbons of smoke still rising from her. With the altar crushed and the toppled gate removed, Sed's newly appointed master of flame stood holding a torch as a general reported to the new governor. Two other advisors were waiting for Sed's directives when a cloaked figure materialized near the smoky chamber's entrance. When a guard stepped in front and raised his spear, the cloaked stranger passed through him.

"It is a spirit!" gasped a slack-jawed advisor, backing away as the cloaked figure approached Sed.

"Where is the child?" asked the ghostly visitor, its powerful voice that of a man.

"Are you a spirit?" asked Sed, his chest heaving as he fought back his fear.

"Where is the child?"

"The Luminaries took him," replied Sed. "They attacked us and killed the governess."

The cloaked visitor studied Sed, its gleaming eyes visible within its shadowed hood. "You claim the governorship?"

Emboldened, Sed straightened on the half-burned throne. "I do."

"You wish to be the keeper of the Dark Gate?"

"*I am* the keeper of the Dark Gate. Who are you?" snapped Sed.

"By what authority do you assume this calling?" challenged the cloaked wraith.

"By the law of succession and the blessing of Ra! Who are you?" demanded Sed.

The cloaked apparition pulled back its hood to reveal the face of a man with white hair and a beard.

Sed eyed the grand overseer, his cloaked personage wavering from hazy and translucent to opaque and distinct.

"Do you not recognize me, Sed, son of Dąbki?"

"You are the one called Cyrus," replied Sed.

"That is right." The overseer's gaze lowered to the glowing orb. "Where is the child?"

"The watcher, Remiel, and his band took him."

"At Mawufe's bidding?"

Sed nodded.

"What of the child's mother?"

"She escaped."

"Escaped?" questioned Cyrus.

"Remiel freed her."

Cyrus's brow furrowed in thought as his gaze turned to the smoldering pile of charred flesh that was Keket. "Ra put much trust in her. Too much." The overseer's dark eyes shifted to Sed. "Do you believe you can do better?"

"Yes."

Cyrus shook his head. "You know so little."

"What do you mean?" frowned Sed. "I have been here from the start. I know the law—the customs—the prophecies."

Cyrus nodded to the orb. "I will grant you the throne in exchange for that ball."

Sed tightened his hold on the sphere. "I think not. I am already the governor. The orb will give me even greater power in this world."

Cyrus's eyes narrowed. "Your time in this world is not long remaining."

"That may be true if the Harbinger were to return to your world and usher in the end time." Sed saw Cyrus's surprise. "I know more than you think. I have an army hunting them down."

Cyrus's eyebrows raised. "An army?"

Sed held up the domain sphere and examined its glowing text. "The ball recognizes you."

"It does," nodded Cyrus. "Give it to me. You have no command of the sphere. It is but a shiny toy to you."

"You and I both know it is more than that."

"I could take it from you," threatened Cyrus.

Sed eyed the wavering apparition. "I do not think you can."

"You forget who I am."

"You are a spirit, not the grand overseer in the flesh."

Cyrus pulled back at Sed's correct assessment. Without the power of the orb, only the overseer's image could visit the abyss.

Sed examined the orb's pulsing characters. "Why do you want it so badly?"

"To access the abyss."

Sed eyed the corrupt overseer. "You wish to build an army. Like before."

Cyrus studied Sed, impressed by his insight.

"Hathor warned me of you long ago."

Cyrus looked at the would-be ruler with disdain.

"Why not use a portal on your world to acquire your army?" asked Sed with a smirk. "Oh, yes, you ordered the star gates dismantled."

Cyrus's eyes narrowed, surprised by the dark dweller's understanding.

"Only one remains, but you don't know where it is. Clever Hathor, hiding it from you."

Cyrus glared at the insolent dark dweller.

"Perhaps you fear the creator gods will learn of your treachery."

"There is no treachery. I am the grand overseer," scoffed Cyrus, his image fluttering.

"Of course," smirked Sed.

Cyrus's glare softened. "If you open the Dark Gate and return me the orb, I will allow you to come back to this world."

"What of my people?" asked Sed.

"They are the keepers of the abyss. At least, they once were," said Cyrus.

"Keket became lazy in her reign. You see what it got her. I will make this people mighty again."

Cyrus's intent gaze lowered to the glowing sphere. "Or you can give me the orb and be free of this awful realm."

Sed considered the overseer's offer. "Unlike you, I am but a man. How long will I live in the otherworld?"

"You will live out your days and then die, like all mortals."

"Or I can stay here and reign forever," grinned Sed.

"So you think."

Sed studied Cyrus. "You consider me primitive and slow-witted, but I know something you do not."

Somewhat entertained, Cyrus asked, "And what is that?"

"Who the boy's mother is."

"She is a mortal whore who bore a watcher a child."

"Not just any child," grinned Sed.

Cyrus's eyes narrowed. "Who do you think she is?"

"The Luminaries say she is Theia, the Awaited One, returned to free them."

Cyrus's jaw tightened. "They are misguided zealots. They understand nothing!"

"But what if they're right?" Sed eyed the overseer. "Which is more dangerous for you? To have the Bringer of Light here in the abyss or in your world?"

Cyrus's brow furrowed in thought.

Sed's face grew serious. "Teach me how to command the orb, and I will see that she has no power in either world."

Cyrus scowled at Sed as he considered the offer.

"And one more thing. Make it give me light," grinned Sed.

————

WHILE THE GIANT'S tracks gave the dark dwellers a clear path to follow, their progress was slow. With only the light of their torches to guide them, the trackers could see barely twenty feet in the darkness. Of the platoon of thirty, only twenty were fighters; the remaining torchbearers provided light and carried the packs of fuel needed to see. The soldiers' foreheads and tattooed eyes shimmered in the torchlight under their peaked helmets, their faces and chests painted black.

"What is this?" asked the centurion as they neared the glowing sea of blue.

"I don't know, but it gives light!" exclaimed a torchbearer.

The platoon stopped at the edge of the vast mushroom sea, their wonder-filled eyes glowing in its light. The centurion pointed his sword at the giant's tracks, which disappeared into the blue expanse. "They went through here."

"How?" asked another, mesmerized by the blue light. "Can we walk through it?"

"I don't know," said the centurion.

"Can we use these things to light our city?" asked a torchbearer.

"Maybe. Will they burn?" asked another.

"Everything burns," scoffed the centurion. "Don't forget, we're following those who murdered our governess!" He pointed to two fighters and their torchbearer. "Clear a path!"

The soldiers nodded, lowered their forked spears, and started into the field, poking and prodding the giant mushrooms as they walked.

When a torchbearer lowered her flame to a knee-high toadstool, it smoked and sizzled. The centurion was about to step into the field when the sizzling mushroom, and those around it, turned red. The torchbearer's eyes widened with the gleam of an arsonist when the mushroom's cap opened. When the toadstool's red jaws burst out and clamped onto the torchbearer's arm, she cried out in pain.

The centurion and the others stepped back as the frenzied mushroom pulled the torchbearer to the ground. The surrounding toadstools sprang open, and their jaws tore into the screaming torchbearer's chest and legs. A fighter fell next. The others watched helplessly as the second soldier leaped back through the field, spearing the snapping mushrooms as he ran. He was nearly free when a jaw grabbed his foot and pulled him back in.

The wide-eyed centurion and the others backed away as the mushrooms devoured the bodies, leaving only their helmets and spears.

The horrified centurion closed his mouth and choked down a swallow. He pointed his sword at the edge of the sea and said, "We'll go around."

LONG PAST THE FUNGUS SEA, Michelle's band was hiking through a canyon with dark, craggy cliffs when Michelle set the heavy Franny down. It felt to her like she had been carrying him for days, and he seemed larger to her now. Michelle gave a worried glance back the way they had come, then asked, "Are we still being followed?"

Remiel shook his head. "I don't think so."

"Good. How much farther to this mountain?" asked Michelle.

"Goash is still quite a distance," replied Gak.

Michelle sighed. "You're really not helpful at all. Are we halfway there?"

Remiel and Gak exchanged glances and nodded.

Michelle watched Franny skip ahead. She thought his pajamas were tighter on him now. She shook off the thought and asked, "What do we do if we get to this mountain and can't find the gatekeeper?"

"We will look for him," shrugged Gak.

"Well, what if we find him, but he won't let us pass?"

"Then you and the prince will not leave," shrugged Remiel.

Michelle stopped. "I'm just worried that we're coming all this way and don't have the orb."

Remiel stopped and turned.

"What do we do then?" asked Michelle.

"Forgive me, but why do you worry about something beyond your control?" asked Remiel.

"I'm not worrying. I'm just planning."

"It sounds like you're worrying," said Remiel.

Gak nodded.

"Well, maybe someone needs to worry a little here!"

"Will it help us to worry?" Remiel asked, turning to the others.

Og shook his head.

"Fine!" Michelle huffed. "But what if we need the orb?"

"Then we go back for it," shrugged Gak.

"Why didn't we get it when we were there?" asked Michelle, not hiding her frustration.

"Because we couldn't find it," said Remiel.

"And the dark dwellers were trying to kill us," added Gak.

Michelle was about to respond when she realized Franny was gone. "Franny? Franny?" she called out, looking to be sure he wasn't behind Og.

"Where did Franny go?" Michelle scanned the canyon walls on either side but couldn't see her son. "Franny!"

Remiel pointed to the boy's tracks. "This way."

"Franny?" Michelle called out. "Come back to Mommy, sweetie!" She followed Remiel toward the massive boulders lining the canyon wall and grew concerned when Remiel removed his sword. "Is something wrong?"

"We are near the Nalidi," said Gak with a hint of concern.

"What's the Nalidi?" asked Michelle.

When Gak spotted a larger set of footprints joining Franny's, he removed his sword.

"What's wrong? Franny!" Michelle watched as Remiel and Gak crept around the enormous boulders with swords drawn. She glanced back at Og, standing in the middle of the canyon, afraid to come any closer. "Og, aren't you coming?"

The giant's sunken eyes widened, and he anxiously shook his head.

Michelle gasped when she turned to a furry little man standing before her. She stumbled backward and fumbled for the blazerod in her bag. The brown-skinned creature was smaller than Michelle and had wispy dark hair on its head, face, and much of its body. It had a receding forehead, a wide, flat nose, and a protruding jaw. "Oh! Who are you?" she gasped, finally pulling the blazerod from her bag.

The hairy little man backed away when he saw the ancient weapon.

"You do not need that," said Remiel, appearing from behind a boulder.

When Michelle saw Remiel with Franny, she released a thankful sigh and rushed to her son. "Franny, you mustn't wander!" she cried, kneeling and embracing him.

"I went to see my friends," said Franny, pointing behind Remiel.

Michelle returned the blazerod to her bag as a bony female hominid with a wrinkled face and sagging breasts, and another male, smaller than the first, emerged from the shadows with Gak. The tallest stood only five feet, and all three had beady eyes and dark leathery skin. "Who are they?"

"They are called Nalidi," replied Remiel.

"Are they-are they human?"

"Nalidi are pre-human. They are part of the process of your world," explained Remiel.

The creation, thought Michelle. She looked at the male, but his worried gaze was on her bag that held the blazerod. Michelle turned back to the female. Unsure of what to say, she nervously smiled. "Hello."

The female cocked her head and looked at Michelle blankly.

"Can they talk?"

"Not in the way you think. They have not yet been endowed with the full measure of intelligence."

"Oh." Michelle didn't know what that meant. She glanced back at the male, still warily eyeing her.

"They are...familiar with the blazerod," explained Remiel.

Michelle glanced down at her bag and moved it behind her back. She then turned to the female, curiously eyeing her. Michelle didn't feel the disgust she often had with halfborns. Instead, she felt an overwhelming sense of sympathy for the creature. Michelle reached out her hand, and the female lifted hers. When their fingers touched, the female smiled, revealing brown, decaying teeth. "Why were they sent here?"

"I don't know. Most of the pre-endowed perished."

"Perished? From old age or something else?" asked Michelle.

"From other things," replied Remiel, looking down.

"The First Cleansing," muttered Gak.

Michelle stared into the darkness, wondering what that meant.

"Mommy, can they come back with us?"

Blinking out of her trance, Michelle looked down at Franny and smiled. "We'll see. We must find the way first."

"To go back to Papa?"

"Yes." Michelle turned to the small, hairy creatures and wondered if they were a family. She wondered if they felt joy or sadness. She wondered how many more there were in that dark and lonesome world.

MANU

SED's scarred face glowed in the orb's golden light as he moved down the dark passageway. In his raised palms, he carried the sphere as his red mantle shawl flowed behind him. Following the new governor limped a cloaked, lanky man carrying a scroll, his bushy white eyebrows and long, thin beard bent in the passageway breeze. The dark wizard's eyes were astute with the secret knowledge of the ancients. Two female guards shod in leather and copper breastplates followed with spears in hand. The last of the procession was the orange-robed master of flame, who carried a flickering lantern raised on a pole.

The governor's procession moved farther into the belly of the underground city until the dark passageway opened to a spacious hall. Inside the arched room, torches cast long shadows behind towering pillars and flickered off the hundreds of faces eager to view the new governor of Manu. But the torchlight was insignificant compared to the orb's radiance, which lit Sed like a tiny sun. The dark dwellers kneeled in awe and touched their tattooed eyes as Sed passed, but his gaze was fixed on the outstretched orb.

At the end of the great hall stood tall bronze doors that reached halfway up the thirty-foot ceiling. Dozens of reliefs depicting a forgotten world adorned the door's faces. Before the arched doorway stood two hulking guards, their forked spears crossed to block entry.

As Sed approached, the guards uncrossed their spears and pushed open the lofty doors to an enormous, unlit chamber. After the procession passed through, the heavy doors groaned closed. The cavern air was dank and brisk and echoed with each step. With only the orb and the master of flame's lantern to light the expansive cavern, much of the underground chamber remained shrouded. Only the marble court and massive pillars that lined it were visible. Bordered by thick stone banisters, the marble court was thirty feet wide and twice as long, but a dark chasm stretched from the railing to the massive pillars and beyond, giving them the appearance of floating in the night.

As Sed walked by the orb's light, the court soon narrowed to a four-foot-wide bridge that spanned the dark chasm. Across the bridge lay a terrace with more stone banisters and columns covered in engraved symbols and glyphs. But the wide-eyed Sed looked past the stone columns to the enormous alloy ring fused into the marble floor. With each step, the orb's light reflected more brightly off the pewter annulus.

Standing just feet from the Dark Gate, Sed's gaze moved to the Eye of Ra carved into the cavern wall beyond. The governor's dark eyes gleamed in the orb's golden light as he raised it to the twelve-foot-tall portal.

After moving beside Sed, the dark wizard opened the scroll. His eyes were sharp and tongue crisp as he read an incantation.

The master of flame's eyes widened when the symbols engraved in the alloy portal shimmered, and a swirling blue cloud appeared inside its ring.

CHAPTER 23
ENIGMAS

It was a moonless night. A chilled breeze shuffled leaves across the empty street as a distant streetlamp glimmered. The large building was dark, except for a few windows that glowed with the light of night custodians. Bundled in coats and hats, Eli and Nazario waited in the shadows of the trees across the street. It was just before midnight that Eli spotted Pellegrini coming down the walk, his rapid shoe steps rupturing the stillness of the cool night.

"Here he is," said Nazario, a slight trembling in his voice.

When the stout Pellegrini reached them, he looked up and down the shadowed walk, then said, "You have it?"

Nazario pulled an envelope from his coat and handed it to Pellegrini.

The assistant curator peeked inside and pulled out three paper notes. When he noticed Eli's satchel, he asked, "You're not planning on taking anything out?"

Nazario's anxious gaze moved to the bag that held Eli's fantastic weapon. "Just our notes."

Satisfied, Pellegrini nodded. "This way."

Eli followed the two as they approached the long, four-story brick building. When they reached a recessed door, Pellegrini knocked three times, and the door swung open to a middle-aged woman in a work smock. After glancing up and down the empty street, she ushered them in and closed the door. The cleaning woman, who had a plain face and red hair pulled back in a scarf, stared at Eli as he removed his hat and nodded.

"Here," said Pellegrini, handing the woman 200 lire.

"Thank you." She pulled her eyes from Eli as she pushed the bank notes down her cleavage.

"You didn't see us," said Nazario.

The woman nodded, then quietly scurried down the dimly lit corridor.

"This way," waved Pellegrini, moving to a marble staircase.

Eli watched the woman disappear, then followed the others down the stairs.

At the bottom was a long corridor with caged lights hanging from the ceiling. Eli hesitated when a round-headed man in a blue uniform with a white sash across his chest and a pistol belt around his waist stepped under a light. He and Nazario watched as Pellegrini clopped down the marble floor and handed the guard money. The guard pulled an attached key from his belt and unlocked a black metal door. Pellegrini waved for Eli and Nazario to join him when the guard pushed open the heavy door. They hurried on tiptoes to the archive's entrance.

Eli breathed in the fetor of antiquity as they stepped into a dark and chilly room and waited for the guard to turn on the light with his key. With a click and a hum, overhead lights glowed to life, illuminating a central aisle with rows of shelves that ran more than two hundred feet.

"You have until six a.m. I will open the door then," said the guard, nervously glancing into the hallway. "If something goes wrong, I've never seen you before. I can't lose my job, you understand?"

"Yes, yes, nothing will go wrong," nodded Pellegrini, pushing the guard out and the heavy door closed.

Nazario waited for the click of the lock, then turned to Pellegrini and said, "Let's get busy. We have no time to waste."

Eli followed Pellegrini down the aisle between rows of shelves packed with dusty artifacts, boxes, crates, and books of all sizes. The watcher marveled at the human tendency to collect any and everything. Eli thought it wasted energy, but, in this case, he was grateful.

"This is only my third time down here," said Nazario as they walked, the end of the aisle coming into sight.

"We're underground?" asked Eli.

"Yes, the Vatican library is on the floors above us," said Nazario.

"This place is enormous. Is the library so large?" asked Eli.

"Four times. It has over twenty miles of shelves with millions of items gathered over the centuries," said Pellegrini.

"Most of it is forgotten and rediscovered every hundred years," added Nazario. "But they're boring things, mainly: the popes' correspondences, histories, treaties."

"Not all so boring," frowned Pellegrini, "Don't forget the Greek and Latin records. It holds the most extensive history of the world known to man."

"Pillaged by the popes' armies and brought back as a prize," smirked Nazario.

"You say pillaged; I say preserved," scowled Pellegrini. "It would all be lost if not for those armies."

Nazario gave a reluctant nod. "I've spent much time up there, most of my career, I'd say, but this is where the juicy stuff is."

"Juicy stuff?" asked Eli.

"The mysteries the popes have kept from the rest of the world," said Pellegrini.

"What mysteries?" asked Eli.

"Artifacts, ancient scrolls, and papyri—books the church removed from scripture that went against their narrative. Skulls of men not from this world. Proof that Jesus never lived. Proof that Jesus lived but had children with Mary Magdalene. Just about anything you can think of," said Pellegrini.

"Juicy stuff," grinned Nazario.

"Here we are," said Pellegrini.

Eli's eyes widened as the aisle opened to a vaulted space. At its center sat two long tables and six wooden chairs. The worn furniture was simple and came from another time. But the most prominent feature of the space was the giant clock built into the twenty-foot-high arched ceiling. The clock's smokey-blue face was a fresco depicting the cosmos with stars, planets, and moons. At its center, a single four-foot-long bronze hand pointed to the ten o'clock position. The clock's face was surrounded by a fresco of men and women clamoring toward its center.

"It's lovely, isn't it?" said Nazario, eyeing the clock.

"Yes," nodded Eli.

"It is said to be the clock of doom. Humanity's time is up when the hand strikes twelve," said Pellegrini.

Eli studied the clock. "But why is it here where so few can see it?"

Nazario shrugged. "Some believe such things are better left hidden."

"The real question is, who put it there, and how is it powered?" said Pellegrini.

"Indeed," nodded Nazario.

"Aw, who believes in such things?" said Pellegrini with a dismissive wave.

Eli turned to the assistant curator. "You do."

Pellegrini huffed.

Nazario glanced at his watch. "It's twelve-thirty. Let's get started."

Pellegrini noticed when Eli set his satchel on a table with a clunk. "What you are searching for could be anywhere in here, but your best bet is starting in the uncategorized section."

"My thoughts as well," nodded Nazario.

"May I look around?" asked Eli, still eyeing the clock.

"Of course," replied Pellegrini. He pulled a pair of white gloves from his pocket. "These are the largest I could find. Wear them to keep your skin oils off of things."

"Thank you," said Eli, taking the gloves.

"Just be careful what you touch. I don't need to tell you these things are irreplaceable."

Eli's gaze turned to a nearby shelf as the two Italians left for another part of the dimly lit library. The shelf stretched forty feet before reaching an end aisle and a wall. Eli walked down the aisle until he saw a stack of dusty scrolls bound by twine. He removed a scroll, but when he untied the twine, the string turned to dust in his hand. Eli's eyebrows raised. He blew the twine remains away and opened the scroll. It too began to break apart, but as Eli carefully unraveled it, he saw its faded text.

Eli looked up when Nazario came around the corner, pushing a cart loaded with books and a crate.

"What are you doing?" snapped Pellegrini, following behind. "That's ancient Egyptian papyri!"

"Yes, I know," nodded Eli.

"Be very careful with it! In your attempt to gain information, you don't want to destroy it!" glared Pellegrini.

"It's a letter from Rameses to Muwatal, the Hittite king, about the Battle of Kadesh," said Eli.

Pellegrini moved closer and looked down at the fragmented scroll. "You can read Hieratic?"

Eli glanced at Nazario, who had also stopped.

"What does it say?" challenged Pellegrini.

Eli turned back to the scroll. "It reads, 'The vile Chief of Khatti stood in the midst of the army that was with him and did not come out to fight for fear of his majesty.' It's missing a part, then 'the wretched Chief of Khatti stood among his troops and chariots... stood turning, shrinking, afraid.'"

"Impressive! You never said your assistant was a paleographer," said Pellegrini.

"Yes, he is full of surprises," replied an uncomfortable Nazario.

"Does it hold any secrets for you?"

Eli carefully rolled up the scroll. "It is no secret Rameses was a braggart and a brute."

Pellegrini laughed. "You say that as though you knew him."

"From his research," interjected an anxious Nazario.

"Of course," said Pellegrini, still eyeing Eli. "You read cuneiform, I'm guessing?"

Eli considered saying he had taught the Sumerians the ancient language but thought better of it as Pellegrini left to gather more artifacts.

"I could live in this place," sighed Nazario, looking over the packed shelves in wonder.

Eli's eyes narrowed when he noticed a worn burgundy book on the shelf between several drab leather-bound texts. He picked it up and blew the dust from its leather cover. He opened it to discover it was written in Occitan, an ancient dialect from Southern France.

"What did you find there?" asked Nazario, looking around Eli.

Eli turned back to its tattered cover page. "The Gospel of the Beloved Companion."

Nazario gasped. "You found it? Just like that? And it's intact! I've spent years searching for that text! What is it doing here?"

Eli shrugged and looked up at the other books and artifacts on the shelf.

"May I see it?" asked Nazario as Eli handed him the book. "Do you know how significant this book is? It is the record of Mary the Magdalene —Mary the Tower—of her accounts as Jesus's greatest and most beloved disciple. Following the crucifixion, when the persecution became too great, Mary, also known as Mary of Bethany, her brother Lazarus, and seventy of Jesus's followers fled Jerusalem for the south of France. She shared the Lord's teachings there, and the Cathar sect was born."

Eli recalled the sadness of the time.

"The Church had no tolerance for Mary's doctrine and what the Cathars called the Sacred Feminine. Their persecution was relentless until Pope Innocent the Third ordered their massacre in 1209 AD. The crusaders murdered twenty thousand men, women, and children—most of them were burned at the stake." Nazario shook his head, shuddering at the thought. "The Church captured this book. It is said to contain Mary's gospel—different from the gospels we now have in the New Testament— and the bloodline of the Lord Jesus!"

"Emmanuel's bloodline," said Eli, realizing the significance of the find.

"Yes! Through his wife, Mary the Tower!"

Eli's gaze grew distant as he wondered where Michelle, a descendant of that very bloodline, was now. With a sigh, Eli returned to the table as a wide-eyed Nazario delicately turned the pages of the ancient text.

BY 4:30 a.m. Pellegrini had nodded off in a chair, and Nazario was yawning as he flipped through a two-hundred-year-old inventory ledger, no closer to finding information on a portal or a domain sphere.

"Here's another reference to *Portam ad inferno*, the gateway to hell. But, like all the others, it leads nowhere," sighed Nazario.

Eli nodded as he sifted through another crate of artifacts.

"Either the references lead to dead ends, or if there is a link, the information is missing. It's as though someone intentionally purged any evidence of your gateways."

Eli wondered if one of his own might have removed the evidence.

"There's no way we can find what we're looking for tonight. It could take days, weeks," groaned Nazario, closing the dusty text.

Eli removed a patinated brass plate and studied its faded engravings, then said, "Ibn Umayl wrote this."

Nazario pulled off his glasses and turned to the plate. "Who is Ibn Umayl?"

Eli glanced at the dozing Pellegrini, then said, "He's a traveler."

"A traveler. You mean, like a nomad?" asked Nazario.

"Not as you're thinking. Travelers have many tasks. They may act as couriers between worlds, or they may be assigned to operate or protect a portal."

"You mean a star gate?" whispered an excited Nazario.

Eli nodded.

"What does it say?"

"It speaks of Hathor's Gate."

"The Egyptian goddess Hathor?" asked Nazario.

"Yes."

Eli turned back to the plate. "It speaks of its use—misuse, really, in sending unpleasants to the dark realm."

"The abyss?"

Eli nodded.

"What are unpleasants?" asked Nazario.

"It's complicated, but in this sense, he's talking about the gate as a punishment for political dissidents."

"They made rivals disappear," said Nazario, with an understanding nod.

"Exactly."

"Does it offer any helpful information?"

Eli shook his head. "Just a reference to the doorway, but..." Eli studied the plate. "This was written around 800 BC, and it speaks as though the portal is still active."

"Where is this doorway?"

"Hathor's Gate was in Egypt. I've traveled it many times, but it was to be deactivated. It shouldn't have still been in use."

"Could it still work?"

"Possibly," said Eli, his eyes shifting in thought.

Nazario looked at his watch. "We have only an hour. We must narrow our search to Egypt."

Pellegrini snorted as he stirred from his sleep. "Yes? Have you found something?" he asked, reorienting himself.

"Perhaps. What else do they have from Egypt?" asked Nazario.

"What do they not have? The ancient Romans were fascinated by that place. They brought shiploads of things back, including the obelisks. There may be as many artifacts in Rome as there are in Egypt," laughed Pellegrini.

"What is there on Hathor? On her mystical doorway or gate?"

"The sky goddess. Hmm. The Egyptians believed she guarded the doorway to the afterlife." Pellegrini sat up, pulled an ancient leather-bound book from under a pile, and opened it.

"What's that?" asked Nazario.

"In the Middle Ages, monks spent their lives copying decaying scrolls. If there is anything on Hathor, it will be in here."

Eli and Nazario moved closer.

Pellegrini scanned the faded, three-hundred-year-old script. His gloved finger stopped on a reference, and he turned back to the rows of shelves. After glancing at his watch, Pellegrini ran down the aisle, leaving Eli and Nazario looking at each other.

"What did you find?" asked Nazario when Pellegrini returned.

"Something I haven't noticed before." Pellegrini set down two thick, dusty volumes with faded Latin script on their spines. He blew off the dust, opened the first book, and carefully flipped through its pages. "Not here," he said, closing it and turning to the next.

Eli watched searchingly as Pellegrini's gloved finger hovered along the pages, careful not to touch the aged ink.

"Here." Pellegrini pointed. "This speaks of the Lateran Obelisk. It's the largest and oldest in Rome."

"How old?"

"From its inscription, at least three thousand years. Some think older."

"How many monuments like this are there in Rome?" asked Eli.

"As I said, the Romans were fascinated by the Egyptian world. We have thirteen obelisks in the city now, but many more were brought from Egypt. Most have been lost to time. In Egypt, these monuments were built and stood in pairs. Each told a story, which pharaoh had it commissioned, which god it was honoring. The Lateran Obelisk is no different. It has a counterpart. It was believed their symmetry gave them power, so the Romans would bring one and not the other to share in that power. To have a connection from Rome to Egypt, you might say."

"To think they so beautifully carved such things from granite so long ago," said Nazario.

Eli nodded.

Pellegrini's eyes narrowed. "Strange. I don't remember this part." He pointed to the copied hieroglyphs drawn in the book, covering the four sides of the stone monument from head to foot. "This bottom part is different."

Nazario moved closer. "How is it different?"

"It's not on the obelisk in front of Lateran Cathedral." Pellegrini sat back in thought. "Of course, Pope Sixtus had it removed."

"Removed?" asked Nazario.

"Yes," nodded Pellegrini, it all coming together for him now. "Constantine's son, Constantius the Second, had this obelisk erected in the center of Circus Maximus in 357. It was the meta, the turning point for the great chariot races. Little is known about what happened to it after that, but in 1500, it was discovered buried in the mud. Pope Sixtus, like the ancient Romans, was fascinated by the Egyptians. He had all the obelisks he could find restored and Christianized. But for some reason, he had the bottom ten feet of this obelisk cut off before re-erecting it."

"Why?" asked Nazario.

"I don't know. But the monks made drawings of it before it was removed."

"Can you read what it says?" asked Nazario.

Pellegrini squinted. "It speaks of Shu honoring his father, 'the great son of the sun,' and his mother Hathor, 'whose house opens to... the heavens,' I think. Curious."

"What?" asked Nazario.

"It doesn't speak of Ra as his father, but of another. I don't know this name." Pellegrini shook his head. "I'm afraid there are others better at reading these things."

"It says, 'in honor of his father, the great shining god, Lu,'" said Eli.

"Who's that?" asked Pellegrini.

Eli sighed and continued. "And his mother Hathor, whose door opens to the world where demons and worshipers of false gods are cast."

"Can you read what it says on this side?" asked Pellegrini, pointing to an adjacent drawing of the obelisk's missing base.

Eli studied the copied hieroglyphs for a moment, then shook his head. "It refers to Hathor's Gate, but some of the monk's text has been scratched out."

"Strange," frowned Pellegrini.

Nazario stroked his mustache. "Do you think its sister monument would tell the same story?"

"Perhaps. If you could find it," replied Pellegrini. "It's no doubt buried under an ocean of sand."

Nazario turned to Eli. "Do you think you could find your answer there?"

"Perhaps," nodded a contemplating Eli.

"Do you know where in Egypt that obelisk came from?" asked Nazario.

"Luxor," nodded Pellegrini.

"So that's it!" said an eager Nazario. "We go to Luxor and find its fellow obelisk. It will lead us right to the gate!"

Pellegrini's eyes swelled with the revelation.

Eli turned to the curator. His brow tightened as he discerned something new in the man.

Pellegrini grabbed Eli's satchel and backed away from the table.

"What are you doing?" scowled Nazario.

A wide-eyed Pellegrini gulped as four German soldiers with pistols drawn appeared from around the row of shelves.

"What?" gasped Nazario as the baggy-eyed Guerre emerged from behind the Nazis.

"I'll take that," snarled Guerre, snatching the satchel from Pellegrini.

"What have you done?" glared Nazario.

Pellegrini shrugged. "The Germans pay well."

"What are you going to do to us?" fretted Nazario, eyeing the soldiers' drawn Lugers. "Turn us over to the Vatican police?"

Guerre laughed. "I think not."

"May I leave now?" asked Pellegrini.

"Not yet." Guerre turned to Eli and sneered, "You have been quite helpful. You have led us along the path every step of the way. I don't think I could have found it without you."

"You've found nothing," glared Eli.

"That's not true," grinned Guerre. "The clues in Scotland were very helpful. It's a shame what happened to your friends after you left."

"What did you do?"

"Let's just say there is one fewer of your ilk to get in the way. And one fewer of mine, as well," laughed Guerre.

Eli's jaw tightened.

"You led me to the orb in the abbey. That was quite a find. Very impressive," nodded Guerre.

"That was me," muttered Nazario, immediately wishing he'd said nothing.

"What happened to the orb in Carnac?" asked Guerre.

"They took it," frowned Eli.

"The Great Ones?" Guerre laughed. "Perhaps they don't want you meddling either."

A fuming Eli shook his head. "Who sent you? Lu?"

Guerre grinned.

"I'm sure he had something to do with the base of the obelisk being cut off."

"I shouldn't have to remind you that anonymity is essential to your kind's success," said Guerre.

"Our success was guiding mortal civilizations to greatness, not exploiting them to satisfy Lu's thoughtless ego!"

"Lu is many things, but he is never thoughtless," said Guerre.

"Cyrus sent you," seethed Eli.

"They are now one in purpose," nodded Guerre.

Eli disdainfully shook his head. "What are you looking for?"

"The same thing as you. The doorway to the abyss. The ability to control who leaves and enters that realm. The resources there are immeasurable when considering world conquest. It's too bad your wretched wife and child wrecked everything. Oh well, a temporary setback, Cyrus says."

Eli's face twisted with restrained fury. "Now what?"

"It is quite interesting seeing the human-polluted part of you creep through."

Pellegrini, who had been following the exchange in wonder, turned to Eli with a gasp. "You! You're a watcher?"

Nazario gave a frightened nod as he eyed the Nazi's pointed pistols.

"All of this time," muttered Pellegrini, his face fading in regret.

"The great and noble Elijah," sneered Guerre. "I'm afraid your feeble and corrupted journey has finally come to an end." The halfborn reached for the blazerod in Eli's bag. "Shoot them."

"What?" gasped a round-eyed Nazario.

"Starting with him."

Pellegrini's eyes widened when a Nazi turned his Luger on him. The curator was about to protest when a bullet pierced his forehead.

Nazario cried out in horror as Pellegrini dropped to the floor.

With his hand in Eli's satchel, the grinning Guerre felt the cold alloy of the blazerod. But when he pulled a flashlight from the bag instead, his eyes shot up to Eli, and he yelled, "Kill them!"

Eli pushed Nazario down before the Germans could fire and tipped the table on its side, knocking off the ancient texts and artifacts. Two rounds struck Eli before he could duck for cover. The remaining pistol rounds shot into the thick tabletop but didn't pass through.

Huddled on the floor behind the table with his eyes squeezed shut, the sound of gunfire rang in Nazario's ears as Eli pulled the blazerod from under his coat.

The frustrated Guerre turned and darted when bolts of light shot through the table, blowing the Nazi soldiers back ten feet into the shelves.

When the shooting stopped, Nazario opened his eyes and gasped at the wood-splintered hole just inches from his skull, an emerging bullet wedged inside. Peeking over the side of the table, the reporter gulped at the four Nazis with smoldering face and chest wounds. He groaned when he saw the dead Pellegrini sprawled on the floor. "What-what happened? Where's Guerre?"

"He's gone," frowned Eli, lowering the blazerod.

Nazario gasped when he saw the bullet mark on the side of Eli's face and the welt on his neck. "Are you okay? Do bullets just bounce off you?"

Eli touched the shallow cheek wound. "I'm fine."

"We must go! The police will come!"

Eli pushed the heavy table aside and searched the toppled books for the one with the monk's drawings. He then shoved it, the brass plate, and the flashlight into his satchel.

With his blazerod at the ready, Eli led Nazario down the long corridor, the reporter's eyes darting from row to row in fear of an ambush. When they reached the metal door at the end, Eli saw it was ajar. He sighed when he spotted the white-sashed guard lying in a puddle of blood.

Nazario looked down the dark corridor both ways, then tugged on Eli's coat. "This way."

Eli hurried with the reporter through the shadows. They had just reached the stairs to the main floor when they heard clomping boots and urgent voices coming down.

"What are we going to do?" strained Nazario, his eyes panicked.

When the cleaning woman who had let them in emerged from the shadows and waved Eli and Nazario to follow, they did.

The Vatican guards had just reached the archive level when the woman pushed the door to the cleaning room closed.

Inside, a wide-eyed Nazario caught his breath. "Thank you!"

"You are welcome," said the woman, eyeing Eli. Her wary gaze lowered to his blazerod.

Eli's eyes narrowed. "You're a halfborn."

Nazario gasped and backed away from the cleaning woman.

"I only want to help," said the woman, suspiciously eyeing Nazario.

"He's with me," said Eli, pushing the weapon into his bag.

Nazario gulped and nodded.

The cleaning woman turned to Eli with the look of an adoring admirer. "We met once before, outside of Troy. You were... It doesn't matter. What of the prince?"

Eli tried to hide his surprise at the question.

"Word has spread among us. We know he has arrived."

"If you're speaking of my son, he's in the abyss," said Eli, trying to hide his pain.

The woman's eyes swelled. "He will prepare the way, then Theia will deliver us."

Eli shook his head in confusion. "What are you talking about?"

"The Bringer of Light and the Harbinger will forever change this world in the end times. That is the prophecy," said the woman, her eyes wide and hopeful.

"The Bringer of Light," muttered Eli, his bewildered gaze drifting.

"We-we're on a mission to find him. A quest, I like to say," whispered Nazario.

"May the Holy and Great Ones guide you," bowed the woman.

Nazario jumped when he heard men's yells from the corridor.

"This way!" whispered the woman. She pushed a table aside, exposing an old iron grate in the floor. "Below is a storm drain. It will take you out of the city, to the river." She grabbed hold of the large grate with a single hand and pulled it free.

Nazario stepped back. He guessed it would have taken two men to lift it. He grimaced as he looked down into the dark, stinky hole.

"Here," said Eli, handing Nazario the flashlight.

When a hard knock came at the door, Nazario took the flashlight and lowered himself into the hole. A moment later, Eli was gone, and the heavy grate was back in place.

BERLIN, GERMANY
20 NOVEMBER 1933

GUERRE GOT up from the foyer bench when the tall chamber doors opened, and Hitler appeared with his aids and advisors. In an instant, the waiting reporters swarmed the chancellor, shouting questions and flashing cameras as those around Hitler guided him along the marble corridor. The eager reporters moved with the chancellor like a rugby scrum, trying to get his attention. When the clump of reporters and the Führer passed, the baggy-eyed halfborn raised his arm and muttered, "*Heil* Hitler."

With no particular allegiance to the German leader, Guerre viewed Hitler for what he was: one of his master's pawns. The greasy-haired halfborn stood a little taller when he spotted Lu following in a fine suit, holding his coat and hat.

Lu waited for the ruckus crowd to move out the door, then stepped to the unsightly Guerre. "Tell me."

"I followed him to Scotland, where I found another."

Lu's eyes narrowed. "Who did you find?"

"The one called Dina. I destroyed her and her child."

"Dina birthed a mortal's child?" laughed Lu. "Their hypocrisy is astounding!"

"Yes, master," nodded Guerre.

Lu studied the halfborn. "What of Eli?"

"He has a mortal with him. A reporter named Nazario."

Lu laughed. "And what are they after?"

"A portal or an orb, just as you thought."

Lu's chest swelled as he looked down the empty foyer in thought.

"I followed them to London. They found an orb in the abbey."

Lu's eyes darted back to Guerre. "They found an orb? Did you get it?"

Guerre gulped. "I did not. They fled with it...and your blazerod."

"WHAT?" bellowed Lu.

"I'm sorry, master!" cowered Guerre.

"It's a good thing I don't have it, or I would reduce you to ash!"

"I'm sorry, master."

"Did they open a portal with it?" fumed Lu.

"No."

"How do you know?"

"It wouldn't work, so they took it to Carnac."

"Why Carnac?" questioned Lu.

"The orb had lost its power."

Lu's gaze drifted off in thought. "Of course, Carnac. Were they successful in re-powering it?"

"They were not. The Great Ones took the orb from him."

Lu gave a bellowing laugh. "Of course they did! Eli has failed them, and they've cast him out!"

The still-cowering Guerre nodded excitedly, but he recoiled when Lu pointed a stern finger at him and growled, "And remember, do not speak the name of those who sent us!"

Guerre gulped and lowered his head.

Lu eyed the halfborn. "Where is he now? Don't tell me you lost them."

"No, master. After Carnac, I followed them to the Vatican."

"What did they find?"

"Books. Relics. A plate from the traveler, Ibn Umayl."

"But you let them go," glared Lu.

"No, master! They escaped! I had our people there helping me, but they had someone helping them too. We searched for them everywhere!"

Lu stroked his beard in thought. "They have the traveler's plate."

"Yes, master."

"Then they are searching for the same thing we are, Hathor's Gate. You will find them in Egypt."

"Where in Egypt, master?"

"They could be anywhere. Send word to our spies there. Have them be on the lookout." Lu's eyes narrowed. "Hathor is a sly one. She moved the gate without my knowledge, so it is a mystery even to me."

"Maybe you could ask her, master," shrugged Guerre.

"I would have to find her first," glared Lu.

CHAPTER 24

THE RIVER BURKOOH

THE ABYSS

The five had just reached the crest of a hill when Michelle noticed a fiery glow from atop a distant mountain peak. "What is that?" she asked, setting the increasingly heavy Franny down. "Is that Goash?"

"No. It is the River Burkooh," said Remiel.

"A river? But it's orange," frowned Michelle, spying the fiery streams flowing down its slopes.

"It is a river of liquid rock," explained Gak.

Michelle's eyes widened. "A volcano."

"It has grown," said Remiel, not hiding his concern.

"Do you think the flaming bridge is still open?" asked Gak.

"We will see."

"What's happening?" asked Michelle, turning from Gak to Remiel. "You said the mushroom sea has grown, and now this volcano?"

"This world is nearing its time," said Remiel.

"But you said this world is frozen in time. That it's a fallen world."

"Just as mortals have a life cycle—birth, life, and then death—so do worlds. They fill their measure, grow old, and die."

"But how can a world be alive? It's only rock and dirt."

Remiel turned back to Michelle, amazed that someone with such light could have so little understanding. "What around you do you see that is not alive?"

"The mushroom sea. That was alive," replied Michelle.

"And connected," added Remiel.

"Yes. But, the rest..."

"See with your true eyes," said Remiel.

Michelle studied the orange shimmering of the elements that comprised the ground on which they walked. She saw sprigs of grass that somehow lived in the perpetual night. She remembered the trees that seemed to breathe. "It is alive, isn't it?"

"Yes," nodded Remiel. "This world's time will soon come, and it will be changed."

"How will it be changed?"

"The River Burkooh will swell to a sea of molten glass. The Sea of Argasay will then seed new life."

"That sounds lovely, but what of those living here?"

Remiel turned to Michelle. "Those not freed will be consumed and become a part of its change."

"Freed?" Michelle gulped, distressed by the thought that so many believed her to be their liberator. "How long before that happens?"

"When it is time," said Remiel.

Michelle sighed and pulled Franny against her as she tried to fathom what it all meant.

As they walked, the landscape came alive with shifting shadows from the volcano's fiery light reflected off the low, dark clouds. The once flat ground was increasingly uneven, and its jagged basalt slowed the band's pace and frequently tripped them. Distracted by the shifting light, Michelle kept one eye on the curious Franny and another on the uneven trail.

When Franny called out in pain, Michelle hurried to him. Upon seeing his pajama feet were torn through, she hefted the boy. But after only a few steps, she put him down. Michelle eyed Franny's tight-fitting pajamas, which were now bursting at the seams. She remembered them baggy on him when they left Manu. "Franny, you've grown! You're six inches taller than when we started! How can that be?" she asked, looking ahead at the others now stopped.

Gak shrugged, but Remiel moved back to them. He studied Franny's features. Before a large toddler, Franny was now a boy. His face had matured, and his curly hair was longer. "He has grown."

"But how? You said nothing changes here," frowned Michelle. "How long have we been walking?"

Gak shrugged.

Remiel looked back the way they had come. "The spores."

"What spores? What do you mean?" asked Michelle.

"It must have happened when we crossed the Sea of Argasay."

"I don't understand?" fretted Michelle.

"The mushrooms end and begin life. Their spores may have done this."

"Did they harm him?" Michelle asked as a button popped off of Franny's front.

"No," replied Remiel.

"But his clothes. He's bursting out of them."

"My feet hurt," whined Franny.

Michelle kneeled and groaned when she discovered his dirty and callused feet. "I can't carry you anymore. You're too big."

"Og can carry him," said Remiel, looking up at the nodding giant.

"I have an idea," said Gak. Stepping forward, he removed his dagger and cut off Franny's sleeves. He stooped and pulled them onto Franny's feet, doubling the extra length under them. Then, moving to Og, he reached for a two-foot strand dangling from his robe. Before cutting the thick thread, Gak looked up at his friend for permission.

Og reluctantly nodded.

After trimming off the strand, Gak wrapped it around Franny's foot, then did the same with his other.

"That was a splendid idea!" beamed Michelle.

Pleased, Gak bowed and stepped away.

"Will you tell Monsieur Gak thank you?" prodded Michelle.

"Thank you, Monsieur Gak," smiled Franny.

"You're welcome, my prince," nodded Gak.

"There, can you walk now?" asked Michelle.

Franny took a few steps and nodded. But then pointed up to Og and asked, "Can I ride on Monsieur Og's shoulders?"

Michelle looked up at the shaggy giant, who nodded.

After climbing up Og's arm, Franny situated himself on a shoulder with one arm wrapped around Og's hairy mane. "Wow, I can see far up here!"

With an approving nod, Remiel turned, and the five continued toward the glowing mountain.

THE STEEP CANYON walls glowed red from the flowing river of molten rock. Michelle shielded her eyes from the heat as she looked down at the lava flowing a hundred feet below. "We have to cross this?"

Remiel's face shimmered in the magma's light as he surveyed the hellish landscape. "Yes, at the flaming bridge."

"I can see why it would be flaming," said Michelle as puffs of sulfur gas and spits of fire shot up from the river. She gasped when she looked up and saw Franny leaning forward on Og's shoulder to see. "Be careful, darling!"

"I will, Mommy," said Franny, his face full of wonder.

They backed away from the edge when a part of the cliff across the gorge fell into the molten river with a fiery plop.

"We should hurry," urged Remiel.

Michelle scurried along the rocky trail behind the watcher with frequent glances at Franny swaying atop Og's shoulder. Her face filled with concern when they came to a partially collapsed stone bridge that arched across the sixty-foot gorge. Split down its length, half of the bridge was missing. The broken and uneven span near the center narrowed to just two feet. Only its stone side wall was intact. "Is that it? We're crossing this?"

"Yes. Quickly!" Remiel glanced back at the others, then started across the bridge.

"Wait!" cried a panicked Michelle.

"There is no time, my queen," said Gak.

A tight-fisted Michelle gasped when more of the bridge fell behind Remiel, tumbling to the flowing lava below. She held her breath as the watcher rushed across the narrowest span, his arms outstretched for balance. She sighed in relief when he reached the far end.

"My queen, you and the prince should pass next," said Gak, motioning for Og to lower the boy.

Michelle's wide eyes shot to Franny as Og set him down. "Take my hand. If the bridge can hold Remiel, it should hold us." She glanced back at the giant. "But what of Og?"

A wary-eyed Og looked from Michelle to the failing bridge.

"We shouldn't linger!" called Remiel from across the gorge. "The air is not good here."

"Come on, Mommy," said Franny, leading the way.

Michelle gave a jittery nod. Then, with Franny's hand clamped in hers, she followed him onto the crumbling stone bridge. "Don't let go," Michelle breathlessly said as she put all of her weight on the cobbled platform. It felt solid, and she took another step. But when the ground rumbled and a wave of hot sulfur gas washed past them, Michelle felt the bridge shift beneath her.

"You must come across!" yelled Remiel.

"Come on, Mommy," urged Franny, pulling her hand. "It will be okay."

Michelle drew in a worried breath and took another step. Franny nodded his encouragement and pulled her along. Choking on the toxic air, they shuffled halfway across the bridge but slowed when they reached its crumbling middle. The stone arch that gave the bridge support from below was all but gone on the left side, leaving the cobbled platform stones teetering. After pulling Franny back from the edge, Michelle glanced at the waving Remiel and cried, "I don't think we can cross here! It's too narrow!" She gasped and pulled Franny against her when another stone fell, leaving only a foot-wide expanse beside the still-solid parapet.

"You must trust in yourself!" called out Remiel. "You must trust in your son!"

"I do! I just don't trust the bridge!"

"Keep hold of the side!" coached Gak from behind.

Michelle gulped as she surveyed the failing bridge. The narrow span ran eight feet before widening again. She felt the stone side rail and thought it solid. "Hold tight to Mommy!" She clutched Franny with one hand and the stone railing with the other. It was warm to the touch. Michelle held her breath as they inched across the narrow span, just inches of stone between them and the molten river below. She tried not to look down.

They were halfway across the narrow strip when Michelle heard a buzzing sound. She froze, fearing the bridge was collapsing, and gasped when she spotted the roiling cloud of black swarming toward them.

"The dark elements!" warned Remiel.

With a new sense of urgency, Michelle and Franny edged along the narrow span. They hadn't reached solid footing when two stones gave way under Franny, dropping him off the bridge. "FRANNY!" shrieked Michelle. She fell to her knees, clutching the dangling boy by the hand. "Franny! Hold on!" she cried as Remiel raced across the bridge from one side and Gak the other. But before they could reach the struggling Michelle, the dark cloud split in two. One cloud rolled in on Remiel, and the other swarmed Gak, immobilizing them both.

"Franny! Don't let go!" Michelle gasped as the hot bridge stone burned her knees. Holding the bridge railing with one hand and Franny with the other, her tipped shoulder bag hung between them, with the blazerod slipping out. With all her might, she pulled Franny up to her.

The dangling Franny seemed unafraid as he reached his free hand to a protruding stone beam and pulled himself up.

But when the blazerod dropped out of Michelle's bag, Franny released the beam to catch it.

"NO!" cried Michelle, as Franny slipped from her grasp. "It's okay; let it go! Take hold of me! I can't hold you much longer!"

Franny shook his head. "No, Mommy, you will need it."

The straining Michelle tried not to look at the burning lava below as she pulled her son up to her. Franny's elbows were on the bridge when the black cloud split again and attacked the stone supports. Michelle gasped when she felt the bridge shudder and saw another piece fall. "No! Leave us!" she cried.

The roiling cloud thinned briefly, then surged back, weakening the mortar that bound the failing bridge. Michelle lost her hold when another stone gave way and fell forward, nearly dropping Franny.

"Leave us!" commanded Michelle.

The cloud backed away for a moment.

She saw a kneeling Gak overcome on the bridge, smothered by the dark billowing cloud. Remiel was just as incapacitated. On the far side, Og watched helplessly.

When the cloud attacked the bridge again, Michelle felt another shudder. She wondered how much longer she could keep hold of Franny.

A major arch stone was working its way free when a glaring Franny yelled, "My mommy said to go away!"

The dark billowing cloud rolled back on itself, faded, and then disappeared.

A freed Gak lifted his head and wheezed, "The prince can control the dark elements too!"

Recovered from the attack, Remiel hurried along the parapet beside Michelle. He reached down to Franny and pulled him up as the bridge shifted under them. "Quickly! To the other side!" exclaimed Remiel as he helped Michelle to her feet. With Franny under his arm, he took Michelle by the hand, and they dashed across the teetering bridge onto solid ground. Remiel turned back to Gak and Og and yelled, "The bridge is failing! We must part here!"

The stubborn Gak charged forward and leaped across the fallen expanse. But when he landed on the other side, the pavers gave way beneath him. Gak lunged for the solid bridge stone but fell short. With his legs dangling, he clawed at the pavers to gain traction and pull himself up, but the halfborn continued to slide back.

When Remiel saw his friend in peril, he started back across the bridge, but stopped when another section fell away. "Hold on!" he yelled, but Gak's grasp was not enough, and he was slipping off the teetering ledge.

Unable to watch the halfborn fall to his fiery death, Michelle was about to turn away when Og charged across the bridge, his mace in one hand, the frays of his tattered robe streaming. Her eyes widened when the giant leaped onto the parapet and scampered along the narrow stone wall like a tightrope walker. But Og's heft was more than the bridge could bear, and the wall crumbled behind him.

Michelle gasped when the light-footed Og reached the clawing Gak. The giant reached down with his massive hand while balancing with his mace. He pulled the wiry halfborn up to him like a hawk snatching a field mouse. Then charged across the crumbling bridge as all but a narrow span collapsed into the flaming river. As Og leaped the final length, Michelle pulled Franny to her. The giant landed on solid ground with the grace of a dancer. But Gak tumbled hard, bouncing off a boulder before coming to a stop at Remiel's feet.

Grimacing in pain, Gak looked up at the shaggy giant and barked, "What was that?"

"He saved you!" exclaimed an astonished Michelle. "You should be grateful!"

Og nodded.

Gak rubbed his head as he climbed to his feet, then muttered, "Thank you, but I was doing just fine."

Og cocked his head.

Gak looked back at the narrow strip of bridge remaining and said, "We won't be going back that way."

"Hopefully, we're not going back at all," said a worried Michelle.

Remiel surveyed her and Franny. "Are you unhurt?"

"Yes," sighed Michelle. "That's twice you've saved me. Thank you."

Remiel bowed.

Michelle brushed the dirt from her dress and cape and looked away, denying her attraction to the watcher. "Now, what do we do?"

"We go to the mountain," said Gak, giving Og a sideways glance as he pushed past.

"Fine, but do you think we can rest for a bit? That was a little draining," Michelle said, glancing back at the fiery gorge.

"Yes, but not here," said Remiel.

A coughing Michelle pushed the blazerod into her bag and said, "Lead the way."

When the centurion and his remaining troop reached the fiery gorge, they looked down at the flowing river in horror.

"How do we cross that?" gasped a fighter.

The centurion scanned the rocky precipice until he spotted the narrow remains of the flaming bridge. "There. That is how they crossed," he said, pointing with his sword. He waved the platoon forward, and they reluctantly followed.

The fighters' resolve weakened with each step closer to the narrow span of teetering stone. "We cannot cross that!" exclaimed a torchbearer, his face glistening in the lava light.

"They crossed it. With a giant!" barked the centurion.

"But it's not safe," muttered his pug-nosed lieutenant.

"You work us too hard," muttered a fighter in the rear.

"Who said that?" snapped the centurion, spinning around.

None owned up to the comment.

The centurion scanned the tattooed faces flickering in the torchlight and sneered, "Then perhaps we should go home and not avenge the governess's death."

A torchbearer said, "The governess would not expect so much from us."

"The governess is dead!" barked the centurion. "May her fire forever burn! Sed is now Ra's appointed governor, and he commands us! He will make our people mighty again! Now, who is with our governor and me?"

The lieutenant looked over the edge into the molten river and shook his head. "We cannot avenge the governess if we are all dead."

"Good point," nodded the centurion. "Who thinks we should turn back without the heads of those who entered the governess's chamber and murdered her?"

After nervously glancing at the others, the lieutenant raised his hand. Several more followed.

The centurion's hand tightened around his sword, and with a quick slash, he sliced open his lieutenant's throat. The lieutenant dropped his spear, staggered back, and clutched his throat as blood surged through his fingers. The others watched round-eyed as the centurion stepped forward, raised his boot, and kicked the gasping soldier off the cliff.

The rest of the platoon watched aghast as the lieutenant tumbled down the canyon wall. He was twenty feet above the molten river when his twisting body burst into flames. The soldiers gasped and staggered back when the river swallowed him.

"Does anyone else think we should quit now?" growled the centurion.

A few shook their heads and backed away, while others stared at the ground.

"We cross here!" roared the centurion. "The longer we take, the farther away they get! You first!" he barked, pointing his sword at a bearded fighter.

The fighter gulped, then turned to the narrow stone arch. After reluctantly moving to it, he looked down at the flowing lava, swallowed hard, and stepped onto the foot-wide arch that spanned the fiery gorge. Using his spear to balance, the bearded fighter scurried across the bridge to the astonishment of the others.

"There, you see! That is how you do it! You are now my second in command!" barked the centurion.

On the other side of the gorge, the bearded fighter raised his spear in triumph.

All eyes were on the torchbearer, next in line. But halfway across, he lost his footing and tumbled, screaming as he fell.

The dark dwellers exchanged nervous glances as the next soldier moved to the failing bridge.

The centurion was the last to cross. Only seven fighters and three torchbearers stood waiting on the far side, the rest having tumbled to their fiery graves. With a confident nod, the centurion moved to the front of his remaining troop, raised his sword, and yelled, "For our governess and the darkness she ruled!"

CHAPTER 25
ACQUAINTANCES

E li breathed in the sweet scent of jasmine and lotus as their boat glided along the western bank of the Nile River. He closed his eyes and basked in the warm Egyptian sun as memories of his time there returned. It had been over eight hundred years since Eli had last been in Thebes, and despite the challenges of that day, he thought it a simpler, more peaceful time.

"You seem to be quite enjoying yourself," said Nazario, eyeing Eli from under his straw hat.

"It is a fine day, wouldn't you say?" But it was not only the weather that calmed Eli. What the rescuing cleaning lady had said about his son had filled Eli's thoughts for the past two weeks. While Eli had never visited the abyss, he had heard the accounts of those fortunate enough to escape that dark and terrible realm, and he could imagine no worse place for his wife and child to be. But the thought that little François might have some purpose in being there comforted Eli and gave him hope.

"It's a bit warm for my liking," replied Nazario, blotting his glistening forehead with a handkerchief.

Eli gazed across the Nile to a fishing boat, its sails full, its four-man crew dressed in long cotton gowns or jellabiyas and their heads wrapped in turbans. "So many things look the same."

"Does impoverishment and lack of progress warm you?"

"Progress is only as good as the purity of intent it is founded on. Change for the sake of change is like a blind man wandering along a cliff's edge. It can go bad quickly," replied Eli.

Nazario's eyebrows raised. "You offer a surprise every day."

Eli gazed across the blue-gray river as they floated past lush green banks lined with shrubs, river grass, and date palms. The desolate brown Theban Hills rippled in the distance under the crisp blue sky.

"This Egyptologist you speak of, do you think he will help us?"

Eli turned to the reporter with a heavy sigh as the peace he had felt for a time left him. "Yes, he will help us."

"Ah, here's the dock," said Nazario as a simple pier stretching along the bank came into view. His eyes widened when he spotted a long, sleek torpedo boat flying the bright red Nazi flag. "What's that?"

"A German attack boat," frowned Eli.

"What are they doing here?"

Eli surveyed the gray boat with its heavy machine guns mounted near the stern. He spotted a single crewman looking at him through binoculars. "From now on, we can assume Lu's spies to be everywhere."

Nazario gulped and glanced down at Eli's shoulder bag. He took comfort in the otherworldly weapon.

A FINE LAYER of dust was pasted to Nazario's face when their horse and carriage came to a stop. When the reporter looked back, he saw only the tops of the palms and a gray slice of the river they had left two hours before. Everything else was brown and desolate. Nazario listened as Eli spoke in Arabic to their dark-skinned driver, whose worn white turban was stained with years of sweat.

"He's working up there," said Eli, stepping out of the wagon, his shoulder bag across his chest. Loaded with his blazerod and sundries, it also held the ancient Vatican text and brass plate. While somewhat cumbersome, Eli never let the satchel out of his sight.

Nazario climbed out with his notebook and brushed the dust off his suit as Eli paid the driver. Ill at ease in the strange environment, Nazario followed Eli up the dusty trail.

As they ascended the hill, Nazario cocked his head at the sound of men singing. "What is that I hear?"

"Men at work."

Upon topping the hill, Nazario's jaw slackened at the valley below. Turned upside down as if by a giant ground squirrel, holes and piles of stony soil lay all around. Here and there stood wood scaffolding and ramps, and white tents and canopies for shade, but everywhere were men in turbans and jellabiyas, swinging picks, casting shovels, or carrying baskets of excavated earth. Nazario guessed there to be a hundred workers between them and the brown cliffs opposite the valley, and most of them were singing. "Remarkable!"

"Welcome to the Valley of the Kings," said Eli, taking it all in himself.

"You've been here before, I'm guessing."

Eli nodded. "Several times."

"Long ago, I suppose."

"Yes. It looks different now."

When Nazario spotted a man in slacks, an open shirt, and a hat over-seeing the sifting of soil under a large canopy, he pointed and asked, "Is that Carlisle?"

"I think so," nodded Eli, descending into the valley.

A few of the workers took notice of the new arrivals as they walked through the site, but most were intent on their labors as they sang in unison.

"What are they singing about?" asked Nazario.

"Right now, they are singing to the ancients of this land, asking that their labors will bring them blessings and not curses."

"Are they superstitious?"

"You could say that," nodded Eli.

When they reached the canopy with the large sifting table, the dusty Englishman turned to Eli with hands on hips and said, "Yes? Can I help you with something?"

Eli studied the man. He had the stern eyes of a foreman, the chest and arms of a man not afraid to do his own work, a nose broken from fisticuffs, and a full mustache. His open shirt revealed tanned skin and a brown hairy chest with touches of gray. "Professor Niles Carlisle?"

Carlisle's bushy brows tightened from under his hat. "Yes, who are you? This is a closed dig."

"We are not here to steal your discoveries but to add to them. My name is Eli Mansel. This is my assistant, Cleto Nazario."

Nazario straightened up, flattered the immortal regarded him as an assistant, then reached out his hand.

"I don't have time for you," huffed Carlisle. "I'm already behind schedule and quite busy, as you can see. So now, if you'll excuse me."

Carlisle was half turned when Eli opened his satchel and removed the patinated brass plate. "Perhaps you will have time for this."

The relic caught Carlisle's eye and turned him back to Eli. His gruffness melted away as he reached a tentative hand to the ancient engraved plate. "May I?"

Eli handed the plate to Carlisle.

"Remarkable," breathed the professor, holding it by its edges. "Where did you find this?"

"That is a discussion for another time. I see you are quite busy here," said Eli, taking back the plate.

Carlisle gulped, "Is that Twenty-Sixth Dynasty?"

"Earlier. What you would call Third Intermediate," replied Eli.

Carlisle's face brightened like a boy on Christmas morning. "Yes, I would like to discuss this further with you." His eyes darted across the torn-open valley in thought. "Could you join me for dinner tonight?"

"Yes," nodded Eli as an amazed Nazario watched.

"Oh," Carlisle reached for his forehead. "I forgot; my daughter is here visiting me. Would you mind terribly if she joins us?"

Eli nodded. "That would be fine."

"Very well then, tonight. Shall we say seven o'clock at the Sofitel?"

"That's perfect! That's where we're staying," beamed Nazario.

"Very well then. Please bring the plate with you," said Carlisle, eyeing the brass engravings as Eli pushed it back into his shoulder bag.

THE SOFITEL WINTER PALACE HOTEL was lavish even by European standards. Built to accommodate the wealthy Western tourists eager to experience that region firsthand, it sat on the east bank of the Nile and had a spectacular view of the life-giving river and the mysterious hills and valleys beyond. Inside, on the west wall of the hotel's sitting room, was a bank of tall windows with gold and burgundy velvet curtains. In the darkness beyond the glass, the city lights shimmered off the placid river. Below the tall windows sat plush couches and cushioned chairs around a lion-clawed coffee table. Lamps atop the end tables glowed off the golden-papered walls.

Nazario's polished shoes clopped on the parquet floor before quieting on the large Persian rug beneath the sitting area. He nervously adjusted his bowtie as Eli, dressed in slacks and a tweed sport coat, sat in a winged-back chair. "It looks like we're the first ones."

Nazario glanced back at the lobby and the grand staircase. He saw hotel workers in suits and red brimless hats with tassels on top, and fine-clothed Westerners sauntering into the dining room through open French doors. While he was always on the lookout for the baggy-eyed halfborn, he hoped they had finally given him the slip. But when Nazario saw a German officer seated beside a bronze-skinned man wearing a red, brimless tarboosh, his heart sank. "The Germans are here." Nazario looked away when the officer's gaze turned to him. "They're everywhere," he added under his breath.

"Their presence will only grow," frowned Eli.

Nazario's gaze moved to a grandfather clock when it struck seven o'clock. He stood when he spotted Carlisle approaching with a woman in a simple blouse and skirt.

"Ah, here are my new friends," said a strangely jovial Carlisle, dressed in an ivory suit, vest, and tie. His curious gaze quickly found the canvas bag at Eli's side.

"Good evening," said Eli, getting to his feet and shaking hands with the professor.

"This is my daughter, Penelope. She's visiting from Manchester."

Eli's jaw fell open when his gaze met the striking blonde-haired woman, her skin like cream, her eyes crisp gray, and her shoulder-length hair curled. She looked much the same as Eli remembered, only older, and her hair was shorter.

Bothered that she and her father would not be dining alone, Penelope gasped when her eyes met Eli's. "Ah! It's you!"

Neither Carlisle nor Nazario could hide their confusion.

"You two know each other?" asked the professor.

The surprised Penelope pulled her hand from her ample bosom. "Elijah is the one who saved my life crossing the Atlantic!"

"When the German U-boat sunk your ship?" asked Carlisle.

"Yes," Penelope breathed. She hesitated, then burst forward and wrapped her arms around the unprepared Eli. "I so hoped I would one day meet you again!"

The curious Nazario eyed Penelope when she pulled herself off of Eli.

"Thank you for saving my daughter," said an astonished Carlisle.

Eli nodded.

"How have you been?" asked Penelope, with the eyes of a still-smitten woman. "I've thought of you often since...since that night."

Carlisle's brow furrowed, even more curious about their connection.

"I've been fine," nodded Eli, unprepared for the distraction. "Niles Carlisle is your father. But, of course, you said he was an Egyptologist. I should have known."

"You-you look just the same as I remember. Not a day older!" said Penelope as Nazario's gaze moved between them. She put a hand to her face. "I must look affright! I thought it was just another fuddy-duddy Father was dining with."

Carlisle wrinkled his nose. "Penelope, we have some business to discuss that may bore you. If—"

"I'll be fine," smiled Penelope, her eyes glued to Eli.

Carlisle sighed. "Well then, let's get seated for dinner, shall we?"

"That's a splendid idea," said Penelope. She took Eli's arm and led him through the dining room's French doors while the other two watched.

Like the hotel's sitting room, the dining room had tall ceilings, flaxen-papered walls, and gold and burgundy drapes lining its tall windows. Their white linen table was near a golden fireplace, and a sparkling chandelier hung overhead.

With Nazario and Carlisle conducting most of the small talk, Penelope, who sat across from Eli, nibbled at her appetizer with frequent glances at the pensive watcher.

Carlisle cleared his throat. "Eli, I know all about Mister Nazario. Tell me about yourself. Where do you come from?"

"Yes. Where do you come from?" asked Penelope, leaning closer.

Nazario's eyes widened, hoping for a morsel of information that wouldn't count against his ten questions.

"Not from here," grinned Eli.

Nazario rolled his eyes.

"France, last I heard," smiled Penelope. "But that was seventeen years ago."

"That is where I still reside," replied Eli.

"By yourself?" probed Penelope.

"I have a dog and a housekeeper."

"His wife is away," added Nazario, immediately wishing he hadn't.

"Oh," said Penelope, her face dimming. "I'd forgotten you were married," she muttered before pushing a mushroom into her mouth.

"Well, now that we are all familiar, let's talk antiquities, shall we?" said an almost giddy Carlisle.

Penelope gave a frustrated sigh.

"My dear, if you think this might be tedious..."

"Yes, I know," nodded Penelope. "Don't mind me."

Eli saw Penelope was hurt but didn't understand why.

"Eli, may I see your plate again, please?"

Eli pulled the brass plate from his bag and handed it to Carlisle.

"I've seen artifacts like this, copper mainly, but the engravings are most intriguing. It appears to be hieratic but different."

Nazario considered mentioning that Eli could read the text but held back.

"Where did you find it?"

"It's from a private collection," said Eli.

"I see. So, this is not a recent discovery?" said Carlisle, unable to hide his disappointment.

"No."

"How is it that I can help you?" asked Carlisle, his interest waning.

"We're looking for something and need your help."

Carlisle studied Eli. "What is it you're looking for?"

"An obelisk."

"Well, there's no shortage of those in Egypt," chuckled Carlisle.

"We're looking for the twin to the Lateran Obelisk in Rome," said Nazario. "We understand the Romans brought it from Luxor."

"Why that particular obelisk?" questioned Carlisle.

"In the hopes it will have on it the information removed from its counterpart," said Nazario.

"And what information is that?" asked Carlisle.

"The location of Hathor's Gate," replied Eli.

Nazario looked at Eli nervously. From his years of researching watchers, the reporter knew he had to disguise his true intent to be taken seriously.

Carlisle sat back. "Hathor's Gate. The goddess?"

"Yes."

"Hmm. Hathor has a temple not far away in Dendera. I think I know the obelisk you're referring to."

Nazario's eyes widened.

"But as for a gate...I can't say I know of such a thing in Hathor's name," said Carlisle.

"In ancient times, the gate was near Giza," said Eli.

"I'm afraid most of my work is here now. After Carter's discovery of Tutankhamen, the Valley of the Kings is now all the rage. Not much is happening in Giza. Why is this important to you?"

Eli looked into Carlisle's eyes and said, "In ancient times, it was a gateway between worlds and dimensions."

Nazario coughed and raised a finger. "According to legend."

"Of course," nodded Carlisle. "Hathor was the keeper of the doorway to the afterlife."

"Yes," nodded Eli. "The plate you hold speaks of that gateway, of its misuse by the pharaohs to punish political rivals."

Carlisle's eyes narrowed. "You mean to suggest that it was a physical place and not just mythological?"

"Yes."

Nazario gulped.

An intrigued Carlisle studied the plate's worn inscription. "You can read it?"

Eli nodded.

"He has many talents," grinned Penelope.

Carlisle studied the plate. "If such a thing exists—and if we can locate it —such a find could rival Tutankhamen's tomb. The mythical doorway to the afterlife," he muttered, his eyes lost in thought.

When Penelope cleared her throat, Carlisle set the plate down and turned to Eli. "What kind of partnership are you suggesting?"

"We would pool our resources to find the gateway," said Eli.

"Hmm. What about the artifacts?"

"They would be solely your finds."

Carlisle sat back in thought. "What's in it for you?"

"Access to the gateway."

Nazario shifted uncomfortably.

"What do you mean, access?" asked Carlisle.

"Just that. The opportunity to use it," said Eli.

Carlisle laughed. "You want to use a mythical doorway to the afterlife?"

"Something like that," nodded Eli.

"And the treasures along the way belong to me?"

"Yes."

"What about Cleto here? What's in it for him?"

"He gets to write the story," said Eli.

Carlisle glanced at the uneasy Nazario, who shrugged and nodded.

"It sounds like a fascinating expedition," said a starry-eyed Penelope. "I want to go along."

Carlisle turned to his daughter. "You're going back to Manchester tomorrow."

"I can wait," said Penelope, eyeing Eli.

"What about your daughter?" asked Carlisle.

Eli's eyebrows raised, and he turned to Penelope.

Nazario noticed the watcher's curious reaction.

"Sybil is fine. She's almost seventeen and nearly on her own, anyway."

Nazario's eyes narrowed as his journalistic instincts kicked in, and he considered the timing. He wondered if more had happened between Eli and Penelope on that voyage than him saving her life. He wondered if Eli could be the girl's father.

"May I keep this plate for a few days?" asked Carlisle. "If I can verify what you say, I'm in."

"Yes," nodded Eli.

Carlisle sat back as the waiter placed his main course before him. He glanced at the mutton and rice, then turned to his daughter. "It would be nice to spend time with you, my dear. We haven't been on a dig together in years."

"Yes, it would," grinned Penelope, slyly eyeing Eli.

AFTER DINNER, they were leaving the table when Penelope took Eli by the arm and said, "Would you care to go for a stroll along the river? I promise not to fall in and drown again."

Nazario watched with wide eyes as Eli gave an innocent nod.

With Penelope's arm around his, she led Eli through the lobby and out the door into the cool night air. After descending the hotel's steps, Penelope pointed toward the river and said, "There's a lovely path right over there by the palms."

Eli looked up at the crescent moon in the clear night sky as they paused for a horse and buggy to pass. They crossed the street and gazed across the smooth, black river, the moonlight gleaming off it as docked boats gently swayed and bobbed.

"You were right, you know," said Penelope, still holding Eli's arm. "I was pregnant."

"You had a baby girl."

"Yes," smiled Penelope. "How did you know so much about me? Even now, it seems as though you can read my mind."

"How is she?"

"Sybil? Well, she's a bit of a chore right now, just like I was at that age, but she's the light of my life," beamed Penelope.

"You married again."

"Yes, but that was another disaster. I seem to have a penchant for choosing unkind men," Penelope said with a glance at Eli.

"I'm sorry."

"What happened to your wife?"

Eli sighed. "She's gone."

"She left you?" asked Penelope, perking up.

Eli nodded, not understanding the connotation.

Penelope eyed Eli. "Do you have children?"

"A son."

"Where is he now?"

"With his mother."

"He went with her?"

"She went after him," said Eli.

"Oh," said Penelope, not understanding. "How long ago?"

"Fifteen years," sighed Eli.

"You still miss her. I can tell."

"More than you know. I've been searching for her all of this time."

Penelope slowed to a stop and turned to Eli, her heart aching for a man with such devotion. She gave a slight shrug and said, "Sometimes people don't want to be found."

Eli studied Penelope. He sensed her intense attraction to him but dismissed it, telling himself it was the same draw that most mortal women had toward him.

"Has there been anyone since her?"

Eli shook his head. "No."

Penelope gulped. Her yearning gaze moved across Eli's broad shoulders and down his powerful chest. Even through his sport coat, she could see the definition of his chest and wanted to run her hands over his naked flesh. Penelope's heart pounded through her breast as she looked into Eli's placid blue eyes, his hair stirring in the breeze, his essence beckoning her. Penelope felt the same unquenchable desire for Eli she had on the transport ship so many years before. She had been with many men before and after meeting Eli, but none did to her what he did. Unable to restrain herself any longer, she raised on her toes, pulled down Eli's face, and kissed him.

When their lips touched, Eli saw a flash of light, and he was suddenly on a bobbing lifeboat in the cold, dark Atlantic, breathing life into the drowned Penelope. He felt her cold emptiness before the warming life force returned to her and her dripping body moved in his arms. Eli was next in his château, kneeling at Michelle's bedside, her lifeless gaze staring past him to the ceiling. Eli cried out from the unbearable pain as a wave of darkness washed over him. As the darkness cleared, a young man with curly blonde hair and steel-blue eyes emerged from the mist, reaching a hand to him. With a flash, the young man was gone, and Eli viewed piles of skulls and bones—more than he could count. Eli felt a terrible foreboding. After another flash, Penelope's visage returned to him, her eyes beckoning as she removed her robe, exposing her curvy, creamy flesh.

With a gasp, Eli opened his eyes. He tasted Penelope's lips. They were warm and full and drew him in. He felt passion and desire he hadn't experienced in years, but Eli stood fast, his chest swelling and his heart pounding.

After a moment, Penelope eased away. Licking the nectar from her lips, she curiously eyed Eli. While he hadn't engaged in her kiss, he didn't refuse her either. Undeterred by his lack of passion toward her, Penelope viewed the encounter as a brief quenching of her desire, a tasty appetizer to what could follow should she play her cards right.

"What was that for?" breathed Eli, knowing full well Penelope's intentions.

"For saving my life," grinned Penelope.

Eli's chest was still heaving as Penelope pulled away. She sashayed a few steps toward the hotel before turning back to him with an alluring smile. "I'm in room three seventeen should you become lonely."

Eli stared at her.

Once Penelope was out of sight, Eli released the pent-up human emotions he so often struggled to understand with a tortured sigh. He considered the strange vision. While Eli dreamed in his sleep, such manifestations were foreign to him. He wondered what it meant as he rehearsed the vivid images in his mind.

Eli stared across the river for a time, then turned back to the hotel's glowing windows. He wondered if it was wrong to allow Penelope to kiss him. But then he remembered seeing Michelle with Remiel in the abyss. He wondered what may have happened between them. Eli told himself Michelle would never betray their love, but he had been around mortals long enough to know their shortsightedness when it came to sexual desire. Eli wondered if Michelle could be so vulnerable.

Eli pushed those thoughts away. Michelle would be his wife and companion as long as she lived as a mortal. But then he wondered what it meant with her being in the abyss. She was no longer in his world. Eli groaned from the pain and frustration of it all. He wondered if he would ever find her again.

WHEN ELI RETURNED to his hotel room, Nazario was sitting near the open balcony door smoking a cigarette. The reporter watched as a pensive Eli pulled off his coat and sat on the bed. After mashing his cigarette in the ashtray, Nazario moved into the suite and eyed the watcher as he untied his shoes. "That went pretty well, don't you agree?"

Eli nodded, his thoughts a chaotic jumble.

"Do you think Carlisle will help us?"

Eli nodded.

"When do you think we will start?"

"After Carlisle examines the plate and is convinced the venture is worth his energy."

Nazario gulped. That was only part of what he wanted to discuss with Eli. "You knew his daughter?"

"Yes." Eli sighed and looked up at the reporter. "We met on a ship from America. She was fleeing a failed marriage."

"I see." Nazario wanted to ask if her child was his, but didn't dare.

"A German U-boat torpedoed our ship. Penelope drowned, and I breathed life back into her."

"I see. That explains her feelings of indebtedness." Nazario looked at Eli questioningly.

"She was already pregnant," muttered Eli.

Nazario's eyebrows raised. He stroked his mustache, then said, "In our weeks together, I have observed your effect on women."

"My effect?" frowned Eli.

"There is something women find irresistible about you. Case in point, tonight." Nazario studied Eli, then asked, "How does it feel?"

Eli turned to the reporter. "How does what feel?"

"To be so sought after? To be adored by women? Lusted after? I imagine it a dream of every man."

"To what end?" asked Eli, irritated by the question.

"To sleep with them, of course."

"But to what end? Satisfying a primordial desire? Do you have any idea what acting on such urges has done to this world? That was the downfall of Lu and the others. They exploited their power, mated with mortal women, and spawned a nation of crossbred halfborns and giants. It led to the Great Purge and nearly the end of this world. My kind swore to follow a code, the Grand Precept. In all of my time, I had never broken that oath...until..."

Nazario sat in a chair across from Eli. "Until you met Michelle."

Eli looked down. "You heard me tell Dina what happened. The German shell took my memory. My identity."

"And Michelle nursed you back to health."

"Yes," breathed Eli.

"That's when I heard of you. Stories of a soldier healing so miraculously."

"When my identity was returned, we were already married, and she was carrying our son."

Nazario's eyes narrowed. "You stayed true to your code before and since."

Eli nodded. "I must say, it has been more difficult since. I never fully understood the draw of sexual intimacy, but I do now."

Nazario longingly nodded.

"The connection, to be joined with another, not just to satisfy a hormonal urge, but to become one, to be complete, is like no other."

"I guess I can see it that way," said Nazario with a slight shrug.

Eli stared across the room in thought.

After a time, Nazario turned to Eli and asked, "Do you think this has all been a test for you?"

"A test?"

"Everything that happened: losing your memory and meeting Michelle. Did God or those who sent you engineer the whole thing?"

"You mean to get Michelle and me together?"

"You told me your son has a special calling. You also told me we mortals are often placed in circumstances to fulfill pre-ordained tasks, like puppets on a string."

"Not like puppets, but agents free to act," corrected Eli.

"You know what I mean."

Eli drew in a beleaguered breath, his gaze distant. "Perhaps."

"I think it's obvious."

Eli considered the notion. "Even so, we are where we are, looking for a way to rescue my wife and son."

Nazario nodded, then asked, "Do you worry Penelope will be a problem?"

Eli's gaze lowered to the floor, and he shook his head.

A knock came at the door, and Nazario got up and answered it. When he returned holding a note, Eli sat up and asked, "What is it?"

"It's from Carlisle." Nazario's eyes widened as he read the note. "He wants us to go with him to Dendera tomorrow, to the Temple of Hathor!"

"I guess he liked what he saw."

An excited Nazario nodded. "I guess he did!"

CHAPTER 26
MORTALS AND GODS

The Abyss

As Michelle sat atop a hill with the others, resting from their narrow escape across the flaming bridge, she surveyed the way they had come. The black hills and gullies glowed with the lava light. So did the low ceiling of clouds set on fire by the volcano's fiery peak. Michelle scratched Franny's back as she listened for sounds of life. She heard only Remiel and Gak's quiet conversation and Og's restful breathing.

Michelle squeezed Franny, kissed his head, and whispered, "You're growing so fast."

Franny gave his mother a curious look.

"How much farther?" asked Michelle, turning to Remiel.

"Two. Or maybe four," said Gak playfully.

"Two or four what?" Michelle shook her head. "You're just saying numbers. Where I come from, it's good to know where you are going and when you will get there."

"Why?" asked Gak.

"So we can plan our time."

"But we have no time here," replied Gak.

"I just want to know what to expect."

"So you can worry about it?" asked Gak.

Remiel scowled at the halfborn.

Michelle sighed. "Perhaps."

"Where you come from, you worry too much," said Gak.

"But that's how we get things done."

Gak turned to her and asked, "But does any of it matter?"

"Yes, of course, it does!" frowned Michelle

Gak shrugged. "To you, maybe."

"It should matter to everyone!" insisted Michelle.

"Remember, you're speaking to the Queen of Light," warned Remiel.

Gak's face dimmed, and he lowered his head. "Forgive me."

"No, really, I don't mind. I enjoy lively conversation," said Michelle.

Gak sighed. "We want to leave this place, but it won't be the same for me and Og."

"What do you mean?"

"We are halfborn. There is no place for us," said Gak.

"That's not true," frowned Michelle.

"It is true. That's why we're here. In the other world, I can at least blend in. But Og? He's hard to miss."

Michelle looked at the nodding giant with compassion. "Where else could you go?"

Gak shrugged. "There are other places, but they are like this. Who wants to be alone?"

"But I know there are other halfborns in my world," said Michelle.

Gak nodded. "Lu summoned many from here and has since sired more."

"Your brother Gik served Lu for a time, but something changed in him when Franny was born." Michelle ran a tender hand along her son's back.

"I saw my brother after Eli cast him here. He wasn't happy about it. I told him the prince was born among men and reminded him of the great prophecy." Gak's face saddened. "Then Lu summoned him back. When Gik saw the prince, he realized the prophecy was true. I'm sure that's what turned him. You and your son are the last hope for us. For those still living," said Gak, his sunken eyes distant.

"What happened to the other halfborns? Those who are not in my world or here?"

"Annihilated," muttered Gak. "By that." He pointed to her blazerod protruding from the bag.

Michelle eyed the ancient weapon.

"You said my brother served you?"

"Yes."

Gak sighed. "That gives me peace." There was a long silence before he asked, "What happened to him?"

Michelle gulped. "Gadreel killed him."

"With his sword?"

Michelle nodded.

"He took off Gik's head?"

"Yes," muttered Michelle. "I'm sorry."

Gak's sad gaze lowered.

Michelle scanned the dreary landscape, then turned to Gak and asked, "Has it been hard for you?"

"To be a bastard? To be despised by mortals *and* gods?" Gak shook his head. "We didn't choose this." He glanced at the listening Remiel. "We should not be punished for others' choices, only our own."

Michelle considered his point. "You say halfborns have a chance at redemption?"

Gak nodded. "That is the prophecy." He turned to Michelle. "Through you and the prince."

Michelle shook her head. "How is it that everyone knows about this but me? I don't know what I am to do!"

Remiel leaned forward. "You have forgotten. Your reckoning with who you are is part of your path." Then, seeing Michelle's confusion, he added, "We all have a path to our fulfillment. Understanding who you are is part of one's journey."

Michelle sighed. "It all makes my head hurt."

Franny leaned against his mother and said, "It will be okay, Mommy."

Michelle looked down at Franny and smiled.

CHAPTER 27
THE TEMPLE

Unaccustomed to seeing a woman in trousers, Nazario's eyes widened when he spotted Penelope walking along the dock with her father. Her silky blonde hair was tucked under a wide-brimmed straw hat. She wore a light coat over a blue blouse, brown leather riding boots, and tan riding trousers that flared above the knee.

"Good morning," said Penelope to all as Eli reached a hand to help her into the boat.

When Eli touched her flesh, a vision of a tall, desolate mountain flashed into his head. Eli blinked away the image as a grinning Penelope brushed by and whispered, "I was cold last night."

Eli only half-heard her flirtation. He was still pondering the vision when Carlisle, wearing a tan suit, stepped into the boat with a man in a gray jellabiya, turban, and striped tunic.

"This is Asim, one of my foremen," said Carlisle. "He will be accompanying us."

Eli studied the bronze-skinned man, who had a prominent nose, a thick gray mustache, and a black eyepatch. Eli tried to discern Asim but was unable. While Eli sometimes struggled to read people, he wondered if this time it was his failing power or from simply being distracted by Penelope. Eli glanced at her, eyeing him.

They weren't far from the dock when Nazario pulled his notebook from his bag and asked Carlisle, "What can you tell me about this place we're visiting?"

"The temple complex?" Carlisle glanced at his daughter, who had moved into the warming sun across from Eli. "Well, it's quite a large and well-preserved site. Nearly an acre, as it stands now. The structures there are from varying periods, some dating back thirty-five hundred years to before the Eighteenth Dynasty. The Temple of Hathor has much newer parts. We think Auletes rebuilt it in fifty-four B.C."

"The Egyptians worshiped Hathor?" asked Nazario, scribbling notes as Eli listened, ignoring Penelope's seductive gaze.

Carlisle nodded. "Hathor was a sky deity. She was the consort of the sun god Ra. This made her the symbolic mother of the pharaohs. She acted as the Eye of Ra, his feminine counterpart. She was rather vengeful and protected Ra from his enemies. Hathor was the consort of other male deities as well, and the mother of their sons."

"Is there any thought Hathor was an actual person?" asked Nazario.

Eli's curious gaze moved to Carlisle.

"She was strictly mythological," replied the professor. "Hathor crossed boundaries between worlds, helping deceased souls transition to the after-life." He turned to Eli. "This gateway you seek intrigues me. I did some research last night and found another reference to it."

"Oh?" said Eli.

Carlisle nodded and put a cigar in his mouth but said no more.

THE MIDDAY SUN had removed the briskness from the air when their boat tied off on the dock.

"It's getting warm. Will you help me with my coat?" asked Penelope, brushing against the watcher.

Eli held Penelope's coat and breathed in her fragrance as she pulled out of it, her unbuttoned blouse exposing cleavage.

"Thank you," she said with a coy grin.

"The temple complex isn't far, but I've arranged for some transportation to get us there," said Carlisle. He turned to the wide-eyed reporter and asked, "Do you ride?"

Nazario gulped when he spotted the waiting mules. "I suppose so."

ELI WAS ENJOYING the lush green fields and the shade of the date palms as he rode the overburdened mule, his feet only inches from the dusty ground. He glanced at a laughing Penelope riding beside him, then turned back to Nazario, four lengths back, holding his reins out like ski poles.

"Are you okay back there, Cleto?" yelled Carlisle, riding in the lead beside the one-eyed Asim.

"Yes," was Nazario's shaky reply, his mule following the others despite the reporter's confusing pulls and jerks on the reins.

"Ah, here it is, the Dendera Temple complex," announced Carlisle. "The tall structure in the back is Hathor's Temple."

Eli's eyes narrowed as the mud-brick walls and towering stone columns came into view. Soon they were out of the lush river valley and into a desolate plain where all was a dingy golden brown.

"Remarkable," called out Nazario, urging his mule on. "Is that the obelisk?" he asked, spotting its tip above the ruins.

"Yes, it is," nodded Carlisle.

After dismounting and tying up their mules, the explorers passed through the remains of the complex's gate past a statue of a headless sphinx and a wall of weathered hieroglyphs.

"Here's your obelisk," said Carlisle, stopping before the towering granite monument covered in engraved symbols.

Nazario's round eyes moved to the obelisk, but his excitement faded when he saw its base was bare. "What happened to it?"

Eli's heart sank as he walked around the obelisk. Its bottom eight feet was worn smooth on all four sides.

"Isn't this what you were searching for?" asked Carlisle.

Eli sighed. "This is the obelisk, but the inscriptions have been removed."

"Just like the one in Rome," muttered Nazario.

"There is still much to see here. There's an entire temple," Carlisle said, pointing to the ruins.

A dejected Eli nodded and followed Carlisle.

Soon they were within the temple's great vestibule, its forty-foot-tall engraved columns supporting a stone ceiling festooned with colorful hieroglyphs and relief carvings.

"Extraordinary," breathed Nazario, forgetting his disappointment as he viewed the ceiling.

"Take as much time as you like," said Carlisle, lighting a cigar. "I've been all over this place. I'd like to see what you can find regarding your mythical gateway."

"Is that Hathor?" asked Nazario, pointing to a depiction of a female with horns atop her head and a sphere within the horns.

"Everywhere is Hathor," replied Carlisle. "The faces atop the columns are her as well."

"What is the meaning of the horns and ball atop her head?" asked Nazario, opening his notebook.

"Hathor was a cow goddess, among other things. The horns depict that with the sun inside them, or the Eye of Ra," explained Carlisle.

Nazario moved closer to the searching Eli and muttered, "It looks like she has an orb atop her head to me."

Eli glanced at the reporter.

"What are the boats?" asked Nazario.

Eli was half-listening to Carlisle's explanation of the funeral boats when he passed the watching Asim. He felt something strange in the man, but wasn't sure what it was.

Penelope, who had been trailing the exploring Eli, perked up and said, "To me, it's just so interesting to think of the people who did all of this work thousands of years ago. Do you ever wonder about them?"

"Yes," replied Eli, studying the engravings and reliefs all around them. He had been there before, but the temple was different than he remembered. He recognized some columns and engravings in the hypostyle hall, but not others.

It was nearly an hour later when Eli started into a dim antechamber. Asim, who had the entire time been following him, handed Eli a flashlight. "Thank you," said Eli in Arabic, but the foreman only eyed the watcher.

"I'm going to wait out here," said a bored Penelope. "I don't care for the dark and cramped parts."

Eli said nothing but made his way through the next antechamber to the mouth of the sanctuary, a forty-foot-long and twenty-foot-wide dark chamber. Eli's conical flashlight beam cut through the blackness and cast shadows across the chiseled stone walls. The circle of light climbed the wall to the high ceiling before lowering and settling on a relief of a funeral boat moving carved figures to the afterlife. Eli moved the beam to a depiction of Hathor interacting with Ra. He saw her with other gods as well. Eli searched the side walls. When he spotted the depiction of an orb emitting rays of light, he paused. He studied the adjacent carvings, but something was missing. Eli shook his head and muttered, "It's not here."

"What is it you seek?" asked Asim from the door of the sanctuary, his voice deep and raspy.

Eli stopped and turned to the one-eyed foreman. Asim had not spoken in Arabic but Coptic, an ancient Egyptian tongue known by few. Eli knew it was a test and considered not replying. He studied the man, then asked in Coptic, "Who are you?"

"I am as my name implies."

"Asim means protector in Arabic," said Eli.

The foreman nodded, then asked again, "What is it you seek?"

Eli drew in a long breath. "Hathor's Gate. The portal to the other worlds."

Asim studied Eli. "You will not find that here."

"Where can I find it?"

Asim's eye narrowed.

Eli was on the verge of discerning the mysterious one-eyed foreman when an excited Nazario burst into the chamber.

"Elijah, I found something you must see! Down in the crypt!"

Eli watched Asim turn and leave the chamber. "What is it?"

"I don't know. Come see!"

Eli followed Nazario down worn stone steps to a long, narrow chamber with a low ceiling covered in reliefs and symbolic carvings.

"Look at this," said Nazario, shining his flashlight on an image of an Egyptian man holding a lotus flower with a long tubular shape and rounded end protruding from it. In its center was a long, wavy snake. "It looks just like a light bulb, don't you think? With the snake as its filament? What is it?"

Eli studied it and several other carvings of men using the same device. "It's a depiction of a blazerod."

Nazario's eyes widened, and he glanced at Eli's shoulder bag. "Of course! A beam with the bite of a snake! How old is that thing?"

"It is very old."

Nazario gulped. "Is there anything else here of importance?"

Eli scanned the crypt. "No."

"I found something else too!" said Nazario, pushing past Eli.

Eli followed the reporter back up the stairs to the hypostyle hall. On its high ceiling were reliefs of winged fowl.

"See there, the center one," Nazario said, pointing to not a winged bird but a winged sphere. "Is that what I think it is?"

"An orb," nodded Eli.

"They're saying it can help one fly, to travel, is that it?"

"Yes."

"Look, there are others!"

"How did I miss this?" muttered Eli as he moved beneath another relief panel with a sky-blue background. On it was a line of fourteen Egyptians ascending a ramp to a giant disk with the Eye of Ra inside. Behind the circular portal stood a watching Hathor. Above and below the ramp of travelers were smaller panels filled with hieroglyphs.

"Amazing," breathed Nazario. "What does it say?"

Eli studied the symbols, then said, "It speaks of the gateway to the other worlds and those journeying there, that Hathor is the keeper of the gate in this realm, and that good and evil pass through it."

"Look, they're even carrying bags!" laughed Nazario. "It's like they're in line to board a train!"

"It speaks only of the gateway and Hathor's command of it. Not its location," said a disappointed Eli.

"Did you find something of interest?" asked Carlisle, with Asim behind him.

Nazario pointed to the ceiling.

"Ah yes, Hathor guiding the dead to the afterlife. Is that the portal you're looking for?" asked Carlisle, his bushy eyebrows gathered.

"Yes," nodded Eli.

"Then there's another thing you would have surely enjoyed. Shame it's no longer here."

"And what is that?"

"The sky disk. The ceiling panel in the great vestibule," replied Carlisle.

"Show me."

"I can't. Not without booking a ship to France."

"France?" asked Eli in surprise.

"Yes. Your Napoleon liked it so much he had it cut and blasted out of the ceiling and took it to Paris! It's in the Louvre as we speak."

Nazario's jaw slackened. "Could that be what we're looking for?"

"Possibly," Eli said, his eyes shifting in thought. He turned to Carlisle and asked, "What can you tell me about it?"

"Well, it's a relief carving of a large round disk with the stars of the zodiac and travelers to the afterlife in its center. I have a copy of it back in Luxor if you'd like to see it."

"I would," nodded Eli.

"Does that mean we get to go back now? I'm famished," said Penelope, brushing up against Eli.

Nazario tried not to stare at Penelope's cleavage as she competed for Eli's attention.

"That depends on our new friends," said Carlisle.

Eli glanced back up at the ceiling reliefs, then said, "I would like to see your drawing."

"Very well," nodded Carlisle. He glanced at Nazario and said with a smirk, "Are you ready to rejoin your friend?"

Nazario looked out at the mules waiting by the entrance and groaned.

LUXOR, EGYPT

THE CALL to afternoon prayer echoed down the narrow street as Carlisle, dressed in his ivory linen suit and straw hat, navigated its littered walk. With a leather case in one hand and a cigar in the other, the archeologist passed a man seated outside his shop smoking a water pipe and another guiding his mule-pulled cart along the dirt street. After turning into an alley, Carlisle walked along the uneven pavers to a shop's entrance overflowing with glistening copper pots, dull horned instruments, vases, and figurines of all sizes and shapes. Inside the antiquities shop, more bright and dingy relics hung from the ceiling or were piled on tables and carts. Carlisle wound his way through the maze of antiques to a man wearing a suit, thick glasses, and a tarboosh. Standing behind a cluttered counter, the shopkeeper examined a coin through a magnifying glass.

"Shakur, peace," nodded the archeologist as he stopped at the counter.

"Ahh, hello, my friend," beamed the yellow-toothed shopkeeper. "I have not seen you for some time."

"I have been busy with my dig," replied Carlisle, his air of superiority on full display.

"Of course. Have you been well? You look well."

"Yes. And how is business?"

The shopkeeper shrugged. "Some days good, some days not. Have you brought me something?"

"How did you know?"

Shakur's dark eyes lowered to Carlisle's leather case. "Why else would you come to visit?"

Carlisle set his cigar on a tray, then opened his case and removed a flat, square item wrapped in a silk scarf.

The shopkeeper's eyebrows lifted when Carlisle opened the scarf to Eli's engraved brass plate. "Where did you find this, my friend?"

"It's a long story," replied Carlisle with a wrinkled brow.

"Meaning, you don't want to tell me," grinned the shopkeeper.

Carlisle's face grew more serious. "What can you tell me about it?"

"Hmm. May I?" the shopkeeper asked, pulling on white gloves.

Carlisle slid the plate across the counter.

The eager shopkeeper took the plate and examined its characters with his magnifying glass. "Yes, it looks first century. Maybe before. Very ancient."

"B.C.?"

"Yes, of course," nodded Shakur, still studying the plate.

"Then, it is authentic."

"Oh, yes," nodded the intrigued shopkeeper.

"Can you read it?"

"Some. It is written in an unusual style." The shopkeeper's eyes widened when he reached the bottom of the plate. "Ah, this explains it."

"Explains what?" asked Carlisle.

"Its author. The plate was written by the hand of Ibn Umayl."

Carlisle shook his head, not knowing the name.

"A very unique character, I would say."

"What can you tell me about the plate? Does it speak of the goddess Hathor?" asked Carlisle, his interest growing by the minute.

Shakur's large eyes narrowed through his thick glasses as he followed the text with his gloved finger. "Yes. I see it here."

Carlisle noticed when the shopkeeper moved the plate closer. "What did you find?"

Blinking in thought, Shakur set down the magnifying glass and looked up at Carlisle. "Will you sell this to me? I have a buyer who would be most interested. He would pay a high price!"

Carlisle shook his head and took back the plate. "It's not mine to sell."

"Shame," frowned the shopkeeper. "May I make a rubbing of it?"

"I don't think so," replied Carlisle, his thoughts going in four different directions.

"Pity. Then please come back with something you will sell me," grinned the shopkeeper.

Carlisle nodded, distracted by what might lie ahead for him, and muttered, "Be well, my friend," as he turned and left the shop.

CLEANED up and dressed for dinner, Eli was seated in the hotel's waiting area, and a saddle-sore Nazario was standing, looking out the window, when Carlisle came through the door. Eli sat up when he noticed the professor holding a framed illustration.

"Good evening," nodded the professor as he laid the colorful representation down on the coffee table before Eli.

"What's that? It's lovely," said Nazario, moving closer.

"This is what I told you about, the sky disk from Hathor's Temple. A colleague of mine in Paris copied and reproduced it. This print is a fraction of the size of the original Napoleon so desperately wanted."

Eli studied the tan disk. It had a sky-blue center with Egyptians traveling along its inner ring. White representations of the zodiac floated like clouds in its sky-blue center. On its outside, twelve Egyptians supported the disk at the clock hours. An outer ring and columns of hieroglyphics formed its perimeter.

"The color is striking," said Nazario, taking it all in.

Eli's eyes narrowed as he followed the copied symbols with his finger.

"Some of that has not been translated," frowned Carlisle. "At least, there is some debate as to what it says. I would like to hear your opinion, Elijah."

Eli studied the engravings for a time, then asked, "You're sure your colleague copied the original exactly?"

"Yes, of course." But when Carlisle noticed Eli's discerning gaze, he shrugged and added, "At least, that's what I was told."

Eli gave a pondering nod, then turned back to the illustration.

The closely watching Nazario recognized Eli's look of discovery. "Let me guess; we're going to the Louvre next."

Eli nodded to the reporter.

"Where is that daughter of mine?" huffed Carlisle, turning to the staircase with hands on hips. "Her tardiness will be the death of me."

"Here she comes," said Nazario, spotting her atop the stairs.

Eli pulled his gaze from the illustration and turned to Penelope, gracefully descending with her eyes on him.

"Nice of you to join us," quipped Carlisle, eyeing his daughter's low-cut dress.

"Oh, am I late? I must have lost track," grinned Penelope.

THE FOUR EXPLORERS were finishing their dinner when Carlisle wiped his mouth with a napkin and said, "Eli, I've given your brass plate much consideration. I've even had two antiquities dealers inspect it, and they assure me it is authentic."

Eli's face filled with concern. He hadn't approved of others looking at the plate and wondered what unwanted attention that might bring.

"As I mentioned, I have seen similar plates. Mostly copper, but a few that are brass, like yours. I think it worth a visit to examine them again."

"And where are these plates located?" asked Nazario, putting down his wineglass.

"At Saint Catherine's Monastery, in the Sinai. The monks there have an astounding collection of artifacts going back to Sumerian times."

"The Sinai Peninsula? Does that mean we're riding mules again?" asked Nazario, his seat still aching.

"No," said Carlisle with a dismissive wave. "That's much too far for them. We'll be riding camels."

"Camels?" gasped Nazario.

"Yes, it's quite a journey, ten days by camel, and we cross the Gulf of Suez in the middle."

"Ten days on a camel," muttered Nazario.

"You don't have to join us," said Eli.

Nazario shook his head. "No, where you go, I go," he said, overwhelmed by the thought.

"You're interested then?" asked an energized Carlisle.

"My only purpose is to find Hathor's Gate," said Eli.

"Splendid! I've already made arrangements. The dig can continue for a few weeks without me. Asim will join us, along with a cook and camel hand. We can leave tomorrow."

"Tomorrow," muttered Nazario, rubbing his sore inner thigh.

"To our expedition!" beamed Carlisle, raising his wineglass.

"To our expedition," repeated the others, raising their own.

After sipping his wine, Eli said, "Tell me about Asim."

Carlisle shrugged. "He's an Egyptian. He's one of my dig foremen. What do you want to know?"

"How long has he been with you?"

Carlisle stroked his mustache. "Asim joined me two, no, three years ago. Why do you ask?"

"There's something curious about him," replied Eli.

Nazario took a bite from a tart and leaned closer, not wanting to miss anything.

Carlisle shook his head dismissively. "Asim is one of my best workers. That's why I made him a foreman. I've found him beyond loyal. He even requested to join us."

Eli sat back and faintly nodded, still uncertain of the man.

Carlisle turned to his listening daughter. "I suppose you will return to Manchester?"

"On the contrary," said Penelope, grinning at Eli. "I enjoy riding camels. I find their humps delightful."

Nazario choked on his tart and coughed as he turned to the unaffected Eli.

Carlisle's bushy eyebrows raised, uncertain what to make of his daughter's comment. "Very well. We'll meet at the boat after breakfast. I'll provide the camels and supplies. Pack for a desert crossing. It will be cool at night but hot during the day."

Luxor, Egypt
4 December 1933

SHAKUR AHMED WAS DUSTING a brass lamp when he heard the sound of customers entering his shop. After setting down his ostrich duster and pushing up his thick glasses, the shopkeeper turned to a baggy-eyed man with oiled-back hair standing in the cluttered entry before two German soldiers. "Oh," he gasped, taken aback. "Can I help you?"

"Yes," nodded Guerre, his dark eyes scanning the hanging and stacked antiques. "Where can I find the plate?"

Shakur nervously glanced at the tan-uniformed soldiers glaring at him. One held a canvas bag. Both had pistols on their hips. "What plate is that? I have many one-of-a-kind Egyptian relics here."

Guerre picked up a figurine of a windup monkey holding cymbals.

"Among other things," shrugged a red-faced Shakur.

"Where is the plate?" glared Guerre.

"I don't know what you mean," replied the shopkeeper, backing away.

"I think you do," replied the baggy-eyed halfborn, stepping closer. "The mystic's plate. The one you told your friend, Yaqub, of."

Shakur's face went blank. "I'm sorry. You must be mistaken. I don't know who Yaqub is."

Guerre's eyes narrowed. "Strange. Allow me to refresh your memory." With the rise of a finger, the soldier with the bag stepped forward and opened it. Guerre then reached into the bag and removed the severed head of a man with bulging eyes and a hanging jaw. "Do you remember Yaqub now?" asked the halfborn, setting the bloody head on the counter.

Shakur recoiled at the gruesome sight and turned away, clutching his stomach.

"I understand Yaqub's antique shop is now for sale. Perhaps you would be interested in purchasing it?" Guerre eyed the squirming shopkeeper. "Perhaps your shop will soon be for sale as well?"

"Please, take it away," grimaced Shakur.

"Will you tell me where I can find the plate?"

"Yes. Please, take it away!"

"Where is it?" glared Guerre, lifting the head by the hair and slamming it down on top of the shopkeeper's magnifying glass.

Shakur shook his head, unable to protect the secret any longer. "There is an English archeologist named Niles Carlisle. He has it!"

"Where can I find him?"

"He has a dig in the Valley of the Kings. That's all I know, I swear it!"

"There, you see. You get to keep your head and can have a new shop too," grinned Guerre, turning away with the soldiers.

"Wait! What about this?" gasped Shakur, cringing at Yaqub's bloody head.

"Do with it what you please," called back Guerre, leaving the shop.

CHAPTER 28

GOASH ARISES

THE ABYSS

The trail had become more treacherous as it climbed the shuddering mountain. Littered by chunks of fallen lava, parts of the path had broken away to the steep slopes and sheer cliffs below. When the travelers rounded a bend, and the looming black mountain came into view, Michelle gasped, "Is that it?"

"Yes," nodded Remiel.

"Goash," pointed Franny.

Michelle looked at her son in wonder.

"The prince knows," said Gak.

"How?" breathed Michelle.

Franny, who had grown to the size of a seven-year-old, turned to his mother, neither troubled nor excited by their dangerous trek.

Uncertain of what to think of her rapidly growing son, Michelle's gaze turned to Goash's shrouded peak. On the mountain's far side, rivers of magma cascaded down. When Michelle inched closer to the trail's edge, she saw another river of lava flowing below. She backed away when a hundred-foot geyser of molten rock shot up from the side of a foothill two hundred yards to their left with the sound of a blowtorch.

"That wasn't here before," frowned Remiel.

Michelle squeezed Franny's hand. "That shower of fire wasn't here before?"

"No, that hill wasn't here before," said Remiel, his face aglow.

Michelle shook her head, awed by the fiery mountain's power. "You didn't say Goash was a volcano."

"It wasn't," replied Remiel.

Michelle gulped. "Where's the portal?"

"On the top," pointed Remiel.

"But how do we get there?" gasped Michelle.

"Very carefully," sighed Gak.

Og nodded.

With Franny's hand clutched in hers, Michelle raised her other to block the heat and glare of the lava fountain. She squinted as its orange flicker competed with her darksight, casting confusing shadows on the switchbacks ahead. Following Remiel, they stepped carefully as flaming bits of lava landed around them. The band stopped and watched when a colossal blast shot up through the clouds and dropped large chunks of burning rock on the trail behind them.

A concerned Remiel turned to Michelle. "We must be swift."

Og swept Franny up in his arms, and the band scrambled up the trail.

CHAPTER 29
HABOOB

THE QENA DESERT, EGYPT
4 DECEMBER 1933

It was late afternoon. The shadows of the winter sun stretched across the desolate plain as the caravan plodded on. Of the ten camels, three carried supplies while the others bore travelers. Carlisle rode in the lead with Asim at his side. Behind them rode Penelope, Nazario, and Eli, with the others trailing. As Penelope and Nazario chatted, Eli's thoughts were on the strange visions he had experienced.

"What do you think of riding camels?" asked Penelope, gracefully bobbing atop hers, a pith helmet with a veil on her head, her riding boots and breeches crossed atop the furry beast.

"I'm getting used to it," said Nazario. "But I don't think he likes me. He keeps looking back and spitting."

"It's a female camel," laughed Penelope.

"Well, that explains it."

Carlisle stopped his camel and waited for the others to catch up. "The sun will set in an hour. We'll camp for the night in that wash up ahead."

"I've never seen any place so brown and dry," said Nazario.

"That's because we're in a desert. An extraordinarily dry one. Here it would take the accumulation of fifty years of rain to equal an inch."

Nazario looked up at the clear blue sky and shook his head. "Was it always like this?"

"No. At one time, this land was green and fertile."

"What changed?" asked Nazario.

"Weather patterns. Time," said Carlisle, climbing off his kneeling camel. He turned to Eli, gazing across the barren landscape. "You've been quiet, Eli."

"Elijah is very mysterious. I find such strong and silent types enchanting," smirked Penelope.

"I've been thinking," replied Eli.

"There's nothing wrong with that," nodded Carlisle. "The world needs more thinking men. Let's set up camp, and you can tell me your mind over a good Bedouin meal."

Nazario delicately climbed off of his camel and stretched. "What do Bedouins eat?"

"You're about to find out," grinned Penelope.

THE SUN WAS SETTING and the air cooling when the last of the three canvas tents were staked and the bedrolls laid across the sand beneath. Asim and another were cooking dinner on a small fire when Nazario approached the laid-out rug outside the tents where the others were resting on pillows.

"Come join us, Cleto," said Carlisle with a wave of his cigar.

"I think I'll stand for now," replied Nazario. He turned and looked across the barren wash. "Is there anything out here we should be worried about?"

"You mean besides me?" whispered Penelope, leaning toward Eli.

Carlisle removed his pith helmet and ran a hand through his thinning hair. "The usual things, snakes, spiders, scorpions."

Nazario gulped. "Are they deadly?"

"Only if they bite or sting you," replied Carlisle.

"Father, you're frightening him," laughed Penelope. "I'm sure you'll be quite safe on a cool night like this. I'm not at all worried if that sets your mind at ease."

Eli, who had been staring across the star-filled horizon, turned to Carlisle and asked, "What can you tell me about this monastery?"

"You've never been to Mount Sinai before?" asked Penelope.

Eli nearly said, "Not since the monastery was built," but shook his head instead.

Carlisle puffed on his cigar. "Mount Sinai is one of the holiest sites in all of Judeo-Christendom. Some believe it to be the very spot God appeared to Moses in the burning bush, where the prophet received the Ten Commandments."

Nazario joined the others on the rug, his eyes wide. "How long has this monastery been there?"

"It was built around five hundred A.D. It's one of the oldest Christian monasteries in the world. Greek Orthodox monks have lived and died there for centuries. There's a mosque there as well. They set a good example in respecting each other's differences, if you ask me."

"Amazing. A mosque in a monastery," said Nazario.

"Local Bedouins worship there," explained Carlisle.

"You spoke of a library," said Eli.

"Yes, I'm sure you can imagine the collection one could amass in four-teen hundred years," said Carlisle. "Priceless things found nowhere else. It's been a few years since I was last there, so I'm quite excited to return."

"Indeed," nodded Nazario.

THEY WERE LONG FINISHED with their dinner of goat meat, rice, and dates when Carlisle mashed his cigar stub in the sand and climbed to his feet. "It's time for me to retire. Tomorrow will be another long day." He glanced at his daughter and the nodding-off reporter, then ducked into his tent.

"I should retire as well," groaned Nazario, rolling onto his knees.

Wrapped in a blanket, Penelope held back a laugh as Nazario crawled to his tent. But when Eli stirred, her face filled with disappointment. "You're not leaving too, are you?"

Eli caught Nazario's wary glance as he disappeared into their tent, then turned back to the pouting Penelope and said, "I should go to bed."

"But I need someone to enjoy this beautiful night with me. Look at those stars!"

Eli glanced at the dying fire and saw the workers in their bedrolls near the camels.

"There! A shooting star!" gasped Penelope.

Eli gazed up into the sparkling night sky.

"I even made a wish," grinned Penelope.

Eli's body tightened when Penelope laid her head in his lap.

"Do you ever wish you could travel to one of those far-off worlds?" Penelope asked, gazing into the starry night. "What wonders would you behold?" She breathed in the cool night air and shook her head. "There must be billions of stars out tonight."

Eli looked up into the night sky. He had just found the Pleiades star cluster when Penelope put her hand on his. In a flash, Eli viewed a dark and terrifying place with lava fountains and magma rivers. When he pulled his hand away, the vision vanished.

"What's wrong?" frowned Penelope, sitting up. She saw Eli's bewilderment, but was quickly swallowed up in his blue eyes. Penelope ran her hand along his square jaw as she studied Eli's handsome features. She breathed in his delicious fragrance, sighed, then breathlessly whispered, "Elijah, when I'm with you…"

Coming out of another vision, Eli stared blankly at the enchanted blonde.

Penelope placed a hand on Eli's broad, muscular chest and closed her eyes. She felt Eli's heart beating through his shirt and breathed in his intoxicating scent. "Elijah, I don't know what you do to me," she whispered. With her face flushed, Penelope eased onto the rug beside him.

"I should retire," said Eli, his wits returned. He climbed to his feet.

"Don't leave me," she softly pleaded.

When Penelope grabbed his hand, Eli saw another flash, then acres of gray-clad soldiers standing at attention, singing an anthem in unison. Hundreds of blood-red Nazi flags lined the mighty throng. He pulled his hand away.

Penelope watched with pouty eyes as Eli disappeared into his tent. She then rolled back onto the rug and groaned.

THE SUN WAS high in the sky when the wind began. With no trees or grass to bend, only dust moved across the travelers' path. Overhead, the brilliant sky had turned a hazy blue.

"That doesn't look good," frowned Carlisle, surveying the looming wall of darkness still miles away.

"Haboob comes! We must make shelter!" warned Asim.

"What's that cloud?" asked Nazario, a little more comfortable on his camel. "It looks as though we might get rain!"

"Not rain, dust!" said Carlisle, dismounting his protesting camel.

"A dust storm is coming," said Penelope, riding beside Eli. "We must get into our tents for protection."

Eli climbed off his camel and watched as Asim and the other workers quickly removed the canvas tents from the pack camels and laid them on the shifting sand.

"It will be here in minutes and could last hours!" yelled Carlisle through the growing tempest as he pulled on aviator goggles. "Take a water bladder, then get atop a tent and pull it around you, like a cocoon. It will protect you from the storm."

"What about the camels?" yelled Eli, helping Asim with a tent.

"The workers will tend to them. Now quickly! It will be on us before you know it!" shouted Carlisle, hurrying to his tent. The archeologist was kneeling on the worn canvas, holding its flapping end as he waited for Penelope to join him, when her pith helmet blew off. "Forget it!" yelled Carlisle, the windblown sand stinging his face and ears.

When Eli spotted Penelope's helmet tumbling across the sand, he charged after it. After fetching it, he pushed against the growing wind and biting sand to Penelope, trying to hold down a tent by herself.

"Haboob!" cried Asim, huddling in the sand between three camels.

"There's no time! It's here!" yelled Carlisle, waving a confused Nazario onto the tent with him. "Eli! Care for my daughter!" Carlisle pulled the tent canvas over him and Nazario.

Eli squinted through the flying sand as he pushed toward Penelope, her canvas tent flapping wildly around her.

"Hurry!" Penelope waved Eli to her and handed him goggles. "Put these on and help me hold it down!" she cried, her voice lost in the ferocious wind.

Eli pulled on the goggles and kneeled beside Penelope. He saw a layer of sand was already building up against Carlisle's tent. Eli's eyes widened when he turned to the rapidly approaching wall of churning sand. It was just fifty yards away and stretched higher and wider than he could see. The coarse granules bit Eli's flesh as he reached for the whipping canvas and pulled it over them. In an instant, the roar of the storm softened to a purr as sand whisked across them.

"I'm happy to be close to you, but not like this," said Penelope with a worried glance.

The wall of sand hit with the force of an ocean wave and knocked them flat onto the canvas floor. The small opening Eli had left blackened to night, and a cloud of choking dust billowed into the tent, filling Eli's mouth and nose with grit.

"Close that up!" cried Penelope, reaching over Eli to secure the hole.

As the storm rocked them and whipped the loose ends of the tent, Eli felt the weight of sand building up behind him. "Are you okay?"

"Yes," coughed Penelope, curled in a ball beside him.

Eli felt Penelope's fear as the sand and wind buffeted them. When she pushed up against him, Eli wrapped his arms around her. When Eli's hand touched Penelope's, the howling storm quieted, and his vision expanded from the murkiness of their shelter to vast fields of devastation. Eli saw toppled buildings and the smoldering remains of blown-open war machines. He thought for a moment he was viewing the killing fields of France eighteen years before, but when legions of bombers filled the sky, he knew it was something yet to come. The vision changed.

Eli saw camps filled with emaciated workers dressed in rags. He heard their agonized cries. Eli's heart ached as hills of rotting corpses grew before him. Stripped nude, their bony arms and legs intertwined with others. He smelled their stench.

The watcher squeezed his eyes closed as the storm pounded them, Penelope's trembling hand still in his. As Eli breathed in the fine dust swirling inside their collapsed tent, he saw another time. It was an ancient time in the land they were now in, but the valleys were lush and green, and the barren desert was far removed.

Eli viewed the builders of the magnificent monuments to the gods. He saw their oppression. He watched their righteous leader, Mawufe, being tortured by the Nubian king, Ra. Eli remembered well the Tassili leader. He had told Mawufe to move his people to avoid the catastrophe of an approaching comet. But Eli's heart ached at the pain he had caused those people. He knew the Tassili would not have survived the comet's strike, but he wondered if their misery and suffering would have been less had they stayed in their own land. Eli's heart sank when he spotted the beautiful yet ruthless Hathor. He groaned when guards threw Mawufe through the portal into the abyss. Then Eli saw only darkness.

ELI'S EYES opened when Penelope stirred beside him. He looked through a crack in the collapsed tent when he heard muffled voices from outside, then pushed the canvas and its inch of sand off of them. The storm had passed, leaving mounds of sand where their blown-over supplies and huddled camels lay. With a snort and a bellowing howl, a camel pulled up from the sand and shook off its humps. Two more followed.

"Are you all right?" asked Eli, careful not to touch Penelope's flesh as he helped her to her feet.

"How long has it been?" she asked, as if waking from a nap.

Eli turned to the sinking sun. "An hour, maybe more."

"Father!" cried Penelope, seeing the moving mound of sand.

Eli trudged across the fresh dune and pulled back the canvas to a tired Carlisle and a sweaty, wide-eyed Nazario. "Are you both okay?"

"Yes." Carlisle climbed to his feet. "Asim! The camels and supplies?"

"Three camels gone, sir," replied the mysterious foreman as he approached through the still-settling dust.

A frowning Carlisle sighed, his hands on his hips. "Find them!"

Asim nodded and turned back into the dust cloud.

"I know there is a blue sky up there somewhere," coughed Penelope, her face and hair covered in beige powder.

"That was quite a storm," muttered a stunned Nazario.

"Not the worst I've seen," grumbled Carlisle. He pulled the dusty goggles from his eyes and looked across the altered landscape to the back-side of the storm, moving away like a towering, black-cloaked demon.

Nazario surveyed his dust-covered clothes. When he brushed away the powdery sand, it billowed around him and left him coughing.

"Now what do we do?" asked Eli, scanning the reshaped desert.

"We set up camp here, then venture on tomorrow," said Carlisle, lighting a cigar. "Hopefully, Asim can find the lost camels."

"What if he can't?" asked a nervous Nazario.

"Then someone will have to walk."

CHAPTER 30
BEYOND THE MIST

THE ABYSS

With the lava fountain well below them and the magma rivers on the far side of Goash, the switchbacks had changed to stone-carved stairs. The ground trembled as they climbed the ancient steps, making Michelle wonder if a violent eruption would claim them before they reached the portal.

With each step, the air turned colder and mistier. When Michelle realized they had reached the dark clouds, she stopped and looked down the way they had come. The molten rivers in the valley had spread and formed long orange fingers that reached for the dark horizon. She glanced at the curious Franny, then looked up at the undulating black layer of vapor that extended above them like a cave ceiling. It reached as far as she could see. Michelle noticed the reflected lava light in places, but most of the cloud seemed impenetrable to even her darksight. She breathed in the cool vapors and tasted the bitterness of ash. Michelle raised her hand to the dark ceiling and ran a finger along the cloud. A faint streak of light followed her touch as the cloud parted and then filled back in, like a ripple across an upside-down pond. Michelle turned to Remiel with a look of amazement. "What's above the clouds?"

"You shall see," said Remiel, offering his hand.

Michelle met eyes with the watcher. She saw his devotion and took his hand. Then, after drawing in an emboldening breath, she tightened her hold on Franny's hand and followed Remiel into the cloud. All went black as the dark vapor enveloped her. Even Michelle's darksight was of no use. She clung tightly to Remiel's hand as they climbed through the soot-filled cloud. Behind her, Michelle heard Gak's steps and Og's breathing. She wondered how long they would climb in darkness.

Soon, the taste of ash lessened and the suffocating blackness thinned. Michelle's eyes widened when her head raised above the mist, and a brilliant, glittering night sky came into view. "Stars!" she gasped. "What a surprise! I'd forgotten how beautiful they are!" Filled with wonder, Michelle hefted Franny and said, "Look at the sky! Isn't it lovely?"

"Yes, Mommy." Franny embraced her as Gak and Og appeared through the mist, gazing at the twinkling stars in awe.

Michelle filled her lungs with the crisp air and looked at the steps ahead. In the starlight, the stairs seemed to stop. She turned to Remiel and asked, "Are we close to the portal?"

"Yes."

As they continued to climb, Michelle noted large brown boulders on either side of the steps. They were not the black, irregular, and jagged boulders from below the clouds, but oblong and smooth, like enormous river stones.

Michelle slowed when the steps turned to level stone. Ahead of them, a dark rectangular entrance led into the mountain like a mine, its side walls and ceiling lined by boulders. Her jaw slackened as she entered. Unlike the smooth boulders outside, the tunnel walls were engraved with flowing lines and patterns. Some lines were circular, some arched like rainbows; others were wavy, like snakes twisting on top of each other. Michelle spotted starbursts and suns among the geometric patterns. Looking past Remiel, she noticed the designs continued far into the passage; its walls, floor, and ceiling were made of individual boulders perfectly fit and aligned. "Who built this place?" she asked in wonder.

"It is thought the Great Ones, but no one knows," said Remiel.

"How do you not know? You're immortal."

Remiel shook his head. "There is much I do not know."

"Does this take us to the portal?"

"Yes," nodded Remiel.

The wide-eyed Michelle moved past Remiel with Franny in hand, the swirling stone mosaics shimmering in her darksight. "What does it say?" she asked, her fingers lightly touching the engraved patterns.

"They are directions. I think," replied Remiel.

"Directions? To what? How to operate the portal?"

"I don't know."

Michelle glanced back at Gak, who shrugged. Behind him, Og followed, hunched low to clear the tunnel's eight-foot ceiling.

When they came to a dead-end, Michelle examined the stone slab blocking them. "The way is closed."

Remiel moved beside Michelle and placed his hand on the large slab. The rock door slid aside with the sound of grinding stone. The corridor continued beyond the door, but it was not as dark.

Michelle felt a *whoosh* of air as she passed the threshold with Franny in hand. Her eyes widened as the brightening passageway opened to a spacious, round court. The huge, patterned boulders made up its floor and side walls, but it was open to the night sky above. Michelle's jaw slackened as she looked up into the endless expanse of space. There were more stars than she had ever seen. Michelle moved from the entry, captivated by the dazzling view, and turned, expecting to see the mountain's peak, but there was only the cosmos. "Where are we?" she asked, backing into the center of the court.

"We are in a star chapel," replied Remiel.

"A star chapel," Michelle whispered in wonder.

All eyes were on the spectacular display above them when Michelle backed into what she thought was a boulder. She turned and gasped at the twelve-foot-round metallic ring standing on end, its base fused into the rock floor. The eighteen-inch-wide and foot-thick annulus had the luster of pewter, and hundreds of embossed glyphs covered its face. Among them, Michelle recognized a fleur-de-lis and an ankh. "Ahh! The portal!" She turned to the others. "I can't believe it! We made it!"

A puzzled Remiel nodded.

"Where's the gatekeeper?" asked Michelle, looking around the court. She noticed no other passages, only the tall boulder walls.

"I don't know," frowned Remiel as he moved closer to the ring.

Michelle sighed. "Will it work without the gatekeeper?"

Remiel shook his head. "I lack the ability, but you..."

"I know nothing of this!" said Michelle.

Remiel backed away to where Gak and Og stood and gave her an encouraging nod.

With a sigh, Michelle turned to the massive alloy ring and studied the glyphs perfectly etched into its surface. She drew in a breath and reached a tentative hand to the portal. When Michelle touched the ring, a bright pillar of light swirled around her. She gasped and pulled her hand away. "Did you see that?"

"See what?" asked Gak, cocking his head.

"There was a light!"

Gak glanced at the others, having not seen it.

"I saw it, Mommy. It was pretty," said Franny.

Remiel, who had been studying Michelle, stepped closer. "Reaching the doorway is only a part of the journey. You must now command the opening. You must set your destination and then go to it."

Michelle gulped. "But how? Can you teach me?"

Remiel shook his head. "I cannot."

Michelle sighed. She touched the ring again, but when nothing happened, her shoulders sank. Frustrated, she asked, "Where's the gatekeeper?"

"Perhaps he has left," said Remiel.

"There has to be a way!" groaned Michelle. All eyes were on her as she studied the glyphs. "What do they say? Can you read them?"

"I can read only some." Remiel looked into Michelle's worried eyes. "Follow your instincts. You have the power in you."

Michelle's brow tightened in concentration. She touched the ring in another place, but nothing happened.

Franny pointed to a swirling pattern of circles within circles on one side of the annulus. "Try this, Mommy."

Michelle examined the circular pattern.

"Put your hand on it," urged Franny.

All eyes were on Michelle as she reached out her hand. When she lay her palm flat on the circles, the space inside the ring turned opaque, and an image within a swirling cloud appeared. Michelle gasped when the ring showed her father, François, as a boy. She recognized Franny in him. Michelle watched spellbound as her father aged. She thought him handsome in his French Foreign Legion uniform. Her jaw slackened as she viewed him fighting in the jungles of Indochina. Michelle beamed when François met her mother. "Mama," muttered Michelle, tears welling in her eyes. François was holding an infant next. "That's me! Can you see?" she asked, tears streaming down her face. Next, Michelle viewed François playing chess with Elijah. Then he was lying in a casket. "Papa," groaned Michelle, remembering her grief. She was about to pull her hand from the ring when she viewed others greeting François, his altered visage glowing. "Papa! He's still alive!" Michelle removed her hand and turned to Franny. "Did you see that? That was your grandfather!"

An engrossed Franny nodded.

Michelle turned to the others. "Did you see it too?"

Gak and the others nodded.

"But why did the ring show him still alive?"

Remiel didn't hide his surprise at Michelle's question. "Because he yet lives in the world beyond."

Michelle shook her head. "What does it mean? Why did the portal show me those things?"

"I don't know," said Remiel.

Michelle's curious gaze returned to the star gate. "I want to see more." She placed her hand on the portal, and its inner ring again turned opaque. Michelle's face lit up when she saw herself and Franny playing in the château's pond. "That's our home!"

"There's Papa!" pointed Franny.

"Elijah!" cried Michelle, seeing her husband for the first time in what felt like decades. He was sitting on the hill near the château, staring blankly across the pond. "He's sad."

"Don't be sad, Papa," urged Franny.

The image changed. "He's working in the vineyard! Elijah! Can you hear me?" called out Michelle, but there was no response.

The image changed again. Michelle's countenance dimmed when she saw another woman walking beside her husband. She was beautiful and had wavy blonde hair. "Who's that?" Michelle's eyes widened when they embraced. She gasped when Elijah kissed the strange woman. When the image changed to them asleep together in bed, a shocked Michelle pulled her hand from the ring, and the vision disappeared.

Franny's uncertain gaze moved from the empty portal to the stunned Michelle as she staggered backward.

"What happened?" asked Gak.

Remiel lowered his head, and Og turned away.

With her eyes round and jaw hanging, Michelle backed against the wall and sank to the floor. When tears spilled down Michelle's cheeks, Franny moved to her with a comforting hand. Michelle lowered her son onto her lap, wrapped her arms tightly around him, buried her head in his, and broken-heartedly sobbed.

CHAPTER 31
BY THE SEA

HURGHADA, EGYPT
7 DECEMBER 1933

Eli led his camel by the reins as they entered the small fishing village. His eyes narrowed as he scanned the flat-roofed adobe buildings lining the dusty road. He saw goats and sheep in simple pens, with some wandering the side streets. Colorful laundry hung from lines strung across the narrow alleys and from worn and failing balconies. Eli heard the chatter of bargaining from a small bazaar. He smelled the tanginess of Eastern spices, which seemed especially sweet after days of breathing dust, camel musk, and unbathed men.

"There's an inn just over there," pointed Carlisle, his face tanned and tired. "The restaurant beside it has decent food. Let's get cleaned up and have a proper dinner."

"That sounds fabulous," said Penelope, her hair and clothes still coated from the dust storm two days before.

"Do we cross the Red Sea tomorrow?" asked Nazario, climbing off his kneeling camel.

"You've gotten quite good on your beast," said Penelope as she gracefully lowered off of hers.

Nazario grinned with pride.

"Yes," said Carlisle, looking toward the docks and the shimmering blue. "After breakfast, we'll take the ferry across to the Sinai." He glanced at Eli and asked, "Are you sure you want to purchase another camel?"

Eli nodded. "You are gracious to lead us on this expedition. It's the least I can do to repay the loss of one of your animals."

Penelope stood with hands on hips, her breeches and riding boots covered in dust, and gazed down the hill across the turquoise sea. "One forgets how lovely water is until you go without seeing it for days."

With his suitcase in one hand and bag of notebooks in the other, Nazario stepped beside her and nodded. "To think Moses led the children of Israel across that same barren desert before parting and crossing the Red Sea. So much history here."

Carlisle set his bag down and huffed, not believing in such things.

"You're not a man of faith, professor?" asked Nazario.

"I'm a man of science. I deal with religion and mythology out of necessity. It is simply a means of unlocking the mysteries of the past."

Nazario glanced at the listening Eli. "Well, I, for one, am a believer. I've seen too much in my research to possibly doubt otherwise."

"How nice for you," muttered Carlisle as he started toward the inn.

Nazario looked around the fishing village and drew in a cleansing breath. "We may be standing at the very spot Moses and the children of Israel camped thousands of years ago. What do you think, Eli?"

Eli pointed to the north and said, "It was further that way."

Carlisle laughed as he walked down the dusty road toward the inn, but both Penelope and Nazario eyed Eli; Nazario like a boy awed by his hero, and Penelope like a woman consumed by desire.

A COOLING SEA breeze wafted through the bamboo shutters as Eli eased into the hot, soapy bath, his thick, muscular body filling the cast iron tub and spilling water. While Eli's face and forearms were tanned dark by the desert sun, his natural skin tone was neither dark nor pale, and his broad chest was free of hair. Eli poured a bowl of the soothing liquid over his full, wavy hair, then washed his face. He settled back into the tub with a relaxing sigh. More water sloshed over the side as his knees pushed out of the tub. With the water to his ears, Eli felt the bath's calming effects and closed his eyes. After walking the last twenty miles, and with dinner in an hour, he thought a rest was deserved.

With his head half-submerged, Eli didn't hear the door to his room open. But when he sensed another's presence, his resting eyes shot open. "What are you doing here?" Eli gasped, sitting up in the soapy water.

Perched on the tub's edge beside him was a wide-eyed Penelope in a pink bathrobe. Its soft collar hung off her delicate shoulder, revealing her creamy skin and the gentle valley between her breasts. Eli gulped. His lips parted at the memory of pulling her from the frigid Atlantic. He saw her drowned body dripping and limp in the lifeboat as he breathed life into her. Eli wondered if he had transferred more than his breath to Penelope when he saved her.

"I just thought I'd check on you," grinned Penelope, her eyes moving down his sculptured chest dripping with water. "I'm sure you're exhausted from so valiantly walking all that way while we rode."

"We lost a camel. It was necessary to carry the supplies," frowned Eli. When Penelope's fingers moved to untie her bathrobe, Eli placed a halting hand atop them. With a flash, his mind filled with the vision of a giant pyramid emitting a brilliant beam of light to a ceiling of black clouds. He saw a glowing Michelle dressed in gold with hundreds bowing at her feet. Eli gasped and pulled his hand away.

Penelope saw Eli's distress and released her robe's tie. "What is it?"

Eli closed his eyes and shook his head.

Intoxicated by Eli more than ever, Penelope's chest heaved beneath the gaping bathrobe. She reached for his hand, but Eli pulled it into the water. "I...I hoped..." Penelope breathed in his essence, her face flushed, her pupils wide. "I hoped we could dine alone tonight. Just...just you and me...in your room," she breathlessly whispered.

Eli shook his head, the full measure of her suggestion sinking in. "I cannot. I am joined to another."

"But she left you. I'm here. All for you!" Penelope pleaded. Desperate to not lose Eli, she stood and pulled open her robe, but Eli was already out of the tub. He hastily wrapped a towel around him and fled the room.

Penelope's shoulders sank, realizing she had lost her chance with Eli, and she pulled her robe closed.

CHAPTER 32

THE TRAVELER

THE ABYSS

S till sitting in the star chapel before the now dormant portal, no one had uttered a word for some time when Gak leaned forward and asked, "Now what do we do?"

Remiel glared at the halfborn, not wanting to trouble the upset Michelle further.

"Are we just going to sit here?" asked Gak with raised palms.

Og sadly nodded.

"It's okay," sighed Michelle, wiping her eyes. "You don't have to stay here with us."

"Our place is with you," said Remiel, his face filled with compassion.

Og nodded.

"So...we're just going to sit here?" asked Gak.

"Yes," glared Remiel.

"Fine." Gak sank back against the wall.

Still holding Franny, Michelle's sad gaze faded, and her jaw tightened in determination. She climbed to her feet, stomped back to the star gate, and pushed her palm against it. When an image of the château appeared, she waved Franny to her. "Come on, François; we're going home."

Remiel and Gak sat up.

Franny joined his mother and looked back at the others.

"Thank you for your help. I'll come back for you if I can," fumed Michelle.

"Goodbye," waved Gak.

The others watched as Michelle pulled her hand from the etched circles and jumped with Franny through the portal. The image promptly disappeared, leaving Michelle and Franny standing on the other side of the giant ring.

"Welcome back," waved Gak.

Remiel shook his head at the halfborn.

Frustrated, Michelle led Franny around the portal and did the same thing. Again, the image of their home appeared, and again, they ended up on the other side of the ring. "I don't understand," said a fuming Michelle. "I can see the château. Why won't it let us through?"

"Because you lack the power to command it."

All heads turned when a man in a flowing blue cloak emerged from the passageway. The stranger had bronze skin, eyes the color of sapphires, and carried himself with a confident swagger. He held a staff in one hand, a bag over his shoulder, and a mandolin strapped across his back.

"It's him, the traveler," groaned Gak, lowering his head.

"Who are you?" gasped Michelle, drawn in by the dashing stranger's bright blue eyes.

The traveler, who wore short hair and a chin beard, looked Michelle up and down. Then, with a gleaming white grin, he said, "Hello. How did someone as lovely as you end up with this sorry bunch?"

"They're my friends," bristled Michelle.

"Are they?"

"Are you the gatekeeper?"

"I was," said the traveler, still eyeing Michelle.

Seated against the wall, Gak hid his face.

"I see you, Gak, twin son of Yima," said the traveler as he strutted to the portal.

Gak looked up at the traveler loathingly. "You look like a gypsy going on holiday."

The traveler huffed.

"Can you help us get back to our home?" asked Michelle, moving closer with Franny in hand.

The traveler's sapphire eyes sparkled in the starlight. "I cannot."

"But we've traveled all this way! Remiel said you could!"

"I cannot because I am trapped here, as you are."

Michelle's eyes narrowed. "Were you banished here too?"

"Not banished, stranded. And for one whose purpose is to travel the cosmos, it's quite unbearable." A crafty grin formed as he studied Michelle's features and proportions. "But to be trapped with you—"

"Be careful what you say," warned Remiel. "She is the Bringer of Light."

The traveler's grin faded. "She is not."

When Gak jumped to his feet and grabbed his sword, Remiel raised a halting hand.

"She is not *yet*," added the traveler. "While her feminine beauty is in full bloom, her brightness has not been realized. She is yet a pupil. Her journey is young."

A fuming Gak took his hand from his sword.

"What happened to the portal?" asked Remiel.

"The overseer decommissioned it," said the traveler.

"Cyrus," huffed Remiel.

"Yes. It seems the child is inconvenient to his plan." The traveler reached for the boy, but Franny stepped back.

"Don't touch the prince," warned Gak, moving beside Franny.

The traveler ignored Gak and asked Remiel, "What happened to Cyrus? Was he not the chief advocate of the Grand Precept?"

Remiel lowered his head and nodded.

"You watchers puzzle me."

Remiel's stern gaze raised to the traveler. "And how is that?"

The traveler motioned to Michelle. "You go to her world on a noble mission of creation and tutelage and fall apart. You can't keep your hands off the females—and for good reason," he flashed a glance at Michelle, "and spawn a nation of freaks!"

Gak scowled at the traveler, and Og growled.

"A hundred millennia later, and your overseer is plotting against the Chosen One's return!"

"It must be nice to traipse around the universe without a care, to come and go as you like," sneered Gak.

"That would be nice, but I've been stuck at this doorway for far too long!" glared the traveler. He turned back to Remiel. "What is most puzzling is why a few of your kind persist in their charade of good while the rest bathe in glory as demigods."

"Power is seductive to even the elect," said Remiel.

"To even the elect," scoffed the traveler.

Remiel sighed. "There are few of us remaining in that world."

"Especially the pious. I understand Lu has summoned an army of half-born. Now, with Cyrus coming forth to lead them, who would not join him?"

Michelle's jaw tightened. "My husband, for one. He has stayed true!"

"Says the mortal who bore the great Elijah a child," scoffed the traveler.

"Watch your tongue!" warned Remiel. "You are standing before the Harbinger!"

The traveler eyed Franny. "Hmm. He looks surprisingly like a boy."

Michelle turned to Remiel. "Do we really need him?"

"Unless you can command the doorway yourself," replied Remiel.

The traveler laughed.

Gak waved his dagger and seethed, "He doesn't need his tongue to open a doorway. Can I at least cut that out?"

"Enough of this!" snapped Michelle. "It's clear you all know each other."

"We do. But the big one doesn't say much," replied the traveler.

Og shrugged.

"If you boys can refrain from any further hostility and posturing, I'd like to ask him some questions."

The traveler gave an exaggerated bow.

"Do you have a name?" asked Michelle.

"Dung brain," muttered Gak.

Og laughed.

"That goes for all of you," glared Michelle. She turned back to the traveler.

"I am called Nixx Trismegistus."

Michelle drew in a ragged breath. "Nixx, my son and I desperately need to return to our world. Will you help us? Will you open a portal?" she asked, motioning to the star gate.

"I cannot."

"Why? Why won't you help us?" Michelle persisted.

"You are beautiful but do not hear well. The portal will not do as you wish!"

"But when I touched it, I saw my home," insisted Michelle.

Nixx's eyes narrowed. "I am impressed. Portals do not recognize most mortals."

"What do you mean?"

"The portal drew from your thoughts. When you imagined your home, it showed it to you. But even if the gate were fully functioning, it would not have formed a travel conduit."

"Why?" challenged Michelle.

"Because you lack the power to command it."

"But you do. Why won't you open it?"

Nixx sighed. "I told you. Cyrus deactivated it. If you must know the details, it's missing a key component that allows for time and space directionality. I could open a portal, but there's no telling where or when it would send you beyond this world. You might end up any place and time, including the center of a sun, which I would imagine is quite unpleasant, even for the Queen of Light."

Michelle's shoulders sank. "Can you repair it?"

"If I could, I wouldn't be here."

With a frustrated sigh, Michelle pulled Franny close to her.

"Well, I guess you'll be leaving now," said Nixx, situating the bag on his shoulder.

Michelle studied the portal. "Before you arrived, I saw something else inside the ring."

The traveler's eyebrows lifted. "What did you see?"

"I saw my father's life. I saw myself as a child, growing up...but then..." Michelle gulped.

"The gate examined you. It showed you your past. Your beginnings." Nixx saw Michelle's discomfort and asked, "Did you view something else?"

"Yes," muttered Michelle.

"Did you view something out of place to your understanding? Something that has not yet happened?"

Michelle nodded, fighting back her tears.

"Her husband in bed with another woman," said Gak.

Remiel looked at the halfborn in exasperation.

"Well, she did," shrugged Gak. "And I thought she was beautiful."

When Gak saw Michelle's heartbroken gaze, he lowered his head and muttered, "Not as beautiful as you, of course."

"You viewed a future," said Nixx.

"A future?"

The traveler nodded. "A star gate has many purposes. It can open a passage through space to different worlds. But it can also function as a window to your past and future—a time mirror."

"You said *a* future. Is there more than one?" asked Michelle.

"Of course. There are infinite futures," replied the traveler.

Michelle shook her head in confusion. "How is that possible?"

Nixx gave a condescending grin. "How many directions can you walk?"

Michelle looked around the stone court. "Many."

"How many words can you speak?"

Michelle shrugged.

"With each action comes a possible future. You could choose to stay on the mountain until Goash explodes and vaporizes you. You could return to Luminah or Manu, where you might die. Or you could travel with me to a paradise world as my lover. I think you would find that last future most enjoyable. I know I would."

Michelle looked at Nixx as if he were joking while Remiel glared at him with clenched fists.

"I forgot what a pompous ass you are," huffed Gak as Og nodded.

Nixx continued, "All of us have such options and with them different futures. There are infinite time threads, each leading to a nexus of limitless possibilities."

Michelle's brow furrowed in thought. "I understand that we have many options, but we can choose only one action at a time. Isn't *that* our future?"

"That is the future for the choice you make, but not for the other choices you do not make," smirked Nixx.

Gak grimaced, trying to keep up, and Og scratched his furry head.

"You're saying what I saw hasn't happened yet?"

"It may have. It may not have," shrugged Nixx.

Michelle studied the traveler. To her, something didn't seem right. She wondered why Nixx had come to the portal carrying his bag, a mandolin, and a walking stick if he wasn't going somewhere.

"Mommy, we need to go," said Franny, tugging on Michelle's arm.

Michelle looked down at her son and said, "We must find a way back to Papa."

Franny reluctantly nodded as Michelle moved to the star gate.

After examining the portal's engravings, she turned to the waiting Nixx and asked, "Where are you going?"

"Me?" asked the traveler.

"Yes. You look as though you are embarking on a journey."

"I always dress like this," shrugged Nixx.

"You always carry a staff and mandolin?"

Nixx grinned awkwardly. "Yes."

Michelle's contemplative gaze returned to the portal, and she placed her hand on a pattern of wavy lines.

Nixx's eyebrows lifted when the annulus filled with dazzling sunlight.

Michelle squinted as the light washed past her into the chapel. "The sun! I've forgotten how bright and warm it is!" To her surprise, when she removed her hand, the window stayed open.

Remiel and the others shielded their eyes from the bright scene as a vast green valley with rivers, lakes, and forests appeared. A gleaming city of glass stood on a faraway hill, and a strange pyramid-shaped flying machine hovered in the powder blue sky.

"It's so light and beautiful," said Michelle. "What am I seeing?"

"The past," said Nixx, looking at the scene with dread.

"The past?" asked Michelle, puzzled by a civilization advanced far beyond what she had known.

Nixx's pensive gaze returned to Michelle. "This world, but long ago."

"It's lovely," said Michelle as a summer breeze moved past.

"Is it?" muttered the traveler. He cocked his head. "How did you open this window?"

"I did what you said. I thought of you wanting to leave and touched it."

"She is the Queen of Light," shrugged Gak.

Nixx's bewildered gaze returned to the beckoning scene.

"This is where you were going when we arrived," said Michelle.

"You are quite insightful," said the traveler. "I considered it, but I'm rethinking that plan," he said with a clever grin.

"You said the portal doesn't work," said Michelle, thinking he had lied.

Nixx sighed. "It only partially works. It cannot project beyond this world and only to this time."

Michelle looked across the inviting valley. "What would happen if we were to step through the window?"

"If you went through, you would be lost in the distant past, even farther from your home, unable to return," explained Nixx. "You and the boy would exist, but not as you are now. You would forfeit whatever calling you may have and forever alter the future of your world."

Michelle gulped and pulled the curious Franny against her. "I just want to get back to Elijah."

Remiel and Gak exchanged dejected looks as the traveler eyed Michelle.

When Michelle backed away from the portal, the window closed, returning them to the chapel's starlight. She sighed and turned to the traveler. "What is it you need to get us home?"

"I need an orb to operate this portal."

"If you had an orb, would you take us?" asked Michelle.

"Perhaps." Nixx's leering gaze moved to the curve of her breasts just visible through her dusty gown. "What would I get out of it?"

"You'd get to keep your head," snapped Remiel, glaring at the traveler.

"And other parts," added Gak, holding up his dagger.

"Please. Tell me you haven't already had your way with her in your mind," scoffed Nixx.

"Watch your tongue! She is the Bringer of Light!" warned Remiel.

"I'll have you all know I'm happily married to the greatest of all watchers," glared Michelle.

"Who, last you saw, was sleeping with another woman," smirked Nixx. He raised a finger to her dress's gaping neck slit and parted it further. "I think that opens the door for me."

"It does not!" fumed Michelle, pushing his hand away.

A grinning Nixx stepped back.

"Mommy, we should go." Franny tugged on the seething Michelle's arm as the others glared at the traveler.

Nixx shrugged off their hostility. "I see I'm not very popular here. Maybe I'll go through that window after all." He touched the ring, and the warming daylight returned.

Michelle's face dimmed as Nixx moved toward the portal. As much as she despised the traveler, she knew he was their only hope to return to Eli. "Wait! What if I told you I have an orb?"

The traveler stopped. "I wouldn't believe you."

All eyes were on Michelle as she pulled the blazerod from her bag.

"Impressive, but that is not an orb. Where did you find it? Was it Elijah's?"

"Yes."

"She can command the weapon," warned Remiel.

"And blow your ugly head off," smirked Gak.

"That is also impressive." Nixx studied Michelle. "Tell me of this orb you say you have."

"I took it from Lu before I came here to get my son."

Nixx's eyebrows lifted in surprise. "You took it from Lu?"

"Yes. Will you take us home with an orb?" asked a hopeful Michelle.

Nixx's eyes narrowed. "Where is your orb?"

"It's in Manu," said Remiel.

"Keket has your orb?" asked Nixx.

"Keket is a pile of ash!" sneered Gak. "The Queen of Light killed her!"

Michelle lowered her head, still traumatized by the memory.

"Then where is your orb?" asked Nixx.

"Somewhere in Manu," sighed Michelle, returning the blazerod to her bag.

"Well, that narrows it," scoffed Nixx.

"If we were to return and find it, you could open a doorway using this portal?"

"There is not time. Goash is alive and will consume this place before you can return!"

"We have to try!" insisted Michelle.

"I won't be staying here. I've waited long enough!" said Nixx with a hint of worry.

Michelle's eyes narrowed, recognizing a conflict within the traveler. "You say you've been here for some time and have a way to leave, yet you haven't. You're afraid to go through, aren't you? You don't want to go back to that time."

Nixx huffed.

"And I think your lewd behavior is an act. No one is that depraved!" added Michelle.

Nixx pulled back, surprised by her assessment. But his bluster quickly returned. "I am the traveler, Nixx Trismegistus! I am the only one who can get you back to your Elijah!"

"Will you?" asked Michelle, not backing down.

Nixx paused, his façade somewhat damaged. "One of your futures is returning to the citadel and finding your orb. Then what?"

"Then you get us home."

"I told you, I'm not staying here," said Nixx.

"Then come with us," said Michelle.

Nixx gulped. "I'm not going back there."

Michelle's shoulders sank. "Then there's no way home."

Nixx's sapphire eyes drifted as he remembered a future.

"Please, we just want to go home," Michelle pleaded, tears filling her eyes.

Nixx snapped out of his spell and turned to Michelle. "Well, that changes everything if you're going to cry."

Remiel's fist tightened.

"I thought you were the Queen of Light! You don't need me! Just open a doorway and take yourself home!" glared the traveler.

Remiel stepped forward, pulled the smaller Nixx up by his tunic, and raised his fist.

"You can strike me if it makes you feel better. Just don't damage my mandolin!" quipped Nixx.

"No, don't hit him. He's not worth it!" said Michelle, wiping away her tears.

"As you wish." A stern-eyed Remiel released his hold on Nixx and moved to Michelle.

The traveler watched Remiel comfort her as he straightened his tunic. "Well, I guess I'll be going then."

"Good. Leave!" huffed Michelle. "I have noble friends that will help me."

"Noble friends with no means of helping you," muttered Nixx as Michelle wiped away tears.

"At least they're my friends," replied Michelle.

Nixx's brashness softened as he eyed Michelle. He sighed, then said, "There may be another way."

Michelle looked at the traveler through teary eyes. "Another way?"

Nixx tried to hide his uneasiness. "I see a future where you return to your Elijah through the Dark Gate.

Remiel shook his head. "The Dark Gate was destroyed."

"It was not," replied Nixx.

"Where's the Dark Gate?" asked Michelle.

"In the depths of the ancient city of Ra," said Remiel.

"We'd have to fight our way back in," said Gak.

"There are other ways into the ancient city," said Remiel.

Michelle studied Nixx, unsure she could trust him. "So you will help us after all?"

"Mommy, no," whined Franny, pulling on her arm.

"As a traveler, it is in my nature to help people."

"You help only yourself," sneered Gak.

"Well, that is sometimes true, but traveling and adventure are in my blood and the past...well, I've already lived it." Nixx's sapphire eyes met Michelle's. "But know this: your desire to return to your home is fraught with hazard. There are powers waiting to use you and your child."

Michelle looked down at Franny, pulling on her arm. "Darling, we must get back to your papa."

After a distrusting glance at the traveler, Franny sighed and buried his face in his mother's cloak.

Michelle collected herself, then turned to Nixx. "You will take us through this Dark Gate?"

Nixx's face grew serious. "Yes."

Remiel turned to Gak and Og with an uncertain look.

Gak could hold back no longer. "My Queen, don't trust him!"

The traveler's brow tightened as his pensive gaze lowered to the uneasy Franny. "Then I guess you can do it on your own."

Michelle eyed the unsavory Nixx. "I don't trust him either, but we must travel back to Manu one way or the other. That gives us time for him to gain our trust."

Nixx sighed. "Are you going to listen to these oafs or me?"

"They're not oafs," glared Michelle. "They're my friends. I will take counsel from those I trust most."

The traveler nodded. "Very well. Then we should depart. We have far to go." After pulling on his shoulder bag, Nixx gave the portal and star chapel a final glance, raised his staff, and started for the passageway.

The others exchanged wary glances and followed.

CHAPTER 33
OBSESSIONS

THE GULF OF SUEZ
8 DECEMBER 1933

Niles Carlisle eyed his daughter as the sea breeze blew his cigar smoke across the ferry's bow. Penelope had barely spoken to anyone that morning, and getting on the ferry was the first he had seen her since they had arrived at Hurghada the day before. With neither her nor Eli joining them for dinner, Carlisle wondered what had happened between them. He knew his daughter's impetuousness well and hoped she would have settled down by now. But then he reminded himself she was *his* daughter.

Carlisle's gaze turned to Eli, who stood by the railing staring at the mysterious mountains of the approaching Sinai. Eli intrigued him. Who he was exactly and how he had amassed such a wealth of knowledge was immaterial to the professor, whose insatiable appetite for lost relics had gotten him into trouble more than once.

Carlisle puffed on his cigar as he considered Eli's brass plate. He wondered where their expedition would lead him. Would it take him to the fabled gate of Hathor and enduring fame? Or would it be another dusty dead-end, with dime-a-dozen artifacts good for only clogging a museum's backroom?

"How long to the monastery?" asked Eli, turning from the railing.

"Three more days. We should be at Saint Catherine's by Tuesday."

Eli nodded.

"We missed you at dinner last night," said Carlisle, studying Eli.

"I hope I didn't delay you."

"Not at all." Carlisle tried to hide his concern. "My daughter—she's a grown woman, of course, and can choose for herself—but she's been hurt by too many men. I trust you would never do such a thing. For if you would, I would end this expedition right now."

Carlisle's empty threat did not bother Eli. He knew the professor was nearly as obsessed over their quest as he was. Instead, he turned to him and said, "I wish the best for Penelope, but my heart is with my lost wife, and my only thoughts are on finding the gateway."

Carlisle pushed his cigar back into his mouth. He studied Eli, looking across the water, then asked, "What happened to your wife?"

Eli's gaze faded in thought. He was about to tell Carlisle the sad tale when Nazario moved between them and pointed, "Look. There's another German ship! A big one!"

Carlisle turned to the German cruiser passing two hundred yards in front of them. "I'm seeing more and more of those dreadful Hun."

Eli surveyed the gray cruiser and its smoke-billowing stack, massive fore and aft gun turrets, and red Nazi flag flying from its stern. Eli turned to the professor when he sensed his animosity. "You despise them."

"Who doesn't, after what they did to the world?" huffed Carlisle.

Eli turned back to the passing cruiser. He tried to bury his sense of responsibility for the last war. "It is unfortunate the actions of a few can cause so many to suffer."

"Yes, it is," fumed Carlisle. "And to think it all started with that damn archduke getting shot."

Eli's heart sank, and his gaze lowered to the ferry's rusty deck as that terrible day in Sarajevo flashed through his mind.

"I wonder what trouble this Hitler will make?" said Carlisle, almost spitting out the name. "What business does he have down here anyway?"

"I don't know," muttered Eli as the cruiser faded into the distance.

CHAPTER 34

THE LAND EAST

THE ABYSS

The mountain was shaking when Nixx led Michelle and the others out of the tunnel. Each looked up into the starry night, savoring the beauty of the lit sky as they made their way down the trail to the dark blanket of clouds.

Gak was the first to descend through them. Like a diver taking his last breath, he paused before lowering into the murky shroud. Nixx and then Michelle followed. She gave one last look at the sparkling stars as the dark mist enveloped Franny and then her. Unable to see by her natural eyes or her darksight, Michelle held Franny's hand tightly as they descended the stone steps through the thick, black clouds. She held her breath but still tasted the bitter ash. When Michelle thought she saw a dimly glowing light below them, she said, "That's odd."

Michelle gasped when she came out of the mist and saw, by the dim light of a torch, a centurion holding his sword to Gak's throat. On the other side of the trail, a soldier pushed up Nixx's chin with the tips of his forked spear. Before Michelle could cry out a warning, a soldier grabbed her from behind and clamped his hand over her mouth. A torchbearer then swooped in and snatched Franny from her.

Michelle watched the dark ceiling of clouds with bulging eyes as four fighters waited for Remiel to walk into their trap, their spears pointed.

When neither Remiel nor Og appeared, the centurion pressed his blade against Gak's throat, drawing blood, and growled, "Where are they?"

"I don't know," wheezed Gak as Michelle fought against her captor, her bag and blazerod hanging inches from her clutched hand.

"They're not coming," said Nixx. "They left through the gate."

"Who are you?" grunted the centurion.

"I am Nixx Trismegistus."

"A traveler? We have another prize for the governor," sneered the centurion.

Nixx's eyes narrowed. "I am nobody's prize."

"We'll see," grinned the centurion. "Let's chop off their heads. We need only the boy alive. Start with the halfborn. Take his arms."

Nixx's sapphire eyes widened when two soldiers grabbed Gak's arms and pulled them tight. Thinking quickly, he said, "A new ruler? What happened to your governess?"

The centurion's annoyed gaze shifted to the traveler. "The witch—" he began. Then, remembering Michelle had used a blazerod to kill his governess, the centurion's eyes shot to her. "Don't let her get her wand!"

The fighter holding Michelle's mouth released her wrist and reached for her bag, but as he did, Michelle spun out of his grasp and yelled, "Remiel! It's a trap!"

The wide-eyed soldier grabbed for Michelle as she pulled the blazerod from her bag and pointed it at him. The fighter stumbled backward to the ground. Michelle turned and shot a bolt past the torchbearer holding Franny and cried, "Let my son go!"

When the torchbearer raised the boy as a shield, Michelle shot a bolt into the dark dweller's leg, severing it below the knee. The torchbearer cried out, dropped Franny, and toppled down the hill. When another raised his spear to Franny, Michelle shot him in the hand, removing it and the spear.

Furious, the centurion was about to swing his sword against Gak's neck when Remiel stepped out of the mist behind him. The watcher's swooping sword removed the centurion's arm at the shoulder, dropping the arm and blade with a *clang*. Remiel brought his sword around in one smooth motion, severing the centurion's head and silencing his agonized cry. The other soldiers turned and lunged at Gak and Remiel, but Og's mace, swinging down from the clouds, struck two of them, knocking them into the others and sending all four down the steep slope. As the dark dweller's torches went out, the fiery glow of the lava fields, hundreds of feet below, lit the mountain's slope.

Michelle pulled Franny close to her and shielded his eyes as Og clubbed two more fighters, and Gak and Remiel silenced the rest, releasing their light into the misty night.

"Are you okay?" gasped Michelle, seeing Gak's throat wound.

"I think so," replied the round-eyed halfborn, feeling his neck.

"It's just a scratch," said Remiel, surveying the sprawled dark dwellers.

"What took you so long?" huffed Gak, still holding his throat.

Og shrugged.

Nixx shook his head at the bodies scattered down the slope, some groaning, most lifeless. "I expect as much from a giant and a halfborn, but how does a mighty watcher, a protector and teacher of mortals, come to such violence?"

Remiel didn't hide his annoyance with the traveler as he wiped off his sword on the dead centurion.

"Thank you for once again saving our lives," said Michelle.

Nixx rolled his eyes when Remiel turned and bowed his head to her.

Michelle kneeled beside Franny. "Are you okay, darling?"

Bothered by the bloodshed, Franny nodded.

"We should go," said Remiel, sheathing his sword.

"Are more of them coming?" asked Michelle.

"No. Look."

Michelle's eyes widened at the hellish scene below. The trail at the base of the mountain was now a lake of magma with fiery spouts of lava bursting from beneath.

"We can't go back that way," said Remiel, moving to the front of the group. "We must go to the east. Quickly!"

Michelle took Franny's hand as they hurried down the soot-covered mountain, cutting through the switchbacks to save time. "What about the survivors?" she called out, glancing back up the hill.

"They won't live long," replied Remiel.

"But...shouldn't we help them?"

Remiel stopped and turned to Michelle. "They should not have come against us. They have earned their fate."

"But..." Michelle glanced up the hill.

"My queen, we must get off this mountain while we still can!" urged Remiel, taking Franny in his arms.

With an understanding nod, Michelle hurried down the hill after him.

When they came to a fresh hill of steaming cinders, they turned off the trail and cut through a forest of charred trees. Michelle glanced over her shoulder when she felt the heat of a surging lava fountain. She gasped at its fury and reached for Franny when flaming rocks landed around them.

"Quickly!" cried Remiel, waving them through the dead trees.

When the traveler tripped and tumbled across the charred earth, Gak stopped and helped him to his feet. Nixx was nodding a reluctant thanks when a flaming rock struck him in the head and knocked him back to the ground.

When Gak saw Nixx unconscious, he turned to the others and yelled. "The traveler's been hit!"

Og shuffled back to them. With flaming rocks bouncing off him, the giant picked up Nixx and carried him to the shelter of an overhanging cliff where the others stood huddled. He laid the traveler down as more chunks of lava struck the ground. When Og's tattered robe lit on fire, he quickly patted it out.

"Oh, that one got him good," grimaced Gak, eyeing the traveler's smoldering head wound. "I can't say he didn't deserve it."

"Be kind," glared Michelle. "We're all together now. Is he okay?" she asked, picking bits of steaming rock from Nixx's scalp.

When the traveler groaned, Gak disappointedly shook his head.

"He's okay," nodded Remiel.

Michelle backed away when the dazed Nixx sat up. Grimacing, he felt his tender scalp. "What happened?"

"You got clobbered," grinned Gak.

Og nodded.

Nixx looked out at the falling rock and spotted his dented mandolin. "Who did that?" he exclaimed, moving to his beloved instrument.

Og looked away.

"It was you, wasn't it?" glared Nixx. "How are we going to have music now?" He picked up the damaged mandolin and strummed it. "It still works! Ha! You're all still in luck!"

Og shook his head.

Franny leaned against his mother as he warily eyed the traveler.

"What do we do now?" asked Michelle, the flaming rock still pelting the ground beyond their shelter.

"We wait until the storm passes," said Remiel.

Michelle moved out from under the ledge for a look. But when Remiel spotted a flaming chunk coming right for her, he pulled her back underneath. Stumbling backward, he fell, pulling Michelle down on top of him.

With their faces just inches apart, Michelle gulped, then pushed away from the handsome watcher.

"Hmm. You have to move fast around here," smirked Nixx as Og and Gak watched.

Michelle gave the traveler an irritated glance, then brushed off her dress and cape.

"I'm sorry. I was protecting you," blushed Remiel as he climbed to his feet.

"I know. Thank you." Michelle looked back the way they had come, then asked. "Why did those soldiers follow us?"

"You killed their ruler," shrugged Gak, sitting on a stack of boulders near the back wall of the overhang.

"Does that mean they will send more?"

Remiel shook his head. "I don't know."

"It means we won't get a warm welcome when we return to Manu," quipped Nixx.

Michelle sighed. "I just want to get home with my son."

"Is that all you want?" asked Gak, trying not to look hurt.

Michelle gulped. "I still don't know what you want me to do."

"You will," nodded Gak.

The traveler's eyes narrowed as he eyed Michelle.

The group huddled under the ledge as chunks of flaming rock dropped from the sky like hail.

"How are we getting back to Manu?" asked Michelle.

"Through the Eastlands," replied Remiel. "But we'll have to wait for it to stop."

"Have you ever traveled that way?" asked Nixx.

Remiel glanced at Og.

"You know that is the land of the Nephilim," said a concerned Nixx.

"I know," muttered Remiel.

"Who are the Nephilim?" asked Michelle as Franny sat beside Gak.

"Giants," grunted Og, his voice deep and ominous. "Mean giants."

Michelle turned to Remiel. "Are those the ones you spoke of in Luminah?"

"Yes."

"You don't want to go that way, trust me," said Nixx.

Gak waved the traveler's warning off and leaned back against a boulder, but when he did, the large rock rolled back into a stack of smaller boulders. The chain reaction caved in the wall behind him, revealing a dark opening.

"What did you do?" glared Remiel as Michelle checked Franny for harm.

"Nothing! I was just sitting there!" exclaimed Gak.

Og shook his head.

"It looks like a cave entrance," said Nixx, moving closer.

"A sealed cave." Remiel pointed to wall carvings.

"What does it say?" asked Michelle.

"It's a warning to stay out." Remiel turned back to Michelle. "Someone purposely closed off this cave."

Og stepped back.

"There is a legend of caves that run underneath this land," said Gak. "It is said they reach all the way back to Manu and beyond."

"There are legends of many things," sneered Nixx.

Michelle took Franny's hand. "It's getting hot. Is it coming from inside there?"

"No. Look," Nixx said, pointing back the way they had come.

Michelle gasped when she turned to a ten-foot-tall wall of magma rolling toward them, not a hundred steps away.

"We have to move!" exclaimed Remiel, his eyes searching.

"Is the storm letting up?" asked Michelle.

Remiel moved to the edge of the overhang but jumped back when a watermelon-sized lava bomb struck the ground just feet away, spraying him with fiery bits. "No, it's getting worse!" he cried, stomping out the flames.

"We can't stay here!" warned Nixx.

Michelle turned to Franny, pulling on her arm and pointing to the cave entrance. While she knew her son had inexplicable abilities and insight, she had not yet placed complete confidence in them. "Franny, do you think it's safe for us to go in there?"

"You're taking advice from a boy?" scoffed Nixx.

"He is the prince and wise beyond his years!" exclaimed Gak.

"Says the halfborn dumber than twice his!" snapped Nixx.

"Stop it! We don't have time for this!" scolded Michelle. "We must work as a team, or we will fail!"

Nixx shook his head. "I see a future where we are entombed in an underground cavern and slowly cook!"

"Do you see a future where we escape from this wall of molten rock by doing nothing?" asked Michelle.

Nixx looked out at the falling lava. The storm had only worsened. "I do not."

Michelle moved to the edge of the overhang. The steaming lava was still rolling toward them. She glanced back at the cave opening, then turned to Og. "Can you fit through there?"

Og cocked his head, stepped toward the opening, and with a swing of his mace, smashed two feet out of the wall. His blow expanded the entrance but brought down dirt and debris on them.

"Okay, let's not do that again!" said Nixx, eyeing the teetering boulders overhead.

When Remiel gave an agreeing nod, Og lowered his mace.

"I'll lead the way," said Remiel, drawing his sword.

"Of course you will," huffed Nixx.

After taking Franny's hand in hers, Michelle ducked her head and followed Remiel through the cave opening. The cave walls sparkled orange in her darksight. But as the passage widened to a cavern with dripping stalactites, the sparkling walls turned turquoise. Michelle looked back to be sure Og had cleared the entrance and found him standing in the cavern with room to spare. "We're all here?" she asked as Nixx came out from behind the giant.

Remiel nodded. "Let's find out where this cave takes us."

Little was said as they crept through the turquoise cavern, and plops of water dripped from the spiked ceiling into puddles on the rock floor. When the level ground began to slope, it grew slick, and Michelle clutched Franny's hand. As they descended, stalagmites appeared on the cave floor, and with each step, the cones of calcified rock grew taller. The rock spikes reached the ceiling in places and joined with the dripping stalactites to form long, hourglass-shaped columns.

"Be careful," warned Remiel from ahead. "It's getting steeper and slippery."

Gak was beside Michelle when his bony legs flew out from under him, and he slid past Remiel, screaming down the turquoise slope out of her view. Michelle stopped and was about to call down to Gak when Og slid past her, snapping off stalagmites on his way. "Oh, no! Are you both okay?" she gasped. But all she heard was Nixx laughing.

Turning to scold the traveler, Michelle's eyes widened when she felt her sandals moving under her. "Oh, no!" she screamed as she slid into Remiel, knocking him off his feet. "Franny!" she cried as she sped out of control down the slope, bouncing and spinning off of the stone pillars.

When Michelle hit the sandy bottom, it took her a minute to realize she was okay. She groaned as she got to her feet and gasped when she spotted Remiel's gleaming sword stuck blade-first in the sand a foot away. After searching for Franny, she looked up the stone slide. "Franny? Are you okay, darling?"

"Yes, Mommy," he replied, walking down holding Remiel's hand. A chuckling Nixx followed.

When Remiel reached the bottom, he released Franny's hand and retrieved his sword. "Lava has sealed the entrance."

"So, there's no going back that way," sighed Nixx.

"Is the lava coming down?" asked a worried Michelle.

"I don't think so," replied Remiel.

After embracing her son, Michelle looked across the turquoise cavern to the stirring giant. "Og, are you and Gak okay?"

Og nodded as he stood, but when he bumped into the low ceiling, he gave a deep, "Ow."

"I was fine until you landed on me," groaned Gak.

"Sorry," grunted Og.

"How is it you didn't fall?" asked Gak, glaring at the traveler as he climbed to his feet.

"Some are more graceful than others," smirked Nixx.

"The universe missed another chance to smash your mandolin," mumbled Gak.

"Any broken bones?" asked Remiel, surveying the band.

"Just those," said Nixx, pointing across the cavern.

All eyes turned to the field of bones scattered down the sandy floor as far as their darksight could show them.

"What happened?" gasped Michelle. "Where did all of these bones come from?"

Remiel picked up a femur and placed it beside his own. It was half the size.

"Are they human bones?" asked Michelle, pulling Franny close.

"Almost," said Remiel.

"Almost?" asked a bewildered Michelle, stepping closer.

"They're Nalidi bones."

"Nalidi? Those small people we met on the way to Goash?"

Remiel nodded.

"But I don't understand. You said people don't age and die here."

Nixx stepped forward. "They don't age, but they still die."

Michelle sighed. "Who killed them? They seemed like a very peaceful people."

"The Nephilim," replied Nixx, pointing.

Michelle's eyes widened at the giant footprints in the sand. She turned to the traveler. "Why would the giants do that?"

Nixx shrugged. "To eat them."

"Oh, that's awful! But they have no need. No one eats here," Michelle insisted.

"I don't think the giants did this," said Remiel.

Gak glanced at Og, sadly surveying the boneyard.

Michelle turned back the way they had come. There was only the slippery climb back up. Grimacing, she looked over the field of bones and asked, "Where do we go from here?"

Remiel pointed across the boneyard. "Through there."

Michelle jumped back when a glowing, five-inch-long cockroach scurried out of a skull's eye socket.

With a swing of his mace, Og crushed the insect and the skull.

Michelle gulped. "Normally, I don't condone harming god's creatures, especially when they're harmless, but I'll make an exception."

Og nodded.

After composing herself, Michelle looked down the long, narrow cavern. While its ceiling was lower ahead, there was still room for Og to walk upright. "Where do you think this goes?"

"We're going to find out." Remiel turned to Og and asked. "Will you carry the prince?"

Og nodded.

Michelle's eyes flashed about as she followed Remiel, carefully stepping around the strewn bones as more of the glowing cockroaches scattered before them. Gradually, the cavern grew in size, and after a hundred steps, there were only a few bones in sight.

Relieved to be out of the boneyard, Michelle glanced back and smiled at Franny riding atop Og's shoulder. They hadn't walked fifty feet when the remains of wooden huts along the cave wall came into view. Michelle stopped and scanned the tattered dwellings. "They lived here?"

"The huts don't appear that old," said Remiel.

"But why would the giants do this?" Michelle turned to Og. "You would never do such a thing. Would you?"

With sad eyes, Og shook his head.

Moving closer, Michelle examined a torn-open hut with a bed of palm fronds scattered out its doorway and drag marks in the sand.

"Come up here!" yelled Gak from a hundred steps ahead.

Michelle and the others moved to the halfborn. She braced for more atrocity, but her jaw slackened when an enormous underground lake came into view. "Look at all of this water!"

"It's like our pond," Franny pointed fondly.

Michelle's heart sank. "Not quite." She looked from one side of the expansive cavern to the next, but there was only water. "How do we get across?"

"I don't know," frowned Remiel. "Gak, search that side. I'll check over here."

Michelle watched them hurry along the shoreline, then kneeled and embraced Franny. "Are you okay, darling?"

"Yes, Mommy."

"I'm sorry," whispered Michelle, her eyes welling with tears.

"Don't cry, Mommy. It's okay."

Michelle sighed. "But it's not. I just want to get you home—back to your papa."

Franny nodded.

"I'm so proud of you," Michelle's smile spilled tears down her cheeks. "You're growing up so fast. I'm sad your papa can't see it."

"It's okay, Mommy."

Michelle wiped at her tears. "I don't know how to get us home."

"We'll get home, but there are things we have to do first."

Michelle's brow furrowed. "What things?"

"Help people."

"Which people?"

Franny smiled. "It's okay, Mommy. You'll know."

"The water goes to the wall," said Remiel, jogging back.

"Same on that side," sighed Gak.

Michelle pulled her gaze from the tranquil Franny. "How do we get across?"

"We build a boat," said Remiel.

"And where do we get wood to build a boat?" scoffed Nixx. "We're trapped in a cave!"

Remiel turned back to the wooden huts. "There."

"Are you sure it wouldn't be easier to swim across?" asked Michelle.

"Do you know how far it is to the other side?" asked Nixx.

Michelle shook her head.

"And some of us can't swim," said Gak, looking sideways at Og.

"If it's not too deep, Og might be able to wade across," said Michelle.

Remiel turned to Og. "Should we try it?"

Og gave a nervous shrug.

"Go on. Walk out there a bit," urged Nixx.

Og glanced at Gak, set down his mace, and stepped into the water. "Cold," he shuddered.

"You can do it," urged Michelle.

With a nervous sigh, Og took two more steps. Knee-deep, he turned back to the others, his shaggy face hiding his worry.

"See, it's not so bad," said Michelle.

Og took another step and disappeared under the water with a *plop*.

Michelle gasped.

"Og!" cried Gak, stepping into the lake after his friend. "It is cold!" he exclaimed, jumping back.

Bursting out of the water, a gasping Og clawed his way back onto dry land as the others grabbed hold and pulled. Rolling onto his back, his robe soaking wet, Og grunted. "Deep."

Remiel nodded. "We'll build the raft."

CHAPTER 35
THE SHADOW OF THE MOUNT

Nazario's eyes widened as their caravan entered the Holy Valley, and a jagged brown mountain, soaring into the brilliant blue sky, came into view. "Is that it? Is that Mount Sinai?"

"It is," nodded Eli, remembering the swarming Hebrew camp that once filled the valley.

"Just think, Moses met God and received the Ten Commandments on that mountain!" exclaimed Nazario.

"Up ahead is Saint Catherine's," pointed Carlisle, amused at the reporter's excitement.

Nazario sat up on his camel when the tall green cypress trees came into view. He gasped when the high walls of the monastery appeared, built from the same stone as the mountain behind it. "I see it! It's even more spectacular than I imagined!"

"Spectacular is not a word I would use," muttered Penelope, still subdued from her failed attempt to seduce Eli days before.

Eli half-heard her as he took in the green cypress spires and clusters of olive trees. Just beyond the garden oasis stood the monastery's sixty-foot

walls, giving it the look of a castle. "None of this was here before," Eli
muttered, spotting the top of the bell tower within.

"What was that?" asked Carlisle, glancing back from atop his camel.

"He said he's never been here before," replied Nazario as Asim, riding
behind, eyed Eli.

"Wait until you see how we get inside," laughed Penelope as their
caravan neared the seven-foot-high garden walls.

"You've been here before?" asked Eli.

Penelope gave the watcher a sideways glance but didn't reply.

"Is this a monastery or a fortress?" asked Nazario, surveying its high
stone walls, turrets, and bastions.

"A little of both," said Carlisle. "It has a fascinating history."

"Please educate us, Professor," implored Nazario, unable to take his
eyes off the forbidding monastery as he bobbed atop his camel.

Always happy to share his knowledge, Carlisle sat a little taller on his
camel. "Egypt was one of the first countries to espouse the cause of Chris-
tianity. But the Romans severely persecuted them, and in the second
century, many Christians fled to the desert to escape the oppression. They
gathered here in the Sinai, but it was not an easy existence. Marauding
Bedouin tribes frequently harassed them. But then, some would say, something miraculous happened. Emperor Constantine became a Christian, and
in three hundred A.D., the monks suddenly had an unlikely ally. The
emperor commissioned the building of the Chapel of the Burning Bush—
supposedly on the spot where God visited Moses. However, the monastery
was under constant assault by the Muslims. It was Emperor Justinian who
finally responded to their petitions, and by the mid-fifth century, Rome
had built a wall around their abbey."

"Remarkable," said Nazario. "But what of the marauding Bedouins?
How did they make peace? You said they have a mosque inside."

"That's another story entirely," said Carlisle. "When the crusaders were
driven back by the Muslims in 1200, those left behind had to make do.
They had to either fight and die by the sword or make peace. The monks
here made peace."

"Remarkable," breathed Nazario.

"Father, how many died in the Crusades?" asked Penelope.

"It's impossible to know," replied Carlisle.

"From my research, some believe up to nine million perished," replied Nazario.

Eli closed his eyes. He remembered those dark years well.

Carlisle shook his head and huffed, "It's a tragedy what some will do in the name of their god. Worship the Christ or off with your head. It's abhorrent and the reason I have no use for religion."

Nazario considered Carlisle's comment, then said, "I, like you, detest the violence men have brought under the pretext of religion, but I have witnessed too much in my days to doubt the presence of a divine being—or beings," he added, glancing at Eli.

"Good for you," muttered Carlisle.

When Nazario spotted a wooden-framed structure suspended fifty feet up the wall, like a bottomless outhouse, he pointed and asked. "What's that?"

"That's how we get inside," laughed Penelope.

Eli's gaze turned to two men in turbans and jellabiyas emerging from the garden entrance.

"Peace, peace," nodded Carlisle to the Bedouins as one gave a toothless smile and reached for the professor's camel. "Asim, will you take care of things here?"

The one-eyed foreman nodded and lowered his camel to the ground.

"Are they standing guard?" asked Nazario.

"No, they stable and tend to the animals of the travelers who come here. Of course, they earn a pittance but should be commended for their industriousness," said Carlisle.

Eli had his bag over his shoulder as he climbed off the camel and followed the others through the outer wall's entrance. When he looked up to the wood outhouse on the tall inner wall, he saw a basket suspended by a thick rope and a bearded man peering down through a small window, fifty feet up.

"Who comes?" called down the monk.

"Professor Niles Carlisle and three guests. Please tell Father Mateo."

Eli felt the monk's scrutinizing gaze before he disappeared from the small opening in the stone wall.

"What a magical place!" exclaimed Nazario, making a quick sketch in his notebook.

With the sound of wooden gears turning, the basket lowered from the elevated outhouse.

"Welcome!" called down Father Mateo, a round black cap on his head, his long gray beard dangling from the small opening.

"I'm sorry for the unannounced visit," said Carlisle.

"You are always most welcome," grinned Mateo. "Perhaps you will discover your faith here this time."

"Perhaps, but I rather doubt it," laughed Carlisle. He turned to the others and said, "The basket can hold two, but you may want to travel by yourself, Eli. No need to overwork the chaps up there on the wheel."

Eli nodded as the wooden basket lowered to the ground beside them.

Carlisle lifted the basket's arm, stepped inside, and motioned for Penelope to join him. The thick rope groaned as it stretched taut, and the gears high above popped and clicked as the basket ascended.

Eli caught Penelope's injured gaze. He wondered what more he could do to appease her without violating his honor.

Soon, the empty basket returned, and Eli motioned for Nazario to go next. When Eli was finally hoisted into the outhouse, he nodded thanks to the four Bedouins straining on the massive wheel that raised and lowered the basket.

"Welcome to Saint Catherine's," beamed the long-bearded Father Mateo. Like the other monks, he wore a long black cassock with a matching brimless hat. His beard was dark near the roots but grew increasingly white through its ten-inch length. Mateo's gray eyes narrowed as he studied the tall Eli. "Have you been here before, my friend?"

"No," replied Eli, shaking the monk's hand.

Mateo stroked his beard as he eyed the watcher. "You look familiar. I'm sure I've seen you before."

Nazario watched the exchange, his reporter mind wondering what the monk had seen.

"It will come to me," smiled Mateo. "Come, I'm sure you would enjoy some refreshment after your long journey. I'll let you sample some of our date wine. It is the best in the Sinai! Of course, that isn't saying much," he winked.

Penelope smiled and flashed a glance at Eli, her bitterness waning.

Eli followed the others as they descended the worn stone steps into the monastery. With a smile and a wave, Father Mateo led them down the path toward the ancient basilica, its brown granite walls rising to a steep copper roof darkly patinated by time.

Eli removed his hat when they entered the 1,400-year-old church. His nostrils flared at the musty air laced with burning incense. Eli's curious gaze moved from the colorful wall paintings to the ornate Byzantine nave. The floor was a vibrant tile mosaic lined by dark wood seats and pulpits. White pillars supported arching plaster walls that stretched to the green and gold ceiling high above. Enormous golden chandeliers hung down, with smaller lamps and incense burners hanging in the side aisles. Rays of light cut across the nave from the high windows, making parts of the already bright and colorful church radiant. At the far end of the nave, behind the altar, stood the apse, a wall of Byzantine paintings surrounded by intricate gilded panels. Hidden beyond those panels was the sacred Chapel of the Burning Bush.

"What treasures hide here?" whispered Nazario, his wide eyes scanning as they passed behind the back pew.

"It is quite elaborate, but a bit overdone if you ask me," muttered Penelope.

"It is a holy place," nodded Nazario.

After exiting the basilica, they followed Father Mateo through a circuitous passageway until it opened to the outside. The monk waved them to a table near an olive tree, then said, "Please, sit. It is a lovely day. We should enjoy God's light."

"Thank you, Father," nodded Carlisle, replacing his hat.

Father Mateo motioned to an aged, bronze-skinned monk passing by and said, "Father Zadith, will you bring wine for our visitors?"

The white-bearded monk stopped when he saw Eli, then gave a slight bow, turned, and departed.

Mateo sat at the table, then motioned to the wooden chairs across from him. "Please."

Eli caught Penelope's gaze as they sat. It was the first hint of longing he had seen from her since fleeing his bath. Eli looked away, but that simple eye movement elicited sadness and uncertainty from Penelope. Eli considered her response. While there were many things he better understood about mortals from his awakening, the driving force of desire was still a mystery to him.

"What brings you to our humble abbey, Professor Carlisle?"

"We are on a search for relics."

"Naturally. You are a man obsessed with the buried past," nodded Mateo. "I only hope your obsession does not blind you to your present."

Carlisle lightly regarded the comment, then turned to Eli. "Show Father Mateo your plate."

Eli opened his satchel and found the engraved plate beside the stolen Vatican book and hidden blazerod. He set it on the table before the monk.

"Father, I recall you having such plates in your library," said Carlisle.

Mateo examined the brass plate as the aged Father Zadith set five goblets on the table with bent and crooked fingers. The monk's eyes widened when he spotted the engraved plate.

"Where did you find this?" asked Mateo.

"Rome. The Vatican, to be precise," replied Eli as the curious monk poured date wine from an aged green bottle.

Mateo thoughtfully nodded, stroked his beard, and then turned to Eli. "We may have similar plates, but you cannot take them from here."

"I understand," said Eli.

"What is it you're searching for?" asked Mateo.

"Information on Hathor," replied Eli.

"The Egyptian goddess?" asked Mateo with a raised brow.

"Yes. In particular, the location of her gate."

Father Mateo casually nodded, but the serving monk stopped pouring and turned to Eli. No one but Nazario saw it.

When Zadith's eyes met the reporter's, he resumed filling the last goblet and left the table.

Father Mateo raised his glass and said, "To my new friends: may your time in the shadow of the Mount be blessed."

The others raised their goblets and drank.

"Oh, it's very nice," said Nazario, smacking his lips.

"That is high esteem coming from an Italian." Mateo's smile faded as he turned to Eli. "So, you seek the location of Hathor's Gate?"

"Yes."

"I thought that was an Egyptian legend. Part of their afterlife mythology."

Carlisle nodded. "That's what I told Elijah, but he's convinced it's not. And this plate gives some tantalizing clues."

"Oh?"

Eli leaned closer and pointed to the engravings. "Ibn Umayl is the plate's author."

"Do you know of him?" asked Nazario.

Father Mateo's brow tightened. "Muhammad Ibn Umayl. Yes, he was a notable Egyptian alchemist. Quite a mystic, I understand. But how does he connect to your mythical gate?"

"On the plate, Ibn mentions Hathor's Gate being used to move people to another world. The dark realm, he calls it," explained Eli.

"Isn't he simply referring to legend?" asked Mateo.

"He speaks as though they used it in his time as punishment."

"But how is that possible?" asked Mateo. "Ibn Umayl lived nine hundred years after the last pharaoh."

Eli studied the benevolent monk. He had said nothing about the gate being abused by a pharaoh. Eli tried to discern him but couldn't.

"It's all very interesting," said Mateo, leaning back in his chair.

Nazario was eyeing the contemplative monk when he noticed Father Zadith's cassock protruding from around a corner. He leaned his head to see the eavesdropping monk better, but when their eyes met, Zadith turned and disappeared into a shadowy passageway.

"How long do you plan to stay with us?" asked Mateo.

"Two, maybe three days, if you'll allow us. That should be enough time for us to conduct our research," said Carlisle.

"You are welcome to stay in the guest house. Your camel hands are also welcome."

"Thank you," nodded Carlisle.

AFTER CLEANING up from their journey, and a simple dinner of bread, goat's cheese, and dates, Father Mateo led the four explorers into the fading daylight for a brief tour of the abbey.

They had just passed the cream-stuccoed mosque when a man's voice rang out from atop the minaret, calling the Muslims to prayer. Eli stopped and listened as the muezzin's song echoed through the monastery and off the nearby mountain slope. He turned to the western gate that led to the gardens and watched tired Bedouins enter for their evening worship.

"This way," called Mateo over the muezzin's beckoning song.

After passing between the chapels of St. Stephen and St. Antony, they came to a long, narrow building with rows of arched verandas stretching across two levels. At the center of the building was a vaulted entry with a large domed top.

Nazario's eyes widened as Father Mateo led them into the medieval library. Inside was a long central hall with rows of dark wood bookshelves overflowing with ancient texts. Nazario's gaze followed the spiral stairs to a second floor of bookcases that were just as full. An ornate tile mosaic covered the narrow hall's floor, and glowing brass chandeliers hung above wooden tables and chairs. Seated at a table, a bushy-bearded monk poured over open books and papers.

"I wasn't expecting this. It's magnificent," said Nazario, his notebook already open. His eyes narrowed when the curious Father Zadith appeared from around a bookcase.

"We are very proud of our library," nodded Father Mateo. "We have collected Greek, Georgian, Arabic, Coptic, Hebrew, and Aramaic texts going back to antiquity."

"I'm sure every museum in the world would love to acquire a fraction of your collection," said Nazario, taking it all in. He breathed in the sweet and sour redolence of aged parchment, ink, and animal hides. "I can smell the history," he whispered.

A less impressed Penelope turned from the rows of books and asked, "Why haven't you sold your collection to museums so the outside world can enjoy them? You would make a fortune and could all retire."

Father Mateo's grin was imperceptible as he turned to her. "There are some things too precious to be squandered on the masses."

"Ah. Pearls before swine," nodded Nazario.

Mateo's eyebrows lifted. "We are all swine when it comes to communing with our God. At least until we are purified and found true."

"Are you purified, Father Mateo? Have you found enlightenment?" asked a scrutinizing Penelope.

Carlisle gave his daughter a warning glance.

"Of course they are!" nodded Nazario. "Look at the monistic lives they lead. They have cut themselves off from all but serving God! Is there any way to become closer to him?"

Mateo gave a slight bow, acknowledging the reporter's compliment, then turned to the others. "The world dulls one's senses and understanding of God's ways. Moses was cleansed and prepared before communing with God, but even that was not enough, and God's radiance nearly consumed him like a burning bush. No normal human could have withstood that." Mateo's gentle gaze turned to Nazario, and he asked, "What happened when Moses came off the mount and returned to the Children of Israel?"

"They had gone back to the idolatrous ways of the Egyptians," replied Nazario. "They had even made a golden calf to worship." His face lit up. "The golden calf! That was Hathor they were worshiping!"

Carlisle stared past the reporter, trying to put it all together.

Father Mateo nodded. "That is right. In the time that Moses had prepared himself to see God, the people he had led from bondage forgot what he had taught them. God gave Moses a higher law, carved by his own hand on stone tablets, but when the prophet descended and saw the Hebrews were not ready, he smashed the tablets." Mateo sighed. "The Hebrews would wander the Sinai forty years and never be ready. The people of the world are no better prepared now. Some might say worse."

"What is it you hide from them?" asked Penelope.

Father Mateo smiled. "We do not hide. We keep sacred."

"What is it you keep sacred, then?"

"That is for the pure in heart to discover," said Mateo with a bow.

Carlisle turned from Penelope and said, "Father, thank you for allowing us this visit. We will be completely respectful of your wishes."

"I have no doubt," said Mateo. His gaze moved to Eli. "I have asked Father Gregory, our utmost expert, and Father Zadith to help you in your search. Now, if you'll excuse me."

Nazario eyed the curious Father Zadith as Mateo bowed and exited the library.

Eli's attention turned to the two remaining gray-haired monks. While they were dressed alike in black cassocks and hats, Father Gregory was shorter, stockier, and had a bushier beard. Zadith was older, his beard longer and whiter, and his wrinkly skin and eyes darker. Of the two, Gregory appeared more confident, while Zadith's beady eyes darted about uneasily before the visitors. Eli wondered why his power of discernment failed him when he tried to read the two monks.

"What is it you wish to see?" asked Father Gregory in Coptic.

Eli cocked his head. He thought of Asim's same question in Hathor's Temple and wondered if the two were somehow connected. *An Egyptian dig foreman and a Greek Orthodox monk? Unlikely.* "Do you have any writings from Ibn Umayl?" Eli asked in English so the others could understand.

Nazario watched Father Zadith fidget at the question.

"We do not," replied Father Gregory, studying Eli.

Eli could tell the monk was lying.

"When I was here last, I saw engraved plates made from brass and copper, about this size," Carlisle said, making the shape of a small book with his hands. "Eli, show them your plate."

Still trying to discern the monks, Eli removed the brass plate from his shoulder bag. "Do you have any plates like this?"

Father Gregory took the plate and studied its engravings. Then he handed it back to Eli with a dismissive shake of his head.

Nazario's shoulders sank at their failure, but Carlisle's brow tightened, sure of what he had seen.

"Don't tell me we came all this way for nothing," sighed Penelope.

"We didn't," said Eli, eyeing the uncooperative monk. He put the plate back in his bag, then said in Coptic, "Why aren't you helping us?"

"What language is that?" asked a confused Carlisle.

Nazario shrugged as Penelope listened.

"I know who you are," replied the monk in the same tongue.

Eli's eyes narrowed. "Who am I?"

The dark-eyed Zadith watched unblinkingly as Father Gregory stepped closer to Eli. "You are one of the fallen. We are sworn to protect the world from you."

"Will someone please tell me what's going on?" asked Carlisle, sensing the tension.

"You're mistaken. I'm one of the true," replied a stern-eyed Eli.

Father Gregory shook his head, his gray eyes piercing. "We do not fear you. You can take nothing from us that we have not already surrendered."

Eli was taken aback by the comment. "Why do you suppose I would ever harm you? It's not in my nature. I'm simply trying to find a portal to the abyss."

"The way is sealed and cannot be opened," glared Gregory.

"You don't understand. My wife and son are trapped there. I must find a way to rescue them," insisted Eli, his fists tightening.

Gregory shook his head. "You seek this for you. You do not seek it for a pure cause."

The allegation staggered Eli. He had been accused of many things over his eons of existence, but being dishonorable was not one of them. Eli's jaw tightened. *How dare he! He has no idea what I've been through!* In a flash of rage, Eli reached for Father Gregory's tunic, believing he could physically bend the monk to his will, but his hand stopped short. Horrified by his emotional outburst, Eli lowered his arm and relaxed his fists. Then, with his jaw hanging, Eli blinked in thought, stunned by the possibility the monk had judged him correctly.

Nazario, who had seen the exchange along with the others, asked, "What just happened?"

Father Gregory turned to the reporter and said in English, "You all appear rather tired. I suggested to your friend that you rest for the night and visit the library in the morning."

A still confused Carlisle turned to Eli and said, "Well, it has been a long day. A fresh start in the morning isn't a bad idea."

"I agree," groaned Penelope, turning away.

Nazario studied his friend, knowing something different was said, then added, "I think a good night's sleep would benefit us all."

Eli's bewildered gaze raised to the two monks, who looked at him not in defiance but with concern, as if for a lost soul. "Very well. In the morning," muttered Eli as he turned to the door.

ELI WAS SITTING in the garden outside the western gate of the monastery, gazing across the tall cypress and bushy olive trees glistening in the moonlight, when Nazario joined him, holding a folded blanket. The reporter set the blanket on Eli's lap, lit a cigarette, and said, "I thought you might be cold out here."

"Thank you," muttered Eli.

"Do you want to tell me what happened in the library tonight?"

Eli sighed. "He thought I was one of the fallen. That my intentions to find Michelle are not pure."

Nazario's eyebrows raised as he drew in burned tobacco.

Eli turned to his friend. "Am I wrong for wanting to rescue my wife?"

Nazario blew out the smoke and tiredly shook his head. "For most men, I would say no. But you are no ordinary man. You have a calling that...that I can't even comprehend." Nazario's gaze moved from the moonlit valley to the steep and jagged slopes of Mount Sinai. "Servants of God throughout time have been faced with a choice. To do their own will or to do God's. I don't think Moses bringing millions of Hebrews into the desert and then climbing that mountain to speak to God was something he wanted to do. He did it because God wanted him to. He was obedient. I think Mary would have chosen another path, but she loved God and bore his son. Even Jesus wanted the cup to pass from him, but he followed God's will."

Eli lifted his head to the starry night.

"The only one I can think of that did what he wanted was Jonah, and we know how that turned out with the whale," chuckled Nazario.

Eli sat quietly for a time, then said, "You don't think rescuing Michelle is what the Great Ones desire?"

Nazario shrugged. "Have they told you what they desire?"

"They have been silent." Eli shook his head. "I thought I was so close when we found the orb in the abbey. But they took it from me."

Nazario studied his friend. The answer was obvious to him, but he knew Eli didn't want to hear it. He took another drag from his cigarette, then said, "Maybe now isn't the right time to save your wife. Maybe they want you to do something else."

"What?" asked Eli, vexed by the suggestion.

Nazario shrugged. "If you were doing your regular job, what would you do?"

"My regular job?"

"You know, your angel job."

"I'm not an angel," muttered Eli.

"Your watcher job then."

Eli sighed and looked down at the ground. "I would try to stop Lu and Cyrus. I would try to restore balance to the world."

Nazario looked up into the stars and said, "Do you think that is what God and the Holy Ones want you to do?"

Eli shook his head and muttered, "I don't know."

Nazario sat beside his friend for a time, then said, "It's getting cold. I'm going to bed."

Eli said nothing as Nazario stood and returned to the monastery. Instead, he brooded over how close he had come, and what might have been had he found the portal and a way to save his wife and son.

Eli was about to return to the guest house when he saw a dark figure moving through the garden shadows. He knew it was a monk from the flowing black robes and round hat. He watched as the monk passed through the twisted olive trees to the main path, where he stopped and turned to Eli. Though thirty yards away, Eli could see the monk's beckoning gesture. Eli set the blanket aside, pulled on his satchel, and started down the path.

Eli was still ten yards away when he recognized the dark-eyed Father Zadith from the library. As he drew closer, the monk nervously waved for Eli to join him in the shadows.

"I can help you with what you seek," whispered the monk, his eyes darting about the murky garden.

Eli's eyes widened. "You can help me find Hathor's Gate?"

Zadith nodded. "Follow me."

Eli glanced back up the hill toward the monastery. There was no one in sight. He followed the monk down the path to a stone wall and through another gate. Soon a long, narrow building the size of two boxcars stacked atop one another came into view, its yellow stucco glowing in the moonlight. Eli watched as Zadith removed a key and approached a door under an arched entry. "What is this place?"

"The charnel house," whispered the monk.

"An ossuary?"

"Yes." The jittery monk opened the door and waved Eli inside.

Eli entered with one hand on his shoulder bag, the blazerod within reach.

After lighting a match, Zadith closed the door, descended some steps, and lit a wall candle.

Eli's curious eyes flickered in the candlelight. Before him was a pile of skulls stacked to the ceiling. *My vision.* It was the same pile of bones he had seen after touching Penelope. "What is this place?"

"This is where we keep the bones of our dead brothers," said Zadith, eyeing Eli. "But that is not what I wanted to show you. Come."

Eli took a step, then stopped when the candlelight illuminated a skeleton dressed in black priestly robes sitting on a chair. The clothed skeleton had a wooden cross around its neck, Greek letters adorning its cassock and hat, and rosaries hanging from its bony hands.

"That is Father Stephanos, Guardian of the Path," said Zadith. "Over here."

Eli followed the monk past more piles of bones to an old wooden chest. After setting the candle down, Zadith pushed the chest aside. Eli stepped back as two rats darted out from under it. In the floor, hidden by the chest, was a square wooden door.

"Help me open it."

Eli grabbed hold of the trapdoor's iron ring. Its hinges groaned when he pulled it open.

With the flickering candle in hand, Zadith's eager eyes flashed to Eli before he climbed down the ladder into the dark crypt.

Eli followed, but the crypt's ceiling was low, forcing him to stand hunched over. Eli's nose wrinkled at the dry, musty air as he scanned the dark and cramped chamber. In it were no bones but dusty shelves stacked with clay tablets and metal plates. "What are these?"

"What I wanted to show you," nodded Zadith. He moved to the shelf, picked up a tablet, and blew off the dust before handing it to Eli.

Eli studied its wedged-shaped engravings. "This is cuneiform, thousands of years old."

"Yes. Do you see its author?"

Eli scanned the text. "Ibn Umayl!"

The monk searched the stacks for another tablet, then handed it to Eli. "In this one, he speaks of the doorway."

Eli read the tablet as the monk dusted off a brass plate. "It says the gate was moved!"

"This is like the one you have, only it tells the gate's location."

Eli took the six-inch by eight-inch metal plate and studied its meticulously carved engravings in the candlelight. "Abydos! It was moved to Abydos!"

Zadith nodded.

"Why are you showing me these things?"

The monk's eyes narrowed. "We are the guardians of the path to truth and enlightenment. But while some among us doubt your quest, I think it a noble cause. Especially with your son's divine mission."

"How do you know of me and my son's mission?"

Zadith closed his eyes as if praying. When he opened them, he turned to the watcher, waiting for Eli's instinct to take over.

Like the sun breaking through a cloud, Eli's discernment returned to him. His eyes widened as he studied the monk. "*You're* Ibn Umayl!"

The monk gave a slight bow.

"You're a traveler. You were blocking me from discerning you."

"There is much danger around us. Even here in the shadow of the Mount, corruption and treachery lurk. The dark forces of evil know no bounds and will stop at nothing to secure their power and control over this world."

"We have seen it for too long," sighed Eli.

"Yes, we have," nodded Zadith. "We met once before, you and I. In Uruk. I was much younger then, but you look just the same."

Eli's gaze turned to the dusty shelves of the crypt. "These are your writings."

"Yes, from long ago. When the world was younger and purer."

"Do the other monks know who you are?"

"A few."

"Can they be trusted?"

"Some."

"Father Gregory?"

"As an ardent protector of the path, Father Gregory's resolve sometimes blinds him."

Eli breathed in the knowledge, then turned to the monk and asked, "What must I do to rescue my family?"

"You must find the portal in Abydos."

"Abydos was buried in a sandstorm that lasted a hundred days," frowned Eli.

"That is where you will find it, in the Portal Temple of Ramses."

Eli shook his head. "But how do I find it?"

"Patience will guide you," said Zadith. "But there is another place you must first go."

"What other place?"

Zadith looked Eli in the eyes. "You will know."

Eli breathed out the angst he had for so long carried. Overjoyed by the prospect of finally finding his family, he asked, "Will you travel with us to Abydos?"

Zadith's brow tightened. "Some will not be pleased with what I have shown you. I must travel separately."

"Will you open the doorway to the abyss once we find the temple?"

"If your work is done," nodded Zadith.

Eli considered the complexity of the situation. "Is there anything else you can tell me? Anything I should know?"

"Much is in motion. The world is changing with each beat of your heart. You must be prepared to alter your course if you are to succeed."

Eli's eyes narrowed, uncertain of the traveler's meaning.

"Tell no one of this until you are well away from here. Spend tomorrow in the library, as planned. You will find little and can begin your journey back the following day." The monk turned to the shelf and handed Eli another plate. "On this, I write of the temple in Abydos. Guard it well, for you will need it to access the portal."

"Thank you," said Eli, eyeing the plate.

"Beware of those seeking the gate."

"Lu and Cyrus," said a pensive Eli.

"I don't have to tell you what chaos they would bring to this world should they have access to the banished souls of that dark realm."

Eli put the plate into his bag.

Zadith placed a bony hand on Eli's wrist, and his dark eyes softened. "Elijah. You are one of the few remaining with the power to stop Lu. While your quest to find your family is just, don't blind yourself to the rising tide of evil filling this world."

Eli locked eyes with Zadith. "You think I can do both? Find Michelle and stop Lu?"

"I believe one will lead to the other."

Eli drew in a ragged breath, then nodded. "Thank you. Thank you for all you've done for me."

"I have done it for all humanity," said Zadith with a tightening brow. "But beware. Danger and treachery lurk in even the purest of souls."

CHAPTER 36
BROTHERS

It was a long and restless night for Eli. Seeing a way forward gave him hope, but knowing the obstacles still in his path filled Eli with trepidation.

After breakfast, Eli, Nazario, and Carlisle returned to the library, leaving Penelope sleeping. When they entered, the bushy-bearded Father Gregory looked up from his table, a quill in one hand and a ledger open before him.

"The day is well spent. I wondered if you had already left," sneered the monk.

"You said after breakfast," frowned Carlisle.

"Breakfast was two hours before the sun rose," replied Gregory.

"Of course. Forgive us for not being on your schedule," smiled Nazario.

The monk set his quill down beside the inkwell and snapped his ledger closed. "Where would you like to begin?"

Eli scanned the study hall. He spotted another monk working on the far table past the spiral stairs. "Where is Father Zadith?"

"He's off on an errand and won't be joining us," Gregory said dismissively.

Nazario leaned into Eli. "Just as well. He seemed off to me."

Carlisle cleared his throat. "Last night, you said you had no engraved plates in your collection, but I vividly recall handling them when I was last here."

"Perhaps your memory has failed you," said the monk.

"I rather doubt that," huffed Carlisle.

The monk raised a hand to the surrounding archives. "I have texts from the region going back four thousand years. Where would you like to begin, or would you care to read them all?"

Eli shook his head, unsurprised by the monk's lack of cooperation.

"I'm afraid we don't have time for that," said Carlisle. "I was rather hoping you might be a good enough chap to direct us on where to look."

"I can show you to the texts that speak of the Egyptian pantheon."

Carlisle glanced at Eli and nodded. "That sounds like a good place to start."

IT WAS late in the evening, and the brass chandeliers were aglow above the study tables laden with books, scrolls, and manuscripts. In one corner, Penelope lay curled up on a blanket. At a table sat a groggy-eyed Carlisle, numbly thumbing through ancient texts. Eli and Nazario sat at the next table. The reporter was studying a tattered parchment, but Eli was staring across the empty library, pondering his encounter the night before with Father Zadith.

"This is odd," said Nazario, eyeing a faded parchment through a magnifying glass. "I can see faint writing in the background."

Eli blinked away his thoughts and turned to Nazario.

"See here," the reporter pointed. "Ghost text behind what is written."

Eli was studying the faded script when Father Gregory appeared from around a wall of books. "Have you found what you seek?" he asked, the wear of the day only making him crankier.

"Father, it appears there is writing in the background of this parchment." Nazario picked up another and scanned it through his glass. "This one too! Did someone write over original manuscripts?"

Gregory bristled at the accusation. "There was a time when parchment was very rare here, and the caretakers of that day chose to bleach certain manuscripts clean and reuse them."

Nazario's jaw slackened. "They destroyed ancient writings to make room for their own?"

"It was of necessity," glared Gregory.

"How much ancient knowledge was lost?" gasped Carlisle, staggered by the thought.

Father Gregory's glare turned to Eli. "Nothing of importance."

"But how do you know? It was all erased!" exclaimed Nazario.

"How many documents were washed clean?" asked Carlisle.

"Hundreds," replied Gregory.

Nazario shook his head numbly. "So much lost because of a paper shortage!"

Eli studied the unmoved Father Gregory. He knew the parchments were not whitewashed by accident. The monks had strategically erased inconvenient accounts from the ancient past, just as the Church had from its canon of scripture.

Carlisle shook his head and groaned, "I'm afraid I dragged you out here for nothing, Elijah."

"That wouldn't be the first time," muttered Penelope, stirring from under her blanket.

"I was certain I had seen the plates here."

"Don't be so sure your memory failed you," replied Eli. He felt Father Gregory's piercing stare, then added, "The journey was not all for nothing."

All eyes turned when the door opened, and the jovial Father Mateo entered. "How are my visitors doing this evening? You've found what you're searching for, I trust?"

"We have not, Father," sighed Carlisle.

"I'm indeed sorry to hear that," said Mateo.

"And we just learned the disturbing news your monks erased and wrote over some of these ancient manuscripts!" exclaimed Nazario.

"Not my brothers," smiled Mateo. "It was done by those who lived a thousand years ago."

A fuming Nazario shook his head.

"If your research is complete, will you be leaving tomorrow?" asked Mateo.

"There's no reason to stay if what we're looking for isn't here," sighed Carlisle. "Don't you agree, Eli?"

Eli nodded, still eyeing the ill-natured monk.

Father Mateo turned to Gregory. "Thank you for your time, Father. I know it is long past your hour."

Father Gregory gave a parting glare at Eli, then left the library.

Father Mateo nodded to the monk as he passed by. Then, stroking his beard, he turned to Carlisle and said, "I've been thinking. With you being an archeologist, you might find Serabit el-Khadim to your liking."

"The ancient Egyptian mines?"

"Yes. It's another route but will take you to the Suez just the same. The ruins of a temple to Hathor still stand there. Perhaps you will find what you seek there."

Carlisle perked up at the suggestion. "What do you say, Eli? Should we visit that place on the way back? I've been there only once and had completely forgotten about the temple."

Eli looked down as he considered the detour.

"And perhaps one last story for you, Cleto."

"Yes," grinned Nazario.

"As long as it takes me back to a soft bed and warm water," muttered Penelope.

THE MORNING AIR was brisk when Eli was lowered down the monastery wall in the basket. Below him, he saw Asim and the others preparing to mount the camels for the long trek home, but Eli's eyes narrowed when he spotted the aged Father Zadith standing beside them.

"Good morning," nodded Zadith. "I thought I would see you off."

"Thank you," said Eli, shaking the monk's hand as Nazario curiously watched. "We're going the way of Serabit el-Khadim."

"Yes, I know," replied Zadith in Coptic. "My brother, Asim, will guide you."

Eli's eyes widened. "You know each other?"

"My young friend, do not suppose anything is without purpose," said a grinning Zadith. "Your footsteps are being guided. But beware, danger lurks all around you. Let virtue and wisdom guide your steps, and you will find your path."

Eli watched in astonishment as Asim and Zadith embraced.

Bundled in a coat atop her camel, Penelope waited for Eli to mount his, then asked, "What was that all about?"

"Just saying goodbye to a new friend," said Eli.

"What language were you speaking?" asked Nazario, puzzled by Eli's connection to the unusual monk.

"A very old one," replied Eli.

CHAPTER 37
THE BLACK LAKE

THE ABYSS

After what felt to Michelle like days of braiding the Nalidi's bedding fronds into rope and binding scavenged sticks, poles, and even the traveler's staff together, the crude raft and oars were finished.

"Well, that should do it," said Remiel, eyeing the rickety bed of bound-together sticks with hands on hips.

Michelle uneasily sighed as she surveyed the crude raft, uncertain it could stay afloat.

"Og, will you move it to the water?" asked Remiel.

Og picked up an uneven end of the roughly twelve-foot-square raft and dragged it through the sand as the others nervously watched.

Nixx shook his head when three poles came loose and fell behind. "Are you sure it will hold us?"

"It should," nodded Remiel, motioning for Og to set it down.

"All of us?" Nixx asked as Remiel gathered up the broken-loose poles.

Og glared at the traveler.

"I mean at the same time. The giant weighs more than the rest of us put together, and it's not that seaworthy. It will fall apart."

"His name is Og," said Michelle. "And we're staying together."

"Do we even know where we're going?" asked Nixx.

"To the other side," shrugged Gak as he helped Remiel tie the poles to the raft.

"We can't see the other side. We don't know how far it is," sighed Nixx.

"It could be just beyond our view," said Michelle.

"Or much farther." Nixx turned to Michelle. "What will you do when the raft falls apart? You've felt that water. How long can you swim before your heart stops? Or your son's? If we all get on that raft, it will surely fail before we reach the other side. Are you willing to take that risk?"

Michelle couldn't hide her concern.

"You and your son should be on the raft, along with whoever can get you back to your world," said Nixx.

Gak rolled his eyes. "I wonder who that could be?"

"Og can stay," grunted the giant, his deep voice sad.

"No. You're an important part of our band," insisted Michelle.

Og's shaggy beard hid his smile.

Michelle considered the traveler's counsel, glanced at Remiel, still repairing the raft, and said, "We're staying together."

Nixx shook his head while Remiel and the others nodded their approval.

"We had a raft once when I was a girl," said Michelle. "It was wobbly if we stood, so we sat or laid on it. Couldn't we do that?"

"We can try." Remiel held up a crudely fashioned oar. "Who will help me paddle?"

Nixx and Gak were arguing about who would be the better oarsman when Michelle felt the ground move. "What was that?"

"A ground tremor," said Nixx.

Michelle looked up at the high cavern ceiling covered in long, pointy teeth and gasped when a second, more violent tremor broke loose a six-foot stalactite. She pulled Franny tight against her as the two-hundred-pound missile fell and speared the sand twenty feet away. "We must hurry!"

"Og, push it into the water!" ordered Remiel. "Carefully!"

The giant dragged the wobbly raft into the lake water as another tremor shook the cavern. A second mineral spear broke loose, this time plunging into the lake.

Michelle held Franny tight against her as the raft settled into the rippling water.

"Everybody on," waved Remiel, steading the raft as he searched the cavern ceiling for falling missiles.

"Og, you should get on first!" said Michelle. "But stay in the middle and lay flat to distribute your weight."

When Og climbed onto the raft, the side under his knee sank while the opposite raised a foot out of the water and everything flexed in between. A worried Og looked back at Michelle for permission to proceed. When she nodded, everyone held their breath as Og placed his full weight on the rickety raft. It groaned, and its sticks and poles swamped with the icy water under Og's knees and hands.

"Og, you must lay flat to even out your weight," said Michelle.

Og did so, and the straining raft raised above the water as it found its buoyancy.

With a relieved sigh, Remiel waved Michelle and Franny onto the raft as the cavern shook. "You and the prince should ride on Og's back to stay dry."

"Are you sure?" asked Michelle as she led Franny onto the raft.

Og nodded.

Sitting atop the giant's massive back, Michelle anxiously waited as the others climbed aboard. The raft settled further into the lake, with puddles of frigid water seeping through in low spots, but it stayed afloat. When Remiel and Gak pushed off with their oars, the groaning and cracking raft moved away from the shore.

"Listen to that," whispered Michelle as a low rumble filled the cavern. "Is it another tremor?"

"It's more than a tremor," frowned Nixx, searching the ceiling.

Remiel and Gak paddled on their knees through the dark water as they scanned the orange-shimmering cavern with their darksight.

"Watch out!" yelled Gak as another massive stalactite splashed into the lake not ten feet away.

"Paddle faster!" urged Nixx as more mineral spears fell around them.

"Watch out!" warned Remiel as a two-foot-long stalactite broke loose above them.

Michelle pulled Franny close and leaned forward as the missile fell toward them. Barely missing Michelle's back, it pierced her cape and speared Og's thigh, causing the giant to bellow in pain.

"Og!" Michelle pulled on the impaling stalactite, but it moved only slightly. "Help me get it out!"

Nixx shook his head at the blood staining Og's wet and tattered robe. "It will bleed more if we remove it!"

"Help her!" cried Remiel, paddling as fast as he could. "The prince will heal him!"

A grimacing Nixx turned back to the embedded stalactite, grabbed hold, and yanked it free. When Nixx saw its bloody end, his face turned gray, and he slumped over on the raft.

"What happened to him?" asked Gak.

"I don't think he likes blood," replied Michelle as Franny placed his hands on Og's bloody wound.

"Hahaha!" laughed the paddling Gak.

"I think the quake has stopped," said Remiel, searching the ceiling.

"I hope so," said Michelle, warily eyeing the shimmering spikes high above. She turned to the unconscious Nixx bent sideways over his mandolin, his hand dragging in the water behind the raft. "Should I lay him flat?"

"Push him in," muttered Gak.

Though in pain, Og laughed.

Michelle ignored the comment and watched in awe as Franny closed the wound. "Does that feel better?"

"Better," nodded Og.

Michelle returned to her spot on Og's back and squeezed Franny. "You are always so kind to heal people in need. How do you know to do that?"

"You taught me."

Michelle's brow furrowed in thought. "How? I don't have that gift."

"You've healed many people. You healed Papa."

"You mean when I was a nurse? That's nothing like what you can do."

Franny smiled at her.

"The quake has stopped," said Remiel, paddling slower.

"Yes, it has." Michelle looked ahead into the darkness but saw only rippling water. "How large is this lake?"

"I don't know," said Remiel.

. . .

As THEY GLIDED across the murky blue, Michelle listened to the *swish* of the oars and the *plops* of dropping ceiling water. The air was brisk and still and stunk of sulfur. She wondered how far they had gone and looked back toward the shore, but there was only water.

"What's that?" asked Gak, looking into the murky lake. "Something's down there."

"In the water?" asked Michelle, turning to the kneeling halfborn.

"Something just swam by."

Michelle leaned closer to the raft's edge and looked into the lake. She gasped and pulled back when a long, slender shape passed by, its luminance just visible in the murky blue. "There is something in there!"

"A fish?" Remiel asked, searching the water from his side.

"A really big fish," said Gak.

"It looked more like an eel or a snake. A twenty-foot-long one!" Michelle returned to Og's back and pulled Franny close to her.

"An Eel sounds better than a snake," muttered Gak.

Og nodded.

"Well, it shouldn't bother us," said Remiel, searching the water.

A loud *plop* turned all eyes to the back of the raft. Remiel scanned the cavern ceiling for more falling stalactites while Gak searched the rippling lake water for the giant eel. It was Franny who noticed the missing traveler and his floating mandolin. "Monsieur Nixx," he pointed.

"Oh! He fell in!" cried Michelle.

"Or he was pulled in," said a wide-eyed Gak. "I like that fish," he chuckled.

Michelle recoiled when Nixx burst to the surface, gasping for air with arms flailing. "Help me!" he gasped before being pulled back under the water.

"Somebody, help him!" cried Michelle, holding Franny tight.

After setting down the oar, Remiel stood and drew his sword, causing the raft to shift in the water. "Where is he?" asked the watcher, searching the murky lake.

"He was there," pointed Michelle.

"I only see his mandolin," replied Remiel.

All eyes searched the rippling water for signs of the traveler.

"There!" Gak pointed as Nixx's head surfaced thirty feet away.

Michelle saw the traveler was drowning and cried, "Somebody help him!"

"He'll be fine," shrugged Gak.

Out of strength and struggling to keep his head above water, the gasping traveler fought his way back to the raft. When Nixx went under again and didn't come up, Michelle set Franny aside, removed the blazerod bag from around her neck, pulled off her cloak, and dove in after him.

"What's she doing?" asked Gak as the traveler's body surfaced.

Remiel sheathed his sword and took up the oar. "Paddle the raft closer to them!"

A gasping Michelle swam back, pulling the lifeless traveler by his blue tunic. When she got to the raft, Remiel and Gak pulled Nixx and then Michelle on board.

"My queen, that was very brave of you, but you should not have done that," said Remiel.

With frantic eyes, the dripping Michelle exclaimed, "He's drowned! We must try to save him!"

Remiel rolled Nixx on his side and slapped his back. The traveler's eyes opened with a cough and then a gasp.

With her hair dripping and her wet dress clinging to her, Michelle surveyed Nixx for injuries. She was relieved to find only shallow bite marks on his forearm. "He's okay."

"Are you unhurt?" Remiel asked Michelle.

"Yes, I'm fine," Michelle nodded, still catching her breath.

"You didn't need to do that," said Remiel.

"But he would have drowned!"

"He is immortal, like me. Like Eli," explained Remiel.

"Some things can kill you; some things can't. It's hard to keep straight," said a frustrated Michelle.

After shaking the water from his ear, Nixx sat up and grinned at Michelle. When his eyes lowered to her breasts, visible through her pasted-on dress, Michelle folded her arms and shook her head. "Immortal or not, some things don't change."

"What's the matter with you?" frowned Remiel.

"Nothing. What's the matter with you?" shrugged Nixx, not taking his eyes off Michelle.

"Are you cold?" asked Gak.

"A little," said a blushing Michelle. "The water feels warmer now."

Remiel put his hand in the lake. "It is."

"My mandolin!" exclaimed Nixx, seeing it floating away.

"Too bad about that," muttered the rowing Gak.

Michelle gasped when Nixx jumped back into the water and swam to his mandolin. "What about the lake monster?"

"It had one taste and spit him out," laughed Gak.

Michelle anxiously searched the murky water for the slithering eel.

When Nixx returned to the raft, Michelle took the mandolin, and Remiel helped the traveler on board. The dripping wet Nixx sat on Og's leg, placed the instrument on his lap, and strummed. "Ha! It still works!"

Gak and Og rolled their eyes.

CHAPTER 38
THE PHARAOH'S MINES

Like a rolling sea of rock and sand, the reddish-brown hills and valleys stretched as far as Eli could see. The dazzling sun, hanging high in the brilliant blue sky, had warmed the afternoon, allowing the travelers to shed their coats.

Eli glanced at Nazario, who had become adept enough at camel travel that he was writing in his notebook as his animal plodded along the dusty trail.

"How much farther to this turquoise mine?" asked Penelope, gracefully bobbing atop her camel.

"Just up that hill," pointed Carlisle.

"It's hard to believe anyone ever lived out here; it's so desolate," scowled Penelope from under her hat.

"Serabit is the oldest turquoise mine in all of Egypt. It goes back to the First Dynasty," explained Carlisle.

"They must have adored the gem to come all the way out here for it," said Penelope.

"Oh, they did. The ancients believed the stone had protective properties. If you were anyone in Egypt, you wore turquoise. If you were of the royal family, you positively bathed in it. But, of course, it was not the Egyp-tians who lived and died working the mines, but their slaves," explained Carlisle.

Eli sat up on his camel when the first of the sandstone monoliths came into view.

"Here we are," said Carlisle as their caravan topped the hill.

Eli scanned the forest of stone that filled the plateau. While many of the four-thousand-year-old monuments were covered in hieroglyphics, all were weathered and worn, some nearly smooth. Not all the stela were standing; many lay toppled and broken in the dirt. Beyond the monoliths stood a hill. But unlike the hundreds of other hills in the area, its brown rocky slopes were dotted by dozens of rectangular mine entrances that gave the appear-ance of dark windows. A large cave entrance stood a little way off from the other passageways.

"As you can see, this temple is nowhere near as pristine as Dendera," said Carlisle. "It was carved in sandstone, much softer than granite, and will take some study to make out the worn characters."

Eli stopped his camel and surveyed the darkened mine entrances. He felt as though they were being watched.

"I suppose this is as good a place as any to set up camp," said Carlisle, motioning to Asim. But the one-eyed foreman was also staring at the hill.

Eli noticed Asim's concern as he climbed off his camel, his shoulder bag strapped across his chest. Eli studied the cave entrance, a long hori-zontal slit halfway up the hill with piles of mined stone spilling from its mouth. He tried to see within its shadows, but there was only darkness. Eli was about to warn against camping there when his sense of danger quieted. He turned to Asim, but the foreman was already unloading a camel.

Eli removed his shoulder bag, filled with the ancient Vatican text, the two brass plates, and his blazerod, and set it near a toppled stone. He then helped the others unload the camels and set up camp.

WITH THEIR TENTS UP and camels secured, Asim oversaw dinner preparations while Carlisle and Eli examined the exposed temple ruins. Nearby, Nazario sketched the faded hieroglyphs from a stone pillar in his notebook while the wandering Penelope scavenged for gems.

"Are you able to make out much?" asked Carlisle, straining to decipher the weather-worn carvings.

Eli didn't answer. He was distracted by Penelope, halfway up the hill. "Be careful." He yelled.

"Are you worried about me, Elijah?" she called back playfully.

Eli watched with concern, still uneasy about the mines.

"Have you found anything?" asked Carlisle.

Eli turned back to the stela and said, "This one speaks of Hathor, 'the mistress of turquoise,' but much of it is missing."

With hands on hips, Carlisle sighed. "I don't remember there being much more than this. Why do you think Father Mateo suggested we come here?"

"Perhaps to get rid of us," chuckled Nazario, still sketching.

Eli glanced up the hill to Penelope bent over a pile of waste stone near the cave opening. He was about to warn her to go no closer when Carlisle said, "Look here. Another mention of Hathor! It seems the slaves adored her. But this is odd."

"What?" asked Eli, turning to the monolith.

"I think...yes, this mentions a doorway! Her gateway!"

Nazario raised his head from his notebook as Eli stepped closer and read, "The goddess who damns and frees souls from the dark world, may the name of Hathor reign from her seat of power in...Abydos." Eli thought back to Zadith's plate.

"Abydos? Interesting." Carlisle stroked his mustache. "Flinders Petrie had a site there, but he found little. It's rumored Seti built a great temple to Osiris there, but if so, it's hidden under the sand, like everything else in this mysterious land."

"I believe we'll find more than sand there," said Eli.

"I hope so," said Carlisle, turning back to the stela. "Strange. With Hathor being the gatekeeper to the afterlife, I can understand the reference to her passing judgment on the damned, but freeing their souls. What does that mean?"

"It means that Hathor's Gate opened both ways," explained Eli.

"Both ways?" repeated Carlisle, not understanding.

When Eli glanced back at the cave entrance, Penelope was nowhere to be seen. At first, he thought nothing of it, but then Eli remembered her saying she didn't like the dark and cramped places when they were exploring Dendera. He started toward the cave, expecting Penelope to emerge any second, but she didn't. Eli passed the sketching Nazario without a word. Still searching for Penelope, he passed his tent with his satchel and blazerod resting outside. When Eli reached Asim and the others preparing dinner, his look of concern was enough to turn the foreman to the cave opening.

"Where is she?" asked Asim

"I don't know," frowned Eli. After surveying the dozens of dark openings in the hill, his worried gaze settled on the cave entrance near where he had last seen her.

"She should not go inside," warned Asim.

Eli hurried up the slope as Asim retrieved his rifle and a lantern. Thirty yards up the hill, Eli was climbing the shifting pile of waste rock when a whimpering came from inside the cave. "Penelope?" he called as he reached the top of the pile. Before him lay a thirty-foot-wide and eight-foot-tall opening. The late afternoon light spilled into the fissure, illuminating the first twenty feet, but beyond that was shadow and then darkness. "Penelope?" Eli called again, stepping into the cavern. He paid no attention to the blue-green mineral veins lining the wall as he searched the shadows. "Penelope! Are you in here?"

Ahead of him, the mine split into two shadowy tunnels. Eli searched their darkness as he stepped further into the mine. When Eli heard a sound behind him, he spun to see Asim climbing over the waste pile with his rifle and a brass lantern in hand.

"She should not be in here," huffed Asim, entering the mine.

"Why? What's in here?" asked Eli.

Asim was about to reply when Penelope's faint cry echoed deep inside the mine.

"Penelope!" yelled Eli, turning to the sound.

"Here, you will need this," said Asim, handing Eli the lantern.

After lighting its wick, Eli held the lantern up and moved further into the cavern. Asim followed close behind, his rifle at the ready. Eli examined the two tunnels. Both were roughly five feet wide and eight feet tall. Chiseled from the sandstone, the uneven walls jogged in and out with crevices and turquoise veins throughout. While the floor was more even, it was littered with rock chips and sand.

"Penelope! Where are you?" called Eli.

"This way," said Asim, pointing his rifle to the tunnel on the right.

With the lantern raised, Eli crept into the tunnel.

They hadn't gone ten feet when Asim pointed to a sandy spot on the floor. "Look there."

Eli lowered the lantern to smeared footprints.

"She is this way," nodded Asim.

"Penelope!" yelled Eli, moving further into the tunnel. He slowed when the tunnel widened and opened to a pit on the left before splitting into another branch on the right. Holding the lantern over the hole, Eli spotted Penelope's pith helmet lying on the rocky floor twenty feet below. "I see her hat!" Eli lowered to a knee, held the lantern over the hole, and called down, "Penelope!"

When a muffled cry came from the shadows below, Eli turned to Asim. "She's down there! She must have fallen!"

"Be careful. She is not alone," warned Asim, his darting eyes scanning the shadows.

Eli gave an acknowledging nod as he reached for his satchel and blaze-rod, but he wasn't wearing it. *I left it at the camp!* Eli surveyed the shadowy pit below him as he considered what to do. When he heard another muted cry, he started down the steep slope, one arm holding the lantern and the other maintaining balance as the rock crumbled underfoot.

"Give me the light," said Asim, reaching down for it.

Eli handed the lantern to the one-eyed foreman, then slid down the slope to the rocky landing below. Once there, he found three branching tunnels and another pit dropping deeper underground. With the light above him, he could see only a few feet into the tunnels. Eli breathed in the musty air, and his nose wrinkled at a scent he had not encountered in a very long time. He called up to Asim, "Drop the lantern, then come down."

After catching the light, Eli raised it to the expanding labyrinth and waited for the foreman to join him. The branching tunnels looked the same as the others, with jagged walls and chipped stone littering their floors. Eli lowered the light over the pit but saw only a bend in that lower level. When Eli heard a muffled cry above him, followed by a thud and the sound of metal on stone, he raised the lantern and looked up, but Asim was not there. Eli saw only the foreman's rifle barrel protruding over the edge of the hole. "Asim!" Eli waited for an answer, but there was none.

Eli lowered the light to the branching tunnels and gasped at the hulking figure standing before him. Dressed in rags and hunched in the passageway, the bearded and craggy-faced giant grabbed for Eli. Eli jumped back, but the rock wall stopped him. The giant's massive hand grabbed Eli's shirt and flung him across the cavern. Eli slammed into another wall before dropping the lantern and falling down the pit. He landed hard on his shoulder and rolled over in pain as the lantern crashed on the rocks beside him, smashing its glass chimney and dulling its light to a flicker.

Eli's eyes widened at the giant dropping on top of him from the level above. He rolled to his side as the behemoth's enormous feet smashed down where Eli had been. The watcher jumped to his feet on the fifteen-foot landing and dodged the giant's swinging arm. The creature's fist, the size of a man's head, struck the wall beside Eli, raining loose rock and dust on them.

With the lantern's light almost gone, Eli knew he would be helpless in the dark. He spotted another pit to his right and leaped across it. When the giant charged him with a swinging arm, Eli ducked and landed a punch in the creature's ribs. The giant barely noticed the blow. Eli dodged another swing and kicked up between the giant's legs with all his might. With a howling cry, the giant doubled over in pain. Eli charged the giant, catching him off balance, and shoved him back into the pit. The grimacing giant fell into the hole but was large enough not to be sucked in. With arms and legs stretched over the pit's sides, the creature roared as he tried to pull himself out, his rage-filled eyes glaring at the watcher.

With his chest rising and falling, Eli was planning his next move when he spotted shadows moving on the walls of the level above. When he heard Penelope's sobbing, Eli lunged forward, jumped on the giant's chest, and leaped up the rocky wall. The giant grabbed for Eli, but when he did, he slipped deeper, wedging himself in the pit.

With the lantern light all but gone, Eli frantically climbed the wall. He was nearly out of the hole when rocks broke loose, dropping him halfway down. Eli was scrambling for better footing when the giant grabbed for him, but he missed Eli's foot by inches. The watcher was clawing back up the wall when more rock broke free. When Eli felt his footing give way, he leaped to an outcropping and pulled himself out of reach of the giant's thrashing arm.

Eli gasped in the musty air as he fought for each hold on the rocky wall, thrusting loose stone down onto the flailing giant still wedged below. The watcher was pulling himself up on the next landing when he felt a second giant's fat, hairy toes. Eli's eyes widened at the monster's hideous face glaring down at him. But before the watcher could respond, the giant pulled Eli from the hole and flung him ten feet across the cavern. Eli bounced off the wall and rolled to his side, groaning in pain as the giant, even larger than the first, glared down at him.

Pushing backward in the darkened pit, Eli stopped when he felt something wet behind him. Eli groaned when he turned to Asim's headless body, his tunic covered in blood, his pulled-off head lying four feet away.

When Eli heard a quiet whimper to his right, he turned to a branching tunnel and saw a trembling Penelope huddled with her knees pulled to her chest. Eli's eyes darted back to the looming giant as it reached for his head. He rolled to the side and kicked the giant, but his blow did nothing to the ferocious beast. When the giant jabbed another hand at the watcher, Eli rolled toward Penelope and yelled, "Climb out to the others!" But she sat trembling in a traumatized stupor.

Eli pushed himself up against the wall as the giant, more than twice his size, eyed Eli like a cat about to pounce on a mouse. The giant's face was pitted and scarred, its yellow teeth sharp and pointed, its robe reduced to threads.

"What are you doing here?" Eli gasped, his hands searching for loose stones on the wall. "Your kind was banished from this world long ago."

"Because of you," growled the fanged giant.

"Why are you here?"

"To do the bidding of Ra and Osiris."

"They haven't ruled this land for thousands of years!"

The beast growled.

Eli found a loose rock and threw it at the giant's warty head, but it bounced off, causing barely a flinch. Eli's eyes widened when he saw the bearded giant climbing up from the pit. He flashed a glance at the curled-up Penelope and cried, "Penelope! Get out! You must climb out while you can!"

"She'll make a tasty meal," growled the sharp-toothed giant, saliva running down its scarred chin. "All of you will."

Penelope lifted her trembling head and shrieked in horror at the craggy-faced giant climbing out of the pit.

"Nazario! Cleto!" yelled Eli as Fangs maneuvered for his kill. Eli knew they stood no chance against both creatures and was searching for a plan when Fangs lunged for him. Eli ducked the giant's swinging arm and spun to the other side of the landing. He grabbed a small boulder and heaved it at Craggy, climbing from the pit. It broke in two over the giant's head and knocked it back into the hole. Craggy's hair-raising howl echoed through the mine.

Eli leaped as Fangs grabbed for him, but this time he caught Eli's arm. With a vicious yank, Fangs slammed Eli into the cavern wall, knocking rocks and dust down. Dazed, Eli punched at the giant's clutching arm but couldn't break free of its grasp. When Fangs reached its other massive hand for the watcher's head, Eli kicked the giant in its shin. But the blow only angered the creature further. "Hold still. I'm going to rip your head off!" growled Fangs.

"Penelope! Get out of here!" shouted Eli as the giant thrashed him against the rock wall, but the trembling woman couldn't move.

Eli was throwing frantic punches with his free arm when a shadow and a light appeared above him.

"Eli!" gasped Nazario, holding a lantern over the pit. The reporter's jaw fell open at the sight below as a wide-eyed Carlisle stood beside him.

"The blazerod!" exclaimed a squirming Eli as Fangs reached for his head.

"Here!" replied Nazario, dropping the weapon into the pit. But when it hit the wall beside Eli, the blazerod bounced away from him and landed beside Fang's large, hairy foot.

When Fangs spotted the ancient weapon, conditioned fear flashed through its face, like a slave seeing its master's whip. The giant's hesitation was enough for Eli to break free of its hold, and he spun under the giant's arm. Now behind the turning behemoth, Eli kicked sideways against Fangs' knee, causing a painful shriek and buckling its thick leg. Eli was charging toward the blazerod when Craggy reached up from the pit and grabbed Eli's foot. The watcher hit the rocky floor hard and gasped for air. He reached for the blazerod, but it was still feet away.

With a vicious kick, Eli broke loose of Craggy's clutching hand and lunged for the weapon as Fangs reached for him.

A wide-eyed Nazario held up a lantern and watched the fight from the ledge above. When Carlisle spotted Asim's rifle, he picked it up and fired at Fangs. The round missed and ricocheted off the walls, nearly hitting Eli. He fired again, this time striking Craggy in the head. The bullet stunned the giant but didn't stop it.

Eli had just reached the blazerod when Fangs grabbed him by the legs and flung him across the landing into one of the branching tunnels. Eli bounced off the wall and rolled to a stop in the shadows, the blazerod loose on the rocky floor beside him.

The furious giant charged the stunned Eli. Fangs was just feet away from the stirring watcher when Eli raised his head, grabbed the blazerod, and fired a bolt through the giant's heart. The blast left a burning hole and dropped Fangs to his knees. When the giant fell forward, its head and torso struck the rock wall above the tunnel, crumbling the ceiling on top of Eli in a billowing cloud of dust.

"Eli!" cried Nazario from above as Craggy pulled himself from the pit onto the landing.

Unable to see through the settling dust, Carlisle held fire. But when Craggy stood on the landing, the archeologist fired the rifle again. The bullet struck the giant in the head, but did little to stop the beast. Craggy hesitated when he spotted the burning hole in the other giant's chest. Then, with his massive fists clenched, he stomped toward the collapsed tunnel. Determined to punish the buried watcher, Craggy threw the fallen rock aside. But when he reached the bottom of the pile and saw Eli wasn't there, he sat back and looked around in confusion.

The bolt of light shot from the shadows of the tunnel through the creature's chest. With a blood-curdling howl, the craggy-faced giant collapsed onto the other before rolling to the ground with a thud.

The dust was settling as Eli limped from the tunnel, his face bruised, his clothing tattered. With his blazerod pointed, Eli warily climbed over the smoldering giants.

"Eli!" exclaimed Nazario, delighted his friend was safe.

"Where's my daughter?" gasped Carlisle, eyeing the gruesome remains of his one-eyed foreman.

"She's all right," replied Eli as he hobbled to the sobbing Penelope, his wary gaze searching the shadows, his blazerod at the ready. Eli kneeled beside Penelope and reached a hesitant hand to her shoulder. She recoiled at his touch and eyed him like a stranger.

Suddenly recognizing Eli, Penelope wrapped her arms around his neck and burst into tears.

"Penelope?" called down Carlisle, still unable to see her.

"I have her. She's safe," replied Eli, lifting Penelope from the rocky floor. When her cheek touched Eli's neck, he saw a flash of light and an expansive grassy meadow. It was a serine image from another time and place, but the vision caused his legs to buckle. Unable to support himself, Eli lowered to a knee.

"Eli! Are you all right?" asked Nazario, sliding down into the pit. When he reached the bottom, Nazario staggered back from the massive, smoking giants, only to turn and recoil from the sight of Asim's ripped-off head.

"Help me," said Eli, guiding Penelope to her feet.

"Are you all right, signora?" asked Nazario, taking her trembling hand and leading her to the rocky slope.

"Here, I have a rope," said Carlisle, dropping it down.

Eli watched Penelope numbly climb the rocky slope with Nazario close behind. When they reached the top, Carlisle embraced his daughter and led her toward the fading light of the mine entrance.

Eli's head spun when he heard movement behind him. It was a shuffling sound from within one of the branching tunnels. The hair on Eli's neck stood at the mournful howl. An angry growl followed from another tunnel. When Eli spotted shimmering eyes in the shadows of the tunnels, he raised the blazerod and boldly said, "I am the watcher, Elijah. I have no desire to spill more Nephilim blood. Grant me safe passage, and you will live."

"Why does a watcher come here and kill our kind?" came a deep, commanding voice from the shadows.

"I acted only to protect those I serve," glared Eli.

"It is true. I witnessed the struggle," said a more feminine voice from another tunnel. Discontented growls from elsewhere in the labyrinth filled the cavern.

Eli's wary gaze shifted, his weapon ready.

"Then go in peace, Elijah, son of the mighty," grunted the commanding giant.

Eli lowered his weapon when the growls quieted, and the glowing eyes retreated into the darkness. He looked up at the wide-eyed Nazario holding the lantern on the level above, then hastily moved to Asim's headless body. After glancing back at the empty tunnels, Eli pulled Asim's body over his shoulder and used the rope to scale the pit wall. After laying the body near the mine entrance, Eli climbed back down into the pit. He kneeled before Asim's pulled-off head, found his eyepatch and turban, and gently wrapped the worn and tattered fabric around the head. Eli then carried it up the steep slope.

The sun was setting when they emerged from the mine. With Asim's body over Eli's shoulder and his head cradled in Eli's arm, he and Nazario made their way down the hill to the camp.

When they arrived, Carlisle was comforting his daughter with one hand while clutching Asim's rifle with the other. The two workers loading the camels gasped in horror when they saw Asim's headless body.

"What happened in there?" asked Carlisle, his face a ghostly white. "What were those things?"

"They were giants," replied Eli, laying Asim's body on the ground.

"Giants?" questioned Carlisle. "What do you mean, giants?"

"Really big scary people," replied Nazario, glancing back at the mine entrances to be sure they weren't followed.

"What?"

"You know. Like Goliath?" said Nazario, still questioning what he had seen.

"That's all mythical hogwash!" exclaimed Carlisle.

"Then I guess what you saw wasn't real," gulped Nazario.

Carlisle shook his head, still not believing. "What did they do to my daughter?"

"She's just frightened," replied Eli.

"Rightfully so! I'm bloody well frightened!" gasped Carlisle. "Are there more of those things in there?"

"They won't harm us," replied Eli, unstrapping a shovel from a camel.

"What do you mean, they won't harm us? Look at Asim!" cried Carlisle. "We need to leave this place immediately!"

"We must first bury Asim," replied Eli.

"Leave him! We must go!" bellowed Carlisle.

"We must first bury Asim," glared Eli.

"Suit yourself." A still-pale Carlisle turned to the stalled workers, clapped his hands, and yelled, "Load the tents! We're leaving now!"

"We should wait until morning," said Eli, searching for a sandy spot to dig.

"Are you mad? I'm not sleeping here!" whimpered Penelope, her frantic eyes scanning the dark mine entrances dotting the hill.

After finding a place to dig, Eli pushed the shovel into the ground, then turned back to Carlisle, wildly pulling his tent down. With an irritated sigh, Eli moved up behind the archeologist, placed his hand to the side of Carlisle's head, and whispered, "Calm yourself and forget."

Carlisle stood and looked around the camp blankly, unsure of where he was.

Nazario's jaw slackened as Eli did the same to Penelope. Her sobbing ceased at the watcher's command, and she sank onto the camp rug with a sigh. When Eli shot a glance at Nazario, the reporter raised halting hands and said, "No, please! I'm okay!"

With a nod, Eli moved to the worried camel hands and said, "All is well. Prepare dinner. We will break camp in the morning."

Somewhat calmed, the two workers turned back to the hastily loaded camel and began unpacking it.

Nazario gulped as Eli returned to the shovel and started digging. He moved closer, scratched his head, and asked, "You haven't done that to me, have you?"

Eli glanced at the reporter as he shoveled sand aside.

"Would I know if you did?"

Eli shook his head and continued digging.

By the time Nazario and Eli laid Asim's body in the hole, night had fallen, and a campfire was burning. After setting the foreman's severed head beside his body, Eli replaced Asim's eyepatch and turban, then refilled the grave. Once finished, Eli leaned the shovel against a monolith and lowered his head.

Nazario watched as Eli uttered a funeral prayer in a strange language, then followed his bruised and tattered friend back to the camp.

At dinner, little was said as Penelope and Carlisle sat staring blankly into the fire. After nibbling on a few dates, Carlisle shook his head and said, "I'm quite exhausted. So much so, I can't even remember what we did today. I think I shall retire."

"Good night," nodded Eli as Carlisle shuffled to his tent.

Penelope's empty gaze moved from the flickering fire to Eli. "What happened to me? I feel as though I'm drunk."

"You'll feel better in the morning," nodded Eli.

With a tired sigh, Penelope stood and shuffled to her tent.

Nazario's worried gaze moved from the mysterious hill to Eli. He noticed the dull luster of the blazerod resting on one side of the watcher and his shoulder bag on the other. Nazario turned back to the darkened mine entrances, faintly illuminated by the firelight, and asked, "Do you trust what they said? Will they come against us tonight?"

"The Nephilim are many things, but I have never known them to be oath-breakers."

Nazario gulped. He noticed the two camel hands talking in the shadows but thought nothing of it. "Will you stay up all night?"

"Yes," replied Eli, gazing into the darkness.

"So will I," nodded Nazario, pulling a blanket around him.

NAZARIO STIRRED from his slumber when the sun broke across the eastern hills. After sitting up and stretching on the camp rug, his tired gaze moved from the cold campfire to the seated Eli. The watcher's legs were crossed, his eyes closed, and his head slightly bowed. Nazario noticed the satchel strapped across the watcher's chest as he leaned toward him and whispered, "Eli, are you sleeping?"

"No," replied Eli, his eyes opening from meditation.

"Sorry. I fell asleep," muttered Nazario as he warily eyed the dark mine openings on the hill. He gulped as he considered the terrible happenings of the previous day. Despite the trauma, Nazario was grateful Eli had not washed away the memory. He turned back to Carlisle's tent when he heard movement from within, then surveyed the pack of camels tied up near the temple ruins. Something was missing. Standing with the blanket wrapped around him, Nazario scanned the hill and plain for the camel hands, but they were nowhere to be seen. "Eli, the workers, I don't see them!"

"They left in the night."

"What?" gasped Nazario. "Why didn't you stop them?"

"It was their right," replied Eli.

Nazario was about to question further when Carlisle pushed out of his tent, buttoned his coat, and grunted. "Good lord, that was an awful night. I had the most wretched dreams!"

Nazario's brows raised as he turned to Carlisle. "What did you dream about?"

Carlisle scratched his head as he tried to remember the details. "We were searching the mines when terrible beasts attacked us."

"Huh. That sounds very unusual. But dreams are like that," said Nazario, glancing at Eli.

"Yes, they are," muttered Carlisle. His eyes narrowed when he noticed the cold campfire. "Asim, why is there not a fire? It's time for breakfast." A stupefied Carlisle blinked numbly when he saw the worker's tent was gone. "Asim, where are your men? Asim?"

Nazario glanced at Asim's mounded grave and wondered if the archeologist would notice it.

Carlisle turned with hands on hips, searching for his foreman and workers. "Asim!" he called out, confused by his absence. "Where is Asim? I can always count on him."

After placing the blazerod into his bag, Eli stood and turned to the head-scratching Carlisle. "They're gone. They left in the night."

"WHAT?" gasped Carlisle. He hurried to the tied-up camels and saw four were missing. "Where did they go? I can always count on Asim. This is so very unlike him!"

Carlisle was still shaking his head in dismay when Penelope staggered from the tent holding her head, her golden hair disheveled. "What's all the noise?" she groaned.

"Asim and the others have left!" blustered Carlisle.

Penelope winced from her aching head as she scanned the half-cleared camp. "What do we do now?"

Carlisle stormed to the supply camels. After a quick survey, he turned back and yelled, "They took most of the food! Damn them! We can't stay here!" He shook his head, fuming. "We're at least two days to El Tor. But we might find a boat in Abu Zenima. That's just one day. We barely have enough water for that. We're going to have to head back. I'm sorry, Eli."

"I understand. Perhaps we should leave this morning," said Eli.

"I'm all for that!" nodded Nazario, glancing back at the eerie hill.

Carlisle scratched his head in thought, then turned to Eli. "Where is it we're going again? My mind's a foggy blank."

"Abydos."

"That's right," breathed Carlisle, fighting to recapture his thoughts. "Abydos."

CHAPTER 39
FORGOTTEN DREAMS

T he sun was low in the afternoon sky when the ragged caravan entered the small fishing village. After bartering for food, supplies, and lodging in a stable, Carlisle went to find a boat that could take them across the Suez while the other weary travelers settled in for the night.

As Eli sat on his bedroll, he heard a merchant outside their stable rolling his cart home for the night and a muezzin calling the faithful to prayer. Eli studied Penelope, sitting six feet away, her head down, her tousled hair in her troubled eyes. "Are you all right?" he asked as a camel munching hay watched from a nearby stall.

Penelope's distressed gaze lifted to Eli, and she gave a faltering smile. "What happened to me in that cave?" she whispered.

Nazario looked up from his notebook.

Penelope gulped. "I keep having these terrible hallucinations. They're like nightmares; only I see them when I'm awake. They're so real."

"What do you see?" asked El, his brow furrowed with concern.

"Huge, awful creatures, ten feet tall, pulling me into the shadows!" Penelope whimpered, tears welling in her eyes. "It wasn't a dream, was it?"

"You're safe now," said Eli.

Penelope wiped away her tears. "It was real, wasn't it? You saved me."

Eli sighed and nodded.

Penelope sank back, relieved to know she wasn't losing her mind. But when her gaze returned to Eli, her face was filled with worry. "Who were they?"

"They were Nephilim."

"Nephilim?"

"Giants."

Penelope laughed and gasped simultaneously. "There's no such thing."

Eli nodded.

Penelope's uneasy gaze moved across the stable as she tried to fathom what had happened. "They-they live underground?"

"Once, there were many upon the earth." Eli shook his head. "I know of no others today."

Penelope's confused gaze turned to Nazario, who could only shrug.

"The pharaohs brought them back to mine their gold, copper, and turquoise."

"Brought them back? From where?" frowned Penelope. "And that was thousands of years ago!"

"There is much to explain when you are ready," said Eli.

Penelope gave a faint nod, then curled up on her bedroll and pulled her blanket around her.

Nazario leaned toward Eli to enquire further about the giants when Carlisle entered the stable and clasped his hands. "I did it!"

"What did you do?" muttered Penelope, staring off in thought.

"I've arranged for a boat to Hurghada in the morning. It will be a tight squeeze with the animals and cost a pretty penny, but it will save us two days. We can restock our supplies there and hire more hands. Damn that Asim! I still can't believe he left us!"

Penelope closed her eyes at the gruesome memory of the foreman's torn-apart body. She was about to speak, but was uncertain what was real and what was not.

"From Hurghada, it will be three or four days back to Luxor, then we can plan a river trip to Abydos," nodded an energized Carlisle.

"I won't be going," muttered Penelope, wrapped in her blanket.

"Just as well," nodded Carlisle, rubbing his hands together. "We're getting close to finding the gate. I can feel it!" Carlisle looked around the stable blankly, then scratched his head. "Where is Asim?"

"He's dead!" exclaimed Penelope, catapulting up from her bedroll. "Don't you remember? The giant tore off his head! Eli buried him while we watched!"

A bewildered Carlisle turned to his daughter. "Are you quite all right? You must have heard me talking about my dream. It was a dream, my dear, that's all."

"It wasn't a dream, father!" cried Penelope.

Carlisle's eyes shifted in thought. He glanced at the watching Eli, then turned to his daughter and said, "My dear, you're suffering from desert fever. I think I may be too. You're dehydrated and exhausted. Drink some water and go to bed. You'll feel better in the morning."

Furious, Penelope threw herself on the bedroll and pulled the blanket back over her.

"Sorry for that outburst," said Carlisle, turning to Eli. "That's the downside to taking a woman on a dig. They're prone to fits of hysteria." The professor glanced at the feeding camels, then asked, "Where are Asim and the others?"

Nazario's round eyes lowered to his notebook as Penelope sobbed under her blanket.

As Carlisle prepared for bed, Eli quietly considered all that had happened. To him, it seemed mortal suffering and turmoil followed in his wake. Eli's mournful gaze turned to the quietly sobbing Penelope. He could bear her sorrow no longer. With a sigh, Eli got to his feet, moved to her side, and kneeled. The others watched as Eli placed a gentle hand on Penelope's tousled blonde hair, careful not to touch her flesh.

A softly whimpering Penelope turned to Eli with red, weepy eyes.

Eli's face saddened at her anguish. "I'm sorry," he whispered. "Be calm and forget."

The turmoil melted from Penelope's face, and she relaxed on the blanket before rolling on her back and gazing into Eli's blue eyes.

Eli felt the pain of her longing. When Penelope reached up and touched his cheek, Eli saw a flash, then an enormous pyramid-shaped hill, its summit hidden in the clouds. Green patches of moss and low-lying foliage covered the small mountain's slopes. Like a bird taking flight, Eli's view swooped up its face, following a narrow path of stone steps. Hundreds of feet up, he broke through the clouds. On its peak, below an azure sky, stood a simple stone house, its walls covered with lichen and moss, its slate roof likewise adorned. When the sun rose behind the stone dwelling, Eli raised his arm to block its blinding light, and the vision left him.

After blinking away the dream, Eli looked deeply into Penelope's grateful eyes.

"Thank you," she whispered.

Eli nodded. Avoiding eye contact with the others, he returned to his bedroll. After lying down, he stared at the flickering lantern shadows on the ceiling as he considered the vision. Unlike the others, Eli thought it was a place he had never been. The lantern light dimmed, and soon the others were asleep.

With thoughts weighing heavily on him, Eli sat up on his bedroll, folded his legs, and closed his eyes.

Eli was meditating when the stable lightened around him. His eyes opened, fearing the lantern had started a fire, but the light came from above, through the stable's ceiling. "Charmeine!" Eli gasped as a woman appeared a few feet in the air before him, her flesh and flowing white gown aglow. Eli's wide eyes turned to the others, but they were fast asleep.

"Hello, Elijah," said Charmeine, her voice soft yet piercing, her long silvery hair gently flowing in the light.

"Where have you been? I've been searching for help for so long!"

Charmeine smiled at Eli knowingly. "I have never been far."

"Can you help me? Can you help me reach my wife and son?"

Charmeine's face filled with concern. "Elijah, I have a message for you."

CHAPTER 40
NEPHILGNAG

THE ABYSS

The traveler's song echoed across the black lake and off the shimmering cavern walls as he strummed his mandolin and Remiel and Gak tediously oared their rickety raft. After Nixx's ninth song, Michelle kindly clapped and said, "Thank you for those lovely renditions. You must be tired. Why don't you take a break?"

"I wouldn't call them lovely," muttered Gak.

Nixx nodded to the snoring Og. "The giant likes my music."

"That's because he has terrible tastes in music," grumbled Gak.

Nixx was about to play another song when Remiel, paddling on one knee, said, "Look at the water."

"Steam is coming off of it," said a curious Michelle.

Gak put a hand into the water. "It's getting warmer."

"That's why," pointed Nixx.

All eyes turned forward when a glowing crevice in the cavern wall came into view. They saw a stream of flowing magma easing into the bubbling lake as they floated closer. Remiel and Gak silently oared the raft past the fiery fissure where the water bubbled and steamed. Michelle coughed when she breathed in the pungent gasses.

"Where are you taking us?" fretted Nixx.

"I don't know," said Remiel, eyeing the blackness ahead of them.

"Look! The cavern splits!" pointed Michelle, spotting an enormous opening to their left. "Which way should we go?"

Remiel studied the dark branching corridor, then pointed ahead. "We should follow this wall."

They were well past the lava fissure and its choking gasses when Michelle felt the raft shift beneath her. "What was that?"

"The ropes are coming loose," said Remiel, noticing the separating poles and branches.

"I warned you," sighed Nixx.

"What do we do?" asked Michelle, pulling Franny close.

Remiel was about to reply when a section of the raft broke free, toppling him into the steamy water.

"It's happening over here too," said Gak, laying down his paddle to pull the unraveling raft together, but when he did, the poles beneath him spread apart, dropping Gak into the lake.

"Is it burning hot?" asked Michelle when Gak surfaced, but the gasping halfborn was too busy trying to swim to answer.

Still sitting atop Og on the largest remaining section of the raft, she reached for Gak, but when the middle of the raft unraveled under the giant, they plunged into the lake.

With one arm around a few of the poles, Michelle pulled Franny beside her as Og splashed and kicked to a larger section. Once there, he laid his dripping mace on it and floated alongside; his hairy mane pasted to his large, craggy face.

Nixx, the only one not to fall in, laughed from his part of the raft and strummed his mandolin.

When Michelle spotted her bag floating away on another section, she called out, "Nixx, will you stop playing and fetch my bag? It has the blazerod!"

With a sigh, Nixx set down his mandolin, then used his hand to paddle closer to the drifting bag. But when something swam by, he pulled his hand out of the lake and sat back.

"It's not too hot. The water's quite comfortable, actually," said Michelle, pushing Franny onto her cluster of poles.

"It reminds me of a bath I once had," said Gak, clinging to part of the wreckage.

A soggy Og nodded.

When Gak felt something brush by him, he gasped, "What was that? Something just bumped my leg!"

"What was it?" asked Remiel, clinging to another part of the failed raft.

"I don't know!" replied a frantically searching Gak.

Nixx laughed and picked up his mandolin.

"Ahh!" cried Michelle, kicking her feet. "I felt it too!"

With one arm hooked around a piece of the raft, Remiel removed his gleaming sword and held it above the water, ready to plunge.

"So now you get your turn with the beast," laughed Nixx.

"I don't think it's the same thing," fretted Gak, pivoting his dripping head to find the creature.

A wide-eyed Og searched the water from his piece of the raft, his mace at the ready.

With all four on or clinging to different parts of the broken raft, they slowly drifted apart.

Michelle screamed when a monstrous alligator head burst from the water and chomped down on her section of raft just inches from Franny.

Remiel swam toward Michelle, but the creature sank back under the water before he arrived.

"Quickly, come up here with me!" exclaimed Nixx, reaching for Michelle.

After swimming her cluster of poles to the traveler's raft, Michelle pushed a dripping Franny up to Nixx. Michelle was pulling herself out of the water when she felt a stabbing pain in her leg. She cried out as the creature pulled her under the water.

"Theia!" yelled Remiel, diving after her with his sword.

Huddled on the raft, Nixx and Franny watched as Og and Gak frantically searched for Michelle. When a long, scaly tail flipped out of the water, Gak plunged his dagger into it. But the blade had no effect on the lake monster, and when its thrashing tail hit Nixx's raft, it knocked Michelle's bag and blazerod into the water. Nixx reached for the bag's strap, but it was gone before he could grab it.

In the murky depths, the creature rolled Michelle; its jaws clamped on her leg. She caught glimpses of the rafts and dangling legs above as she spun. When she spotted Remiel swimming toward her, she reached for his hand, but the creature pulled her away faster than he could swim. With her air nearly gone, Michelle fought with all her might, kicking with her free foot and dragging her hands along the silty lake bottom, stirring up even more murkiness. Michelle reached for her sinking bag when she spotted it, but her fingers fell inches short.

It was Remiel's sword plunging into the creature's side that released its bite on Michelle. When she felt its jaws open, she kicked the monster in the head and lunged for the sinking bag. Michelle had just reached the bag when the creature's tail struck Remiel, knocking him back. When the monster bit down on Michelle's leg again, she cried out in pain. With the last of her air gone, Michelle pulled the bag toward her. She fumbled for its opening and the blazerod inside as the monster tumbled her. Disoriented and with her darksight dimming, Michelle thought all was lost when she finally felt the blazerod. With her strength waning, she pulled it from the bag, pointed it at the thrashing creature, and fired a bolt.

On the surface, Nixx jumped when a flash of light shot out of the water and struck the cavern ceiling.

"She has the blazerod!" cheered Gak.

Two more blasts followed. One knocked a ceiling stalactite into the lake.

When Michelle burst from the water, gasping for air, Remiel swam to her. "Are you hurt?" he asked, pulling her to Nixx's raft.

A sobbing Michelle nodded as Nixx reached down to her from the raft and a worried Franny watched.

Michelle cried out in pain when Remiel pushed her onto the raft, her dress torn and gnawed with blood and light streaming from deep puncture wounds in her thigh and calf. Still clutching her blazerod, Michelle writhed in pain as she lay on the raft.

Nixx eyed the ancient weapon, envious of its power.

"Young prince, can you help her?" urged a worried Gak, floating nearby.

Only slightly distraught, Franny moved to his mother's mangled and bloody leg. He pulled a broken tooth from a wound and placed his small hands on her.

Nixx and the others watched as the bite marks glowed from within, and the wounds shrunk and then closed. But their eyes swelled when the radiating light spread to fill Michelle's leg and then the rest of her body. Soon Franny's arms were glowing.

Remiel shielded his eyes from the brightness and gasped, "Theia's light is filling the prince!"

When Franny let go, the light faded, and the drained child nestled against his sobbing mother, her chest heaving.

Still catching his breath, Remiel lay his sword on the raft and shook his head in wonder.

"Are you okay?" asked Gak, floating on the other side of the raft.

Remiel nodded.

"What if there's more of them?" worried Gak.

"We must get out of this lake," said Remiel. "Can you see the shore at all?"

Nixx turned from the exhausted Michelle and scanned the dark horizon. "No. I see only water."

"Let's try to bind these raft sections back together. We can't drift apart," said Remiel.

The others nodded and went to work.

A MIST HAD SETTLED across the lake when Nixx sat up.

"Do you see something?" asked Remiel, holding two sections of the disintegrating raft together.

"I think so."

"What is it?" asked Gak.

"I'm not sure. It looks like...a boat," said Nixx.

"A boat?" frowned Remiel. When he noticed more of Og out of the water, he asked, "Can you touch the bottom?"

Og nodded.

"The lake's getting shallower!" exclaimed Remiel.

Now chest-deep in the water, Og pulled the remains of the raft that bore Nixx, Michelle, and Franny while Remiel and Gak kicked alongside.

"It is a boat," said Remiel as the tilting wreckage grew larger.

"A giant's boat," breathed Gak.

With a groan, Michelle sat up on the fragmented raft and looked at the leaning boat half-submerged in the lake. It was thirty feet long and curved at its stem and stern. It had no mast but oar guides, with a broken oar dangling in the water. "I didn't know giants could build such things," she said, eyeing the workmanship.

Og nodded as he pulled the raft past the wreckage.

"We must be very close to Nephilgnag," said Remiel, not hiding his concern.

"Nephilgnag?" asked Michelle.

"The city of the giants," said Remiel.

Huddled under her wet cape with Franny tight against her, Michelle heaved a sigh when the misty shore came into view and impatiently waited as Og pulled them closer.

When the raft hit the rocky shore, Michelle climbed off into the knee-deep water, her wet and blood-stained dress clinging to her. With the blazerod in one hand and her cloak tucked under an arm, she took Franny's hand, and they waded to the shore.

The mist made it difficult for Michelle to see the cavern ceiling and walls as she scanned the rocky beach, littered with boulders and rocky outcroppings.

Once on dry land, Michelle gave a grateful sigh and turned as the others joined her. Og was the last to come out of the water, dragging his mace. All were dripping wet except for Nixx, who had mostly dried since his time in the lake. Standing in silence, they surveyed the expansive cavern.

"We made it," said Remiel. He surveyed the band and asked, "What did we lose?"

"My bag," sighed Michelle, holding up her blazerod.

"Any weapons?" Remiel asked, his hand on his sword hilt.

"My dagger," sighed Gak, holding his short sword.

"I still have my mandolin," grinned Nixx.

Og raised his mace.

"How were you able to swim with that thing?" asked Nixx.

Og shrugged.

Looking through the mist, Michelle's gaze followed the stalactite-covered ceiling as its mineral-rich walls arched down to the rocky cavern floor a few hundred feet to either side. "What's that smell? It's bitter, like camphor or myrrh."

Remiel shook his head. "I don't know."

"Now we just have to find a way out," said Nixx.

"It looks like there might be a way out over there," pointed a relieved Gak.

"Those look like steps carved into the rock," said Remiel.

Through the haze, Michelle spotted the chiseled staircase a hundred feet away. Beside the steps were stacks of large boulders neatly arranged along the cavern wall. "What is this place?"

"I don't know," replied Remiel.

"At least we're out of the water, and the ground's not shaking," sighed Michelle.

"I, for one, am ready to get out of this hole," said Nixx, starting toward the stone stairs.

Michelle wrung the water from her cloak. "Can we start a fire and dry off first? My dress is soaked," she said, shivering.

"We all are. Well, most of us," said Gak, eyeing Nixx.

"Mommy, I don't like this place. We should go," said Franny, tugging on Michelle's arm.

"We will. We're just going to dry off first," nodded Michelle.

Nixx eyed Michelle slyly. "I think a fire is a fine idea."

"We just need something to burn," said Michelle, searching the rocky shore.

Remiel's brow furrowed, concerned what attention a fire might bring.

"I bet his mandolin will burn," sneered Gak.

A scowling Nixx turned his instrument away from the halfborn.

"What about the raft?" pointed Michelle. "If you'll gather what's left of it, I think I can set it ablaze."

Remiel glanced back toward the stairs. "I think the prince is right. We should leave here."

"We'll leave just as soon as we're dried off," Michelle reasoned. "We'll be much more comfortable."

"Give the queen her fire," urged Nixx.

After reluctant glances, Remiel and Gak gathered the remains of the raft and placed them in a pile. Then Michelle lit it on fire with a blast of the blazerod.

Michelle shielded her eyes from the fire's brilliance, having gone so long using only her darksight. Upon feeling the fire's warmth, she gave a contented sigh.

The fire was popping and cracking when Nixx picked up his mandolin and began strumming. His brows raised when Michelle motioned for the drying Remiel and Gak to turn around.

With her just visible behind the turned Og, the traveler pretended not to stare when Michelle pulled her wet dress off her shoulders and stepped out of it. He watched as she examined her mostly healed bite marks, wrung out her dress, and shook it open. When the naked Michelle glanced back at him over her shoulder, Nixx's gaze was elsewhere. But it quickly returned to her exquisite form. When Michelle moved further behind the turned Og, Nixx leaned to see her. But when the giant opened his robe to dry off, exposing his hairy loins, a repulsed Nixx set down his mandolin and turned away. "I'm going to explore."

"Good idea," glared Remiel, his back still turned to Michelle.

By the time the fire died down, Michelle's gown was mostly dry. She was pulling it back on when Remiel asked, "May we face the fire now?"

"Yes, thank you," said Michelle. Their eyes met when the bare-chested watcher turned, holding his drying cloak in front of him. When she saw Remiel's broad, muscular chest, she pulled her gaze away and thought of Eli. She wondered if all watchers were so powerfully built.

"The fire feels good," said Gak, stretching his bony arms.

"Yes, it does," said Michelle, trying to hide her revulsion at seeing the naked halfborn and open-robed giant. When she turned to see Franny also stripped down, she sighed. "Well, we're all more familiar now."

The five were mostly dry and dressed when Nixx yelled back, "You should come see this!"

Michelle pulled on her cloak, took Franny in one hand and the blazerod in the other, and started toward the carved staircase. As she drew closer, the details became more visible through the haze. She counted forty steps before they reached a terrace atop the rocky slope. To the right of the stairs was a string of boulders arranged like enormous tables. Though hard to visualize in the flickering shadows of the dying firelight, each had a large flat slab supported by two boulder ends. She guessed the tables to be ten to fifteen feet long and four feet off the ground. Michelle was twenty steps away when she stopped and gasped. Atop each of the tables lay a giant. Michelle's eyes widened as she studied the first of the sleeping behemoths. It was a female, proudly wrapped in her tattered robe. Her large, worn face was peaceful, and her hair was carefully braided. "Nixx, where are you?" she whispered.

"Over here."

With the firelight still competing with her darksight, Michelle pulled her gaze from the giant. She spotted Nixx near the far wall, examining another. "Are they sleeping?"

"They're dead," replied Nixx as Remiel and the others joined them.

Michelle's jaw slackened, amazed at their size. "This one is even larger than Og. Are you sure they're not just sleeping?"

"They're dead," said an uneasy Remiel. "These are sepulchers."

"Were they just laid here? There's no sign of decay," said Michelle.

"Remember, in the abyss, life is static. There is no natural death or decay, only that which is forced," said Remiel.

"But what about the Nalidi bones we saw?" asked Michelle.

"They were eaten clean," replied Remiel.

Michelle shook her head. "Then how did these giants die?"

"Battle." Remiel pointed to a head severed from its body but laid back in place.

Michelle grimaced. "Who would fight the giants?"

"Other giants," said Gak.

"They are a contentious and warring race," explained Remiel.

"But not Og. He's sweet as can be," said Michelle, turning with a smile, but Og's attention was on the dark terrace above them.

"We shouldn't be here," warned Gak, backing away.

"No, we must leave," said Remiel, his hand on his sword hilt.

"That sounds fine to me," whispered Michelle.

Og nodded, his eyes wide and searching.

Michelle took Franny in one hand and tightened her grip on the blazerod with the other as she followed Remiel, watching the resting giants to be sure they didn't move.

After hurrying to the massive stone staircase, Remiel led the group up while a wary-eyed Og followed at the rear, his club at the ready.

Michelle marveled at the chiseled stone rails and balusters as they climbed the tall steps. When she looked up, she noticed the cavern ceiling atop the terrace had no stalactites, but was carved and vaulted like a cathedral. Thick stone columns shaped like tree trunks lined the sides. "What is this place? A mausoleum?" she whispered.

"Maybe," said a wide-eyed Gak, not knowing the word.

As they neared the top of the steps, an eager Remiel pointed ahead. "I can see the cave opening! Quickly!"

"We're almost there, Franny!" whispered Michelle as his short legs leaped the last of the steps beside her.

The band had just reached the terrace and the vaulted chamber when a mammoth figure stepped out from behind a column in front of them.

"Watch out!" warned Remiel as the giant's six-foot-long club swung at them. Gak and Nixx jumped aside, and Remiel ducked with Michelle in time to escape the massive club, but it struck Og squarely in the chest and tumbled him back down the stairs to the crypt.

"Giant!" exclaimed Remiel, reaching for his sword. But before he could draw it, another giant stepped out of the shadows, his robe flowing, and knocked Remiel ten feet back into Gak, sprawling them both on the stone floor. The nimble Nixx dodged the first swinging club, but the second giant's blow knocked him sideways into a carved pillar.

Huddled on the floor over Franny, Michelle screamed when the giant lifted its foot to stomp on them. She rolled to the side with Franny as the giant's foot came down. The giant's sandal barely missed Michelle as it hammered the stone floor with a loud *thump*, but it caught her cape. She released her cloak and rolled again as the giant's club came smashing down, missing them by inches. The giant was raising his club when Michelle pointed the blazerod and fired a bolt through its chest, but the blast continued into the vaulted ceiling. Dust and debris rained on the giant as it staggered backward. Still clutching Franny, Michelle fired again. With two smoldering holes in its chest, the giant fell against a pillar before toppling onto the floor. When the pillar collapsed, it brought with it part of the ceiling. The giant raised his arm and cried out as a massive stone slab crushed him.

Michelle was turning the blazerod to the second giant when its club struck her arm. The blow spun her around and knocked the weapon across the floor and down the stairs. "Oh, no! The blazerod!" cried Michelle as the twelve-foot-tall behemoth raised its club, but more stone fell when the giant's mace struck the vaulted ceiling, causing the creature to stumble backward.

Michelle rolled across the floor and pulled Franny to her as another wedge of the ceiling fell, smashing in pieces beside them.

"It's caving in!" warned Nixx. After scrambling to his feet, he snatched Franny off the floor. "This way!" he yelled, running through the chamber with Franny under his arm and his mandolin across his back.

"Franny!" Michelle hobbled to her feet and chased after them as the cave ceiling rained rocks and debris. Michelle screamed when she glanced back at the pursuing giant just feet behind her.

When the giant's club caught the back of her sandal, Michelle spun to the floor. She screamed and rolled to the side as the giant's foot stomped on the floor beside her. Michelle spun again as his club hammered down, smashing a chunk of fallen rock.

Michelle scrambled to her feet and charged after Nixx, still fleeing with her son. Her eyes widened when a massive iron gate descended from the vaulted ceiling. Knowing the gate would seal her inside, Michelle ran with all her might. Nixx and Franny barely cleared the dropping gate, but it slammed to the stone floor before Michelle could reach it. "Wait! I can't get out! Franny!" Michelle cried, reaching for her son.

Standing outside the cave, a huffing Nixx stopped and turned with Franny still under his arm. "Mommy!" Franny called out, reaching for his mother.

Michelle felt the giant's ferocious gaze from behind her and looked back in time to duck as its spiked club swung past her head. "Franny!" she exclaimed as the traveler backed away with her son.

"Sorry," Nixx shrugged. "The prince is my way out of this place."

"NOOO!" cried Michelle as Nixx turned and ran into the shadows with Franny reaching back to her. "Franny! FRANNY!"

Michelle heard the angry giant pull back its club. With terrified eyes, she bent down as it swung for her head. When the giant's mace struck the gate just inches away with a thunderous *clang,* she spun under the creature's legs. Pushing backward on all fours as fast as she could, Michelle gasped when she bumped against the cavern wall. She screamed and raised a shielding arm when the giant came after her with its club raised.

The giant's mace was swinging down when Remiel leaped through the air, his glistening sword, E'atura, over his head. With a mighty swing, the gleaming blade sliced through the giant's thick forearm, sending it and the mace spinning in the air. Michelle tucked into a ball as the massive club fell to one side of her and the giant's hairy arm to the other.

The giant's agonized howl echoed through the cavern as he spun and struck Remiel in the chest with his other arm, knocking the watcher backward and sending his sword across the floor.

Undeterred, the giant reached for his fallen club, but before he could grab it, a shrieking Gak leaped onto his back.

Michelle's panicked eyes shot from the stunned Remiel to Gak. Clutching the giant's thick neck, the halfborn punched its head with blows that were more irritating than harmful.

"Watch out!" cried Michelle as the giant grabbed Gak's tunic, pulled the halfborn from his back, and flung him across the shrine.

Michelle searched for Og, hoping he would appear with the blazerod, but he was lying at the foot of the stairs, and the blazerod was hidden behind a burial slab.

With a ferocious roar, the giant reclaimed his club, his severed arm gushing blood and light. When the giant's glaring eyes moved to Remiel, staggering to his feet, Michelle shouted, "Watch out!" But by the time the dazed watcher looked up, the giant's club was swinging for him. The mace's impact threw Remiel backward into a wall.

Michelle's horrified gaze turned from the motionless watcher to the giant, its eyes dark and menacing, its lip snarling. The growling giant raised the club and charged her.

When Michelle spotted Remiel's shimmering sword near some fallen rubble, she leaped for it, stumbling as the giant hammered his mace down, missing her by inches.

Sobbing with fear, Michelle grabbed hold of E'atura's hilt. At her touch, its blade glowed even brighter. With eyes wide, Michelle pulled the beaming sword over her head. She gasped and jumped back when the giant's mace swung by, grazing her gown. The heavy blade fell in her arms and crashed to the floor before she could raise it again. Michelle locked eyes with the wounded giant. She saw its fear and rage and knew she could be smashed in an instant, leaving her Franny an orphan.

With a fierce cry, Michelle lunged the sword forward, piercing the giant's robe and side. She feared the stab would only agitate the creature further, but the glowing blade had a much more powerful effect and caused the one-armed giant to stumble backward.

Michelle gulped as she pulled back the heavy sword, its shining blade burning off the giant's blood. She stepped back when the giant, even more furious, charged her with the mace raised. Michelle cried out in fear, nearly turning and running, but held her ground.

The giant was just feet away when he began his swing. Rather than recoiling, Michelle leaped forward, meeting the creature mid-swing. This time, the radiant sword plunged deep into the giant, and as it did, a burst of luminance shot forth, filling the creature with a dazzling light.

With a mighty howl, the impaled giant fell back.

Michelle staggered backward, horrified by what she had done. But her sickened look of fear changed to astonishment as the giant's hideous body morphed. As the glowing giant whimpered in pain with the shining E'atura still lodged in his belly, his enormous form diminished until the creature was the size of a large man. Michelle's jaw hung as the giant's shrunken body ceased writhing, and its life light wafted into the shrine's dank air. She gasped as the giant's body withered on the cavern floor, and in a few blinks, only the creature's tattered robe remained. It startled Michelle when Remiel's sword clattered to the floor, and its shining blade returned to its usual luster.

"What just happened?" asked Michelle as the gaping Gak climbed to his feet behind her.

"I don't know," said a battered Remiel on a knee.

"You have freed Da'roonk," came a raspy woman's voice.

Michelle's head spun to the closed gate, and her eyes widened. Beyond its bars towered eight more giants, their robes torn and tattered, their craggy faces glaring. Michelle gulped when the beardless one in the middle, who wore a mantle across her shoulders and held a wooden scepter, stepped forward.

"Who are you?" asked the queen of Nephilgnag.

Michelle moved her lips, but no sound emerged.

"She is Theia!" proclaimed Gak. "The Bringer of Light!"

CHAPTER 41

GREAT EXPECTATIONS

THE GULF OF SUEZ, EGYPT
18 DECEMBER 1933

Eli looked across the smooth blue water as the fishing boat, loaded with their camels and supplies, puttered across the channel. It was a lovely morning, and the brisk air made Eli feel alive. But at the same time, he felt a growing foreboding and a sense of inevitability. Eli surveyed the barren shoreline, just five miles away, like a mountain climber eyeing an impossible peak.

When the boat's captain barked, "Get out of here!" Eli turned with the others to see the captain face to face with Carlisle's camel, its curious head inside the crowded wheelhouse.

The others laughed.

Eli understood humor better now, and the watcher would have considered the scene funny if not for the weight of his thoughts. He wondered how long it would be before he would laugh again.

Eli turned to Penelope standing beside him. He could tell she was less confused and frustrated, but was still troubled. Eli wondered how she had escaped his first mind-clearing and was glad his second attempt gave her peace. He told himself there were some burdens mortals didn't need to carry.

Eli studied Penelope's smooth skin and silky blonde hair. He knew there was something unique about her but didn't understand what. He wondered if their crossing paths twice was a coincidence. But above all, Eli wondered what the visions he had when touching her meant. He wished Charmeine had given him more answers.

Eli turned to Nazario, sitting on a pile of smelly fishing nets, writing in his notebook. Eli had come to think of him as a friend. He wondered how many volumes the reporter would fill on their quest. He wondered if Nazario would ever get to ask his ten questions. There were so many things Eli wondered.

The watcher turned to Carlisle, enjoying the last of his cigars. Eli was grateful for the archeologist's help and hoped he and Nazario would be successful in the next stage of their expedition. Eli sighed as he considered his quest. He had hoped he was on the verge of rescuing his wife and son, but that success now seemed further out of reach.

Eli's breath shortened at the trepidation growing within him. For days, he had considered Ibn Umayl's words. Eli had supposed the traveler was referring to the turquoise mines as the place he must first go, but Eli now understood the monk was referring to another place—an even darker, more sinister realm. Charmeine had confirmed that much, at least.

Eli stared across the water as he considered his existence. For eons, he had prided himself in his work guiding humans, but everything changed the day that German shell struck. Since his awakening, Eli had come to understand that, even as an immortal, his life was no more predictable than the humans he was sworn to serve. He hoped his final effort would be enough. Eli drew in a fortifying breath and closed his eyes. His purpose was now clear.

When a shadow and then a German cruiser pulled alongside their small fishing boat, Carlisle pulled his cigar from his mouth and muttered, "What's this? Lousy Hun."

Nazario looked up from his notebook and gasped at the looming cruiser, ten times larger than their boat, pushing through the water just thirty feet to starboard. His wide eyes raised to its massive deck guns and the dark-clad sailors looking down on them from twenty feet up. When the cruiser slowed to match their speed, Nazario looked back at their wild-eyed fishing boat captain, barking orders to the scrambling crew. The reporter jumped when an Arabic voice boomed over the cruiser's loudspeaker. "What's happening?" gasped Nazario, clutching his notebook.

"They just ordered the captain to stop his engine. They're going to board us," replied a calm Eli.

Nazario's worried gaze moved to the satchel across Eli's chest. He had no doubt the blazerod could deliver them from the Nazis.

Eli watched as armed German sailors scrambled down rope ladders like crabs, then leaped onto their bobbing fishing boat.

"What's the meaning of this?" exclaimed Carlisle as sailors aimed rifles down on them from the deck above.

"We can do nothing," shrugged the helpless fishing boat captain as the German sailors swarmed his vessel.

Eli's jaw tightened when he spotted a man in a suit, hat, and long leather coat climbing down the rope ladder.

When the baggy-eyed Guerre stepped onto the fishing boat, Nazario gasped and pointed. "It's him!"

Glaring at the halfborn, it was all Eli could do not to reach inside his bag for the blazerod. He thought of the satisfaction he'd feel blasting the halfborn out of existence, like Guerre had Dina. But Eli knew he couldn't let human emotions overpower him. Not now.

When a German sailor sprang up behind Penelope, wrapped his arm around her chest, and put a Luger to her head, Eli bellowed in German, "Let her go!"

"Raise your hands, or she's dead!" barked the sailor.

Eli lifted his arms.

"You can't board us like this! We're British citizens! And let go of my daughter!" yelled Carlisle. He started toward her, but abruptly stopped when he felt a pistol against his head.

A grinning Guerre stepped over the cluttered deck past the wide-eyed Carlisle. "So nice to see you again, Elijah. Once again, I thank you for doing all the work for me. Now I will take that plate."

"I won't give it to you," seethed Eli, fighting against his emotions.

"You will," chuckled Guerre. He pulled his dagger from his belt and held it against Penelope's delicate throat. "Or you'll watch your lovely friend die."

Penelope closed her eyes and whimpered with fear.

"How many mortals have already died because of you, I wonder," sneered the halfborn.

Eli's face twisted with emotion. It was all he could do not to pummel the vile creature.

"Such control. So very unlike you lately," grinned Guerre. He lowered his glistening blade down Penelope's coat, slicing off her buttons. "Or should I start with her belly? Does she carry another of your bastard offspring?"

"Don't harm her! She's innocent!" seethed Eli.

"No one is innocent," laughed Guerre. "Now, give me the plate."

Eli glared at the halfborn as he pulled the satchel over his head.

"And don't even think of throwing it into the sea. Your friends will die for sure," snarled Guerre.

Eli's face was contorted with rage as he handed his bag to the halfborn.

Nazario, held between two sailors, gasped, "Eli, don't!"

"There, you see, no one has to die today," grinned Guerre. When he opened the satchel, his eyes widened. "Ah, here it is." The halfborn pulled the brass plate from the bag and examined it. "This was quite a find in the Vatican. We would have discovered it eventually, but you saved us considerable time."

"I'm sorry for that," fumed Eli.

"And I even get my blazerod back!" gloated Guerre, holding it up for all to see.

"It's not yours," growled Eli.

Carlisle's brow wrinkled when he saw the strange rod. He jumped when Guerre fired a blast at his camel at the rear of the fishing boat, and watched in horror as the beast tumbled over the side into the sea. "Bloody hell! What was that? You shot my camel!"

"I'm sure you'll find another," sneered Guerre, pointing the blazerod at Eli's head.

"Eli, what have you done?" groaned Nazario.

"He saved your miserable life," replied Guerre, looking down the weapon at Eli. "Do you know there's only one other thing besides this that can kill a watcher?" smirked the halfborn. "A watcher's sword."

Carlisle and Penelope looked from Guerre to Eli in confusion.

"Oh, yes. Eli is an immortal. Did he not tell you? Maybe he did, then washed your minds clean," laughed Guerre. "It's an old trick. One I wish I could use."

"Eli," groaned Nazario, devastated for his friend.

Guerre turned to Nazario. "That reminds me, take his notebook!"

"What? No! You can't have it?" cried Nazario.

"So clever of you, Eli, employing a journalist to document your findings. The Führer will be grateful."

Nazario's chin buckled with emotion.

Eli gave his friend an encouraging nod and said, "It's okay, Cleto."

Nazario shook his head, as if giving up a child. But when a sailor jabbed his pistol into the reporter's temple, Nazario's shoulders sank. Then, with a painful groan, he surrendered his notebook.

Taking great pleasure in his cunning, Guerre looked into Eli's bag for the monastery plate, but it wasn't there. "Where is it? Where is the plate you received at Saint Catherine's?"

"We found nothing there!" exclaimed Carlisle.

"You're lying!" snapped Guerre.

"No, it's true! We came back with nothing!" insisted Nazario.

Guerre's baggy eyes narrowed. "Convincing, but I know you have it. And the book you took from the Vatican. Where is that?"

"That's all I have," replied Eli, nodding to the empty satchel.

Nazario's eyes shifted in thought as he wondered where the ancient text could be. Eli had kept it in his bag with the plate since acquiring it.

"Search them! Go through all of their things!" ordered Guerre.

As German sailors emptied the explorers' bags and searched their clothes, Penelope's fear changed to anger. She struggled against the sailor holding her, then glared, "How dare you empty out my things!"

"If you know where they are, Fräulein, tell me, and it will go better for you," snarled Guerre.

Penelope gulped. "What are you going to do with us?"

Guerre turned to her. "Tell me where to find the relic and the book, and you will live."

Penelope's eyes widened. "I don't know what you're looking for."

"A very old book and a plate, like this one," said Guerre, holding up the brass plate. He studied Penelope. "Search her."

"Keep your bloody hands off my daughter!" bellowed Carlisle before a sailor thrust a fist into the professor's gut, doubling him over.

"Father!" Penelope cried as a scruffy-faced sailor roughly searched her pockets. When the grinning sailor popped the buttons off her blouse and squeezed her breasts through her silky bra, Penelope gasped. "How dare you!" She kneed the sailor in the groin, doubling him over.

The other Germans laughed, but when the grimacing sailor flashed a switchblade knife at Penelope's face and barked something in German, she pulled back in horror.

"I suggest you cooperate, Fräulein," warned Guerre. "There are four hundred men on that ship who would love to have a turn with you."

The color emptied from Penelope's face as her father helplessly fumed.

"Eli, do something," muttered Nazario.

"Yes, do something," grinned Guerre, the blazerod still pointed, but Eli didn't move.

After another twenty minutes of searching, the sailors turned to Guerre with empty hands and shaking heads.

"Maybe it was in the pack of my camel you shot," seethed Carlisle.

Guerre glared at the professor before shaking the blazerod in Eli's face and bellowing, "Tell me where the book and plate are, or I'll end you right now!"

Eli studied the halfborn, then calmly replied, "What chance do you have of ever knowing their secrets if you do that?"

Guerre's face twisted with rage, and he lowered the weapon. "Take him!"

Nazario's round eyes moved from the halfborn to Eli, waiting for the watcher to fight back, but Eli stood calmly by.

"You are a prisoner of the National Socialist Party of Germany!" fumed Guerre. "We'll see what you have to say to your old friends!"

Penelope, Nazario, and Carlisle watched in disbelief as the sailors grabbed hold of the larger Eli and led him across the bobbing deck to the cruiser's rope ladder. Nazario waited for his immortal friend to explode in a fit of rage, throw the sailors aside like rag dolls, and reclaim the blazerod before blasting a hole in the awful halfborn. He imagined the surprise the others would have when the dazzling light bolt blew Guerre over the side. But none of those things happened.

When Eli reached the top of the rope ladder and climbed aboard the German cruiser without a fight, a confused Nazario sank onto the pile of fishing nets.

The three explorers helplessly watched as German sailors aimed their rifles down at them from the cruiser's deck, wondering if they would fire. When the cruiser pulled away from their boat, Penelope rushed into her father's arms and burst into tears. The Egyptian captain barked frantic orders from the wheelhouse as the fishing boat motored away. Nazario saw the captain's worry as smoke billowed from his engine, straining to push them away from the warship as fast as possible. Nazario gulped when he considered the cruiser's large guns and wondered if anyone would know should the Germans blow their little fishing boat apart.

Penelope wiped at her tears as the German cruiser steamed north. "What will they do to him?"

"I don't know," replied Nazario.

"What do we do now?" she sobbed.

"I don't know," muttered Nazario.

Unwilling to face the realization that his great find might never be, a determined Carlisle shook his head and huffed, "There's only one thing we can do: go back to Luxor and file a complaint with the authorities. We'll get the diplomats involved. They'll get Eli back!"

Nazario watched the cruiser fade into the distance, then muttered, "I'm afraid these powers don't respond to state threats."

EPILOGUE

Cleto Nazario stood at the hotel's balcony, smoking a cigarette as his gaze stretched over the Nile. He watched boats glide across the shimmering water and wondered what it was like back home in Rome. He imagined it would be like any other Christmas, with the faithful attending mass the night before to praise the Nazarene's birth. For the rest of the Christian world, it was simply a day of giving, with excited children opening presents and reveling. In other parts, it was just another December day. It felt like that to Nazario. He wondered if anything would change if the masses understood the true history of the world. But then he reminded himself he didn't fully understand it.

Nazario's heart ached at how close he had come to uncovering the mysteries that had for so long captivated him. He thought of the captured immortal and sighed. Without Eli's help, Nazario feared the truth that angels still walked the earth and that a war raged for control of humanity's destiny would remain a clouded myth.

Nazario turned from the open French doors, mashed his cigarette in a full ashtray, and looked at his packed bags on the bed. He had even loaded up Eli's things and planned on returning them to his château in France.

Nazario sighed. It saddened him to be leaving this remarkable land with so much left undiscovered. His lonely gaze moved to his open notebook on the writing desk. He had spent the past three days recording everything he could remember from their nearly three-month quest, but he feared much was forever lost. While the reporter had so desperately wanted to share his understanding and accounts with the world, much of it was now a fading memory—a tale fit only for a fiction author.

Nazario thought back to that awful day in the Gulf of Suez. He still didn't understand why Eli gave himself up without a fight. Was it to protect them? he wondered, or was it for another reason? Nazario remembered Eli's final glance down at him from the German cruiser. It was not a look of surrender but one of resolve. He wondered what the immortal watcher was up to.

While Nazario had little doubt Eli would survive his encounter with the Nazis, he feared he might not see him again in his lifetime. Now fifty-six, Nazario hoped he had another two decades in him, but that was a blink in the life of an immortal. Nazario sighed and shook his head, desperately wanting to believe his life's pursuit had not been in vain. He turned back to his notebook, stretched his stiff hand, and sat at the writing desk.

When a knock came at the door, Nazario glanced at his wristwatch. The bellmen weren't due to come for his bags for another hour. Nazario got up from the desk with a groan and moved to the suite's door, but no one was there when he opened it. He looked up and down the hallway and spotted a man in a gray jellabiya and striped kaftan walking away. About to close the door, Nazario noticed a package on the doormat. Frowning, he brought it inside, untied its twine, and tore open its brown wrapping. Nazario's eyes widened when he saw the ancient book from the Vatican Archive. Resting atop it was a dull brass plate covered in strange characters. With mouth gaped, he studied the plate. Its patina and shape differed from the relic they had stolen from the Vatican, making Nazario wonder from where it had come. He rushed back to the door and looked down the corridor, but the man in the striped kaftan was gone.

Nazario locked the door and raced down the hallway after the presumed deliverer, but when he reached the stairs, they too were empty. Undeterred, the reporter hurried down the stairs, jumping three at a time until he reached the lobby. With his heart pounding, Nazario's eyes darted across the crowded room. He saw roaming Westerners in suits and workers in tarbooshes carrying guests' bags. When Nazario spotted the man in the striped kaftan exiting through the tall front doors, he cried, "Wait!" and charged after him.

Nazario was halfway down the hotel steps when he finally caught up to the strange deliverer. "Wait! Who are you? Where did that package come from?" called out the reporter, but the stranger kept walking.

Nazario put a hand on the man's shoulder and spun him around. He gasped at the familiar face and black eye patch. "Asim?"

I hope you enjoyed *Elijah's Quest.*
I would love to hear what you think about it.
Please leave a rating and a review!

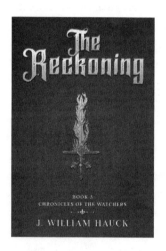

Be sure to read *The Reckoning*
Book III in
The *Chronicles of the Watchers* series!

Please enjoy these excerpts from *The Reckoning:*

Eli stepped in front of the cowering professor as the jailer fired into him. Three rounds struck the watcher's chest, penetrating his tweed coat, but only slightly moving him. When the German saw his bullets had no effect on the large worker, he pulled the inner gate closed, locking them inside. But Eli lurched forward as the jailer backed away from the gate, reached through the bars, and grabbed the jailer's arm.

When Yavin realized he was still alive, he opened his eyes to the stunned guard, still holding his rifle. He then turned to Eli, struggling with the jailer. Yavin jumped when another round fired, ricocheting off the stone walls, then watched wide-eyed as the jailer pulled away from Eli. Yavin gulped as he waited for the German to finish off the new prisoner, but the dazed jailer looked at them in shock as he held his pistol.

"Put away your weapon. You do not need it," said Eli.

Michelle sprung to the side to avoid the retreating Og, but tripped on entangling debris and fell with a cry.

When Og glanced back at the fallen Michelle, Mog lunged forward and, with a mighty swing, landed a blow squarely against the side of Og's head.

The scampering Michelle looked up to see Og's eyes roll back as he toppled toward her like a falling tree. She screamed and leaped out of the way as Og's 800-pound body slammed to the ground with a *ca-thump*.

"Og!" Michelle cried as the attacking giant glared down at her. When Mog raised his club and started for her, Michelle tried to leap off the debris mound, but slipped and rolled down the pile instead. She scrambled to her feet but didn't notice her bag had fallen from under her cloak, exposing the dark pewter base of the blazerod.

When a soldier in a khaki German army uniform moved out from behind the temple with a rifle, Carlisle pulled back on his reins. "What is the meaning of this?" he cried.

Two more soldiers appeared, one barking orders in German and pointing back the way they had come.

"Bloody Germans! You have no jurisdiction here!" bellowed Carlisle as his horse fidgeted under him.

Nazario maneuvered his mount in front of the frightened Penelope.

"I demand to speak to who's in charge here!" yelled Carlisle over the barking German.

When a dark-haired man with a pipe appeared from around the wall, wearing a suit with putties wrapping his boots and calves, Carlisle shook his head. "Ludolf Horst. I should have known."

"Hello, Carlisle," grinned the German. "What brings someone of your age to Abydos?" he asked in English, his accent thick.

"The same thing that brings you," bristled Carlisle. "The hidden mysteries of the past. Only, I don't need soldiers to guard my work."

AUTHOR'S NOTE:

We live in a wonderful and mysterious world. The locations Eli visited, Rosslyn Chapel, Carnac, Westminster's Cosmati Pavement, Dendera, St. Catherine's, and Serabit el-Khadim, are factual.

Made in the USA
Middletown, DE
05 August 2024

58559605R00217